THE MAN HIMSELF BROKE THE SILENCE

"You know, I don't think I really believed they could do it. Shut down the Arab nations, I mean." He sounded like he was talking to friends, comrades in the face of adversity. "I guess they really can, unless somebody can tell me I'm wrong."

"You're not wrong, Mr. President," Brognola stated. "If that weapon detonated in Baghdad, Iraq would have been half-depopulated, minimum. The nation would cease to exist, and it would splinter into small states. If the device in Egypt is detonated anywhere near Aswan, even if it doesn't take out the dam and disrupt the Nile's flow, the water supply will be poisoned for a century. Seventy million people will be an impossible number for all the humanitarian efforts in the world to save. In Iran—we don't know the target there. We can assume Tehran, which means Iran loses a quarter or a third of her sixty-six-million population and falls into anarchy."

"A nonfunctional Iraq was what we were hoping for awhile back, but never at the cost of ten million lives," the Man mused. "Tell me how Israel comes out of this if both the Egypt and Iran devices go off."

"Israel will get nuked."

Other titles in this series:

DON PENDLETON'S

STONY

AMERICA'S ULTRA-COVERT INTELLIGENCE AGENCY

MAN®

THE THIRD
PROTOCOL

A GOLD EAGLE BOOK FROM

WORLDWIDE®

TORONTO • NEW YORK • LONDON
AMSTERDAM • PARIS • SYDNEY • HAMBURG
STOCKHOLM • ATHENS • TOKYO • MILAN
MADRID • WARSAW • BUDAPEST • AUCKLAND

First edition June 2003

ISBN 0-373-61949-9

THE THIRD PROTOCOL

Special thanks and acknowledgment to
Tim Somheil for his contribution to this work.

Printed in U.S.A.

THE THIRD
PROTOCOL

CHAPTER ONE

Tel Aviv, Israel

An unprecedented thirty days had passed without an episode of deadly violence between Israel and the Palestinians, a twenty-first century milestone that was celebrated with the announcement of yet new peace talks, to commence immediately in Washington.

The news was greeted with speeches and accolades. At last, the optimists declared, the Israelis and the Palestinians had agreed to peacefully settle their disagreements and come to a permanent plan for peace.

The word of the hour was compromise. It was used by the Palestinians, it was used by the Israelis, and it was used by the Americans who applauded this hugely positive step. There would be a new openness, a new willingness to put all options on the table in hopes of forging a final agreement.

To most, compromise was the only hope for a final settlement. For some, compromise was robbery. Blasphemc. Anathema.

The promise of peace negotiations was enough of a spark to set these forces in motion.

The news of the bombings exploded around the world in minutes. Before the series of blasts had even ended, four minutes after they started, the Israeli prime minister was given the word. Before the smoke pall began drifting out of the small West Bank settlement that had lost eighteen of its population, the Palestinian Liberation Organization command received the news. Before the last of the wounded had been dragged out of the rubble and loaded onto the fleet of ambulances, the U.S. President knew all about it.

The West Bank and Gaza were immediately subjected to the equivalent of a lockdown. No traffic was allowed into or out of Palestinian cities and villages. The borders into and out of Israel, West Bank and Gaza were closed, cutting off thousands of Palestinians from their employment.

The U.S. President begged the parties to look beyond the violence perpetrated by the few and carry through with the plan to meet. Let peace win, he said. Amid the fury of accusations flying around the Middle East, the President was ignored. The talks were canceled.

The violence escalated, and the death toll rose by the hour. It was the same Israeli-Palestinian story of violence all over again, with one critical difference: the Palestinians had suffered tremendous economic losses during the years of sporadic isolation at the hands of the Israelis. When the borders and roads of the occupied territories were locked down yet again, the Palestinian people had no economic cushion. The impact was immediate. Some Palestinians began to starve to death. Humanitarian aid didn't seem to be reaching them.

Somehow, though, the media was getting in, and global news broadcasts of dying Palestinian children set off an uproar of reaction across the Middle East. Mideast tensions escalated. Iraq, Iran, Syria and Jordan made immediate demands for the opening of the occupied territories for true humanitarian aid, but the belief in Israel was that the Arab nations wanted to use recent events to steal Israeli land.

When it was learned that those guilty for the settlement slayings that started it all were a group of refugees, fearful of having their right to return to their ancestral homes traded away at the bargaining table, it no longer made any difference. The hatred was rekindled. The wave of violence was still gathering steam and was unstoppable.

The outcry from the Arab states throughout the Middle East was peppered with rhetoric more threatening than had been used during past crises. The message was clear. The Arab world intended to involve itself militarily in this conflict.

It was only a matter of time.

Stony Man Farm, Virginia

"RESPONDING TO YESTERDAY'S border attacks and car bombings, Israel cracked down on the West Bank and Gaza with a strict quarantine. In what is said to be the toughest restrictive measures ever imposed by Israel, Palestinians and Arab Israelis have been banned from crossing any Israeli-imposed borderlines, regional or national. All other country borders are off-limits, and travel within the regions is unconditionally prohibited. Palestinians are not allowed to leave their city of residence or travel on any of the roads linking Palestinian population centers. Palestinian officials who have traditionally been granted VIP passes to allow travel throughout Israel and the occupied territories without stringent security checks have had those passes revoked. It is said that even the highest ranking leaders of the Palestinian Authority have no special privileges.

"Confiscation of Palestinian Authority VIP passes is seen as a rare and extreme measure. While the Palestinian Authority has called it an action designed to further demean the Palestinian people and their right to leadership, the Israelis have called it a self-defense policy. They say Palestinian officials are using the passes as a tool for smuggling weapons and explosives into Israel."

YAKOV KATZENELENBOGEN wasn't facing the wall screen as it played the CNN report for the third time in an hour, but he heard every word.

He had lived through war and personal tragedy. He had buried much of his family, including a son who died on the battlefield, and he had even lost an arm while fighting for Israel. Even after all that, he had dedicated himself to the continuation of the fight for peace and spent years going head-to-head with what he considered to be the true villains—any person who perpetrated terror against the innocent.

Katz was once confident in the righteousness of the Israeli cause—confident enough to fight in the wars against the Arab nations.

He hadn't lived in Israel for quite some time, and that changed his perspective. Now he could see clearly that what he hated about the conflict was true of both perpetrators.

What he hated was the dogmatism of the Israeli and Palestinian tenets—the intransigence of their belief systems. It was this intransigence that kept the hatred and conflict alive and passed it down through the generations. There seemed to be no clear-cut solution.

He had been on the phone with a handful of old contacts inside Mossad, the Israeli Central Institute for Intelligence and Security, and even Shin Bet, or General Security Services, which was responsible for Israeli domestic counterintelligence. No one could give him the answers he wanted. He was now trying to make use of his older, less reliable contacts.

The computer at last yielded the security code he was looking for. He could have saved four or five minutes of work by asking one of the computer team to help him crack it, but since becoming the Farm's tactical adviser, time spent behind a desk had taught him new skills, including some of the latest hacking techniques. Akira Tokaido was always a cheerful tutor on that end.

Katzenelenbogen selected the complicated number string and clicked it to have the number dialed out, with full tracing by the computer system just in case the source might be needed again sometime.

The voice that answered said simply, "Yes?"

"Hello, Ori," Katzenelenbogen said.

There was an intake of breath. "My God, Yakov, is it really you?"

"It really is."

"I was sure you were dead. I heard rumors you've been in contact with some old friends, but I didn't believe it. Where are you? What are you doing?"

It was the kind of question one didn't ask in their line of business. Katzenelenbogen's old acquaintance was clearly taken off guard. When he only received silence for an answer he retracted the question. "Sorry. Stupid of me. I also won't ask you how you got this number, old friend."

Katz smiled without humor. He and Ori Flatt had

never quite been friends. In fact they'd been on opposite sides of the fence on many issues. Flatt was technically one of Katz's subordinates when he was an Israeli intelligence chief, and he'd always known that a man with Flatt's cunning and political finesse would either crash and burn or make it far up the Mossad ranks. Once or twice, as he followed the man's career, it had looked as if it would be crash and burn. But when Flatt did in fact became a top-level Mossad official, Katz hadn't been shy about making use of him. It had been years since the two had communicated.

"Tell me what's really happening there, Ori," Katz said.

"You know as much as I do if you've been watching the news, Yakov."

"That's bullshit, and we both know it."

"And it's bullshit for you to try to get more than that out of me, Yakov," Flatt said. "Even if you were still with Mossad I wouldn't answer such a question, because if you asked it would mean you aren't supposed to know."

"I've got a bad feeling about what I'm hearing, Ori," Katz said. It was a rare and strange admission from a man like him, especially to a possible adversary.

"You've got a bad feeling?" Flatt demanded, perturbed. "How should I feel when a possible traitor to the state phones me out of the blue and asks me to spill state secrets? No I said nine days ago, no I say now. Listen to me, Yakov. No I said nine days ago, no I say now."

"Fine, Ori. Thanks for nothing," Katz retorted, and severed the connection.

Then he typed the words on the workstation screen: *No I said nine days ago, no I say now.*

It was an odd word order, even for a native Hebrew speaker who was speaking English. He translated it to telephone numbers and added the Israeli country code. Far too many numbers for a phone number. When he dialed it he got a No Such Number message. He dialed again, adding the country code but starting at the nine. It was answered during the first ring.

"You treated me like a peon when we met last face-to-face, General." It was Flatt speaking through a voice scrambler that made him sound like a moaning phantom in a bad horror movie.

"I was a colonel. And you *were* a peon," Katz replied.

"Give me a number to call you back."

Katz provided it, and the connection clicked off just as the last digit left his lips.

"Lots of cloak-and-dagger stuff going on at Mossad these days, Ori?" Katz asked when the line rang through a minute later. It was one of the cache of numbers Stony Man kept prepared for emergency use. It was highly secure, untraceable.

"These days, yes," Flatt said. "You're working with the U.S. now?"

"I am in the U.S. now," Katz admitted. The number he had provided was a U.S. number.

"I have heard through the rumor mill that you have the ability to call up special operations forces of some kind. I have heard you were partially responsible for identifying the group that wanted to arm the people on the streets of Israel and send them into the West Bank to start a war by the citizens against the Palestinians. Is any of this true?"

Katz didn't answer. In fact, Stony Man Farm had been instrumental in that action. When a group of rich young men in the Israeli technology sector had decided they had enough with sending Israeli defense technology to China and other foreign nations, they had funded the manufacture of thousands of kits to outfit Israeli citizen soldiers. High-technology weapons systems, communications systems, battlefield armor, assembled with usage instructions that the average person could have understood. Then, through manipulation of the media, the group had raised anti-Palestinian sentiments to a fever pitch. The result nearly started a war. Stony Man Farm had managed to locate and destroy the weapons and the group behind their manufacture before they could get into the hands of the people. It had been a near thing.

"Who says I had anything to do with that?" Katz asked.

"No one says. But you were in contact with some of the people in Mossad. That's what I heard. And we—the Israelis—couldn't do anything to stop it. Even those of us who wanted to stop it. And then a day later some sort of a special operations outfit was known to be in Israel, eluding Mossad and solving the problem most effectively. You level with me, Yakov. Did you have anything to do with that?"

"Yes."

"Can you do it again?"

Katz didn't answer that.

"I hope you can, Yakov, because this time I'm sure someone has gone too far."

"Explain that to me, Ori."

Flatt sighed, his voice full of weariness. "We were never really friends in the old days, Yakov, but I had respect for your ethics and that's why I'm telling you this, and that's the only reason. I'm hoping you're still

the man now that you were then. If you helped stop
the criminals who would arm the citizens of Israel for
a war, then maybe you're still that man. This's what I
am pinning my hopes on.''

It was a heartfelt declaration—or a well-acted ploy.
Katz couldn't think of a reason this man would be trying to fool him, but there could be many reasons. He
answered noncommittally. ''I like to think my ethics
haven't changed, Ori.''

''Mine have,'' Flatt admitted, sighing, as if revealing
this flaw to himself for the first time. ''Once I was
dedicated to Israel, and only Israel, and now I feel I
am a traitor to her and to thousands of years of Juda-
ism.''

Katz could tell that the man was struggling to come
to terms with his inner turmoil. If he was genuine, it
was difficult for him to speak now. He nudged the man
gently. ''Ori, are the threats sincere?''

He didn't have to explain what threats he was talking
about. Everyone knew what the threats were. They had
been the subject of news and debate for the past forty-
eight hours. They had resulted in the largest air deployment in recent years and had been denounced from
virtually every corner of the globe.

''Yes,'' Ori Flatt said, swallowing the words. ''The
threats are sincere.''

The news reports had made the gravity of the situation crystal clear:

*Israel is coming to its most dangerous hour as mil-
itary readiness operations proceed throughout the
Middle East.*

*Israel is facing growing problems on every one of its
national borders as well as internally. Nowhere is the*

situation more dangerous than on its northern boundary with Lebanon. Hezbollah guerrillas have been hitting Israeli military vehicles with rockets at an escalating rate. Until this morning, Israeli forces had been steadily dropping back through the disputed Chebaa Farms area, then military officials suddenly ordered the troops to stand their ground and return fire at will. Israel has promised to cross once again into Lebanon and hunt down the guerrillas if the fire is not stopped.

Hezbollah spokesmen promise that any incursion by Israel into what is currently Lebanese-controlled Lebanon will result in immediate and massive retaliation.

Shifts of Israeli combat helicopters have been monitoring the Chebaa Farms area, at the Golan Heights foothills, constantly over the past two days. The Golan Heights was taken by Israel from Syria in 1967.

Israel occupied south Lebanon for eighteen years until pulling out in 2000 to a border demarcated by the United Nations. The Hezbollah insist that territory currently occupied by the Israelis is Lebanese and should be returned to Lebanon.

While no one seriously believes Lebanon has manpower or firepower enough to stand up to Israel, it does have growing support across the Middle East. In what is seen as a tightening coalition, Lebanon has been witnessing a growing level of support from three of the strongest militaries in the Middle East: Iraq, Iran and Egypt.

It is a curious mix of states, to be sure. All three are predominately Muslim, but their orthodoxy and politics are quite different. Egypt has been an active participant in the peace process with Israel, signing the groundbreaking Israel-Egypt Peace treaty in 1979. Iraq and Iran have both maintained a vehement anti-

Western, anti-Israeli stance for decades and even denounced Egypt for its peace initiatives, even as they battled each other over boundaries in a war during the 1980s.

But the people of Egypt have been increasingly critical of the government for refusing to stand up to Israeli violence against the Palestinians, especially since the renewal of violence during the summer of 2000. It's new hard-line stance is seen as the will of the people superseding the cooler heads of the government. In Iran and Iraq, we are seeing years of resentment against Israel coming to a head.

If Hezbollah continues to harass the Israeli military, Israel will invade Lebanon. If Israeli invades Lebanon, Egypt, Iran and Iraq have promised the action will be considered an act of war against all their countries.

Israel's response has been terse and unclear. It has threatened, and I quote: "If faced with a war on multiple fronts, we will have no choice but to permanently neutralize the aggressor nations to preserve our own sovereignty."

How legitimate a threat is it? Is it as dire as it sounds? Would Israel actually use weapons of mass destruction against its enemies? These are the questions being argued on all corners of the globe.

"ARE YOU TELLING ME Israel intends to use weapons of mass destruction against Iran, Iraq and Egypt if and when war starts?" Katz asked coldly.

"Not what you're thinking. There are many Israelis at the highest levels, including Mossad and the other intelligence and military offices, who think we can't use these weapons under any circumstances. Even if it means surrendering to the Arabs and allowing the destruction of Israel. From a practical standpoint it is a foolish act. We would become worse butchers in the eyes of humanity than Hitler himself. We could do nothing worse to turn the world against us as a people."

"So who's behind it?"

"I can't tell you. By that I mean I don't know. But a plan is in motion."

"How?" Katz demanded.

"Again, I don't know," the Israeli intelligence officer admitted. "What I'm telling you is secondhand information, Yakov. But I believe it is correct. There is *some* plan in motion, using our moles inside these three nations already."

The Stony Man tactical adviser was growing more alarmed by the moment. His worst fears were being realized. "No way they could deliver weapons of mass destruction by air," he guessed out loud. "Not with every aircraft in the Middle East in the air around the clock watching for trouble, including the U.S."

"Maybe, maybe not. But I think the attempt was made already. And I think it failed. There've been rumors of an Israeli air crash in Iran. But that isn't important. What is important is that the plan now relies on undercover agents on the ground, moving invisibly through these nations. That's what I've heard, anyway."

"To what end?"

"I can only guess. As can you. They are carrying some sort of weapons. Something small enough for transport in any car. Maybe small enough for men to carry in packs."

"Could be anything."

"I have a code name to give you," Flatt said. "But first I have a promise to extract from you."

Katz stiffened. "What is it?"

"HE MADE ME PROMISE to stop the Mossad agents," Katz reported minutes later. He was sitting in the War Room with Barbara Price, Stony Man Farm mission controller, and Aaron Kurtzman, head of the Farm's cybernetics team. "I told him I would do everything in my power."

"That sounds awfully damn righteous of him. What's your read on this man, Katz?" growled the voice out of the speakerphone. Hal Brognola, director of the U.S. Justice Department's Sensitive Operations Group, served as Stony Man Farm's White House liaison. It was he who obtained presidential sanction for the Farm's covert activities, most of which violated the sovereignty of other nations or were outside the boundaries set forth by the constitution.

Katz shrugged. "I wish I knew what to tell you, Hal. I barely know the man. We butted heads a couple of times, years ago when I was with Israeli intelligence. I've kept tabs on him over the years, just as I have a hundred others who were my peers at the time. We've communicated once or twice. What little intelligence he's provided me has been legitimate. None of this adds up to a conclusive portrait of the man by any means."

"What's your gut tell you?" Brognola demanded.

"He's legit."

"What reason would there be for him to lead you astray?" Kurtzman asked.

"He knows something about the Farm," Brognola responded. "Maybe he's trying to draw us out into the open. There have to be some people in Jerusalem who're pretty pissed at whoever it was who stopped those idiot Soldiers of Solomon. If they know Katz is tied to the group responsible, well..." He left the conclusion unsaid.

"If we were to follow the intelligence that Ori Flatt provided, we wouldn't be sending our people into Israel," Price said. "Wouldn't they set the trap on their home turf?"

"If they wanted to catch us, sure," Brognola growled. "If they just wanted to expose us they would send us into the god-awfullest places on earth, then anonymously blow the whistle."

"So we get caught red-handed sneaking around in Iran," Price finished. "Or Iraq. Our people wouldn't stand a chance."

"Even Egypt would be bad news, with the U.S. struggling to keep all the friends it can among the Arab states," Katz said. "If we were captured inside Egypt, it would strain the relationship, maybe past the breaking point."

Everyone was considering the dire consequences for a few seconds when Brognola said, "Bear, what do we know on this code name Coldman?"

"We're working on it now, but so far there's nothing, Hal," Kurtzman replied as his hands brought up a screen of active searches and data culls being performed by Carmen Delahunt and Akira Tokaido. Kurtzman had started them on the search the instant he had the word from Katz, knowing any information that could be gleaned instantly would be useful in early decision making. "We've found brand names, surnames, but nothing and no one that relates to this project as far as we can tell."

"Katz, does Coldman mean anything to you?" Brognola asked.

"Not a thing."

"What's our best guess for a weapon that can be packed in to the target site by a group of fit men?"

"Biological would be the obvious guess," Price stated. "A couple of pounds of anthrax fed into the limited water supply of the desert nations would wipe out hundreds of thousands. Lob one chunk each into the Tigris and Euphrates, and you've neutralized Iraq. Put another into the Nile above the dam, and Egypt is essentially wiped out."

"Iran isn't as dependent on a limited number of water supplies," Kurtzman added. "Still, a biological element could bring down Tehran, wipe out the Iranian president and Assembly of Experts. The chaos would bring the nation to a standstill. It would probably dissolve into civil war in short order."

"Problem is, we have no evidence of the Israelis developing biological weapons," Brognola said. "What else could it be?"

"Magnetic pulse generators? Radioactive contaminants?" Price suggested. "The Israelis have the technology to put together some of the most advanced weaponry on the planet. We've seen enough evidence of that. We can only guess without more information."

Another moment of silence. "Goddammit, this isn't a lot to go on!" Brognola erupted.

"It's enough in my book," Katz stated.

"Yeah. I guess it has to be," Brognola admitted. "I'll go to the Man. I'll see what he thinks. Will we be prepped?"

"Yes," Price replied. "We've got all personnel from both teams on the premises or en route. The blacksuits can be mobilized in twenty minutes if needed. We have a call out to Mack—he's a question mark at the moment."

"I'll get back to you when I can. If you get any more information—I mean even a shred—I want to know about it."

The line went dead.

THE CALL BACK CAME within the hour. The President hadn't required a face-to-face meeting. He was more than disappointed at the failure of his Mideast peacemaking efforts, another line item on the "unhappy about" checklist the nightly news rattled off every time another presidential popularity opinion poll was released. The Stony Man Farm conclusions sounded farfetched, but at least it was *something* the U.S. could do in response to the current situation.

"I think the Man sees this as a wild-goose chase, and I'm not sure I can argue too strongly. But the word is given," Brognola said, again over the speakerphone, this time to a packed house. Around the table were gathered the five men of Phoenix Force, the three members of Able Team, as well as Kurtzman, Price, Katzenelenbogen, Stony Man Farm pilot Jack Grimaldi and armorer Cowboy Kissinger.

"Who goes where?" Carl Lyons asked.

"We're putting all of you, Able and Phoenix, on the plane to Kuwait," Price announced.

Lyons nodded. Although Able Team was once dedicated almost entirely to the North American sphere of operations, the team increasingly found itself heading overseas.

"I get to play chauffeur," Grimaldi announced.

"It's a military jet for VIPs. Get you to the Middle East in a big hurry."

"But what will we do when we get there?" asked Phoenix Force leader David McCarter.

Price nodded to Kurtzman, who tapped at the keyboard in front of him and brought the big wall monitor to life as he maneuvered the wheelchair away from the table. "We think we have a lead on one of the groups of Mossad agents. Katz's intelligence says there are three teams. All are described as 'en route' to their destinations, which might be Baghdad, Tehran and Aswan. All are equipped with the matériel necessary to perform some sort of large-scale sabotage."

"Such as?" McCarter probed.

"Unknown," Kurtzman said. "Could be anything."

"Something doesn't gel," Lyons said. "Two capital cities, Baghdad and Tehran, and Aswan, at the butt-ugly end of Egypt. If their targets were big cities, Cairo would be the logical Egyptian target. That must mean the dam is the target."

"We've considered it," Price said. "We simply don't know. Could be there are different types of targets in each country, to make each team harder to trace should one of them be discovered."

"We think one of them has been discovered. By us," Kurtzman added. With the tap of a finger a topographical appeared on the wall monitor. The block letters in the corner said Iraq.

Someone groaned.

"We've been tracking the activity of all known and suspected Mossad agents in and around the Middle East. So has everybody else. Everybody is afraid of the Israelis right now," Kurtzman said. "Luckily, somebody spotted this bunch in Istanbul a week ago. That somebody happened to be MI-6. British agents kept tabs on the man for a week, then decided they had bigger fish to fry. We raided the Brits' database this morning and did a hasty job of rationalizing their reports and ours and found a number of missing links, obviously. Eventually we were able to track down the whereabouts of every agent on the list. Except him.''

The map became a man, arms crossed on his chest as he waited on a city street. He was dark-skinned, with straight black hair and dark eyes. His expression was bland, his frame small and almost delicate.

"Tamar Strasler," Kurtzman announced. "A naturalized Israeli, fluent in at least four Arabic dialects, with a doctorate in psychology. Specialist in personality profiling but with a penchant for undercover work. Died in 1989."

"That's a '97 Mercedes he's leaning on, Bear," Hermann Schwarz said.

"I'm telling you what the official records say. Mossad reported him killed in 1989, and there's been no mention of him since."

"That's a dangerously long time to stay undercover," Lyons said, shaking his head slightly.

"Apparently his loyalties are intact as far as the Israelis are concerned. We traced the registration on this car to a fake name, and through that name tracked him to a truck rental in Istanbul. Our friends at the CIA managed to get a GPS transceiver on the truck during a rest stop just before it entered Syria."

"Hell of a long drive," Gary Manning commented.

"We know there are at least three men in the truck, maybe as many as five," Kurtzman added, changing the monitor back to the map of Iraq, now expanded to include neighboring countries. A small white dot moved across Turkey and partially through Syria. "They'll cross into Iraq in just a few hours."

"They must be good to dupe the Syrians," McCarter said.

"They must be dedicated to the cause, no matter how good they are," Hawkins added. "You gotta be motivated to go sneaking into Iraq, for God's sake. Of all places to try to get inside of."

"Maybe they're more than motivated," Price said. "Maybe fanatic."

"You mean these Israelis are on suicide missions," said Rosario Blancanales. "These guys intend to die along with all their victims."

"Could very well be the case," Price stated.

"Which means they won't hesitate to kill themselves and us if we get them against a wall," McCarter concluded.

Price nodded.

"This could be nothing." Brognola piped up over the speakerphone. "This could be a wasted trip. Bad intelligence. Or it might be one of our most dangerous undertakings. Dangerous for us. Dangerous for countless innocent people if we fail to stop what might be happening." The words fell on a grim, silent audience until Manning spoke up.

"You saying we can opt out, Hal?"

Brognola made a snorting sound. Almost a laugh. "I'm saying be careful."

Now it was Manning's turn to snort. "When I'm hunting terrorists in Iraq, I'm *always* careful."

"So what's the lowdown, Barb?" McCarter asked.

"You go in," she said simply. "Take the Mossad unit by surprise. Disable their hardware. Ask some pointed questions. We'll improvise and make new assignments when we see what kind of intelligence we get. Sorry, Able, but for the foreseeable future you get lumped in with Phoenix.''

''Hey, it's better than sitting home with our knuckles up our noses,'' Schwarz said.

McCarter shook his head. ''*Anything* is better than going to Iraq.''

CHAPTER TWO

Iraq

Saeed Obeid heard the approaching gunships. He saw the flash of a rocket, no more than a streak of white fire cutting through the haze of the diminishing sandstorm like lightning. An idle fact crossed his mind in that hour-long microsecond: if he could see the aircraft, it meant the Americans weren't relying on the sophisticated, satellite-guided missiles launched from miles away. This was a likely a Hellfire, a laser-targeted missile. They rarely missed.

Still, it was possible the sandstorm would foul up the works and send the Hellfire off target.

Launched from a U.S. Air Force AH-64A Apache, a laser seeker in the nose of the rocket locked on to the targeting laser that took it to the radar station without varying more than a few meters.

Obeid was an electronics and radar expert. At least, by Baghdad standards he was an expert. The truth was, he had just two years of electronics training, and it was more in the field of machinery repair than advanced radar maintenance. So how did he end up chief electronics supervisor at New Radar Watch Station 14 in the middle of the desert, smelling like funk from too many weeks without a bath and living off canned soup and old, stale bread?

Had he really had a choice? Why hadn't he refused the invitation to take the post at New Radar Watch Station 14? What was the worst they would have done, imprisoned him?

Saeed Obeid the electronics expert was snuffed out so quickly he didn't hear the noise or feel the heat, and Iraq's newest station ceased functioning just as abruptly.

Kuwait

"WHOA," THE COLONEL grunted to himself.

He had made the mistake of watching the video monitoring built into the gunship as the Hellfire homed in on its target. He saw the man emerge from the front of the metal shack that housed the latest Iraqi radar post. The Iraqi had stared into the face of the oncoming missile. The video feed didn't have resolution anywhere near sharp enough to get a read on the man's expression, but the Iraqi had known the missile for what it was. He witnessed the flash of his death, coming at him at meteoric speeds. Somehow, the colonel and the Iraqi had shared the intimacy of death for a fraction of a second.

And that was getting just a little too close to the enemy for the colonel's tastes.

"The station is out," he reported.

"You sure about that?" demanded the leader of the special operations unit.

He was sure. Just to follow protocol he turned to one of his monitoring operators and got the official word. "Yeah, I'm sure," the colonel said.

"Then we're going in."

"Good luck," the colonel said, but it sounded more sarcastic than sincere. He wished he hadn't been flip. Those commandos might be going to their deaths.

Might be, hell, probably. They were going into Iraq, in a hurry, without much military support. In fact, he wasn't at all sure they were military themselves. But they were armed, they were trained and they sure carried themselves like a bunch of guys with battlefield experience.

Whoever the hell they were.

Over Southern Iraq

"YOU'RE MAKING a mess of the place," T. J. Hawkins shouted over the steady throb of the rotors as the U.S. Army CH-137 raced over the dry landscape of the Mesopotamian plain, raising sand that billowed behind them in hazy clouds.

"With their radar out in this vicinity, it just might look like more of the sandstorm to them," the pilot commented.

"Just as long as it doesn't gum up the works," Hawkins said.

"They've been flying this beast around the Middle East for a lot of years. I think they've got it pretty well desert-proofed. It's our Air Force pilot in the rear bird that worries me. Not that I have anything against Air Force pilots," he added for the benefit of his USAF copilot. "But nobody's very good flying in this junk."

"Yeah," Hawkins said, recalling photos of Air Force choppers that went down after drifting into one another in a sandstorm during the Iran hostage rescue attempt in 1980.

"This is a really just a *dust* storm—dust, shale and shell particles," the pilot said with a grin, clearly in his element. "They have *real* sandstorms in the Sahara. Those last hours. This is nothing like a *haboob*."

"Say what now?" Hawkins asked, growing a teenager's smirk, but David McCarter, the team leader, materialized and cut him off.

"ETA?"

"Five minutes," the pilot replied.

"Then let's be ready," McCarter said to his teammate, and they ducked into the rear of the Sikorsky helicopter. There the Briton scanned the group of men quickly. None appeared to notice as a flash of introspection appeared in his eyes, a somber reflection on the consequences of what might happen. They were performing last-minute checks of gear and electronics.

It didn't seem possible that the time had passed, but McCarter's watch wasn't lying, and the pilot confirmed it. "Thirty seconds," the pilot announced, his voice coming through the earpiece the team leader had put in place.

He felt like a cyborg going into the field with this level of sophisticated electronics, even though he was checked out on all of it. "Confirm. Let's be ready."

His words were wasted. The team was more than ready, and when the forward momentum of the chopper slowed to a hover and the pilot gave them the verbal okay, the doors were yanked open without hesitation or discussion. The thrum of the rotors became a chaos of swirling beige sand riding hot, biting winds. The first commando jumped out of the helicopter when it was hovering twenty feet off the desert floor, riding a slim cord to the ground so quickly he might as well have been falling. But his feet touched the earth smartly, he stepped back, and a second commando was right behind him. Soon the entire team was on solid ground.

They made quick work of radioing guidance to the pilot to carefully bring down the car that was dangling underneath, then dismantled the harness in seconds. The second CH-137 was waved in right behind the first and freed of its burden. The two ground vehicles were undamaged from their flight, and the pair of transport helicopters spun and headed for home.

Their chaperon, an Apache AH-64A, wasn't as quick to leave. The gunship hovered in the clouds of its own downdraft, the pilot and gunner watching the team for a moment as if they couldn't believe they were just going to leave them there in the middle of Iraq. Then it, too, spun, agile and quick, and sped back across the desert sands.

Leaving eight men alone in the Iraqi desert.

"Lets do the Iraqi people a huge favor and take out some of the national bureaucrats while we're here," Hawkins suggested.

"Let's can the chatter and get moving," McCarter stated.

"Stony Base here," a voice said in McCarter's headset as he jumped in the passenger seat of the Hummer, which had a desert camou paint job.

"Phoenix One here," the Briton replied, speaking loudly as the man behind the wheel cranked the vehicle to life with a huge roar. "We're on the move." As the Hummer pulled away, he glanced back to be sure the second vehicle wasn't left behind. The Chenowyth Advanced Light Strike Vehicle was rolling along just a few yards behind them, with a grim-faced figure standing at the M-2 .50-caliber machine gun mounted in the rear.

"What's the situation?" Barbara Price asked.

It was an unnecessary question. If there was any situation, McCarter would have reported it immediately. But the conversation was a way of maintaining a sense of equilibrium as the team entered a highly volatile situation.

"Nothing to report, Stony Base," McCarter said. "What are our friends up to?"

"They're sitting on their thumbs," Stony Base replied. "Looks like they pulled off the side of the road. Probably got word of the strike on the radar station and are waiting out the response. The last thing they want is to get into the middle of the excitement."

"That's good news, if they succeed in keeping to themselves."

"That's what they think, too, I imagine," Stony Base said. "They're behind a chunk of rock to hide them from the road. Looks like its shaded from the sun and there's enough tracks visible to make me think it's a regular stop for desert traffic."

"Phoenix Two here," said Rafael Encizo from behind the wheel of the Hummer. His dark complexion and black hair, graying at the edges, spoke to his Hispanic ancestry. "How about some coordinates?"

The woman responded with a set of Global Positioning Satellite coordinates, which Encizo plugged into a dashboard computer without looking. The map that blinked onto the monitor showed him the distance, major features of the landscape and estimated ETA. The driver gave it a quick glance but saw nothing of interest. The graphics representing geographical details of the landscape between here and there were fairly bland. If there was a canyon that was in his way, well, that might provide a bit of a challenge. But there was very little topography the Hummer and the Chenowyth were going to have trouble negotiating.

As it turned out, they covered the fourteen-mile distance in an almost direct straight line. There was no landscape feature that caused them to veer off. Only as they were coming upon the highway did they begin to see the geologic breaks in the rock strata. The extended panel truck was parked near one of these rocky mounds in the desert floor just ten yards off the Damascus-to-Baghdad highway. Indeed, a well-worn trail showed it was a frequent rest stop for vehicles, where they found shelter from the sun during the hottest period of the afternoon.

The panel truck had once been painted red and blue but was bleached into faded slate colors by years of exposure. A single figure crouched near the rocks in the shade, smoking a cigarette and watching a battered VW van at least thirty years old rattle down the highway and drive past, en route to the Iraqi capital.

He didn't see the new arrivals coming at him overland. They waited just beyond a low rise in the land as they assessed the situation. Phoenix Force leader David McCarter touched his headset. "Stony Base?"

"Go ahead." The voice of the mission controller was as clear as if she were speaking from just a mile away, when she was actually sitting belowground on the other side of the planet, in a communications center beneath a wood pulp plantation at Stony Man Farm in Virginia. The satellite uplink in the back of the Hummer served as a base station for the radio communications coming from the commandos' radios. Even as McCarter was evaluating the parked panel truck, another commando, T. J. Hawkins, had removed the uplink equipment and was placing it on the ground.

The servomotors inside, controlled by a computer tied into a gyro, did a good job at maintaining a robust uplink to the satellite, but it wasn't dependable during a probe in which the vehicles might be moving erratically and quickly.

"We've got the truck. It's alone and there's a single figure on guard."

"Affirmative, Phoenix One," the mission controller responded. "Our eye shows just one other vehicle in the area. That's on the highway and appears to be heading away."

"Just a passerby, Stony Base," McCarter confirmed, turning his field glasses on the van to confirm it was heading away. His words went from his headset to the satellite uplink behind the Hummer, into orbit, across the satellite network, down to a retransmission device sitting on a Virginia mountaintop. The retransmitter sent the signal to the Annex communications equipment, which sent it to Mission Controller Barbara Price. She heard it with virtually no delay, despite the six thousand mile distance, and despite the complexity of the signal from mixing satellite systems to make automatic use of various military and encryptable military communications systems.

"How about your readings, Able Three?" Price asked.

"Clean," answered Able Team commando Hermann Schwarz. "No chemical, no biological, no radioactive."

McCarter nodded. That was good news, because those enemies couldn't be fought by his teams, no matter how good they were.

"Go when you're ready, Phoenix One."

"Affirmative, Stony Base." David McCarter turned

his field glasses to the extra-long panel truck. The guy with the cigarette was lost in thought, staring at the desert floor. At least that was how it looked. It would be very dangerous to underestimate that man. Or the truck. Or anything about the situation.

"Phoenix. Able. Let's make our move, mates. And let's make it carefully."

THE CHENOWYTH Advanced Light Strike Vehicle was a high-performance, all-terrain military vehicle made for the battlefield. Its purpose was to penetrate and to survive. There was virtually no wheeled vehicle on the planet that could outmaneuver it on virtually any terrain, and do it in a hurry.

The unit succeeded the Chenowyth Light Strike Vehicle, a three-seater that gained a solid reputation during the Gulf War, on these very sands, allowing U.S. Marine and SEAL squadrons to penetrate and operate without detection deep behind Iraqi lines, performing reconnaissance and other missions.

The lessons learned in Iraq during Desert Storm, and the advances in technology, meant that the next-generation Advanced Light Strike Vehicle had significant advantages in terms of speed, agility and firepower. The main fire station could mount either an M-2 or a MK-19 automatic grenade launcher and utilize it with a 360-degree arc of fire. David McCarter had requested a pair of the ALSVs for Phoenix Force, as well. He had known success taking a pair of the vehicles into the field, one with the M-2, one with the MK-19. A better variety of bang for the buck. The problem wasn't the availability of the vehicles but getting the vehicles to where they wanted them.

Schwarz tried not to grin like an idiot. This was a

sweet ride, and he was pretty pleased to be at the wheel
of the Chenowyth. As a soldier with a realm of experience in the field, he had operated more types of vehicles than he could remember. The new generation
Chenowyth put most of them to shame. The ALSV was
designed for battlefield insertion and mobility, pure and
simple. Some would have called it an unattractive piece
of mechanics, but a person had to admire its clarity of
purpose.

But when Schwarz powered the Chenowyth over the
sand hill and saw the elongated panel truck sitting in
the shallow shade of the rock hillock below, silent and
motionless, with a single guard crouched and puffing a
cigarette, thoughts of enjoyment vanished. It came to
him again that they were driving themselves into an
unknown situation. Unknown and potentially dangerous.

Between the rumble of the Chenowyth and the thrum
of the big diesels powering the Hummer, it was a surprise it took the smoker as long as it did to hear their
approach. His head snapped up and he jumped erect as
the pair of military vehicles bore down on him. He
strode forward two steps, and Schwarz could almost
see the wheels spinning furiously in his brain, then his
head snapped toward the highway as if he expected to
find more military vehicles coming that way. Then he
sprinted behind the truck and was gone.

Schwarz's moment of elation had grown cold. He
didn't like the looks of that guy, the smoker. He wasn't
sure why, but he long ago learned to trust his battlefield
instincts.

Before he could say a word, the occupant of the
passenger seat spoke. ''Be ready to make a dodge,
Gadgets,'' he ordered quickly, then spoke into his ra-

dio. "Able One here. That guy's going on the defensive!"

There was no answer over the radio, but even as Schwarz yanked the wheel hard to take the Chenowyth into a sharp right veer the Hummer changed direction agilely, the vehicles separating like a pair of well-rehearsed fighter planes at an air show.

A puff of smoke emanated from what appeared to have been the solid metal roof of the truck, and in the flash of propulsion fire they saw the roof grow a giant hole, as if a massive fist was just punched through it. Schwarz didn't see any more than that because he was concentrating on maneuvering the Chenowyth over uneven ground without even thinking of taking his foot off the gas pedal.

"Go, Gadgets," urged the man in the seat beside him.

Schwarz could have come up with a colorful retort if he'd had time to get the words out of his mouth, but that was when the earth belched open at their backs and the sand and rocks chased after them, flaying the skin of their exposed necks and arms. Then the sound was gone and Schwarz pulled the vehicle in a sudden left, heading back toward the waiting truck. He wasn't going to stay on the path long enough to let them get a fix.

And then he did an anatomical inventory. No parts missing, as far as he could tell, but it felt like acid had been misted on his nape.

"Gadgets?" Carl Lyons demanded.

"I'm fine."

"Pol?"

There was no answer this time, and Lyons twisted hard to get a look into the rear of the ALSV. Schwarz couldn't look and didn't have time to wonder what was going on with his teammates as he took the Chenowyth into a series of hard twists and turns. Whatever had just been fired was heavy duty. If one of those deals landed on top of them, they were all dead meat.

"Talk to me, Pol."

"I'm okay," the man in the rear replied, but his voice didn't agree with the statement. "I took a rock. How's Phoenix?"

"Still on all fours," Schwarz grunted. He'd spotted the Hummer making its own crazy path down the long, boulder-strewed incline. Schwarz's mental stopwatch reached eleven seconds from the explosion before the second puff appeared, and he straightened the wheel and found the smoothest course available to get them out of there fast. If they had been targeted, if the targeting was good…

He spotted a belch of smoke, fire and earth, and the Hummer was gone from sight. Impossible to tell how close the round had detonated. No time to worry about it now.

CARL "IRONMAN" LYONS saw it happen, the quick mask of fire and dirt that blocked his view of the Hummer. It was close. How close he couldn't tell. Whatever they had inside the truck had been fired accurately. Was it high-end weaponry or an expert at the controls or both? He didn't have the three or four seconds to spare to watch the result of the blast, to find out if the Hummer and its occupants were still alive and kicking.

"You fit enough?" Lyons demanded of the groggy-looking figure in the rear of the ALSV.

"I'm fit," Rosario Blancanales said as he pulled himself into a standing position.

"Good, 'cause we're going in!" Schwarz stated as he pulled the ALSV into a hairpin curve and sent it barreling down the last ten feet of the slope onto flat land and directly at the truck. A driver was in the cab now, wrestling with the wheel, and another man jumped onto the driver's-side step and targeted the ALSV with an assault rifle.

Lyons triggered his M-16 A-2 at the same instant the M-2 machine gun rattled to life over his head. The man with the assault rifle never knew what hit him as a pair of 5.56 mm rounds slammed into his chest and a trio of .50-caliber machine-gun shockers crashed into his shoulders. The next pair of machine-gun rounds took the driver in the chest, and by the time the flying shrapnel of glass splinters bloodied his face he was already dead. When his body went limp his foot slipped off the clutch. The truck jerked forward and began to roll before the engine died. With the movement of the vehicle the dead driver bounced upright for a second or two, eerily pantomiming a living man.

"Engine," Lyons shouted over his shoulder.

"Done," the gunner replied, unleashing another barrage as the ALSV closed to within a few paces of the truck. The rounds crashed through the grille and vanished. Lyons strained for the sound of the impact and could hear it, his ears ringing from the close proximity of the M-2 fire. He couldn't tell if the machine-gun rounds were hitting an engine block or armor.

Then a small, matte black metal object arced out of the top of the truck and landed on the sandy soil just in front of them. Schwarz had slowed to under forty miles per hour, and they were going to be on top of the grenade in under a second. Lyons tried to shout even as he saw the second and third rounds tumbling through the air, but the words turned to a grunt when his body was pushed into the door by the abrupt spin of the Chenowyth. Schwarz saw the grenades at the same time and didn't need Lyons to tell him how to react. Twin billows of dust came from under the wheels as the ALSV struggled for traction on talcum-soft sand, and when it finally shot away at a right angle from the truck the dust cloud became a fireball that burst once, twice, three times in quick succession. This time the rounds were smaller, but they were much closer, and Schwarz felt the shock wave lift the rear end of the vehicle. He experienced a sudden drop in acceleration and checked his gauges, but there was no useful information. When the first aural aftershocks of the explosion faded, he could hear the engine rumbling evenly. He pushed the pedal and got a good response. The problem, whatever it had been, was gone for now.

He accelerated, nosed up the incline and sent the vehicle on a sharp, high-speed turn that brought ninety percent of the weight off the inside tires. He needed to get the ALSV into cover, behind the rock wall that protected the truck from the highway. Just for a moment.

A moment would be long enough to get his bearings and find out if Rosario Blancanales was still alive in the back seat.

CHAPTER THREE

Stony Man Farm, Virginia, U.S.A.

Barbara Price was looking at a live video feed of the battle, as viewed from near Earth orbit. In fact, the orbit was a lot nearer than the National Reconnaissance Office would have liked.

The U.S. government National Reconnaissance Office operated the nation's most capable spy satellites, including an electro-optical satellite currently orbiting low over the Middle East. It often took major arm-twisting to get the NRO to provide access to its satellites at all, let alone to some nameless black-budget outfit. To actually turn the total *control* of the satellite over to these strangers was unheard of. Ridiculous.

Yet it was happening, right now. Stony Man Farm, an agency of the U.S. government that most of the government knew nothing about, was firmly in control of one of the most advanced spy satellites in existence. Key-D, as the NRO had code-named it for the time being, was being operated by the skillful hands of Aaron "The Bear" Kurtzman.

"That's it," Kurtzman said. "We get any closer to Earth and we won't be able to fight off gravity."

"We drop that eye and we'll make NRO angry,"

the young Japanese-American man at the next work-station said in a low voice. Then he smirked. Maybe he liked how he had understated the situation, or maybe he liked the idea of getting the National Reconnaissance Organization hot under the collar. One thing that definitely gave Akira Tokaido a thrill was knowing he was a key push away from sending the billion-dollar satellite into catastrophic free fall.

Kurtzman was rock solid in his wheelchair, eyes locked and unblinking on the monitor as it displayed the Key-D telemetry, plotted and actual. The satellite's variance from the safety parameters Kurtzman had committed to was minuscule, but even that was almost too much. They were well beyond the NRO's operational parameters on the Key-D. With no more than a nudge in the wrong direction that bird would stall and fall like an experimental aircraft when the designer's calculations went wrong.

The computer expert felt the responsibility for the satellite as if the entire heavy metal mass of it rested on his shoulders, and the tension was so thick he was tempted to pull the thing up higher, just for *some* margin of safety. After all, he was no expert in the sort of anomalies a satellite could expect among the upper ionosphere, the band of atmosphere 50 to 250 miles above Earth's surface where X rays and ultraviolet radiation continually split the molecules and atoms of the atmosphere into negative electrons and positive ions. Did this ongoing ionization make shifting winds at an altitude that would be sufficient to buffett the Key-D? Kurtzman didn't *think* so....

But his results were breathtaking. By moving the Key-D lower in its orbit than any NRO restriction would have allowed, they were getting extremely vivid shots of the Iraqi desert. Kurtzman was sure they had achieved nine-centimeter resolution. He'd analyze the digital recording of the shots later to be sure, when he had time for trivialities.

At the empty workstation to his left, the screen showed the raw monochrome image being fed to them from Kcy-D, while the third workstation and the wall screen displayed a computer-enhanced image for mission control purposes. Kurtzman and his team had designed software that added contrast and color, then blended in a digitized, to-scale, high-resolution photographic geographical survey of the territory for added detail—if such a detailed analysis was available. Virtually every square foot of Iraq had been digitally photographed by various military agencies, eager to know when and where the Iraqis started to make suspicious holes in the sand, so for this mission the data was very good.

The software also added the signals coming in from the members of Phoenix Force and Able Team, as well as their vehicles. Their GPS-generated positions were superimposed on the screen. Stony Man Farm mission controller Barbara Price knew at any given second where each of her eight men was on the landscape. She could even see the figure of the smoker as he moved in the direction of the truck in response to the arrival of the two vehicles over the top of the incline.

She heard a quick whispered radio communiqué from Carl Lyons, Able Team commander, to David McCarter, Phoenix Force commander and the leader of the joint mission. She didn't quite catch what he was saying, but there was a note of urgency in his voice. She could see the big dark box of the Hummer on her screen and the smaller, spiderlike image of the Chen-owyth ALSV.

"Stony Base, here," she radioed. "What's up, Able—"

Price stopped and stared at her screen as the jerky, slow image-refresh showed her the two vehicles split apart and head in opposite directions, then suddenly disappear in the thunderhead of an explosion.

Iraq

THE ALSV SKIDDED to a stop the moment the rock wall separated it from the truck. Lyons and Schwarz twisted in their seats almost in unison and found Blancanales collapsed in the rear. He pushed himself into a sitting position and stared at the blood coating his hands, blinking as more of it trickled along the corners of his eyes.

"It's kind of like a roller coaster when you drive, Gadgets," Blancanales said with a grin as he wiped the blood on his shirt. "I've been hit in the head with flying rocks before, but never twice in the same minute."

Relief flooded through Schwarz. Blancanales wasn't seriously hurt. Two close-proximity blasts in the rear of the ALSV, which didn't offer any protection, was really pushing their luck. "Hey, I wasn't the one who said we should go to frigging Iraq for the weekend," he said.

"I know," Blancanales replied. "But with you it's *always* Wisconsin Dells."

"Can it," Lyons muttered. It got on his nerves when Gadgets and Pol started trading quips when things got hot and hairy. He knew it was their way of easing battlefield stress, but couldn't they at least wait until the battle was done with?

"Able One here—talk to me, Phoenix."

"Phoenix One...shi—"

It was McCarter, and his last profanity was cut off, followed by a percussive burst from beyond the rock wall. It sounded very big and far away.

"*Now* what are they using?" Blancanales demanded as he pulled himself to his feet by the straps of his quick-disconnect harness, the only thing that had kept him from flying out of the rear end of the ALSV a half dozen times since they came down the hill. It saved him again when Schwarz stood on the accelerator and spun the Chenowyth in a tight circle. Blancanales knew better than to fight it, hanging on and going for the ride as his body tried to lift out the rear of the vehicle, dangling in the harness like a horse in a veterinarian's sling. The desert-camou nylon was pulled tight, creaking like stressed leather, and Blancanales held hard on to the M-2's handgrip. If he ended up going out the back of this dune buggy he was going to take the machine gun with him.

"Able One here. Stony Base, what's Phoenix's situation?"

"Unknown," Price said. She sounded cool, in control. She was the backbone of stability when the Farm's special operations groups were in the field. "We just spotted another rocket launch from the truck. Wait— Phoenix is still rolling."

"Yeah, we're here, Stony Base," McCarter shouted, his voice coming over their headphone speakers under the rattle of automatic rifle fire. "We can't get close to that truck. We can barely outrun the rounds they're firing at us."

"Able One here. We're making a run, Phoenix," Lyons declared into the radio as they turned sharply around the rock wall and faced the hood of the panel truck. Schwarz accelerated directly at it, alert for telltale signs of the inhabitants. He could see no windows or access openings for weapons, just the slack-jawed corpse of the driver. When he was just yards away he swerved to the left, bringing the ALSV alongside for a second, and Blancanales unleashed a .50-caliber stream that zigzagged over it, stem to stern, Then the fire halted as the truck fell behind them and Schwarz took a right, putting them again behind the protection of the rock.

"Able Two here—bad news, Stony Base," Blancanales radioed. "All I did was dent the metal. That truck is well armored."

"Hell," Lyons muttered.

"Incoming, Phoenix!" Price said suddenly, and the three members of Able Team heard another explosion beyond the wall. Schwarz turned the wheel and was about to hit the gas when Lyons halted him with a gesture.

"Keep them distracted," Lyons said with characteristic brevity.

"Keep who distracted and why?" Schwarz demanded incredulously, then realized Lyons was removing his seat harness.

"The truck, so they don't kill me," Lyons said through gritted teeth. Then he was jogging away from the ALSV.

"I guess he'd rather walk home than drive with us," Blancanales said.

"Stony Base, here," Price said sharply in their ears. "Report, Phoenix."

"Phoenix One here. I sure wish our intelligence had included the fact that these guys have rockets, Stony," McCarter growled, a hard edge to his voice. "We're staying outside their range. Able, you ready to make another pass?"

There was a slight pause, during which Blancanales decided that Lyons wasn't going to answer. "Able Two here," he said. "Negative, Phoenix One. We could drain the gun into that truck, and I don't think we'd get inside. We're going to do some attention-getting, instead."

"Attention-getting?"

"To distract the guys in the truck," Blancanales explained reasonably. "You know. So they don't kill Ironman."

Stony Man Farm, Virginia

"ABLE ONE?" Price asked, furrowing her brow as she zoomed in the display on the small digital A1 icon clearly moving away from the ALSV. "What's going on?"

"Able One here." Lyons was breathing heavily. "I'm going to get inside the truck."

"How are you going to get in if we couldn't break in with the M-2?" Price demanded.

"I can't exactly explain it all right now, Stony Base. I'm climbing a big rock in a big hurry."

Price felt her blood run cold. She *knew* what Lyons was going to do. The picture of it blossomed in her mind vividly, and instantly the mental image changed to its potentially deadly outcome.

"Negative, Able One," Price said. "Do *not* attempt to penetrate the truck."

"Somebody's got to do it," Lyons responded, his breath labored. "Can't talk. Going off-line temporarily."

"Able One, do *not* go off—" It was too late. The A1 icon on her screen turned red, indicating a malfunction, and a glance at the more detailed auxiliary status screen showed her that Lyons's communications link wasn't functioning.

"Able Two—" Again it was too late. As she was about to order Lyons's teammates to go back and get him, she saw the arachnid-like image of the ALSV on her display career around the rock and pass in front of the truck at an angle, putting distance between themselves and Lyons. If she ordered them back now, they would fail to provide the distraction Lyons requested. The men in that truck were highly trained professionals, and if they realized Lyons was coming at them on foot, they'd be able to gun him down in a heartbeat. She was sure of it.

But they might gun him down anyway. Lyons could still be spotted. The truck might be guarded by a security grid of some kind. Laser motion detection. Sound sensors. Who knew?

Price halted that line of thinking. Since there was nothing more she could do, every second she spent thinking about it was wasted effort better channeled to providing the assistance that would be constructive to her men in the field.

Lyons was on his own.

Another puff on the display. For a second Price swore she saw the streak of a projectile on the satellite feed. If she did, it meant the projectile was better than 9 cm in size. That was as sharp as the Key-D resolution could possibly see. Nine hundred millimeters was a fairly large projectile.

"Able, incoming!" she radioed sharply, but it was too late to be of help. Even as she spoke the explosive detonated, and a fuzzy sphere appeared on her screen, engulfing the Able Vehicle icon on her screen as it wiggled away from the dark rectangle of the truck. She held her breath as she stared at the blocky display, praying for the ALSV to emerge from the fuzzy sphere.

What seemed like a minute was under two seconds. Then the ALSV icon emerged from the sphere. Was it slowing? Coasting?

"Report, Able Two," Price said in a level voice.

"Able Two here, Stony Base, and we're tired of getting the back of our necks singed," Blancanales replied.

"Phoenix One here," McCarter interrupted on the line, speaking fast. "You're pushing your damn luck, Able. Stay the hell out of their range. They're compensating for your speed, and the next time they'll guess your dodge and you'll be nothing more than a hole in the desert."

"Understood, Phoenix One, but I think we need to make one more run."

"Able, do not make another run, understood? Able?"

Price watched the small, fragile-looking spindly shape of the Chenowyth on her display make a hard turn to the right and head broadside at the truck. This time they weren't playing games. Schwarz was driving a straight line at the side of the truck. No swerving or zigzagging. What was he doing? Why?

Price saw another insubstantial puff appear at the top of the truck.

Iraq

SCHWARZ HAD BEEN making a subconscious study of the terrain in the past few minutes and picked his approach path carefully. The way was clear of obstructions and smooth as a parking lot as far as the ALSV was concerned. He knew the gunners in the truck, either the operators themselves or their computerized control systems, had evaluated his speed and come up with a good guess as to his top speed. Now he was planning to befuddle them. Heading on a direct path, he could bring the ALSV to even faster speeds and outrun their aim yet again. He hoped. Overhead he heard the M-2 rattle to life as Blancanales picked a spot and worried it with a continuous stream of .50-caliber rounds, impacting the same point on the side of the truck van with terrific force.

It was a furious onslaught that only increased in intensity as the ALSV's proximity rapidly grew, and Blancanales was wondering just how good that armor inside really was. Tough enough to stand up to this kind of abuse? More important, were the inhabitants so confident in their truck's armor that they would have the wherewithal to make a tactical response while that kind of sleet pounded against the window?

For three long seconds Blancanales thought the truck van had to have some sort of bombproof shielding as he watched the big dent just keep getting bigger and deeper. Then there was a glimmer of darkness in the middle. The metal gave. At the same instant smoke erupted from the roof of the truck, and Blancanales dropped as he felt the ALSV veer away, swinging him into one of the support girders. Before he could get his arm in front of his face the explosion came.

But Schwarz had guessed correctly. Blancanales could tell from the sound that the round was farther away than the last two, and the blast of flesh-peeling sand and pebbles never came.

"Able Two here. I put a hole in the truck before that round hit," he said rapidly into the radio.

"Able, this is Phoenix One. Get out of range now. Do you understand?"

"McCarter ain't a happy camper," Schwarz called over his shoulder as he steered them out of range and slowed.

"Able Two here. We got those guys if I can widen that opening and get some rounds rattling around inside that truck," Blancanales radioed urgently.

"No way, Able," McCarter shot back. "You guys are pushing your luck way too far. Stay out of range, do you understand?"

"Do we understand?" Schwarz called to Blancanales.

Blancanales made his decision in a heartbeat, but he never got the chance to say so before Lyons was on the air.

"Able One here. Don't do it, Gadgets. I'm going inside."

"Oh, shit," Schwarz said, "there he is."

CHAPTER FOUR

There Lyons was, dangling from a big rock on Kevlar rope like a lunatic spider. He wasn't directly over the truck, but he was close enough. If the occupants realized he was up there, all they had to do was turn their rocket launcher in his direction and he was dead. They wouldn't even have to aim. Any shot would probably throw enough rock shrapnel at him to chew him to pieces even if it didn't dislodge him. But why waste a good missile? They'd probably just tag him with an assault rifle and watch him drop.

Lyons descended another ten feet and paused again, low enough to get a good view of the cliff side of the truck. It was as featureless as the front. No way in. There might be an entrance in the truck cab. He might be able to blow that or the rear doors if he had the time and didn't get shot dead first. Too risky to try it. The truck and its contents had to be stopped, and it had to be done very soon.

Because the Iraqis were on their way by now.

Lyons decided he'd worry about that problem later. He was going to have to drop in on this crew from the roof and hope they didn't decide to launch a round while he was at it. If nothing else, he wanted to survive to hold this escapade over the heads of Cowboy Kissinger and T. J. Hawkins, both known to climb big rocks in their off hours.

The Able Team leader shifted his weight, gripping the rappel line with one hand as he swung his body far enough into space from the overhanging lip of cliff to show him a few inches of the interior of the truck.

The top of the truck used some sort of roll-away armor panels, which he could see nested against the side of the interior, leaving only a thin fabric covering on top for appearances. This shredded when the first round was fired from the inside. He also saw the weapon hardware, smaller and closer to the roof than he had expected. Then he was swinging away again. The next swing showed him just a little more of the interior and the weapon, as well as the shielding and an electronic box adhered to the shielding with cables running into the walls of the truck. He also saw the top of a man's head and his hands on the controls of the weapon.

Some sort of launcher for small rockets, with a targeting system requiring sensors on the side panels of the truck. Lyons didn't have time to feel foolish as he swung back and then again found himself over the truck, looking even farther into the interior. Three men. Two standing below, arguing in front of a small bank of displays and other electronics equipment, while the third crouched on the elevated platform some six feet off the floor. Lyons heard a snatch of the angry words and didn't understand any of it. It was Hebrew.

Which was to be expected.

Were there others inside? Only ten or twelve more gunmen could have been lurking in the sections of the truck interior Lyons couldn't see. He swung away, did some quick thinking and performed a quick equipment prep. He sure wasn't going back the way he came.

"Able One here," he said. "I'm going in."

He swung over the truck and eased up pressure on the rope. The man behind the rocket launcher saw something and turned to look straight up, getting a very good view of the soles of the boots that crushed his forehead.

Lyons heard the crunch, then widened his stance as the figure crumpled and he fought for purchase on whatever platform was underneath him. One ankle twisted as he landed on the crumpling body of the gunner, and he fought to clear it while his eyes furiously sought the details of the interior. The truck was dark compared to the sun-drenched desert outside.

The pair of arguing men at the controls stared at Lyons in blank amazement while another pair hidden in the darkness made a grab for weapons strapped on their shoulders, separating to make themselves harder targets. Lyons's reaction was instantaneous. The Atchisson Assault 12 shotgun came off his shoulder. It roared in the dim light and slammed into the gunner on the right, dropping him like a bag of rocks. In his left hand Lyons held the Colt Python. The big handgun bucked in his grip, and the second gunner went down as he triggered his subgun. The quick burst went wild.

Lyons spun to face the far end of the truck interior and tossed himself off the platform in the same movement to avoid a spray of machine-gun fire from the darkness. He hit the truck floor heavily, rolled to dissipate the energy and was on his feet again, backing into a corner as he liberally filled the interior with shotgun pellets.

The machine gunner hurried away from Lyons, but

the next blast from the Atchisson cut his knees out from underneath him before he could get Lyons into target acquisition.

Lyons was pretty sure the guy was completely out of the picture, but the next blast from the Atchisson caved in his back and made the gunner a confirmed nonfactor.

Then Lyons was alone.

He wasn't convinced of it at first. Where had the two arguing men gone? How had they escaped without him seeing? Only seconds had gone by and there had been no light from an opened door. He stepped quickly into the back end of the truck, scrutinizing the dark interior. He was convinced they would fire from some concealed hiding place at any moment.

He heard the engine start up, and the truck van lurched. The floor tilted under him, and Lyons fell back on one hand to avoid sliding. Lubricated on its own blood, the nearby corpse snailed several inches down the floor then stopped, its head dragged from one side to the other so that the glassy, wide eyes stared at Lyons.

The Able Team leader ignored it, leaping over the blood and making a grab for the small ladder used to mount the firing platform. He manhandled the operator into a sitting position, then saw just how heavily caved in the man's skull was. The operator wasn't going to be spilling any intelligence, ever. Lyons tipped him over the low wall of shielding, dumping him to the floor, then stepped up to balance with both feet on the top of the shielding, his head protruding from the roof of the van.

"Able One here. The truck van is secure, but I let two or more of them get away."

"Phoenix One here. They're in the truck cab. That engine must have been armored just as well as the van. They had it rigged for quick disconnect from the van."

"Able Three here. We're coming in to pick you up."

"Stony Base here with bad news," Price said evenly. "I have one low-flying aircraft headed your way."

That would be Iraqi military. They were coming out to investigate the destruction of their radar stations. They'd be sending surveillance teams to look for suspicious activity in the vicinity, using aircraft that could fly too low and slow to get a reaction out of those enforcing the No-Fly Zone.

"Able One here. Give me a fix on them, Stony Base," Lyons radioed.

There was a moment of silence as Price thought that through. "You're going to shoot them down?"

"I'm going to try. It'll sure buy us time."

Price didn't argue or ask for an explanation but quickly read off the coordinates of the incoming aircraft. "It's heading at you right out of Baghdad, Able One. Does that put her behind the cliff?"

Lyons had been on the platform studying the controls. More Hebrew. He stepped up and poked out his head, looking for the aircraft and seeing nothing. If the Iraqis were coming in from behind the cliff, then he wouldn't be able to see or fire on them until they swept around to his side of the rock. By then they could have radioed home with a report of two non-Iraqi military vehicles trespassing in their desert.

Then he saw a hovering speck. It was still a few miles away and looked like it was coming right at him.

"Able One here. I see the bird, Stony Base. Patch me through to Cowboy."

An unusual request, and again there was no time-wasting interrogation. "Here he comes. Cowboy, I have Able One, code red."

John "Cowboy" Kissinger was on the line in seconds, as if he had been standing by waiting for the communications link. In reality he was probably in the Stony Man armory, wrapped up in a customization project or reverse-engineering new weapons technology. As Stony Man weaponsmith and armorer, he was also an expert in defense-attack systems.

"Kissinger here."

"Able One. Cowboy, I have some sort of a rocket launcher here, probably Israeli, and I need to be proficient using it in about forty-five seconds."

"Understood. Describe the general layout."

"It's tied to some sort of electronics, and a series of cables run to the walls of the truck I'm in, probably sensors. Computer tower bolted alongside. The readout is in Hebrew. One rocket in the tube and three in the cradle alongside, reading to fire out the roof."

"Any numbers or legend on the controls?"

Lyons read out a serial number and could hear Cowboy typing into his ID database. "Here's something. MAPATS. I'll spell it—"

"Man Portable Anti-Tank System," Kissinger interrupted. "Israeli made. The missile rides a laser beam to the target to a range of about three miles, depending on the warhead you're using."

"No markings that I can see on the rocket itself, Cowboy," Lyons said, peering closely at the nose cone nestled in the steel cradle at his side.

"Then wait until your target is within two miles, Able One," Kissinger replied. "Even closer if it's moving rapidly. This weapon is only as good as its target fix and range.''

Lyons considered that. These rockets had failed to hit the Stony Man vehicles at close range and hadn't even tried for a hit when they were more than a few hundred yards away.

''Cowboy, you sure we're talking about the same piece of equipment?''

''There's not all that many rocket launchers in the world today, Able One, and only one MAPATS with those model numbers,'' Kissinger replied evenly. ''This one must be customized to link to external sensors, maybe an external auxiliary laser.''

Lyons bent and did a quick underside examination, enough to verify that it did appear to have a modular mounting mechanism and electronic connectors. ''Okay, Cowboy, let's do the drill.''

''Describe the display.''

''Large type that says Auto Mode.''

''Status or situation displayed nearby?'' Kissinger said.

''Yeah. 'Status locked.'''

''Is there a prompt in the lock field?'' Kissinger demanded.

''No.''

''Can you tab a prompt to the lock field?''

''There's no keyboard. It's not a damn PC, Cowboy!''

''Then what's the input device?'' Kissinger shot back.

''Hold on.''

Lyons was unclear as to the passage of time and he needed to know the proximity of the Iraqi aircraft, so he stepped on the shielding edges and looked out of the top of the truck again. The aircraft was gone. Disappeared.

Then it came into view from behind the cliff edge. It was a helicopter, small, flying low, meandering at a leisurely pace over the desert. If it didn't move a little farther to the east, Lyons was never going to be able to get a rocket past that rock wall.

"Able One here," he radioed as he dropped to the platform. "Stony Base, what's the distance on the Iraqis?"

"I put her 2.6 miles from your position," Price answered.

"I don't have much time, Cowboy. I need to get this launcher operational! Can you or can you not—" That was when he dropped down and kicked something plastic in the darkness on the platform, hanging on the end of a coiled cable. He grabbed it and saw a Compaq logo.

"Hey, Cowboy, I found the keyboard." It was about as sheepish as Lyons ever got. "I'm tabbing to the lock field. Okay, I have it unlocked."

As the weapon unlocked, the cylinder beneath the modular mounting socket extended with the whine of a servomotor, settling in seconds into an elevated position above the roof of the truck. As it was painted black, Lyons realized it would be virtually invisible against the truck without close inspection.

"That's not standard equipment," Kissinger said when Lyons described the servo positioning of the weapon. "I hope everything else works the way the factory designed it."

The small digital sight that was a window on the display showed him the distant helicopter. Between the two of them, it took just seconds for Lyons to find the correct targeting procedure and direct the laser mounted on the launcher to locate the helicopter, still hugging the edge of the cliff from Lyons's perspective. He achieved a Target Lock message and promptly lost it when the helicopter dipped lower. A red *X* appeared on the screen, only to be replaced again by the Target Lock message as the Iraqi aircraft bobbed up.

"They installed it for antiaircraft, but they assumed those aircraft would be attacking the truck, not hanging around a few miles out," Kissinger hypothesized. "It's angled up so it can't get a good laser lock on a target so low."

"That explains their trouble tagging us," Lyons agreed. It sounded logical, but it was all guesswork. He watched the helicopter drift to his left, almost disappearing again behind the cliff wall. If he hit the cliff with the rocket, would he go, too? Maybe. Then the helicopter sank, hovered and rose again. It was as if the pilot were drunk.

"Let's get on with it," Lyons said to himself.

Then the perfect shot presented itself as the helicopter drifted higher and farther to his right. At the moment Lyons realized he had been given a perfect target, he also realized that the helicopter's new behavior came from the fact that it had spotted their activity and was coming at them. The helicopter pilot would be grabbing for the radio. Somebody in Baghdad would get an alert. Lyons didn't bother to consider the consequences of that before stabbing at the key he hoped was the trigger.

Above his head, the rocket flashed and sizzled and was gone in a plume of white smoke. On the small digital sight display Lyons saw the helicopter turn to a cloud of smoke and gray fire.

DAVID MCCARTER STOOD inside the crook of the passenger door of the Hummer with the field-hardened GeoVid pressed to the bridge of his nose, trying to get a reading on the digital distance meter, but the Iraqi helicopter was outside the thousand-meter range of the field glasses. Around him he noticed the uncomfortable quiet.

There had been no contingency plans possible for the arrival of Iraqi air forces. A small special operations group simply couldn't carry antiaircraft weaponry with them and have any hope of moving fast. Now the weapon had been fortuitously delivered into their hands.

"Come on, mate," McCarter muttered, swinging the glasses across the expanse of tan sand to the silent truck trailer.

"What *exactly* is he waiting for?" Gary Manning demanded somewhere behind him.

Manning, a big Canadian with piercing gray eyes and the weather-battered complexion of an outdoorsman, knew as well as the rest of them that Lyons was having trouble getting his sights on the helicopter. If he fired at the wrong moment and that rocket grazed the cliff, it could very well destroy the truck. And Lyons with it.

The helicopter wasn't cooperating. It was veering aimlessly back and forth. If it hadn't been crawling along at a leisurely pace, McCarter would have guessed the pilot was avoiding the imminent attack.

Then the helicopter moved up and forward, looking to McCarter like a hunting dog suddenly catching a scent and coming to the alert. They'd spotted something. They'd be radioing their base. It had to be clear of the cliff by now.

The youngest man on the team, Thomas Jackson Hawkins, was sitting in the window on the opposite side of the Hummer, assessing the scene with his own field glasses. "Is he waitin' for Christmas?" Hawkins demanded. The words were still coming out of his mouth when the air was slashed by the ignition of the missile. The white streak of the rocket covered the distance to the helicopter in a heartbeat, and the Iraqi bird ceased to exist.

"All right, Ironman!" Hawkins blurted.

McCarter didn't hear him. Even before the burning image in the binoculars descended halfway to the desert sands he saw the second aircraft emerge from behind it, coming out of the sandstorm wake of the first bird.

"When it rains it craps," Manning declared. He swung himself bodily into the Hummer. McCarter was already inside, pulling his door shut viciously, and Hawkins saved himself from a neck injury by sliding into his seat just before the driver gunned the engine and sent the Hummer barreling over the sandpile that had been partially shielding them.

"Stony Base here, I've got a second aircraft coming in fast," Price reported.

"We see it," McCarter shot back, biting back the urge to demand an explanation. If Stony Man Farm could see people on the ground with their special little spy toy, why couldn't they see an extra few tons of aircraft? He'd save it for later.

"Able Two, Phoenix One here. What's your position?"

"Moving around the back of the rock," Rosario Blancanales stated. "You'll see us in a minute. The new bird is already coming over to say hi."

"Run distraction. We'll get Ironman," McCarter replied. He pointed out the windshield, and the driver didn't need further instructions. He veered off his head-on course with the new helicopter and headed toward the truck.

"Able One, your ride is here. Copy that?" McCarter added on the open frequency.

"Understood," Lyons answered. "Give me a minute."

"Give you a minute?" McCarter said, unable to believe what he had heard, then he saw Lyons poke out of the top of the truck van and hoist a gangly metal apparatus over the side. It hit the dry earth hard, and Lyons landed in a crouch next to it with a piece of tubular weaponry slung on the same shoulder as his combat shotgun.

"What's the deal?" McCarter demanded.

"Going to take out that second bird," Lyons responded grimly as he hoisted his hardware through the back-end window of the Hummer and jumped inside, sitting on the rear window ledge and holding on to the roof racks for support.

"How the bloody hell are you going to do that?"

"Drop me out there," Lyons responded shortly, giving a wave into the open, empty desert. "They saw the first bird go down, and they'll never risk exposing themselves to the truck."

"You'll get chopped to pieces, mate!" McCarter said, and that was just his first argument in a long series he could have used to describe the foolhardiness of what Lyons was proposing.

"We have got to get that bird down, David," Lyons replied. "We still have the truck to catch up to."

"It's very risky, Able One," Price intoned.

Hawkins snorted in the back seat and started to add his thoughts to Price's understatement, but McCarter's hand went up, flat. Without speaking he was saying simply, *stop,* and the Hummer full of commandos fell into silence.

McCarter had to think.

He had been known as a man with a temper during his earlier days as a commando on Phoenix Force, when it was under the leadership of veteran soldier Yakov Katzenelenbogen. When he was put into a position of command he had been forced to mature quickly, but sometimes the old temper flared. Now he was fighting it, packing it down. He would *not* allow himself to lose control and make a bad decision. He mentally ticked off the facts as he knew them.

Was what Lyons proposing viable? Yes. This weapon was theoretically portable, and he had evidence it could down a helicopter. But would Lyons survive in the open long enough to fire the thing? That was the big *maybe.* How fast could it fire? How close would the helicopter need to be and how quickly could a target lock be established? These he didn't know. Lyons knew, and he thought the option was viable.

In the midst of combat the seconds could seem like minutes, and it had taken him a full three seconds to decide he would allow Lyons to go out into the desert and maybe to his death.

"We'll do it."

The driver hit the accelerator hard, and the Hummer fishtailed on a patch of loose sand before rumbling into the open.

McCarter heard the rattle of machine-gun fire, and he spotted the Chenowyth bounding over the rolling sands with tiny geysers of dust chasing it every foot of the way.

CHAPTER FIVE

Despite sanctioning by the UN and years of U.S. intelligence effort, Iraq inevitably rebuilt its military arsenal after the heavy losses incurred in the early 1990s. Iraq's Air Defense Force was especially hard hit during Desert Storm, and for years there hadn't been enough hardware to support the staff, so pilots and ground crew were left sitting on their thumbs. But where there was a will there was a way. Iraq's dictator had the will and he found the way. Making use of a network of illegal arms traders, guns, ammunition and even aircraft had been purchased, sometimes one and two at a time. The prices were high, but the power base had to be restored. The common people of Iraq paid dearly for the rearming of their despot.

The Eurocopter Fennec AS 550 C3 was equipped for lights-out night flight with the pilot wearing night-vision gear. This particular Fennec had been purchased when just a year old, in France, by an oil company that didn't exist, then transported to the oil company's non-existent Azerbaijani oil field. Then the arms traders who perpetrated the forgery sold the Fennec, in a batch of eight mismatched aircraft, to Iraq.

The arms trader had been forced to deal a little on the Fennec—the buyer really wanted it with antitank missiles or a 20 mm gun, and all he could offer them was the side-mounted machine gun. But he still made 150-percent profit.

The Turbomeca Arriel 2B power plant could bring the Fennec to a speed of roughly 150 miles per hour even when loaded, and right now it was having no problem following the vehicle that was doing its best to maneuver away on the desert floor below. The Iraqi pilot was grinning as he banked the Fennec to follow a sharp swerve by the open combat vehicle. He'd seen them before. He knew those were Americans. He didn't know what the Americans were doing on Iraqi soil, but it was clearly a violation of Iraqi sovereignty. The president might pin the medal on him personally as reward for putting a halt to this invasion.

"Follow him!" his copilot blurted as the vehicle swerved sharply again, taking the pilot off guard. He banked as the vehicle traveled directly underneath the Fennec in a narrow hairpin and was suddenly traveling back the way they had just come.

"You are letting them get away," the copilot said accusingly.

"Shut up," the pilot said, his face hot. His copilot was a young hotshot, rising fast through the ranks of the Air Defense Force through a mixture of viciousness and salesmanship. The pilot couldn't keep up with these idiot self-promoters who always outranked him in the end. He knew he was a better flyer than his copilot, but the younger man was right. He should have expected the dodge and been ready for it. Instead he was playing catch-up as he banked too sharply.

"You will lose control!" the copilot exclaimed, clearly in fear of his life as the aircraft shuddered to stay on course.

The pilot fought the Fennec to level flight, enjoying the copilot's terror even if he had been momentarily petrified himself. Then his fear redoubled as he realized he had been tricked again. The hasty move had brought the Eurocopter to a near standstill. It was a sitting duck. Any moment—

The thump of .50-caliber machine gun rounds traveled across the underside of the aircraft, and the pilot swore he felt the hits through his boots. The copilot was shouting at him, swearing vehemently, and he heard the thump of the gunner slamming into his seat when he pushed the aircraft in a near vertical ascent, rotors straining. The desperate move kept the belly of the aircraft pointed at the gunfire, and the machine gun pounded into them relentlessly as the seconds stretched to infinity. The heavy rounds would chew their way into the cockpit or tear out some vital parts at any second.

Then the aircraft gripped the air and shot up as if getting a fresh burst of adrenaline, and the pounding fire fell away. Despite the roar of the stressed Turbomeca powerhouse, the cockpit was blessedly silent.

"God in heaven, he is dead!"

It was the gunner, who had crawled into the cockpit to find out what was going on. The pilot hadn't even noticed that at least one of the machine-gun rounds had penetrated the cockpit. It had wormed its way through the floor into the copilot's abdomen.

The pilot went through a gamut of emotions as he stared at the wide-eyed corpse. Satisfaction dominated. But then he got worried, trying to picture the schematics of the aircraft and what vital components were in the floor where the round had penetrated. He couldn't remember.

"We will kill them!" the gunner was exhorting. "We must slay them all. I hate the Americans!"

The pilot nodded, feeling more confident as the Fennec responded perfectly to the small adjustments he made to her flight. The helicopter seemed unfazed by the barrage, and there was still a good prize to be claimed on the ground.

"Get the doors open," the pilot ordered the gunner. "We will make them pay their debt in their own blood."

"Understood," the gunner replied. "Let us take care of him first."

The gunner pointed to the south. There was one man, standing in the open, waving his arms at the big Hummer that was circling around him.

Yes. One man, in the open, unprotected. An easy target and far more satisfying than taking out a vehicle. He brought the Fennec into a dive.

"Ready," the gunner radioed.

"Target the car first," the pilot said. "Do not let them reach that man."

He leveled the helicopter and brought her broadside to the scenario on the desert floor, then heard the rattle of his deck-mounted machine gun behind him. The Hummer was out of range, and the Americans inside had been convinced to stay there. So much for their helpless comrade standing in the middle of nowhere. The patrol vehicle was also keeping her distance. The Iraqi gunner fired another burst of machine-gun fire, going for the lone figure, but before it reached the solitary American he raised his own weapon and triggered a round at the Fennec.

The pilot was startled, and he veered away, then realized it was a feint as the round arced well underneath them and hit the ground with a crack. The round was fired out of a grenade launcher mounted on the soldier's M-16. It would never reach the aircraft, and he was acting like a gun-shy rookie pilot. He pulled the chopper around again and lined up as before, creeping closer.

"What are you doing?" the gunner demanded. "He's got a grenade launcher!"

"It is an M-203," the pilot assured him. "It won't fire more than four hundred meters."

"You better be sure of that," the gunner said nervously as the American triggered another round into the sky. It never came closer than thirty meters before falling to the earth and blowing a crater in the sand.

"Now take that piece of swine down," the pilot said with satisfaction.

"Gladly."

"OKAY, ABLE ONE, give me an explanation," McCarter said coolly, fighting to keep the top of his head from blowing off as the pressure inside his skull seemed to grow exponentially.

"The targeting is nonfunctional on the rocket launcher," Lyons reported tersely. "I've got to bring them in close, so I'm playing with their heads."

"You idiot!" McCarter bellowed. He'd been had. "Rafe, we're going in to get him."

"Right," said the powerful figure behind the wheel, dragging the Hummer into gear.

"Able One, be ready for a pickup, and that's an order," McCarter said.

"Too late," Lyons responded, and then McCarter saw that it *was* too late.

The Iraqi helicopter returned to a broadside posture,

looking down on Carl Lyons, who responded by firing another 40 mm grenade from his M-203. It never came close. The machine gunner was getting the gun lined up on the Able Team leader as the helicopter sank even lower, just above the top of the grenade arc.

Lyons played his only card. Dropping the M-16/ M-203 to the ground, he twisted and fell on his stomach behind the Israeli-made rocket launcher, mounted on the field tripod he'd found in the truck. He'd been forced to rip out the sensor connection when he extracted it from the van. He hoped it would fire on manual; he hoped his aim was good; he hoped he had time to find out before the machine gunner got him.

He quickly adjusted the tube and fired. From five hundred yards he could still see the expression of shock on the face of the helicopter gunner when the rocket launched in a burst of smoke. Lyons never saw the terror on the face of the pilot, who never even had time to take evasive action. The rocket smashed into the raised landing gear and detonated, tearing into the power plant, the hydraulics, the electronics, turning it all to scrap. The gunner and the pilot were dead so fast they didn't feel it happen.

The packed sand of the desert came up to meet the wreckage and turned it into a conflagration.

CHAPTER SIX

"Able One," David McCarter said, "you're a son of a bitch."

"Affirmative, Phoenix One," Lyons answered tersely.

"Stay there. We're coming to get you."

"Uh-oh," Schwarz said to himself. He didn't like the sound of that. He'd known McCarter—and Lyons, for that manner—for years, and knew that the two of them had the perfect personalities to butt heads when the opportunity arose.

He was the first to admit that Lyons had the personality to butt heads with anybody. Ironman was this very grim, very determined guy. Still, he and Lyons had a kind of bond that went beyond friendship. It would take an accountant to add up the times each had saved the life of the other, same as Blancanales. There was a closeness to the members of Able that he was sure couldn't be found in a bigger team like Phoenix Force.

"I've got him, Phoenix One," Schwarz radioed hastily and shot toward Lyons, swerving to give the flaming carcass of the Iraqi chopper clearance. Schwarz was relieved to hear Barbara Price come on the line before McCarter could protest. She was asking for a report.

"Good shooting, Ironman," Blancanales said with a

grin as the Able Team leader pulled himself into the passenger seat.

"Thanks," Lyons replied, refusing to break a smile. "I just wish there were more rounds for that launcher. It might come in handy later."

Schwarz cocked a head at him. "So you pulled that stunt knowing you had only one shot at bringing down that chopper?"

"I can't wait until David finds out," Blancanales said.

"He doesn't need to know right now. We've got to stop that truck."

McCarter was finishing a summary of recent events by the time Able Team's Chenowyth pulled alongside the Hummer. The Phoenix Force leader had managed to get through it without making any accusations, but Schwarz knew that when this ordeal was over there was going to be some hell to pay.

"Iraq always this much fun?" Schwarz asked T. J. Hawkins, who was looking morose in the rear window of the Hummer.

"Don't ask me," Hawkins said. "They haven't even let me out of the back seat yet."

"Okay, Able and Phoenix, the good news is that our truck isn't looking healthy. We're tracking it moving at less than thirty miles per hour," Price reported. "Bad news is that it turned off the main highway to Al Hindiyah. They're taking a shortcut dirt road to meet up with another highway going directly north into Baghdad. And you need to stop them before they get there."

"Into the fire," Blancanales said in a resigned murmur.

"It's a mixed blessing. If you can catch up to the

truck on that road, you'll be less likely to be seen. It's empty wasteland there. Once they reach the highway north the task becomes more challenging."

"Understood, Stony Base," McCarter said. "We're moving out now." The Briton pointed ahead, and Schwarz steered the Chenowyth around the rock and onto the highway. Following Price's instructions, they left the pavement almost immediately and started overland on a faint, ancient trail.

"You're on the path of history," Price said. "It's a trail used by the Persians for centuries. Now its mostly forgotten and erased, but we can see it pretty well from our eye in the sky."

"Population in the vicinity?" McCarter asked.

"Almost none for the next ten miles," Price reported. "Just before the highway, though, you leave the desert and enter pastureland irrigated out of the Euphrates. That's when you'll start running into locals."

"What about the military?"

"We're monitoring all the military activity that we can from here," Price said. "As far as we can tell, there's nobody coming yet."

"But you couldn't see that second helicopter when it came at us, am I right Stony Base?" McCarter said testily.

"Correct, Phoenix One. They were too low, and the dust clouds raised by the first chopper camouflaged them. We're trying to compensate for that situation now so we won't be caught off guard again." There was a hint of an apology in her voice.

"I know you'll do the best job possible, Stony Base," McCarter said.

Schwarz was concentrating on keeping the Chenowyth on all four wheels as they rocketed over the dry terrain of the desert, but even so he could hear the doubt in McCarter's voice. Was it disappointment? Chagrin? Stony Base had kind of let them down.

"This is turning into a real downer," Schwarz said quietly.

Somehow, Lyons heard him. "Yeah," he answered icily, "not like the happy, carefree terrorist hunts we usually go on."

Blancanales, unlike Schwarz, knew when it was smart to say nothing.

They didn't call him Politician for nothing.

THE END OF THE CASE came quickly, almost anticlimactically.

Rafael Encizo jumped out of the Hummer's driver's seat and jogged to the chosen pile of rocks with the Ruger Model 77 Mark II Magnum sniper rifle gripped in both hands. Assembled by Manning during the drive, the weapon was loaded with a trio of rounds. There were more rounds in Encizo's pockets.

"You made good time, Phoenix Two," Price said in his headphones. "You've got a two-minute lead over the truck."

Two minutes wasn't a big advantage, but enough, Encizo was thinking as he laid himself out on the earth behind the small rockfall, peering down the ancient path where the truck would appear. He judged the distance at 350 yards, confirmed it with the digital distance monitor on his field glasses and readied himself as the other members of Phoenix Force sped away.

"Able One here. We're in position."

"Phoenix One here. We are in position. I have the truck in sight, Phoenix Two."

"I'm as ready as I'll get," Encizo replied.

He heard the truck now, the rattle of the diesel. He saw the shadow appear on the level ground on the tracks where countless men and women and pack animals had walked over the course of centuries. Then the truck came into his sights.

Encizo's torso was rigid as he squeezed the trigger and rode out the stunning Ruger recoil. Even wearing the custom protective cushion it was like a hammer slammed into his shoulder socket.

But the 500-grain, copper-clad bullet was a crushing force that sliced through the truck cab frame around the window and slammed into the driver, killing him instantly.

The man in the passenger seat was staring dumbstruck at the bloody corpse when the boom of the Ruger finally reached him.

Then he reacted, bursting out of the door as the truck swerved and crunched to a halt against a pile of rocky rubble. He tried to run, but he was burdened by the pack slung over his shoulder and the suitcase in each hand.

"Stop."

The runner came to a halt as if relieved to have been caught, and he faced the business end of Gary Manning's handgun. He appraised the commando shrewdly—and his weapon, a Heckler & Koch Mk 23 Mod 0. It was the U.S. Offensive Handgun Weapon System, or OHWS, designed for a level of accuracy usually only found in competitive shooting firearms, but with combat handgun operational and durability characteristics. It was developed specifically for U.S. special operations units throughout the military, and this variation was subtly upgraded for Stony Man Farm field units by Cowboy Kissinger.

"You aren't a SEAL," the man said, breathing hard but speaking perfect conversational English. "And I doubt you're a Ranger. Are you by any chance from the U.S. Air Force Special Operations Wing?"

Manning grimaced, refusing to be drawn into a pleasant conversation that would lower his guard. "I'm Canadian."

Despite his skill, the agent's shock showed on his face. "Canadian?"

"Go figure."

The agent thought about it.

"And that guy's a Brit," Manning added, looking pointedly over the agent's shoulder.

The agent didn't fall for the amateur's trick until he heard the throat-clearing of the man behind him. When he spun he found a second Mk 23 aiming confidently at the place where his eyebrows met.

"Good afternoon," McCarter said, playing up the accent.

The agent was having a tough time dealing with it. He was trained to perform amid violence and high-pressure fieldwork, but this sudden bizarre turn of events had him confused. "What's your unit?" he demanded.

"Royal Fusiliers," McCarter said, then gestured slightly with the muzzle of the handgun. "Step away from the cases, please."

"We're allies, for God's sake. You just murdered one of my men in cold blood."

"The hombre who shot your friend is a Cuban. I don't think y'all have a mutual nonaggression pact with Cuba."

If McCarter had been playing up his accent, Hawkins was going for pure cornpone Texan, but it got the effect he was after. The agent with the suitcases was flabbergasted, as much by the fact that he'd been completely surrounded as by the real or assumed identities of the commandos surrounding him.

But he was a professional, and his mind cut through the fog of bafflement. The odd facts didn't matter. His mission had failed, and all he could hope to do now was erase its evidence.

"You have me, gentlemen," the agent said politely as he unhurriedly lowered his suitcases and backpack to the sand. "I will surrender myself to you and show you my identification." He spoke like an East Coaster, with a trace of a Harvard accent.

Now who's hamming it up, McCarter thought. "Stop now. Step away from the luggage."

"I need to show you my identification, sir," the agent insisted as he put his fingers on the release catches on a suitcases. He sounded so reasonable, and he moved with such confident casualness, that he might have gotten away with the act. McCarter had seen enough.

He triggered a single round. Even without its suppresser the Mk 23 Mod 0 was amazingly quiet for a .45-caliber handgun. About like the bark of a .22. But the results were what one would expect from a .45 triggered into a human wrist from less than three yards.

The Israeli Mossad agent gasped as his hand left his body and a huge volume of blood issued from the stump.

He knew he had just seconds before the pain and shock rendered him senseless, He had to act now. No more pretending he was on the same side as these agents from—wherever they were from. He wedged the stump into his stomach and grabbed for the suitcase latch, then spotted the pinprick of light from one of the handguns' Laser Aiming Modules, stuck on the back of his hand as if it were adhered there. The Mossad agent met the gaze of the British commando, who was shaking his head slightly. "Give it up."

"Cannot give it up." His words were already clipped by shock, and strangely enough he couldn't be sure if he was feeling the pain from the missing hand or not. He feinted for the latch, then grabbed at the weapon tucked inside his belt and squeezed the trigger as he targeted the Briton.

But the gun was gone, lifted out of his hands. It was the man who claimed to be Canadian, flicking away the handgun with a slap. Then the Mossad agent felt his good arm get locked into place at the square of his back. Seconds later, as his vision blurred, he felt what he knew were disposable handcuffs tightening around his wrist stump as a tourniquet, and his good hand was bound up somehow behind his back. Then he was on the ground, tasting hot, gritty sand.

He felt the pain of the wound now. It was terrific, yes, but it was nothing compared to the misery of having failed his mission as completely as possible. He didn't deliver his package; he didn't escape undetected; he didn't erase the evidence of his mission.

He had even failed to kill himself before being questioned.

CHAPTER SEVEN

The Mossad agent was uncooperative, and David McCarter was running out of patience, striding away in disgust.

"Anybody got a rack?"

"The medieval kind?" Lyons asked.

"Yeah. You know, Spanish Inquisition. Bones pulled apart at the joints. Screams of agony. Got one?"

"No."

If it had been anybody else making the exchange, it would have comes across as lighthearted banter. Somehow between McCarter and Lyons it wasn't.

Blancanales was looking at the man, who was bound by his wrists, biceps and ankles to a support on the side of the Chenowyth. They knew he was a pro and weren't taking chances by underestimating his ability to free himself from bondage, even with a hand missing.

"You need to look at it from his point of view."

McCarter stared. "*His* point of view?"

"Sure, David. The guy has been undercover for maybe as long as fifteen years, perfecting himself, devoting himself to a single goal. Then, as all that work and devotion is finally about to come to a climactic ending, he gets stopped in his tracks. He never gets to make the final play he's been working for all these years.''

"I dunno, mate, it's kind of tough for me to feel sorry for the bastard.''

"You don't have to feel sorry for him or agree with him," Blancanales said, sliding off the hood of the Hummer, which had been his seat. "But you do need to empathize. Mind if I give it a shot?''

McCarter waved extravagantly, and Blancanales approached the silent, self-absorbed prisoner. Blancanales couldn't do any worse. He had managed to get zero out of the Coldman-Mossad agent. They had no more intelligence now than they had before arriving in Iraq.

They had to know—and they had to know now—if, where and when more weapons were entering Iraq.

"You guys having any luck?" he asked Gary Manning and Hermann Schwarz. One of the two men grunted noncommittally as they carefully pulled open the titanium casing on the second suitcase.

The first suitcase was open, showing a custom-compartmentalized interior composed of stiff, sculpted foam cushioning, inside of which nested components of stainless steel, wiring and plastic composites. The wires were all ivory colored and had no numbers, bar codes or other identifying markings. The electronic components were all housed in composite plastic containers. The plastic was the same ivory color as the wires.

Manning and Schwarz gazed at the contents, then looked at each other without comment and moved on to the third suitcase. The locking mechanism was the same as that on the first two, strong and tough to break but without booby traps or tricky mechanics. The keys from the dead driver had opened them all. Inside the third suitcase was more of the same. Hard white cutouts. Ivory-colored plastic. Some wires and an ivory-colored plastic connector, with some stainless steel parts.

Schwarz and Manning stood over the three open cases, looking first at one, then another.

"Well?" McCarter asked.

"You got me," Schwarz said.

"Is it a bomb?" McCarter demanded.

"Maybe," Manning said with a nod.

"Anthrax?"

"Possible," Manning admitted.

McCarter caught himself before he made an unreasonable demand. This wasn't the time to be pushing for answers, because the answers had to be right.

Manning was using a Bruker IMS 2000, designed to detect a variety of chemical warfare agents, to test the components in the suitcases. It sniffed the air, drawing in the atmosphere, ionizing it using a low-energy beta source and using ion mobility principles to differentiate the gases in the atmosphere as they passed through an internal membrane. The handheld unit fed into the portable computer Manning wore on his hip. He glanced at the instrument several times without getting a reading. If there were toxins in the canisters, they were perfectly sealed.

"Could this be an aerosol dispersal unit?" Schwarz asked, bending again over the odd steel-domed device in the first suitcase as he used his digital field camera to carefully snap monochrome, high-contrast, thermal-imaging and standard high-resolution images of the devices, which went immediately over their communications link to Stony Man Farm.

"Maybe," Manning admitted, "but does that mean

this is the chemical agent?'' He gestured at the larger container in the third case. ''If it's GF or VX, this could hold enough to kill hundreds. Some kind of more exotic and toxic chemical agent, and it could kill thousands. If so, where is the plumbing to get it from there to here?''

''These could be high-pressure conduits.'' Schwarz touched one of the connector devices, then bent over and snapped a tight shot of it. ''The connectors are stainless steel and what looks like a fiberglass composite. Whatever's inside could be just as strong.''

John ''Cowboy'' Kissinger spoke up on their headsets. ''I'm seeing your snaps, Gadgets. Is it my imagination or are all the connectors designed for the same socket configuration?''

''Huh?'' Schwarz grunted in surprise. He took the camera away from his face and leaned close to the devices in suitcase two. ''You're right, Cowboy. What's *that* mean?''

''I'm not seeing this,'' Manning interrupted them.

''Look,'' Schwarz said, pointing at one of the exposed ends of the connection devices, which protruded from a component housed in a plastic cylinder eight inches long. ''The connectors are all the same. Exactly the same. So are the sockets. You could plug any connector into any socket on any other component.''

''What the hell for?'' Manning demanded, understanding the explanation but not the purpose. ''Look, there's electrical connections. That looks like high voltage DC. And this is a data port of some kind. And this has a flexible seal.''

''Yeah. Could be gas. Could be liquid. Could be anything,'' Schwarz said. ''And they are all quick connects.''

They weren't even aware David McCarter was standing there getting more and more frustrated at their lack of progress. They had been parked for nearly twenty minutes, and anywhere in Iraq wasn't his first choice for a picnic. But Manning was an explosives expert. Schwarz seemed to know a little about anything and everything technical and electric. And Kissinger, monitoring them back home at the Farm, was a sort of weapons genius. If the three of them couldn't figure out this thing, nobody could.

"It's to confuse us. Or anybody who's trying to put the thing together," Manning said. "You've got to know the system in order to know how to assemble it or even to figure out what it does."

"I may have something for you," Kissinger said. "There are symbols embossed into the stainless-steel canisters, hidden under the plastic shielding. The infrared is picking them up as variations in the heat of the metal."

"Is it legible?"

"Almost. We're trying to clean it up. Gadgets, give me another IR shot of the big canister in the third suitcase."

Schwarz took the shot and transmitted it, and as he waited for more from Kissinger his eyes fell on an extra set of latches on the second suitcase. He used the keys to unlock them, Manning watching him curiously and he lifted the second suitcase. The bottom came off. This suitcase was just an outside shell.

McCarter felt like a fifth wheel, standing there like an idiot unable to offer help. Blancanales, he noticed, seemed to be getting somewhere with the Mossad agent—at least the man was talking to him. Blancanales nodded, his expression grave. The Mossad agent seemed to be pleading, begging.

Now Schwarz and Manning were cautiously positioning the topless and bottomless second suitcase on top of the first. The two units fit together, the components meshing. Clearly the third suitcase would fit on top of these two, forming a single, enclosed case. They were getting somewhere. At least they were getting an idea how the device was assembled. Maybe that would get them closer to figuring out what the device actually did.

"With the IR I was able to read the markings on the big canister," Kissinger said in a clipped voice. "I see 'H3' and 'U.'"

McCarter saw the change. Schwarz and Manning went rigid, like a brief electric shock had gone through each of them, locking their muscles. Schwarz mouthed the word, "Shit."

They were quick and even more careful as they detached the two suitcase sections and examined the contents again with fresh eyes.

"This would be the fissile core," Manning said quickly, fingers pointing out components, "and this is a tritium boost."

"So what's the compressing agent?" Schwarz asked.

"You want to explain what's happening here?" McCarter demanded, frustration mounting, but they didn't hear him.

"It's this stuff," Manning said.

"The foam?" Schwarz asked.

"Look at these slots. They're connections into the case itself. There must be igniters inside the foam, which I'll bet is some sort of CO_2 foamed casing around a moldable, cyclone plastic high explosive. Maybe they can foam-blow plastic explosive itself now. The igniter blows the plastic, the plastic compresses the fissile core.''

The vocabulary made sense now. McCarter didn't have to ask again what they were talking about, and he knew why they looked worried.

"Stony Base here." Price's voice came over their headphones. "Able, Phoenix, we think we may have tracked down the identity of Coldman. And you're not going to like it."

"Phoenix One here," McCarter said, his words almost breaking in his throat. "We know what it is. Our worst fears confirmed."

"You do?" She was surprised.

"It's a bleeding nuclear weapon," McCarter said, staring at the suitcases sitting on the desert sands.

ABDUL JA'AFAR HAD BEEN up for a promotion a few minutes ago. Now he was watching the promotion, and maybe his very life, slip away without even a whimper.

He was sweating, getting close to panic. Everything was falling apart with the sudden eruption of silence.

"I want a lock on that signal!" he shouted over his shoulder.

"There's no signal to lock on to," replied the operator in a controlled voice, very aware that Ja'afar wanted an excuse for a shouting match and a place to lay blame.

"Then get it back up!" Ja'afar snapped. The operator didn't reply, but even in this state of mind Ja'afar knew the statement was foolish. There was nothing they could do to receive a signal that wasn't being broadcast. He was frantically trying to get the auxiliary

GPS tracker to function, and it was just as lifeless. The signal that had been coming in from the small device planted on the truck thirty-six hours ago had simply vanished.

Ja'afar knew he had risked too much. He should have turned this over to his superior officer in the Al Hadi, the Iraqi Project 858 charged with monitoring communications within the country. He could have easily divested himself of all responsibility the moment he realized the truck was full of Israeli terrorists, but the opportunity had been too rare, too big.

It had started just yesterday. It was a few hours before dawn when one of the operators on his watch handed over a priority report coming in from a night commander at the ground collection facility outside Mosul.

The Mosul station was the only station as well-equipped as the Al Rashedia headquarters for listening to latent radio signals. Al Rashedia had been completely refurbished after the Americans blew away this section of the building during the war against the Iraqi people, then upgraded two years ago when new technology became available. Mosul received the same equipment, which had to be extremely expensive if purchased on the free market. Which of course it wasn't. It was U.S.-made. Mosul was chosen because the Iraqi president saw the Turkish border as a potential entry port for troublemakers.

The president was right. It looked like the Mosul listening station had picked up some sort of an encrypted radio transmission. Nobody encrypted radio transmissions in Iraq if they knew what was good for them.

Whoever it was didn't know they were being monitored by some of the most sophisticated radio listening hardware on the planet, whisked away from its intended destination in Australia and brought here for the service of Iraq.

"What do you make of it, Abdul?" asked the watch commander from Mosul when they conferred on the phone minutes later.

"Nothing yet. Are you certain of the translation?"

"As certain as I can be. The signal was very hard to hear clearly even after we did a radical process job on it."

Ja'afar requested the electronic files, and the watch commander sent them immediately. Ja'afar was his superior, if not in rank then in seniority. This looked like a dead end. If Ja'afar wanted to hog the credit for it, he could go ahead and do it.

After listening to the heavily processed audio file extracted from the encrypted message, he was no closer to clarification. Ja'afar performed his own processing on the original file, concentrating on optimizing vocal gradations in the least distinct sections of the recording. He identified another word or two the original transcriber had missed, but he got something more important.

An accent. He heard it slip into the voice of the speaker. The words were Arabic but the accent was non-Arabic.

The speaker was an Israeli.

Probably even a native-born Israeli, if he was reading the accent correctly, and a part of his studies since joining Project 858 had involved the identification of potential enemies based on their diction, even when they tried to disguise their voices.

This man was disguising his voice and doing it expertly, and he spoke Turkish Arabic fluently. Even while stringing together nonsense combinations of words in whatever code he was using, the vocabulary rolled off his tongue. The man had to be an expert undercover agent of some kind. He would have thought that the chances of his radio signal being detected, let alone intercepted and decrypted, were almost nonexistent. He had underestimated the capabilities of Project 858 and their new U.S.-sourced technology.

And the agent, feeling overconfident, had slipped, allowing a twinge of his past to emerge in his voice.

The discovery was like a revelation to night watch commander Abdul Ja'afar. With the renewed tension blossoming between Israel and the Arab nations, the implication was obvious. The intruder was a spy or a saboteur.

Ja'afar had a decision to make.

Protocol demanded that a discovery like this be turned over immediately to his superior and then passed on to an appropriate security agency, which would track down and expose the agent.

The security agency would get the credit for the apprehension. Project 858 would indeed receive acknowledgment for identifying the spy, but Ja'afar knew his name wouldn't be found on the reports issued to the president. And with a situation of this magnitude, the president's eyes would be all over the reports, scrutinizing every word. He would be looking for loyalists. Unless everything backfired, then the president would be looking for the names of those who were at fault.

Ja'afar also considered that. If he did report this now, his name would be on the report, only to be removed when the questions were answered and the potential for a successful outcome was assured. That was simply how bureaucracy functioned under a desperate dictator.

That was when he decided to say nothing until he knew for certain. After all, what evidence was he going on?

The negotiations with the watch commander at the Mosul listening station were brief and productive, and within minutes, the Mosul commander had a pair of field agents chasing down the truck being driven into Iraq by the Israeli spy.

The bug was a simple GPS sensor with a transmitter inside a steel case. From the moment the device was attached under a rubber seal behind the cab at an improvised roadblock he had a lock on the position of the truck. His watcher could perform regular spot checks on its activity without tailing the vehicle and alerting the spies. The watcher was also a part of Project 858, but was Ja'afar's personal assistant and nephew, ordered out to Mosul when Ja'afar dedicated himself to the undertaking.

There were no problems in the first twenty-four hours, and his nephew proved he could do the job well enough, which was a relief. The boy had been slated for Project 858 by his politically connected family because he lacked the guts for real military work.

Ja'afar used the time to carefully develop the rationale he would use if things should go sour. He hadn't alerted any of his superiors because the evidence of impropriety was too slim. He wouldn't waste their time. He didn't truly believe there was a risk here, so he had simply ordered a low-priority tracer put on the vehicle.

But these were excuses. They wouldn't be acceptable if things went bad.

If things went as Ja'afar hoped, then he could turn over his findings to his superior's superior, a breach of protocol but permitted when emergency action was immediately necessary. It was politically imprudent, since it made his superior officer look useless. It was a stab in the back. His career would go into the toilet unless the gamble was a winning one.

But if the gamble paid off it would pay off big. To be named publicly as the man who identified and tracked down Israeli spies operating within Iraq would result in an instant promotion and high favor among the top ranks within Project 858 and within the inner circles of presidential influence. Then he wouldn't have to worry about the man who was once his superior officer.

But into the toilet it all went, starting with the unexpected attack by the Americans on one of the new radar stations monitoring the No-Fly Zone. This one had been designed to provide pinpoint targeting accuracy for Iraqi antiaircraft weapons. Never mind that the weapons themselves weren't capable of following a target that precisely. There were always new weapons coming in.

At the same time as the radar station went down, Ja'afar got a call from his nephew. The truck had pulled off the road and was under attack.

So the Americans had attacked to cover the insertion of an armed force, but why attack their allies, the Israelis?

He thought up a quick lie and was on the phone to his superior, who would serve as Republican Guard liaison in a time of crisis. "I have picked up an encrypted radio signal in the vicinity of the bombing," he reported with professional brevity, hoping to avoid questions. ''These are ground-based signals, and we show no more aircraft in the area.''

The computer tracer records wouldn't back it up, but maybe they would never be examined. Maybe he could stage a malfunction to explain their nonexistence.

His superior officer took details on the location and hung up, but Ja'afar's relief was short-lived when he monitored the downing of the search aircraft sent to the truck site. The second helicopter managed to get off a report of antiaircraft weapons fired from the truck, and the words became a short shout of terror before the signal vanished. But by then the GPS signal told him the truck was moving and had made too much distance to be the source. So where were the rockets coming from?

Of course more search aircraft were sent at once, and Ja'afar was cursing his ambition as he monitored events. The GPS was still on the truck and would be found eventually. It would be traced to Project 858. The Mosul commander would be held accountable when the component was sourced to his listening station, and then he was sure to implicate Ja'afar, whose silence about this matter would be interpreted as treason. He would be labeled a conspirator with the Israelis. He knew what his reward would be in the end.

He had to cover his tracks. He had to get his nephew to the truck, get that GPS and get away before the Republican Guard found the thing.

The boy was a weasel. A simpering whiner. A woman with a man's genitals. Would he have the courage for this task? The GPS signal had come to a halt in the desert by the time Ja'afar was on the radio giving his pep talk to the simpering whiner upon whom his life now depended.

Then the signal blinked out like a piece of tumbling space dust flaring out in the desert night sky.

CHAPTER EIGHT

The number of surprises coming out of this mission continued to assault David McCarter. The latest wrinkle was more unanticipated than the discovery of the suitcase-size nuclear weapons. That had always been a possibility. The kid with the .45, on the other hand, had come entirely out of left field.

"Who are you again, son?" McCarter demanded.

"I am Hany Alsalleh," the youth said in perfect English, then he realized he had made a mistake and the look of self-incrimination clouded his face. "I am the one who is asking the questions!"

"What I meant to ask was who you are with," McCarter said. "You Republican Guard?"

The Briton knew there was no way on earth this kid was from the Republican Guard. Even the leader of Iraq wasn't that desperate for soldiers. But the youth was flattered and slipped up again.

"I'm with Al Hadi," he offered.

"Since when does 858 field agents?" Schwarz asked.

Alsalleh's handgun shifted onto the one who spoke, then onto the next one who spoke.

"They must send out service technicians," Manning said. "I didn't know they armed them, though."

"You alone, Hany?" McCarter asked, and the business end of the M-1911 swung in his direction.

The Iraqi youth was about to reply when he caught himself, and his brow clouded with anger. "Shut up! All of you shut up!"

"So you are alone," McCarter said with a nod. "You know you are going to get yourself killed. Why are you playing hero for that loser you people call a president? You don't really believe the propaganda, do you?"

"If you do not shut up and start answering my questions, I am going to shoot you dead and move on to the next man!" Alsalleh was enraged. He had been terrified when he made the assault, but the attitudes of the terrorists were too much like the attitude he got at home. Condescending. He was sick of being condescended to, and he was going to prove to his father and his uncle and everyone else that he wasn't a woman, which they called him behind his back.

"Sorry, Hany, you just surprised us, that's all." The British commando raised his palms to shoulder level. "We're trying to figure out what in the world you're doing here."

"Apprehending terrorists on Iraqi soil, it looks like to me," Alsalleh said, sounding proud of himself.

"Maybe. Maybe not."

"No maybe. No maybe not. I want your affiliation. Are you British SAS?"

"Every danged one of us," Hawkins drawled.

"What's your mission? Who is your prisoner?" the young man demanded.

"What prisoner?" McCarter looked genuinely alarmed.

"That man!" The ancient M-1911 waved at the figure of the bound Mossad agent, and that was all it took. McCarter stepped forward and swooped in with one big fist that slammed into the youth's grip on the handgun, which plopped into the sand. Rafael Encizo snatched it up before the Iraqi had time to be surprised.

But he did have time to break into a run, his legs flying over the sand as he grabbed the radio and shouted at it. Then McCarter brought him down to the ground so hard the Iraqi felt his ribs cracking, and the pain hit him. He had no air, so his mouth gaped silently.

"Time to go," McCarter said with a wave toward the vehicles, tossing the youth's radio to the ground and stomping it.

He didn't know how the Project 858 boy fit into the picture, but he did know that radio cry had called in help. The Guard would be on its way. Within seconds the vehicles were speeding away, with their prisoner and his contraband. Hany Alsalleh was still lying there, overflowing with shame and pain, when the first aircraft buzzed overhead.

"THEY AFTER US YET, Stony Base?" McCarter demanded as Encizo muscled the Hummer up a steep incline and the cloudless desert sky filled their view. Then the ridge was crested, and the front wheels fell out from under them, and they rolled down an even steeper rock wall at increasing speed. Encizo managed to keep the vehicle under control, just barely, but couldn't avoid slamming the front end into the sandy floor when they hit bottom.

"No evidence of it yet, Phoenix One," Price replied. "But there's aircraft all over the desert."

"Let me know when we're spotted," McCarter said.

"Um, you're spotted, Phoenix One. Two aircraft turning in your direction. One's a fighter jet, judging by its behavior. I think he got you on his scope and he's called in low-altitude support craft."

"ETA on the low flyer?"

"Under a minute. He's moving fast. Take cover."

McCarter scanned the partially enclosed valley into which they had descended. It looked like every other corner of the Syrian Desert, from there to Damascus.

"What cover is she talking about?" Encizo asked, threading his way around the spines and humps of rock, but only when he could make the dodge without slowing. Otherwise he went over and hoped for the best.

"You got me—find some!" McCarter said.

Encizo shrugged and steered toward a thousand-foot-wide gap of flat land between a pair of rocky banks, which opened into miles of featureless flat desert. As the Hummer jounced over a smooth oblong of stone protruding from the floor, he felt as if he were steering a raft over the last few rapids on the river before it emptied into a becalmed sea. The next thing he knew the bouncing had stopped, and the ride became smooth as a newly laid highway.

"This your idea of cover?" Hawkins asked from somewhere behind him.

"Smart-ass," Encizo muttered as he checked the mirror for the Chenowyth's position, then manhandled the Hummer into a sharp right that had the vehicle traveling sideways for a full second, a sort of miraculous event for a vehicle that grossed six-tons plus and was specifically designed not to lose traction. Ever. Then the low-lock setting Encizo had engaged on the Venture Gear transfer case locked out the internal differential, providing equal torque to all four wheels, and the vehicle grabbed at the surface of the unblemished desert like a bobcat engaging his claws in the bark of an evergreen trunk.

Exclamations filled the interior. One wordless shout from Hawkins brought a grin flickering across Encizo's mouth as he stomped the accelerator again, and the Hummer was suddenly flying back the way it had come. The Chenowyth had been lost during the momentary chaos, and the little Cuban spotted it in the mirror. Schwarz was at the wheel, and he wasn't about to send his vehicle into an end over end, but he managed a rapid U-turn and came up fast on the rear of the Hummer.

Manning voiced Encizo's thoughts. "Is one lousy overhang too much to ask for? A cave or a grotto or anything?"

"All we need is a wall," McCarter said, then added quickly, "and there it is, Rafe."

"I see it." The rocky ridge that had grown out of the desert had expanded for a short time into a real cliff face. Not much cover, really, but it would have to do.

"Follow us in, Able," McCarter radioed.

"It might be too late, Phoenix," Lyons retorted, and they heard the aircraft a second after Able Team heard it in their open ALSV.

Encizo was going as fast as he could safely control the vehicle, but anything was safer than being located by the Iraqis. McCarter started to say something when Encizo pushed the 6.5-liter V 8 turbo diesel into the upper reaches of its manufacturer specs.

The Cuban braked and turned, and for the second time in the same minute had the six-ton vehicle traveling in a sideways skid on loose sand. The skid ended with the broadside of the Hummer crunching against the nearly vertical cliff edge, pushing the body panels an inch, but by then their speed of travel had been reduced to almost nothing. The sound of the impact was blotted out in the roar of the aircraft thundering over their heads. The dark shape that appeared suddenly from behind the cliff face became a MiG-31, racing hard over the desert.

The appearance of velocity was deceiving. It was crawling along, as close to stall speed as the pilot dared. The Russian-built plane was designed for better performance at slower speeds and lower altitudes than the rocket-fast MiG-25 model it was derived from, but not ideal for a ground search.

McCarter exhaled as the jet shrank to toy size and didn't waver in her course. "Phoenix One here," he reported, briefing Price on the flyover. "He didn't see us, Stony Base, but he'll figure that out soon. Then he'll be back."

"He might be late to the party," Price said. "Sorry to tell you this, but there's three choppers on the radar, and they're coming at you almost as fast as the fighter. One of them," she emphasized, "is moving very fast."

"We're dead meat if a gunship gets a lock on us," Encizo muttered.

"Yeah, I know," McCarter retorted. "Stony Base, what's the status on the United States Air Force? Didn't I hear Dan Rather saying something about them enforcing a No-Fly policy in this part of the world?"

"I've been reminding them of their international obligations for hours, Phoenix One. They're on their way now."

"What the bloody hell does that mean, 'on their

way'? When will they get here? What kind of incentive will they be packing?''

"That's all I know. We're trying to track their birds. Meanwhile, my best advice is to get out.''

That was no advice at all, but McCarter saw no reason to point that out. He gestured out the windshield in frustration. "Go.''

Encizo went, quickly but carefully, hugging the cliff on his right-hand side as he put distance between himself and the flyover point. Any minute now the MiG-31 was going to double back. Any minute and the helicopters following in its wake were going to come bearing down on them.

ROSARIO BLANCANALES shielded the glare and squinted into the sky, staring at a dot so small he'd never have been able to find it in his field glasses in the jostling Chenowyth. "Able Two here,'' he radioed. "Phoenix, Stony Base, we've got some sort of high-altitude recon aircraft keeping an eye on us.''

"Affirmative, Able Two,'' Price replied. "Looks like he's relaying your location to the others. The MiG's coming around, and the three choppers are altering to an intercept course.''

"Where's the bleeding USAF?'' McCarter demanded.

"Fighters are en route. We're seeing them now,'' Price said. "The warnings are already being broadcast to the Iraqis.''

"Lot of good that will do,'' Schwarz said as he allowed the Chenowyth to slow behind the braking Hummer. They had just run out of cliff.

Ahead of them the rock wall tapered off until it descended to the level of the sandy earth. The landscape for miles ahead of them was as empty and flat as the stretch to their left. If they headed into it, they'd be as visible as a bull's-eye on a white archery target. If they stayed there, they were at least shielded from one side by the cliff face.

Stony Man Farm, Virginia

BARBARA PRICE WATCHED the screen with a knot of dread balling up tighter in her stomach. The radar feed from the USAF in Kuwait was being digitally mixed into the master display, transposing the icons of the aircraft on the screen with the GPS feeds from the Stony Man teams and the stored digital geographic detail of the landscape. Their satellite window had expired more than an hour ago, but that was almost a relief. It wouldn't help them now. Price wouldn't have to watch what might be about to happen.

One small icon for the reconnaissance craft at a twelve-thousand-foot altitude directing in the other Iraqis. A fast-moving gunship and a pair of unknown helicopters coming in from the north. The MiG-31 closing in fast, maybe a minute away…

"Here we go," Kurtzman said over her shoulder. She had almost forgotten he was nearby, struggling to maintain the various signals he was mixing like a recording studio engineer, getting the mix just right. Now she saw them, the little green airplane icons that began to pop up on the screen with tiny numerical designations for their approximate altitude.

Two. Then four. Drifting across the monitor lethargically like the electronic Ping Pong ball in an antique computer game, but that translated to an actual speed of hundreds of miles per hour.

Which might not be fast enough.

Then the Iraqi reconnaissance aircraft at twelve-thousand feet seemed to break out of its trance, pouring on the speed, and the quartet of green aircraft icons moved in close after it. The USAF nipped at the Iraqi's heels as it fled.

"Phoenix, Able, come in," she radioed. "The recon plane has turned tail. Get a move on, back the way you came. The MiG's closing in. Stay by the wall and you might keep him from homing in."

"Understood, Stony Base."

Price could do nothing but watch. It was a feeling of helplessness she'd become accustomed to, but she despised it when she was stuck staring at a screen while the forces of death closed in on her teams. Now the tiny icons representing the Hummer and the Cheno-wyth were crawling along the shading of the cliff so slowly they were barely moving on the scale of the display. Compared to the pace of the Iraqi fighter they weren't moving at all.

The MiG-31 was screeching across the desert toward them, its display showing a measurable altitude. Now that it found its prey the pilot had brought himself to a better operational height.

Price wished they had a lock on the radio exchange going on between the Iraqis. She wouldn't understand what they were saying, but maybe she would know if the MiG pilot was trying to get the recon aircraft to help pin down the Stony Man teams. Coming in that fast, that low, could he be able to lock on to a ground target moving against a rock wall? She just didn't know.

The MiG fired, and it was a move born of frustration. The rocket slammed into the cliff where the vehicle had been a half-minute earlier, then sped away as three more green icons appeared from the southeast, out of Kuwait. As the fighter ripped past them, two of the helicopters on the radar screen were also making lazy U-turns that would take them back to Baghdad. The fast mover was gone, disappeared from the screen.

"Stony Base here," she radioed. "The gunship's gone low, off the radar. I'm not tracking her."

THE IRAQI Mil Mi-24 Hind was designed for attacking armored vehicles. The Soviet-made helicopter was a fast and lethal killing machine, with antitank missiles on its short, stubby wings. The pilot was confident he would take out the American spy team when he found them. All he had to do was avoid the American fighter jets for a few more minutes. Keep his radio silence. Stay very low. He brought the gunship down until he was hovering low over the desert, raising a cloud of sand to further camouflage his presence but not so low he couldn't see out of the cloud himself. His copilot got worried when they spotted the trio of U.S. and British fighter aircraft streak overhead in pursuit of the MiG.

"Didn't even know we were here," he said assuringly. The copilot nodded but said nothing. Their radio feed was full of static and confusion as their command attempted to gain control of the crisis.

"There they go," the pilot said, his voice dripping with the loathing he felt for the Americans. The two spy vehicles were racing away from the cliff, exposing themselves.

The pilot pushed the Mi-24 into a fast pursuit, closing to within a mile of his prey before he knew the truth. The Americans hadn't been so stupid after all.

The trio of fighters had sent the MiG-31 fleeing for home and were on their way back. The pilot had been lured into exposing himself on the radar.

They would be on to him long before he could hope to lose himself in the desert again. As capable as the gunship was, it could never outrun and outgun three fighter aircraft in the open desert.

The pilot cursed, staring at the receding dust clouds from the pair of American spy vehicles. For a moment his copilot watched him warily. The copilot could see the man's temptation to go after the vehicles and run them to ground. They just might be able to accomplish it before they were blown out of the sky by the fighters.

Then the pilot saw the futility of it. He banked the Hind and headed away.

His copilot breathed a sigh of relief. One of these days the pilot was going to get him killed, but at least it wasn't this day.

CHAPTER NINE

Stony Man Farm, Virginia

The Annex Computer Room at Stony Man Farm was double the size of the old facility in the main farm house. Bigger size and a nearly constant hardware upgrading initiative meant that the Computer Room's equipment could handle huge and ever-expanding data stores. Aaron Kurtzman still wasn't used to his new spacious work environment.

Kurtzman's task of managing information had benefited tremendously with the explosion in computing power and Internet expansion. There was a time when just a fraction of the data he wanted could be found electronically. Now it was rare that he couldn't find information he needed on-line. If it was available anywhere, it was probably accessible from the Farm.

More than that, the data was probably already stored at the Farm, for now, with ballooning terabytes of electronic storage available on-site, Kurtzman's cybernetics systems actively explored and duplicated the word's intelligence and security data networks in-house.

Kurtzman had become a designer of virtual copy machines. He, along with a staff of brilliant cybernetics experts, found themselves increasingly in the business of creating applications that could evaluate, map and then download copies of other computer systems, even the highly secure systems. Only by mirroring entire server networks in-house could Kurtzman guarantee that the information he might need from that system would be available when he needed it.

Key to this effort was the young Japanese-American programming genius named Akira Tokaido. The man had a global reputation under various user names as an unbeatable hacker. He had accessed the most secure systems on the planet, and he counted it as a point of pride when entire national defense systems were powered down in last-ditch efforts to shut out his probes. But he was even prouder when he got in and out of the same systems without being detected.

Tokaido wasn't the kind of hacker who broke into the world's biggest systems just for kicks or to launch destructive viruses. But he did *look* the part of a starving hacker. He was to be found at any hour dressed in ragged blue jeans. Kurtzman considered it a great unsolved mystery that, during the time they'd worked together, he had never seen Tokaido in *new* blue jeans, and finally decided he had to purchase them pre-worn at Salvation Army stores.

Tucked into the pocket of the well-used jeans would almost always be an audio player of some kind, feeding a pair of tiny earbuds invariably tucked into his ears and usually blasting out some sort of music designed to fill huge arenas.

Huntington Wethers was Akira Tokaido's polar opposite. He was an older black man, solidly built, tall, hair graying at the temples. A dignified man with a steady personality, rarely seen in a state of agitation. His gentlemanly ways complemented a brilliant mind.

As a former cybernetics professor at Berkeley, he had designed some of the founding architecture of the digital communication protocols that brought the Internet to the masses in the last decade of the twentieth century.

The final member of Kurtzman's cybernetics support trio was a small, vivacious redhead, Carmen Delahunt. Unlike the two men, Delahunt had been recruited to Stony Man Farm by Hal Brognola instead of by Kurtzman.

The big Fed found Delahunt stuck in a Federal Bureau of Investigations cubicle, performing brilliant feats of computer investigation and getting nowhere because she wouldn't play the bureaucratic games needed for FBI advancement. The more Brognola learned about Delahunt's record of successes with the FBI, the more he knew she was an underutilized resource. He gave her the opportunity to do some real good with an organization that didn't require political maneuvering for career survival. She excelled at the Farm, with a reputation for being unperturbable in any high-stress operation.

With the brilliant Aaron Kurtzman at its head, the cybernetics staff of Stony Man Farm was a digital intelligence powerhouse. There was no governmental organization on the planet, large or small, with a more efficient digital investigations department.

And there was almost nobody in the world who even knew they existed.

Including Israel.

Right now Israel was the target, and it wasn't an easy one. Israel had made itself formidable as a Middle Eastern military force by becoming a technological powerhouse in its own right. Now Israel was so advanced it supplied governments worldwide with its military technology, including the Chinese, to the chagrin of the United States. Between the independent industry of military and electronics technology flourishing along the Haifa to Tel Aviv corridor and the advanced development work within the military and intelligence bureaucracy, there was a higher level of military technological sophistication in place than in most nations outside the superpowers. Maybe even including some of the superpowers.

Tokaido was inside, somewhere at Mossad. Mossad didn't know it. Searching with impunity within the intelligence systems of foreign nations was the de facto standard of excellence among system invaders, yet Tokaido wasn't a happy hacker. The words that were coming out of his mouth were vivid Japanese expletives.

"I don't know what that means, but I'm glad I'm not the one you're saying it about," Huntington Wethers said in a neutral, somehow sympathetic voice.

Tokaido dragged the tiny earbuds from his head and tossed them onto the desk, stretching out in his chair to get out the kinks of too many hours spent hunched over the keyboard.

"No Coldman," he complained. "No matter how you spell it or what language you spell it in. It's got to be here!"

"It was there. You found it," Wethers reminded him, referring to the one reference Tokaido managed to unearth. It was an ancient Israel Defense Forces file, so old it was probably entered into a computer via punch cards, before there was such a thing as electronic spying.

It was a reference to funding arranged for a small

group in Tel Aviv to continue research based on data pertaining to the U.S. Special Atomic Demolition Munition, or SADM, a low-yield device based on the W-54 warhead. Another reference in the ancient files referred to a Soviet device based on stolen W-54 schematics but with unique Soviet innovations.

At the same time Cowboy Kissinger had been identifying the device from its hidden markings, Wethers had done enough quick on-line research to come up with the specifications on the SADM. So small it was used at one time in the Davy Crockett recoilless rifle by the U.S., with a 51-pound projectile that was twenty-six inches long and eleven inches wide. The W-54 warhead had a variable yield of as much as one kiloton—the explosive force of one thousand tons of TNT.

What the Israelis intended to use the weapon for back in the 1970s, when the files were written, was unclear. But once the Farm had all the details on the weapon they knew they had the right animal. The Coldman of thirty years ago had been the starting point for the device they had now.

Now it was much improved.

HAL BROGNOLA'S VOICE bristled with anger. "What do you mean he's dead?"

"Heart stopped beating." McCarter sounded tired. Sounded like he'd had a hard day.

"Who killed him and why?"

"He did it himself, probably to avoid getting reamed out by his boss for perceived screwups. These guys were very prepared, Hal. They took poison as soon as they realized they were under attack. Slow-acting stuff, so if they got through it they could take the antidotes they had with them. It was a way of guaranteeing their deaths if they got caught, and they wouldn't have to depend on popping a cyanide tab at the last minute.''

"This guy had already killed himself before you even caught up to him?" Brognola said.

"Yeah. We just didn't know it. Then we're driving cross-country and he's in the back end in cuffs and we realize we haven't heard a word out of him the whole time. Doesn't take long to figure out he's in a coma. He stopped breathing before we got lifted out of Iraq.''

"You get anything out of him before that?" Brognola asked.

"Pol did."

"I'm here, Hal," Blancanales said over the speakerphone.

"What did you manage to get out of our friend before he checked himself out?" Brognola asked.

"Not as much as I would have liked," Blancanales admitted. "He was deeply depressed. He might have killed himself even if his orders hadn't required it. Once he knew we had IDed him and the Coldman device his confidence went in the toilet and I was able to finesse some details out of him." Blancanales's voice dropped, and the roar of the transport chopper that was taking them back to the U.S. Air Force facilities in Kuwait almost muffled him out. "It's grim, Hal," he said after a moment.

"Tell us," Brognola urged.

"Tamar Strasler said he was part of an Israeli group that consists mostly of Mossad agents. Their goal, according to Strasler, is to make sure Israel doesn't go down without taking the rest of the Middle East with her."

Price and Brognola met eyes across the table, both

with question marks on their faces, but it was Katz who said, "Could you explain that, Pol?"

"I didn't spend a lot of time poking around this area. Strasler said something like, 'Some of us are just petty, some of us want to neutralize the Arab states to make life easier for the Israel that will follow once this Israel is wiped out, and some of us want to bring on the end times.'"

Katz blanched. Kurtzman's hands froze over the collapsible keyboard he was using to enter notes on Blancanales's brief.

"Biblical end times?" Brognola asked.

"I guess," Blancanales said. "We didn't get into it."

Katz was nodding. "Yes," he said. "That's what he meant. Judgment Day follows the war in the Middle East. That's in Revelation."

"This is a core belief to many Israelis," Kurtzman said with a nod. "That the Middle East will soon be the source of the fire that will consume most of the world, but ushering in the arrival of the Messiah."

"Kind of fatalistic. Almost a suicidal philosophy in itself," Brognola said. "Living with the assurance of looming death?"

"It's not necessarily imminent, depending on who you're talking to," Katz explained. "But the tumult of the twentieth century for the Jewish population furthered the belief that the end times were coming soon."

Brognola shook his head as if freeing himself of the thought. "Names? Ranks? Anything on the group directors?"

"Nothing," Blancanales said. "I got the impression most were or are Mossad. But Strasler did say some were outside Mossad, in government. He used the word bureaucrats.''

"What do they plan to do?" Price asked. "What are their targets?"

"Three targets," Blancanales said. "That much he confirmed. Iraq, of course, as well as Iran and Egypt."

"Those are big targets," Kurtzman said. "I don't care how potent the Coldman devices are, they're not going to wipe out an entire nation. Not even a major city."

"Bear's right. They've got to have more specific marks," Brognola stated.

"He wasn't willing to be more specific, and I pushed him on it. He was still loyal to the cause. If he hadn't been so spirit-broken, I wouldn't have got what I did."

"Are there multiple groups penetrating each nation, perhaps?" Kurtzman asked. "Maybe that's what we're missing here. This was just one of several Coldman devices being planted in Baghdad."

"I don't think that's the case," Blancanales replied. "Strasler said something like, 'We are the last resort, and now we've failed in Baghdad.' I took that to mean we had stopped their Iraqi efforts. Unless he was totally bullshitting me, I'd say this was the only Coldman team penetrating Iraq."

"What did he mean by 'last resort,' though?" Price pondered.

"I'm betting the Coldman organization tried to get teams in by air," Katz suggested. "Flatt suggested as much. Bear, remember those reports from NRO?"

Kurtzman nodded quickly. "You're right. We saw them yesterday, Barb. NRO watchers spotted what they thought was a low-flying aircraft penetrating Iran from the Gulf of Oman, seventy-five miles east of the Iranian city of Bandar-e Abbas. The only likely point of origination was an Israeli shipping vessel. It vanished into the Zagroz mountains. Later they thought they glimpsed it with a couple of Iranian fighters tailing it, and it went down. NRO went on a high-level watch and started looking for similar instances. They were just in time to see another attempt into Egypt only a few hours later. Same result. The aircraft went down. No explanation out of Iran or Egypt.''

"Those were ill-advised incursions. Mideast airspace is locked down tighter than a funeral drum," Katz said. "If that was the Coldman first attempt, what about the Iraqi air probe?"

"If you characterize an attempt at air penetration of Iraq and Egypt 'ill-advised,' trying to get past the U.S. eyes on the Iraqi No-Fly Zones would be wasteful," Brognola said. "Might as well dump your men and equipment in the Gulf and be done with it."

"Right, and the Israelis would know our capabilities as well as anyone," Kurtzman agreed.

"Well enough to attempt to evade our Iraqi eyes?" Price said.

"I doubt it."

"So we go on the assumption that no air penetration in Iraq was even attempted?" Katz posed.

"If you want my two cents, I'd say yes," Blancanales stated. "As I said, I got the impression that Strasler's team was going in independently, not as a part of a two-pronged approach."

There was a moment of consideration.

"Unless he was totally bullshitting you," Brognola said finally.

"Yeah," Blancanales agreed. "Keep in mind that we're talking about a top Mossad agent. Training, education, conditioning. In almost every aspect they train some of the best intelligence and undercover agents. Strasler successfully lived a lie for years and years, so we know he was damn good at spinning untruth.''

''You're good, too, Pol,'' Price reminded him.

''Who's better?'' Blancanales offered. ''We'll never know.''

''Give me your gut feeling,'' Brognola said impatiently.

''My gut tells me he was telling the truth. Even a pro would have tried to steer me in a more definitive misdirection if he wanted me off the trail. He gave us too little for a ruse.''

''Okay, if we go by that, what's our next step?'' Brognola addressed Price.

''Try to get a line on the teams going into Egypt and Iraq.''

''Easier said than done, I take it.''

''Of course. We have nothing definite to go on. We're doing background investigations on Strasler under the fake name he used on his travel documents. We took prints off the corpse of his companion. Neither of those avenues is likely to tell us where the other teams are headed now. We can send in Able and Phoenix to find any acquaintances and search their homes, but these aren't the kind of guys to scatter incriminating evidence.''

''Katz?'' Brognola said. ''Ideas?''

''No. I've got only one contact on this inside Israel. I'll get in touch with Ori Flatt again and maybe he'll have more to tell me, but don't count on it.''

''What about the Iran and Egypt angle?'' Brognola suggested.

''What about it?'' Price queried. ''Iran's huge. Slap

it on top of the U.S. and it would cover eleven north-
east and midwestern states. In Egypt, you're talking
about an area two hundred miles wide and seven hundred miles long—if you discount the arid western dis-
tricts and the Sinai Peninsula. A lot of area to search
when we don't know what we're looking for.''

Kurtzman's hand went to his chin and rubbed it as
he focused on the far wall, the quick processing of facts
almost a blur in his eyes, and his expression was a
beacon that got the attention of everyone in the room.
That look was as much a part of the Aaron Kurtzman
they knew as were his wheelchair and his horrid coffee.
When the blur focused and he found he was the center
of attention he looked slightly startled.

''Maybe,'' he ventured, ''we *do* know what to look
for.''

CHAPTER TEN

Kuwait

"There's Jack. I think we're gonna blow him on his ass," T. J. Hawkins stated, watching out the small port-hole window of the transport chopper as it descended rapidly onto the concrete landing pad.

Gadgets Schwarz leaned into the window. "He's got all those big MPs to hold him up. Well, isn't he just special?"

Jack Grimaldi did look like a small, even frail figure as the blasts of helicopter downdraft pulled his light-weight civilian clothing against his frame, making him look like a stick man. His black, close-cropped hair tumbled and tossed but somehow managed to stay curled in the wind blast. He seemed a head smaller and fifty pounds lighter than any of his eight MP escorts. The emergency lights on four vehicles were flashing, and just beyond them sat the dark hulk of the small transport jet. The cockpit door was open, and the pilot was waiting behind the controls.

"How's Iraq?" Grimaldi shouted with a grin, jogging up to the chopper doors as the big beast was still settling her weight on solid ground, fighting the gale force wind every step of the way. The eight MPs stayed in a tight circle around him, no more than a few feet away.

"Shitty!" Schwarz said as he pushed the big cases into the waiting hands of the Stony Man pilot, who latched on to them with more strength than his thin build suggested he had. The third case was draped by the straps over a shoulder.

"See you around!" Grimaldi yelled, but the words were lost in the wind roar. He jogged to the aircraft, his MP escort scrambling to keep up with him, and slid the suitcases into the small cabin, belting them down. He slid into the copilot's seat and within a minute of Phoenix's landing the aircraft was accelerating for takeoff. Within two minutes, his plane had disappeared into the skies of Kuwait, heading for the Gulf.

USS Carl Vinson, *Persian Gulf*

"He's coming in?" Admiral James Weyer said as he strode onto the vast bridge, still flicking rye bread crumbs from his mouth. He'd been eating lunch in the executive galley. Even his best estimates hadn't led him to expect the aircraft for another twenty minutes.

"He's here already, Admiral," Captain Frank Furcas answered, nodding toward the deck, where the aircraft was coming to a standstill.

"Hmph. I think I'll check this guy out for myself," Weyer said acidly. "See what he's got to say for himself."

"Good idea, Jim."

The admiral hurried out of the bridge, and Furcas grinned. As if Weyer had a choice. The admiral had been ordered to attend to the new arrival personally.

And there weren't a lot of people who had brass

cajones big enough to tell a U.S. Navy admiral to play chaperon to some visiting civilian.

"MR. HALLDORSON?" The Admiral introduced himself to the civilian. "Let me get somebody to take one of those for you."

"Thanks, but no thanks, Admiral," said the tall, rangy man who jumped to the deck of the Nimitz-class aircraft carrier. The muscles in his lean forearms were pulled tight, but he didn't seem to be struggling with the heavy cases. In fact, it was three cases, one hanging from a shoulder. The whole set had to have weighed over a hundred pounds.

"I think we ought to at least get those onto a cart," Weyer said, without showing his uneasiness as they headed to the entrance that would take them below-decks.

As soon as Jack Grimaldi saw that was where they were heading, he sped up and forced the admiral to hustle.

"We've got to get these to their destination soonest."

Weyer glared at the cases. He knew what they were and why they had been transported to his ship. What he didn't know was this man's identity. Why and how he had come by the cases. And why he had been granted the full cooperation of one of the highest-ranking naval officers in the U.S. Navy, who was following the orders of *the* highest authority in the U.S. military.

Admiral Weyer held the door for the civilian because he had no staff with him. He knew when not to have an entourage. The new arrival nodded his thanks and maneuvered the cases through, bumping them. Weyer winced.

"You arrived sooner that I expected," the admiral said, steering them into a large elevator.

"Your pilot let me take the stick, and I pushed her."

The admiral didn't know how to respond to that. "You're checked out on military aircraft like that?" he asked.

"Yes."

When the elevator doors opened again, they were deep in the bowels of the vessel. A pair of armed MPs put them through the ID process. Somehow, the civilian's retinal and palm scans were in the system, and he was passed through.

"I don't think I've ever seen an admiral without a retinue," Grimaldi commented as they headed down the silent, cool, wide hallways. It could have been interpreted as a gibe, but the slight grin told Weyer it wasn't an insult.

"I'm to keep you out of contact with all ship personnel," the admiral said. "Hell, even I don't know who you really are. You're not really a civilian?"

"Yeah, I am. Anyway, since I left the Mob."

Weyer looked at the guy again as they stopped at the next security check, allowing them deep into the off-limits suites of the carrier. Halldorson was smiling, sort of. Weyer was surprised to realize he actually liked this guy.

They were inside a minute later, surrounded by the two civilian researchers and two naval doctors who comprised the entire staff of this high-security suite. They brought the admiral and the civilian to a dead halt with an assault of electronic devices, including a handheld digital Geiger counter that began to beep. The sounds it made were quiet but piercing, and the team exchanged glances as the beeps grew in intensity.

"I'm not getting fried, am I?" Grimaldi asked.

"How long have these been in your possession?" one of the researchers asked, a severe young woman with dark eyes.

"This close? Maybe fifteen minutes total."

She shrugged. "It won't kill you, but try not to father any children for the next couple of months."

Grimaldi nodded sincerely. "I know good advice when I hear it."

"Come on," she said, snatching him by the elbow. "You get decontaminated anyway." She dragged him in the direction of a bank of stainless-steel showers visible through the doors to an adjoining section of the lab. "The clothes will have to go."

"Doctor, you're giving me mixed signals," Grimaldi said.

Just before the Strong Man pilot was ushered into the showers, the admiral said, "Mr. Halldorson?"

"Admiral?" Grimaldi grabbed the door, and the muscles seemed to be straining in his arms to keep himself from being forced inside by the stern researcher.

"Do you enjoy Jack Daniel's?"

"You like boats?"

"Since you'll be confined to the lab, I think I can stop by and pull out a bottle without the other brass witnessing it. We'll have a belt later. If you've survived."

On that note of finality, Grimaldi was thrust into the showers.

GRIMALDI'S FACE had once been tanned and dark. Now it was a sort of muddy pink. He ruefully wondered if it was from embarrassment. The nurse had stripped him to his birthday suit before the detox process, which involved a very thorough scrubbing with a stiff brush that hurt.

"I could probably do this on my own," he protested at one point. She washed his hair with what smelled like burned motor oil for the third time and was now using a new kind of round, pneumatically powered spinning brush to exfoliate the skin of his face, ears and neck. The device beeped every minute. At each beep she thumbed off the brush, sending it into a stainless-steel trash can with a thick plastic bag liner, and popped on a new brush from a sealed plastic bag.

"No, you couldn't," she said simply. "Not well enough."

"I use those to get the crud off my barbecue grill," he said, as another brush went into the trash. "I don't think this is even needed. I wasn't in contact with the suitcases for very long."

"You're right. Probably not needed," she said, stopping for the only time and explaining herself patiently. "But if we find out you were exposed to dangerous radioactive particles offgassing from that device, every moment we delay removing those particles from your skin increases the danger."

"More dangerous than you and your disk sander?" Grimaldi asked, trying to keep his sense of humor. His eyes happened to fall on her name tag. She was a doctor, not a nurse as he had assumed, and apparently a civilian.

"Far more dangerous than me," she said offhandedly as she strapped a face mask around his head. "Breathe deeply. This'll help detox your lungs if there are particles, and we'll proceed to phase three." She was grabbing a new, stiffer, bigger brush. The doctor adjusted the speed on her power tool, making it spin faster, whining angrily.

Soon other parts of Grimaldi were just as red as his face.

"HOW DO YOU FEEL?" asked an older male doctor as he emerged from the showers in a disposable jumpsuit.

"Like an old T-Bird that's just been stripped of forty years of paint jobs," Grimaldi complained.

"That was nothing. When you get exposed to heavy radiation and go through *real* detoxification, then you can complain about it." He was smiling as he came around to take Grimaldi's hand. "Dr. Lawrence Claire."

"Jack Halldorson," Grimaldi said.

"Happy to say that's all you'll have to endure," Claire said. "I'll show you."

"There's no radiation?" Grimaldi asked as the doctor led him to the rear of the lab.

Claire looked at him curiously. "It wasn't the radiation exactly that we were worried about, Mr. Halldorson."

"Jack. Then why the free shower?"

"Particles," Claire said. "I'm Larry unless the Navy brass is hanging around. Then we keep it formal. Yes, particles is what we were worried about. We could tell in an instant that the device you carried wasn't dangerously radioactive. It was the particles that might have been emitted that we were especially concerned about."

Grimaldi looked at him expectantly, and Claire shook his head.

"Guess you need to be brought up to speed, Jack. I assumed with your security clearance you were well-briefed on what was going on."

"I think they told me all they knew," Grimaldi said, "which wasn't much. Without going into it, Larry, the people who got their hands on that thing were in a hell of a big hurry."

Claire nodded, understanding that Grimaldi couldn't give him details on who had procured the suitcases. Or who the authorizing agency was behind the operation. But he wasn't stupid. "I can imagine," he said. "I have to tell you that I do know the basics of your mission. A woman named Barbara has been on the line with us briefing us on it."

Grimaldi said nothing, neither confirming nor denying.

"She deemed it necessary. We needed to know how the devices were to be used in order to make the best analysis."

"Makes sense," the Stony Man pilot said.

"When we learned of the scenario, we assumed the suitcases were made to be some sort of device for dispersing a lethal agent. And who knew how well the agents were contained? That's why you got the free shower when you got here."

"It's not biological or chemical, though," Grimaldi said. "It's a freaking nuclear weapon. I hope you guys are treating it as such."

Claire looked at him oddly again. "Of *course* we know that."

Grimaldi realized he was way, way out of the loop, and it frustrated him. "I get the impression I don't know enough about what's going on. Not that I need to.

I'm just the delivery guy. But the folks back home have a lot riding on what you people come up with."

Claire nodded. "Understood. Come on."

The rear of the central lab branched into three separate laboratory rooms stocked with rows of electronic devices in racks, monitors at workstations, and enclosed transparent cubicles that Grimaldi recognized as containment cubicles for dangerously radioactive items. The rubber gloves and internal tools allowed the technicians to work on the items inside and stay protected. Grimaldi had always wondered how good those rubber gloves could actually be at keeping radiation from leaking out. He looked inside the cubicle they were walking toward, but it was empty. Dr. Claire gestured at a porthole in the wall.

The amber-colored glass was clear but an inch thick. Inside was a chamber with walls and floors as reflective and seamless as polished glass, and in the middle of it sat the suitcases. They were laid out in all their component pieces while a mechanical arm moved over them with a sensor probe. Another face was looking through a window on the next wall, operating the arm.

"Just about done," Dr. Claire said.

"Uh-huh. Done doing what?" Grimaldi said.

"Figuring out," Claire said, "what that thing *tastes* like."

Stony Man Farm, Virginia

"JACK HALLDORSON here."

"Hello, Jack. It's Barbara," Barbara Price said as the phone connection linked them to the radiation lab on the USS *Carl Vinson*.

"Hi, Barb. I'm here with Dr. Lawrence Claire and Dr. Sandra Shorn." The two doctors said hello.

"And I'm with Aaron."

"Hello all," Aaron Kurtzman said. "Doctors, I'm interested in hearing what you've found."

Dr. Claire spoke first. "We performed a spectroscopic analysis on the suitcases, as you requested. We came up with the profile you requested on the device. I'm sending it now."

Kurtzman saw the file appear on his workstation. He opened the text document, scanning the fields. "Yes. This is exactly what we'll need."

"Make sense to you, Aaron?" Dr. Claire asked curiously. Kurtzman knew the man wanted to know if he was talking to a fellow radioactive researcher.

"Just enough to do what I need to do. I hope," Kurtzman replied. "I'd like your advice on this, if you are willing to listen and understand this is still a top-security issue."

"Of course."

"Dr. Shorn?" Kurtzman asked.

"Yes, sir."

Kurtzman grimaced at the *sir*. The doctors assumed he was some sort of U.S. general, maybe a high-ranking CIA director. That was fine if it insured they would treat this as top secret.

"Let's get everybody up to speed," he said. "Dr. Claire, please give us the layman's version of this for Barb, who's not as familiar with the technology."

Claire started without preamble, as if he were a narrator in a documentary. "We have the potential at this moment for two more devices, identical to that one, running loose, one in Iran, one in Egypt. We don't know where they are. We need to find them and find them fast. Barb, the spectroscopic analysis of the suit-case devices essentially sorts pulse-height spectra, de-fining each pulse according to its amplitude. When you've got every pulse sorted, you have a radioactive profile of the device. A profile—not a fingerprint.''

"Why not a fingerprint?'' Grimaldi asked.

"A fingerprint would imply it was unique to the de-vice,'' Dr. Shorn said, her voice warm and feminine beneath her matter-of-fact enunciation. "The radio-active profile we developed from this device, measured generally, would be the same as that of a device built at the same time to the same design and using the same materials.''

"Got it,'' Grimaldi said.

"Barbara?'' Dr. Claire asked. "You getting this?'' He wasn't condescending but, talking to strangers whose background he couldn't know, he wanted to be sure he was communicating clearly.

"I'm following you so far,'' Price said.

"Well, then, Aaron,'' Claire went on, "I think it's your turn.''

"Yes. So here's what we intend to do, Doctors,'' Kurtzman explained. "We have the capability to locate small radioactive sources from the air using slow-moving aircraft. Once we find a source that is approx-imately strong enough to match the suitcase, we home in with more sensitive airborne instruments and try to match the signature. Not as simple as it sounds, of course.''

"We thought this was what you might have in mind,'' Dr. Shorn said. "There are a number of diffi-culties in making it work. First of all, you say you want to pinpoint a source from the air with the radioactive intensity of the suitcase we have, but once you compensate for shielding, such as the roof of the building or the steel body of the car that the suitcase might be inside of, then you've really widened your search parameters to include every radioactive source larger than a smoke alarm.''

"We think we can weed out most of those. We'll be using very discriminating sensors.''

"They'd have to be. And I think I'm up to speed on the military's current state of the art in airborne measurement of ground radiation sources, Aaron, even still-developing technologies.'' Claire paused.

Kurtzman nudged him. "Tell me what your best guess is for our success.''

"One in ten of identifying the device, if and when you actually stumble over it.''

"That's not encouraging.''

"But it is realistic. Your chances are better if the thing is in a car, better still if it is being carried around in the open, and that seems unlikely.''

Kurtzman looked at Price. They knew it wasn't a sure thing, but the odds Claire was giving them were less than they had hoped.

"We're going to give it a try, anyway, Doctor,'' Price said.

Justice Department, Washington, D.C.

HAL BROGNOLA STOPPED what he was doing to watch the display coming from Stony Man Farm.

Knowing what he was looking at, Brognola still had a hard time seeing what he was supposed to be seeing. Even if an outside entity had somehow accessed the transmission and broken Kurtzman's encryption, they'd have been mystified by the swimming sea of graphics that might have been infrared images of a coastline or might have been radiopictographs of a dermatological carcinoma.

The image shifted slowly as he was watching. The curving lines of the red mass seemed to waver and swell, growing bulges and shaded projections, while the deep fluorescent blue mass remained featureless except for the occasional pinprick of white starlight that twinkled into existence and blinked out again.

"How long will this take?" he said into the phone when Kurtzman came on the scrambled line. Before he got an answer he amended the question. "I mean, how long *could* this take?"

"Depends how good our guesses are and how well our luck holds out."

"That doesn't tell me much."

"As much as I can tell you. This is new territory, and chances are it won't work."

"We have anything else at the moment? Anything new?"

"No."

"What's that?"

A white flash had appeared on the screen, brighter than any of the pinpricks so far. The lower left quarter of the screen opened into a new window covered with a grid, and the image of the white flash grew larger inside it. As the image grew it became less perfect, the edges yellow and blurry. A series of rapid-fire numerical displays played between the grid lines for what seemed like a quarter of a second, froze on a complicated trio of numerical strings, then vanished along with the close-up window. It had all happened so fast Brognola hadn't had time to get his hopes up.

"Didn't taste right," Kurtzman explained. "It wasn't the needle we were looking for."

"You sure it's not making rash decisions?" Brognola was only half kidding. It was hard to believe the system zeroed in on a potential target, evaluated its radioactive signature and decided it wasn't a match to Coldman, all in that brief spurt of activity.

"I'm sure," Kurtzman said patiently.

"Dammit." The big Fed's eyes traveled to the time display. "I've got the meeting now. My phone will be on. If you get a positive hit, call me."

"While you're in the meeting with the Man?" Kurtzman asked.

"I'm going in with nothing," Brognola complained. "You'd be doing me a favor if you interrupted with good news."

"Understood," Kurtzman said.

Brognola watched the screen for ten seconds more. Another brief starlight flash in the middle of the red. The red was actually on the coast of Iran, the southernmost strip of the Sistan va Baluchestan province, a likely landing point for a clandestine Coldman team. The flash was gone in a blink. The system hadn't even regarded it worth a closer look.

"Dammit."

He went to his meeting, hoping Kurtzman's call would come through, but it never did.

And the meeting went on for a long seventeen minutes.

CHAPTER ELEVEN

Caspian Sea

The sea was empty, silent except for the murmur of swelling waves. The overcast night sky was featureless, a blanket of clouds blocking the glimmering stars and glowing moon. Without the faintest illumination, the sky and the sea merged in blackness.

Then there was a distant hum, so faint that had anyone heard it, they might have deemed it to be a figment of the imagination.

Then there was a detail in the sky where there had been none. In the vast blackness a tiny small rectangle of deeper blackness materialized and increased in size, followed by three more, melting into the sea with the sound of disturbed water. The splashes were instantly lost in the murmur of the ocean.

Ten minutes later, incongruously, there was a light. Tiny, steady, green.

And out of the oblivion of blackness, voices.

"On target?"

"Couldn't be closer."

"Time?"

"Zero-three-twenty-three."

Carl Lyons nodded. When Gadgets Schwarz released

the illumination switch on his wrist GPS, the utter blackness was back. Sitting in the Zodiac inflatable raft, unable to see his hand in front of his face, he glared into the darkness, as if daring something, anything to disturb the void.

That disturbance was just seven minutes away, if the pattern was followed.

Not much of a pattern. Every hour on the half hour since Stony Man located it. The previous appearance had been fifty-three—no, fifty-four—minutes ago.

If the pattern wasn't repeated, it was going to be a long night sitting on the surface of the Caspian Sea— a fool's errand undertaken on the advice of a man who was already dead.

YAKOV Katzenelenbogen's contact provided the intelligence, and then the contact died for doing it.

The man called Katz on the secure line that the Stony Man tactical advisor had provided him. The line came into the Farm only after filtering through a CIA switch box and a half-dozen cutouts across the nation, untraceable from the outside in. Even the CIA wouldn't have been capable of following the line if they were to discover its inexplicable presence in their secure phone net.

"Yakov?" It was his old Mossad acquaintance, Ori Flatt. After speaking with him only briefly the one time after so many years Katz could still make out the quaver in his voice.

"Ori, what's wrong?"

"Shut up and listen. You did it in Iraq. I know about it. So do the others. Joseph Devorha knows, and he somehow knows I provided the intelligence. Maybe you have a leak. Probably it was on my end. It doesn't matter why the leak happened, and I don't blame you if it's your fault. The point is this—Ill be dead in five minutes.''

"What?" Katzenelenbogen said. "Where are you, Ori? I'll see what I can—"

"Shut up. Running away would be futile, and it would be an undignified way to spend my last precious minutes on this Earth. I can do one more good thing before I die, and that's pass along what I know.'' Flatt's speech became more rapid, but precise, and Katz grasped the urgency of his words. Flatt was speaking with maximum efficiency. If he really had just moments to live, he had to make every second and every word count. There was no time for misunderstandings. Katz checked the phone monitor and was reassured to see the small blinking circle-and-arrow icon that told him the automatic recording function was active.

"Joseph Devorha is the man with the plan," Flatt said. "He runs Coldman. He's the brains.''

"What we really need most is a lead on the Iran and Egypt teams," Katz said, his mind racing. Was Flatt exaggerating? Was his assassination just minutes away?

"I know, and I have just one piece of intelligence to offer you. I pray it is enough to get you a lead on them.'' Flatt read out a series of numbers and letters, and Katz wrote it down. Only when he was on the final digit did he realize what they meant.

"It's latitude and longitude.''

"Of course it is," Flatt snapped. "I broke into Devorha's office, hid myself like a fool in the damned closet while I listened to his conversations, and eventually I heard him on the line with a field operative.

This position is where one of the teams was dropped off. I saw Devorha find it on a map. He made the smallest mark, just a dot, but it was enough for me to find the spot again on his map after he left. I grabbed it and ran. Set off some sort of a damned alarm, but I got out. That wasn't twenty minutes ago.''

Katz pictured it. He didn't know yet who Devorha was, but surely he was a leader in some aspect of Israeli military or intelligence. Had to be Mossad. ''They must have had security cameras, wherever his office is.''

''Of course,'' Flatt replied impatiently.

''They'll know your face. They'll ID you in no time.''

''They already did, I'm sure of it,'' Flatt said almost offhandedly.

''Listen, Ori, get out of there now. Get into hiding. We'll arrange for protection—''

''Forget it, Yakov. There's no time left. I think my ride's already here. Yes. Two cars out front. Looks like I rate pretty highly. Must be seven or eight of them.''

''Ori—''

''Yakov, do something with the information I gave you. It cost me my life. Make sure it was worth the price.''

''I will,'' Katzenelenbogen promised.

''Time to say goodbye, Yakov.''

Katz heard the phone hit the floor, and he listened to a tinkling crystal sound. Ice in a glass. The sound of Ori Flatt taking a sip of a drink.

Then there was a series of thumps. Flatt called out, ''Come on in.''

Katz listened with a sort of stunned amazement as a door crashed open. There was a quick burst of suppressed machine-gun fire followed by a sigh that was endlessly long.

Then another tinkling sound and a thump.

On the other side of the world, Ori Flatt's lifeless fingers had just released his drink and allowed it to fall to the floor. The line went dead.

Katz hung up the phone and stared at the deceptively simple series of numbers on the notepad.

An ethical man had died to get these numbers, had begged Katz to make the death worthwhile.

It was the least he could do.

THE SPOT the numbers pointed to proved to be in the Caspian within sight of the Iranian shore, fifty-odd miles south-southeast of the twin Azerbaijani-Iranian cities of Astara. Within a minute of hanging up the phone, the auditory shadows of the hit still echoing in his thoughts, Katz had explained the situation to Kurtzman and Price. They soon had access to a satellite and were staring at the spot provided by the late Ori Flatt.

And they saw nothing.

It was empty ocean. Evening in the Middle East, the fishing vessels that were in the vicinity had all returned to port for the night. Others wouldn't have cause to be this close to the shore. Just an occasional cargo vessel could be spotted cruising idly through the vicinity.

Then the first appearance came, almost exactly on the half hour, so small it might not have been worth paying attention to—except that it materialized out of nowhere.

"A sub. A small one," Katzenelenbogen muttered as they stared at the warm spot.

"Maybe ten, eleven meters," Kurtzman said, running some quick identification diagnostics on the image. "Two-meter-diameter hull. Cozy. I wonder if they can even stand up inside that thing."

"Big enough to do the job," Price said. "Our own SEAL minisubs will fit six and all their gear."

"I think," Kurtzman said, staring at the blobs of whiteness that materialized on top of the image, "that we have at least that many."

Katz and Price leaned close as Kurtzman played with the image compensation software. The bright, blurred oval became more dim, and the tiny dots that had to be humans grew defined as the contrast increased.

"I count seven," Price said. "It's got to be damn tight under there. I think this is good news."

"I agree." Katz nodded. "It makes sense that this is how they're getting their saboteurs into Iran, and that sub can't hold more than seven people. So it is the Coldman team, not yet landed. We're not as far behind as we thought we were."

"Any communications coming out of there?" Price asked Kurtzman.

"I'm not getting anything," he replied, switching to the display coming from one of the NRO communications eavesdropping satellites. Kurtzman had slaved it to the visual-infrared sat system.

"You won't get anything. They'd be foolish to use radio." Katz grunted. "Even an encrypted signal might be picked up and investigated by one of the patrols skirting Iran."

"They'd be foolish to do *anything* right now," Kurtzman added. "We've got an air patrol in the area." He pulled back the view and they could see the aircraft, moving slow enough to tell them it was a prop plane, making a surveillance run a few miles off the Iranian shore.

"Not close enough for them to see or hear. Not yet," Price observed. "Think they're getting reports broadcast to them?"

"They don't need it," Kurtzman said. "They know. Look."

As he tightened on the sub again, it was clear the pinpricks of white that were human beings were disappearing into the white oval of the minisub.

"They're going to try to land using an inflatable, I'd guess. They'll need plenty of time and clear skies to do it," Katz stated. "Looks like they'll wait a while."

"Their chances of running into nonmilitary watercraft will be better later anyway," Price said. "Still, it's got to be pretty stuffy inside that hull. I just hope their caution is stronger than their discomfort."

Price was on the line to Kuwait, and minutes later Able Team was in the air.

WHEN THEY WERE FINALLY over the Caspian they got the bad news from Stony Man. The half-hour pattern of surfacing had commenced until local time 0230. The window of opportunity the crew had been patiently waiting for presented itself. Five of the seven men departed the sub in an inflatable raft that took them quickly toward the Iranian coast. The boat ran in darkness, masked thermally by the spray of water it raised around itself. The satellite lost it and couldn't find it again. The sub vanished. They had no reason to expect it would surface again—unless they were waiting for a report of safe arrival from the raft crew.

"It's possible," Schwarz had said with a shrug as they geared up for their drop in the Caspian. "The landing party can run at thirty knots or less. It'll take them an hour and a half or more to get onto dry land,

and we know they communicate using low-power radio that's unlikely to be noticed or traced. The sub will have to surface to get the message.''

''Yeah. Maybe.'' Lyons wasn't happy about it, but he knew the job had to be done, even if it meant they'd spend the next twenty-four hours floating around the Caspian with nothing to do except wait for a pick-up.

How had the Israelis managed to get a sub into the Caspian? Even a small one had to displace fifty tons.

''Maybe they brought it here in pieces,'' Schwarz suggested when he brought it up. ''They take preassembled parts to a secret Caspian boathouse. They'd be parts small enough to fit into ground transport or maybe airdrop. Then they weld them together and make the electrical and mechanical connections, and you've got a working sub.''

''That sounds a little far-fetched,'' Lyons stated dismissively.

Schwarz shook his head. ''We're building componentized Virginia-class submarines now, a lot bigger and more complicated than this one.''

Lyons had his doubts, but he hoped Schwarz and the others were on target on this one. If it didn't pan out, they had nothing to go on.

The countdown in Lyons's head said he had two minutes more to wait, but then the LED on Gadgets's wrist computer, plugged into the microphone he had dropped over the side, glowed to life with pinhead-size squares of red.

''Got something,'' Schwarz said, his eyes seeing nothing as he concentrated into his earphones. ''Sounds good.''

''How good?'' Lyons asked.

''Give me a minute.'' Schwarz glanced at the device,

but the screen showed him no positive ID. That was to be expected, since they were on the trail of an unknown type of minisub.

But they had made a number of educated guesses about the craft, using their knowledge base of Israeli technology. A top-secret Israeli special operations sub in the Caspian would be a political powder keg if the news got out, so it would have to be very secret. It would almost certainly employ very quiet engines for stealth running, which implied batteries. But if it was used for long-distance silent running to place commando teams, it would need something that lasted longer. The answer was probably fuel cells, a technology the European navies were increasingly adding to their submarines.

Diesel subs traditionally used lead-acid batteries to store power, but the output didn't offer a lot in terms of submerged distance travel. Next-generation subs were powered by hybrid diesel-electric propulsion systems, and the fuel cells made for farther stealthy submerged travel than the best battery technology. They stored power in liquid oxygen and metal hydrides, more dense and offering greater capacity.

Running on fuel cells, a big sub made less noise than a nuclear sub. But a sub as small as this one might make no noticeable noise unless someone was within a few yards of it.

Schwarz's underwater microphone was dangling on a thirty-foot line over the side of the Zodiac raft, wearing a protective basket of soft, acoustically inert foam to keep it from clanging if it hit the minisub. It was feeding into the waterproof computer Schwarz was wearing on his wrist, the device comparing the sound signature to sound signatures of known submarine types and engines.

But this was a case in which the ability of a human to make a good guess was far more valuable than the precise brain of the CPU, which had to be forced and cajoled to make any sort of a guess.

Schwarz grinned. "We have a submarine," he said, so quietly that his voice came over their headsets more clearly than Rosario Blancanales could hear him at the end of the raft.

"How big?" Blancanales asked. The size of the thing was critical.

"Big enough," Schwarz replied uncertainly.

Lyons looked at him sharply. "*How* big?"

"Give me a tape measure and a snorkel and I'll go find out," Gadgets shot back testily.

"If it's big, it sure isn't Israeli," Blancanales commented.

"Maybe it's Iranian," Lyons suggested.

"Or an old Soviet boat being used by Azerbaijan," Blancanales said in a low but conversational voice. "Or Khazakstan or Turkmenistan. Maybe Russia herself."

"Whoever it is, if it doesn't have a Star of David stenciled on it somewhere, we're in a hell of a lot of trouble," Lyons said. "Gadgets, can you tell me *anything* about this boat?"

Schwarz looked up sharply as the red dots on the tiny panel of his wrist computer became brighter and changed to orange, then yellow. "Yeah. I can tell you it's coming up right now. Here we go."

The gentle Caspian Sea began to boil. Lyons heard the cascade of water and saw the dim glow of a small porthole rise above the surface just five yards from the raft, no more, and that was all he saw before he flipped himself backward into the water.

The reaction by all three members of Able Team was the same and was instantaneous, using the noise of the surfacing minisub to disguise their entry into the water in case the Israelis had sophisticated listening devices of their own.

Blancanales had the most formal training in the water, coming from his special forces experiences, but Lyons and Schwarz had both been through SEAL training regimens throughout their years with Stony Man Farm and were comfortable in water, even in the blind darkness as they rocketed toward the sub far faster than a human could swim. Blancanales was less trusting of the electronics controlling their moment of approach than Schwarz, who had designed the system they were using.

The propulsion units, harnessed between their shoulder blades, were four-inch-diameter cylinders about a foot long, and they looked like small household fire extinguishers. The similarities were more than skin-deep. When activated, the unit provided propulsion through shaped nozzles, releasing high-pressure CO_2 foam that pushed the device and its passenger through the water with amazing speed for short distances. Controlling the system was a highly tuned underwater proximity sensor and CPU.

Schwarz built the units long ago, never knowing if they would be useful in the field, and had assumed they would be used for a quick escape, with the proximity sensors preventing them from banging into underground obstructions. He had adjusted the programming on the flight from Kuwait to do the job they now needed. He couldn't know how distant they would be from the sub when it surfaced. All he knew was that they would need to get to the sub as fast as possible. Now the units sought out the nearest and only obstacle—the minisub—and aimed right at it. They pulled the Able Team warriors through the water only ten feet below the surface and homed in like a torpedo. Then, at a distance of just a few yards, they would automatically stop working.

Blancanales felt his equipment dangling behind him as the wall of water was forced past him. It seemed to go on for minutes. Their tiny air bottles were also disposable and were only meant to keep them alive underwater for five minutes or so.

Then he felt the pull on his scuba harness stop and the line went slack. He pulled the quick-release and kicked for the surface, hands outstretched to prevent an impact with the hull.

As he brought his eyes above the surface, he saw he was right where they'd intended him to be—alongside the center of the hull, an arm's length from its black mass, which seemed to absorb the small glow of yellow light from the single porthole. A hatch was creaking open under the small tower. Blancanales spit out the mouthpiece and yanked the handgun from the waterproof pouch strapped on his shoulder blade, and he bobbed out of the sea to expose the weapon to the least amount of water. Then he waited, adjusting the flotation devices in the harness. They provided almost neutral buoyancy, despite the extra weight of his equipment.

What was going on? Had they been detected? Schwarz had warned them not to touch the hull, but could the minisub security system be sensitive enough to detect intruders who were floating nearby?

Maybe they'd made a mistake in approaching the minisub *too* fast. If the crew realized they were about to be attacked, all they had to do was submerge again and move off.

Then the hatch swung open, and Blancanales heard the hiss of a man speaking angrily in a near whisper. It was Hebrew. The Able Team commando didn't know Hebrew, but he could tell an argument when he heard one. Probably one wanted to stay inside, the safest course, while the other wanted to get a taste of fresh air while he could.

The man emerged from the hatch and stood on the deck, stretching his arms high, rolling his shoulders—and then he froze.

The crewman has just spotted a trail of froth from the propulsion devices. The Able Team commando lined up his sights and tried to compensate for the wave motion. As the crewman wheeled, Blancanales fired the suppressed handgun and saw the submariner's leg bend the wrong way, bringing him to the deck with a shout and the gonglike sound of his head hitting the thick, hollow metal.

There was a quick answer from inside the sub, but as Blancanales grabbed for the handrails he saw that the fallen crewman wasn't out of commission. He'd forced himself onto one hip, grunting from the pain of the ruined knee, and was grabbing for the gun under his arm. He reached over his head, somehow aware that was where Blancanales was coming aboard, and triggered a round that flew out into the ocean.

He was too weak to force his head back far enough to aim, so all he could do was shoot wildly, and even that was a huge effort. Blancanales heaved himself aboard between shots and put the conning tower between himself and the wounded man.

Shouts were coming from inside. The wounded man began to drag himself toward the hatch, yelling for his crewmate to help him inside.

When Blancanales heard the crewman come to the hatchway, he stepped around the tower to find a head and arms sticking out of the hatch, dragging at the wounded man. Both of them reacted to the sound coming from behind them. The wounded man twisted his head to witness someone else coming out of the sea, climbing onto the deck. It was Lyons.

Blancanales was in the way, so Lyons couldn't return fire on the two crewman. As the wounded man struggled to free his hands from the crewman inside, Blancanales reached for the steel hatch cover that leaned against the tower and shoved hard. The weight of the hatch was immense.

The wounded man didn't have time to react, but the crewman saw the hatch coming and gave a shout of surprise. It cracked into his head, then smashed both his arms before they slipped through the opening, and Blancanales felt a heavy thud from the interior. He disarmed the wounded man with a viscous snap of his foot, sending his handgun into the ocean. The crewman's eyes rolled into his head as Blancanales snapped plastic cuffs on his wrists.

His eyes snapped open when the thrum of an engine vibrated the deck. He realized the sub was about to submerge.

Schwarz appeared from the front end of the craft and heaved the hatch open, disappearing inside.

Blancanales was right behind him, and he felt the engines growl as he landed inside the cramped interior of the minisub. He was in a compartment no bigger than an airplane washroom. Schwarz was aiming a gun at him.

"Out of the way!"

Blancanales crouched, and Schwarz fired into the locking mechanism in the aluminum bulkhead. The lock shattered, and Blancanales followed it up with a bash from his elbow that sprang the panel out of its tracks, crashing it to the floor in the room beyond.

There was a sudden wail of a siren, and a small screen flashed a big red WARNING at the operator. The crewman was gasping with every small movement as he forced his crushed and broken arms to work the controls. A voice alert was added to the strident siren, but it spoke Hebrew. Then the message was repeated in English. "Do not submerge! Do not submerge!"

"Stop," Blancanales commanded, leveling the handgun at the operator as he moved in and made room for Schwarz.

The operator looked at him, then he gritted his teeth and forced his hands to move across the electronic keypads. There was something on the screen about an override, and when the operator pressed the next key Blancanales heard the hum of pumps and the rush of water into the sub's ballast tanks.

Blancanales cracked him in the side of his already bloodied skull, then Schwarz stepped over the falling body and stabbed at the keyboard. The rush of water halted, then reversed to empty the ballast tanks.

The operator went into convulsions at their feet.

THEY DUMPED the operator unceremoniously into the Caspian. After losing pints of blood he had gone silent while his internal injuries finished bleeding him to death. The wounded crewman on the deck watched the body sink into the blackness with sick terror.

Lyons lowered into a crouch, his face inches away, and said in a low growl, "We have some questions."

The crewman stared at the grim, silent man and nodded vigorously. "I will answer."

CHAPTER TWELVE

Bandar-e Anzali, Iran

The fishing vessels were full of activity, noisy and lit, with shouting men and swarming activity. Behind them crouched the sleeping coastal city, cool and quiet.

Schwarz grinned. "Nice scenery."

"Huh," Lyons said.

"Pol, I've got a guaranteed money-making business idea. Caspian Sea Cruises."

Blancanales nodded. "I see where you're going with this. Cruise the Picturesque Iranian Coastline by Submarine?"

"Of course."

"We'd need a new toilet. That latrine's smaller than a cereal bowl. It wouldn't support the posteriors of the cruising clientele."

"Minimal renovation costs," Schwarz declared.

Blancanales poked a thumb at the open hatchway, where below the Israeli crewman, named Rosner, was blindfolded, gagged and trussed to the wall fixtures. "Do we have to let that guy in on it?"

"Well, it is his submarine."

"Gadgets, that guy is an asshole. I don't think I want to go into business with him."

"Oh, well. Another capitalist venture goes down the drain."

Lyons waited, then demanded, tight-lipped, "Well? You done?"

"Yeah," Schwarz said.

The fishing boats were heading out, making their way through the dredged channel to the open water, and the Israeli sub was parked a full half-mile away. Black in the blackness, she was invisible. They would wait out the fishing traffic, then move in. Unless they were spotted first.

"Able One here," Lyons radioed.

"All clear, Able One," Price responded. He'd been asking for reports every five minutes.

Lyons wasn't into this sitting-duck crap. He'd rather take the chance of a Zodiac raft landing, no matter how exposed it was. Trouble was, none of them knew for sure how stealthy the Israeli sub was and how good the Iranian coastal monitoring was around here.

But there was no sign of alert as they waited out the last of the fishing boats and submerged for the slow cruise in. They stood in the crammed cubicle, staring at one another and the flat panel displays showing them the images from the video array on the sensor pod that passed for a periscope. The wharf was quiet now, and the humming of the electric engines was almost silent, even inside the boat. The infrared display revealed no warm bodies waiting in the shadows on the docks. Schwarz turned off the engines and allowed the sub to drift until she stopped, moving gently in place between a pair of empty slips.

"Stony Base here," Price said.

"Go ahead."

"I think you've been spotted."

"Huh?" Schwarz asked, scanning every display and screen again.

"We've got a large vessel headed into the dock. Could be an Iranian shore patrol. Boats don't usually come in before dawn, so it is definitely suspicious."

"ETA?"

"Twenty minutes."

"We can be out of here in five," Lyons replied.

"What about him?" Blancanales asked. The crewman was staring at them with wild eyes, convinced that his usefulness was done and he would be disposed of.

"Rip out the radio and let him make a run for it," Blancanales said. "He won't make contact with anyone soon enough to cause us trouble."

"Wishful thinking," Lyons said.

"He'd never make it past the patrol boat," Price said. "If they've spotted the sub already, they'll home in without trouble and send it to the bottom."

"Take me with you," Rosner blurted, his face shining with sweat. "I will help."

"How?" Lyons demanded.

"I know where the team will be."

"That's not what you said a couple of hours ago, friend."

"I was trying to buy them time. I will tell you where they are going. I will tell you what kind of defenses they have in place."

"You're going from patriot to traitor just like that?" Schwarz asked.

The crewman swallowed the hurtful words. "Not just like that," he said. "I have become afraid of this sub. I have started having nightmares."

"You've become claustrophobic?" Blancanales asked.

"No. Not the space! The cold. I'm afraid of the freezing."

Lyons and Blancanales looked at Schwarz.

"Yeah. I forgot. We're standing on enough liquid oxygen to turn this end of the Caspian into a skating rink."

"We're not sure about the integrity of the system," Rosner said. "There have been leaks and accidents. A depth charge would burst the LOX tank before sinking the sub itself. When that happens, the liquid oxygen fills the sub all at once. Everything freezes solid. Everything. But they say your brain is the last thing to freeze and you are aware of it happening."

The crewman was whispering the words, and Lyons thought he was either on the verge of a mental breakdown or was a hell of a good actor. He was a notorious skeptic, but he didn't have time to contemplate the pros and cons.

"All right friend, you come with us," Lyons said. "But I want you to understand—you are no longer loyal to the Coldman project. From now on you are loyal only to *me.* You'll give me all the information I want, when I want it, no game playing. If you give me anything less than one hundred percent cooperation..."

Then Lyons did some acting of his own. He leaned close to the crewman and spoke in a very low voice. Schwarz and Blancanales didn't hear a word of it.

When Lyons finished the crewman was pale as the belly-up fish carcass that was nudging the hull in the darkness.

THEY LEFT the minisub right where she was, between the docking slips for the big fishing boats. Here the water was dredged deep, but the vessels would tend to miss the wreckage during their maneuvers in and out. Unless the Iranians staged a search with divers or magnetometers they might not stumble upon her remains for weeks, or months, or until the next dredging.

They silently paddled the crowded inflatable to the dockside, mounting the sea-slimed ladder. Lyons was first, scanning their dark corner of the wharf for a full minute before being satisfied that it was deserted. Then he gave Blancanales a wave. Hanging on the bottom of the ladder with gentle Caspian waves wetting his feet, Blancanales knifed the inflatable until the weight of her anchor dragged her sputtering into the black water.

Schwarz had been assigned the task of bringing the wounded crewman up the ladder. No easy task. Schwarz had removed a strap and steel hook, used to secure loose components inside the sub, and tied it around his chest. A rope also went through the strap. The crewman stood in place on the ladder with the hook keeping him upright. Schwarz looped the rope on an upper rung, then hauled down to lift the guy as he hopped, laboriously, up the rungs. Progress sped up considerably when they were close enough to the top that he and Lyons could stand there and haul him in.

Then they stood on the dock and saw the lights of the vessel coming inshore. Maybe just a fishing vessel with some sort of a problem. Maybe not.

"Signing off now, Stony Base," Lyons radioed. Once the satellite uplink in the submarine was destroyed, they would have sporadic contact with Stony Man Farm.

"Good luck," Price said.

The crewman had been freed of all his bonds except for his wrist cuffs. He was staring with a kind of fearful fascination at the gray-on-black outline of the minisub, the upper quarter of it riding above the surface.

"Go ahead," Lyons said.

Schwarz touched the remote that detonated the explosives planted inside the sub. The open hatch became a searchlight, sending a beam of yellow light into the clouds then disappearing as quick as a lightning strike. The crack of the explosions was muffled by the water, and the hull came apart at every rivet. Inside, the charges were designed to obliterate the electronics and penetrate the bottom bulkhead, cracking the fuel cells and opening the liquid oxygen tank. The water entered the hull in a sudden flood, bubbled white, releasing a cloud of fog, then became solid.

The night became silent again, leaving only the wreckage embedded in an ice sheet on the surface of the warm Caspian.

"They saw the flash," Blancanales said, observing the ship turning toward them.

Lyons and the minisub crewman were regarding each other. The Israeli looked at once relieved that the object of his phobia was destroyed but knowing that a new and greater fear might have replaced it. He looked at Lyons, then the frozen wreckage, then at Lyons. A heavy section of the sub tore loose from the ice with a screech of metal that made the crewman jump.

Now unstable, the ice mass began noisily releasing its hold on the metal parts as Able Team stepped into the blackness of the Iranian night.

When the approaching ship halted and sent a dingy to investigate the source of the strange flash, the first mate came back towing something totally unexpected.

It was a latrine, an extremely narrow toilet made from brushed aluminum. What was really odd, though, was that it was encased in a shapeless chunk of ice as big as a steamer trunk.

And it was a warm night.

CARRYING A SATELLITE uplink just wasn't practical, and without it they couldn't establish the kind of secure communications channel they liked with Stony Man Farm. They would have to rely on commercial satellite phone service. It wasn't one-hundred-percent reliable, especially inside a building, but it was portable, encryptable and their radio systems were programmed to tie into it.

And it wasn't working.

Lyons didn't worry about it. Eventually they'd get through. Right now he was more concerned about his captive. The man presented all sorts of problems. He was barely mobile, untrustworthy and probably mentally unstable. But he might have the key to tracking the Iranian Coldman team, which meant Lyons couldn't afford to get rid of him. The crewman's phobic behavior wasn't an act—he was sustaining it too consistently. Lyons was almost certain he was genuine, but the man's fear was so intense he could act irrationally and impulsively, which was dangerous, too. Right now he was in control of himself if only because of the threat Lyons made.

The Able Team commander told the crewman that if he screwed up or gave them bad intelligence, he was going to be trussed up, gagged, blindfolded and deposited in a back corner of one of the industrial freezers at the Bandar-e Anzali fish processing plants. There he would freeze to death, but not like on the minisub. It would be slow, lingering and he would be *aware* of it for hours instead of seconds.

It was the right button to push, and it was probably cruel, but Lyons didn't care. He cared about doing his job. He cared about not letting a thousand or ten thousand innocent Iranian families die in nuclear fire.

Before dawn they had wheels, a four-cylinder hunk of junk with an unpronounceable name and a shape like a station wagon. Lyons had to sit with his knees against the dashboard. Schwarz, in the driver's seat, was straddling the steering wheel and having trouble getting the clutch pushed down.

But it got them where they wanted to go and had been free for the taking. They waited in it, watching a small bakery that looked like a house with a storefront, situated on a street with especially heavy foot traffic even this early in the morning. When the sky was getting light, two employees were spotted working inside.

"That is them," the sub crewman said. "The older man is the owner. It is his shop and his house, and he does all the baking."

A minute later the front doors were propped open. There was a quick rush of business from the small queue of patrons that had formed in front.

Schwarz maneuvered the station wagon into an alley behind the bakery and parked next to a delivery van. He eyed the van almost lustily, and Lyons read his mind. The van would be better cover and a lot more comfortable than the station wagon.

Time to make their entrance.

AMIR KADIVAR WAS WIPING his hands on a flour-covered apron when he came in the back and found himself staring down the extended barrel of a suppressed handgun.

"Speak English?" Lyons asked.

The man stared at him. "A little bit English."

"Speak Hebrew?"

"No! What question is that?"

The sub crewman was walked out for the baker. Kadivar lifted Rosner's head by the chin and muttered darkly to himself—in Hebrew. Rosner kept his eyes closed.

"You're military," he said accusingly to the submariner. The baker's English was suddenly unbroken, almost unaccented. "We need them, but they are always the weak link. They do not have the dedication to the cause that gives us our perseverance. So they reveal our secrets with a twist of the arm."

"We want the team and the device," Lyons said.

"Why?"

"If you don't know, then I'm not going to be able to explain it to you, and I really don't want to even try."

The baker was in midfrown when he heard the thunk of metal on bone. It was from behind him, from the front of the bakery, then Rasool Far, his assistant, brushed against his shins as he collapsed on the floor. A red knot already marred his forehead. Far was a trained assassin, one of the most capable agents Kadivar had ever known. For somebody to get the drop on him was startling.

The baker heard another American voice. "He was going to whack you with a croissant, Ironman."

Kadivar didn't turn but looked down to see hands that efficiently removed the hidden 9 mm pistol from his assistant, then flipped him and trussed him in plastic handcuffs.

"Thanks for the assist, Gadgets," said the leader, the dark grim figure.

Kadivar stared at the man in front of him, clearly an American, probably from the West Coast originally if his voice identification skills were still sharp. And Kadivar knew they were. The third man, the American's companion, was darker-skinned and hadn't said a word, but he wore a complicated personality on his face, an inexplicable combination of friendly and deadly. He could slap your back over beers in a bar and take you out with cold-blooded efficiency the moment you put your hand on your weapon.

That was the read the baker got, and he was an expert when it came to analyzing personality types. It was part instinct, part doctorate in psychology from Tel Aviv University.

"I just don't understand why the Americans would want to stop this," the baker protested.

The leader, Kadivar thought, was one grim human being. He wore a shroud of malevolence, fueling his drive against his enemies. Maybe one of those enemies was himself. The baker was coming slowly to terms with just how skilled and deadly this little group was. If he was to trust his first impression.

The leader was also smart, refusing to allow himself to be dragged into a distracting conversation. He stood there, waiting with unnerving patience. Even Kadivar, an experienced intelligence analyst and a master manipulator of most personality types, became agitated at the man's implacability and malice.

"Are we just going to stand here?"

"The team and the device. I want to know all of it."

"I won't tell you any of this. Why should I? Are you going to shoot me?"

"I'm going to make you famous," Lyons said, his head turning a fraction. "Smile for the camera."

The baker saw it, the tiny video pickup mounted on the commando's headgear, and his stomach became cold. "You're taping this? You'll never get it out of Iran."

"It's already out," Blancanales said. "We're compressing the data and feeding it in packets over four phone lines. Good thing for us your house doesn't have a lot of steel in it to block the signal. How's it look on your end, Barb?"

"The audio is great," Price replied. "The video is clear enough. The guys at the networks can clean it right up. The first clip of *Israeli Spy Runs Bakery in Iran* is already attached to an e-mail and ready for me to hit Send."

"Send where?" Kadivar demanded. The cool voice of the woman had come through a small speaker the darker-skinned commando attached to his headset.

"I have contacts all over. Reporters at ABC and BBCWorld.com, a video segment producer at MSNBC, an anchor at CNN.com, six or seven more."

The man who was both baker and an Israeli intelligence mole looked sick.

"You have thirty seconds," the dark, grim man said. "That's all it will take for us to expose you and ruin you. You will be responsible for creating holes in Israel intelligence that will take decades to plug. Mossad and Israel will revile you. All your work, everything you've ever accomplished, will be shit."

"What right do you have to do this?" Kadivar demanded. It was a stupid thing to say, the kind of thing that trapped victims were always saying.

"I have the right to do anything I can to prevent genocide." The grim figure spoke the words like he was biting them out of uncured leather.

The baker looked the dark man in the eyes, no longer seeing the big handgun that was a finger twitch away from blowing his brains out. His eyes narrowed and he said, ''Genocide?''

CHAPTER THIRTEEN

Cairo, Egypt

It had been a long, unproductive day already, and it was still morning. The street vendors and small open food kiosks were starting to cook midday meals while the sun ripened the streets. The smells got thicker as the air got hotter.

David McCarter knew there were nice parts to this city, because they had been in one a few minutes ago, but so much of Cairo, and Egypt, was below an economic level that the world labeled poverty.

"I thought we were looking for a family of wealthy Egyptians," Gary Manning said as they sat in the Land Rover at the side of the street, taking in the ambience of the neighborhood.

"Yeah."

"This is a slum."

"Family ties. They're supposed to have extended family around here," McCarter reminded him.

"If I had rich cousins and they let me live *here,* I think it would strain the family relations," Manning said.

"It's all just for cover," Price told them. "And it looks like they're not using it at all anymore."

Rafael Encizo and T. J. Hawkins emerged from the ramshackle building fifty feet ahead of them. Despite the sagging second floor and the broken windows, the structure was well-maintained compared to other buildings. To Manning they looked like homeless derelicts squatting together with their shoulders touching, breath bad with the previous night's alcohol sickness.

Encizo and Hawkins wore the voluminous robe that was standard Middle East dress. It helped them to blend in with the locals and concealed a variety of weapons. The two men climbed into the old Land Rover.

"It's been weeks since the place was used," Encizo reported.

"By humans," Hawkins added. "It's too clean, in terms of possible leads."

"We're batting zero," Manning complained.

McCarter was driving, and he headed through the slum toward their next stop. "Stony Base, how sure are we about the cover story Able got from the sub crewman?"

"Not sure about that, Phoenix One," Price answered. "The crewman believed that the Egyptian Mossad moles are posing as a wealthy family returning home after a three-week holiday in Sydney to visit family. We're trying to confirm that through airline records. There's an airline mainframe failure somewhere, and that's slowing us down."

"They sure must have a lot of family," Manning grumbled.

"But the crewman thought the moles would have returned to Cairo by now," McCarter added. "So far, we're not seeing it."

"Sounds like they were in place for years," Price

reminded him. "You invest that much time establishing an identity you're not going to trash it without good reason."

Phoenix Force had made short work of getting into Cairo, where they began their search for the deep-cover Coldman team. The first stop was across the Nile, at a two-story villa in Garden City that was listed as the primary residence for Nibal Eissa and wife Mona. But the villa was locked up tight. Their next step was to check out the residences listed as belonging to Eissa relatives.

None of the properties was a known Mossad safehouse, which could mean they were on the right track. Coldman would have its own network in place. Two of the other places they checked were stocked as if for a siege. Weapons and ammo, medical kits, food, clothes, and cosmetics and clothing for quick disguises.

Maybe the Coldman team wasn't back in Egypt yet. Maybe these safehouses were for some other purpose. Maybe they were on the wrong trail.

"Are we making progress on getting solid IDs, Stony Base?" McCarter asked Price, who was communicating with them through a secure link that fed into the wireless phone on the dashboard. It looked normal, but the acoustics were superior, and the electronics in the dashboard were much more sophisticated. The system automatically used the best of whatever local wireless phone technology was offered, expanding the number of lines to accommodate the amount of data, voice and video transmission that was needed, all sent over the lines using high-speed data switching. This sent the information in bursts, or packets, which were so brief that no audio quality was lost. Kurtzman and Huntington Wethers had developed their own encryption methods to make use of the Wireless Access Protocol without risk risking their data security.

"Some, Phoenix One," she said. "We've got global searches ongoing, based on fingerprints Able got off the minisub interior. We're trying to make them correlate with the sub computer's data and what we learned from the crewman."

"And?"

"It's not that easy, Phoenix One," Price replied. "We're trying to put our finger on agents who have been in deep cover of some kind for years, maybe since the Gulf War. That was before a lot of this information was digitized by the Israelis. It's hard to find even falsified data on agents who were supposedly killed or left the agency that long ago."

"Since we have even less evidence on the Egyptian group, how confident can we be that we're looking for the right people?" McCarter asked.

"You want numbers?" Price sighed, her frustration beginning to tell in her voice. "I'm guessing eighty percent."

Manning groaned. McCarter shot him a glare. "Tell us about the next stop."

"It borders a part of the city called Misr al-Qadimah, which is Old Cairo," Price said. "We think it's unknown to Mossad or other Israeli intelligence. Any amateur would blow his cover in an Old Cairo neighborhood. It's one of the most densely populated parts of the city."

"These Eissas sure don't live like rich folks," Manning said.

"Can't be any worse than the last place," Hawkins stated.

He was wrong.

CAIRO WAS CONTRAST. Every element of the city possessed an opposite. Every statement ever made about Cairo could be contradicted by another.

In a nation known for its ancient civilization, Cairo was a new city. Yet it was an ancient city by any other measure, founded as a military stronghold and encampment in 641. It was planted with trees and even some lawns, and the sprawl of the metropolis on either side of the great Nile River was cushioned with irrigated fields. But on the outskirts, where the irrigation stopped, the desert recommenced. One moment the ground was lush and green, the next it was desiccated, a delineation so clear it could be seen from space.

The people were contrasts, too. Arab, Bedouin, Nubian and European, all juggling for a position in the convolution of Egyptian society.

And her wealth was a contrast, perhaps this more than any other thing. Under her sands and decorating her history were the most valuable and renowned archaeological treasures, made in priceless gold and gems. But most residents of Cairo drowned in poverty.

As its name implied, Old Cairo contained ruins dating back centuries to the city's medieval splendor, but most of the buildings were dilapidated versions of the same two-, three- or four-story walk-ups that seemed to house most of Cairo's population. The same crude red brick was used for these flats, but somehow it looked more crude and crumbling, and in this part of the city few buildings had the decorative plaster exterior seen elsewhere.

Among the apartment buildings were more small factories and shops than one could count. They were forging antiquities, baking bread, weaving rugs, slaughtering sheep. The effluence mingled with the trapped

smoke of countless cooking fires and the stench of rip-
ening garbage, all of it heated to oven temperature by
the midday sun, until the atmosphere swirling among
the buildings was thick and nearly unbreathable. Almost as oppressive was the discordant wail of Arabic
and Western pop music coming out of cheap boom
boxes in every window and shop.

Walking in and crowding the streets were people by
the thousands—the poor of Cairo. They were newcomers by the standards of Cairo's settlement. Once farm-
ers or desert dwellers, they hadn't moved off the bottom rung of Egypt's ladder of social status even after
several generations, and few dreamed they ever would.

The people parted for the Land Rover, some glaring
at the occupants behind the shaded windows. The de-
cade-old rental SUV was worth more than many of
them saw in a lifetime.

When Phoenix Force came to the address they
wanted, it looked much like other walk-ups on the
block except that it lacked the droves of children and
families on its steps and in its windows.

"Too many people," McCarter commented. "Not a
good place for an altercation. We can't endanger these
people."

"I'm seeing a courtyard or a car park—something,"
Rafael Encizo said, peering through binoculars. "It's
guarded."

"Guarded?" Price responded. "That could be good
news."

"Hold on." Encizo rolled down the window just
enough to poke out the lenses of the field glasses. The
smog still made it look as if he were looking through
a film, but he could see better than through the shaded
car windows.

It was a decorative iron gate set into a wall of the building that faced an alley. The alley was so narrow and the gate so far back it was almost hidden from the street. Through the bars he made out a man on a stool, his arms folded as if napping.

Encizo described it as he closed the window. "Doesn't look like standard equipment for this kind of housing."

"Locked?" McCarter asked.

"Yeah. A big box lock and a heavy steel beam across the gate. I don't know if we could get up enough speed to push through."

"Promising, but how to get in?" Manning asked.

McCarter craned his neck and took in the street's layout. "The building on the far side might be close enough to give us access."

Manning gave the Phoenix Force leader a disbelieving look. "You can jump first."

"We might not have to," Calvin James observed. "Look what's coming."

Up ahead they saw the crowd parting smoothly around a car that was rolling down the street at a walking pace, low-riding under the weight of suitcases and a pair of steamer trunks that looked like they were from the nineteenth century. A spiderweb of ropes snugged the mass of luggage to the roof. When it was close they made out the Mercedes emblem and the fresh shine.

"It's them," Manning said. "It has to be."

"What's up?" Price asked. Manning briefed her.

McCarter thought Manning was right. This was the Coldman mole team. His thumb banged the steering wheel as his mind whirled. The Mercedes was going to enter the secure lot, and this might be their best and only chance to get past the barred gate. Another thought: if the team was just returning to Egypt, then the Coldman device was in that car. They couldn't let this opportunity slip away.

"We're going in," he stated, interrupting Manning as he was shooting Price a digital image of the license plate from a portable digital camera, with an extended zoom lens for quality close-up zooms. "Rafe, T.J., get out there and be ready to provide cover and backup."

"What's the plan?" Price asked.

"I plan to improvise, unless somebody has a viable strategy." Nobody answered. Hawkins pulled his robe closed around his hardware and opened the door when McCarter said sharply, "I'm issuing just one directive—we don't shoot until they do. I want to be sure—one hundred percent sure—that this is who we think it is. I won't have the blood of an innocent Egyptian civilian on my hands. That understood, mates?"

"Understood," Hawkins and Encizo said in unison, then the doors shut behind them.

"Suit up, please," Price said. "I'd like full data feeds."

McCarter absently pulled on his headset, watching the Mercedes and the gate. The driver showed no evidence that he was aware of the parked Land Rover. Occupants in the rear were hidden behind black glass, although he thought he saw the profile of a young woman turning to look at him as the Mercedes entered the alley with a brief beep of the horn.

McCarter drove the Land Rover after it, moving just fast enough to encourage the locals to scramble away as he approached, and then he was nose-to-rear with the Mercedes as the gates swung open.

"Play it cool," he muttered just loud enough for the

others to hear. "No weapons necessary." As the gates slid away ponderously and the Mercedes rolled through with the effortless, silent drift that was a standard feature on very expensive automobiles, McCarter stayed close. He got the nose of the Land Rover inside before he tapped the brake and jerked it to a stop in response to a sharp word from the gatekeeper. It was the man Encizo had spied napping.

McCarter nodded, but the gatekeeper looked resolute. The Mercedes was pulling across the car park, and McCarter gestured at it, showing irritation. The guard motioned for him to roll down his window.

The Briton opened it. "What's the problem? We're bringing luggage for Mr. Eissa."

The guard's look darkened when he heard the English, and McCarter watched the furrows of suspicion grow deeper as he examined the other occupants of the Land Rover. "Why don't I know about it?" he replied, his English heavily accented.

"Sorry you didn't get the memo," McCarter replied. "Are you going to let us in so we can drop of Mr. Eissa's luggage, or should we just dump his stuff in the street?"

"I will not let you in until I know more who you are."

"So find out more," McCarter said impatiently.

"Back up so I will close the gate."

"Look, pal, if you kick me out of here I'm leaving. I can come back in—" he looked at his watch "—three hours. I'll let you explain to Mr. Eissa why half his luggage is missing."

"No, no, just wait one second," the gatekeeper said quickly, and then he tried to do what McCarter had been afraid of. He turned and opened his mouth to shout at the house, where the back end of the Mercedes was protruding from a too-short niche under the second story.

While he was drawing the breath to yell, McCarter's hand shot out, grabbed the waist of his baggy linen trousers and pulled him into the side of the Land Rover with a movement so powerful the man never quite realized what was happening. His chest and head were whipped into the roof.

McCarter held the limp body against the window as he steered the Land Rover close to the building, against the wall on the street side and out of the line of sight of the Mercedes in back. He dropped the guard, and the man fell against the wall, but his knees wedged against McCarter's door and kept him half standing upright. With a sigh of exasperation the Briton shoved him out of the way, stepping out as the man scraped slowly along the wall and crumpled on the brick pavement with a groan. McCarter had him cuffed in seconds, with gray tape covering his face. The only thing to secure him to was the corner of an exposed aluminum electrical conduit.

"That's too flimsy, mate," McCarter told the guard as he struggled weakly against the cuffs. The guard's wrists were dragged over his head and linked with another pair of cuffs on an exposed suspension spring behind the front wheel. "Can't have you running around loose. Sure hope we have time to let you off the hook on the way out." He relieved the gatekeeper of a snub-nosed .38.

"With the gate open and the guard missing, it won't take long for them to figure out there's a problem," James stated as they listened to the activity in the car park around the corner. There were snatches of English mixed with Arabic.

"I'm counting six or eight people," James added.

"At least two women."

"I promise you will like the house, Gamal," a female voice said enthusiastically in English. "Just wait until you see the garden. Come on!"

"She sounded young," James observed.

"Too young," Manning muttered. "But this guy was armed." He looked at the gatekeeper, then shook his head. "That means nothing. If I had any money in a neighborhood this poor, I'd keep armed protection, too."

"Phoenix One here," McCarter radioed. "We're getting a bad vibe here. We may have a kid on the premises."

"Stony Base here," Price replied. "Understood. But the kid could be part of the cover."

"We're not making overt moves until we're convinced," McCarter stated. "Phoenix Two?"

"Go ahead," Encizo replied immediately in his earpiece.

"Watch the place. We don't want to lose the Coldman device if they try to use an escape route we don't know about. Don't come in unless we ask for help."

"Understood."

McCarter led the stealthy approach as the sounds of conversation faded. They moved to the car park and saw no one. The mounds of luggage were still in place on the vehicle. If the suitcase weapons had been in the car, they surely would have been hand carried, and the interior of the Mercedes was as empty and clean as it had been on the showroom floor.

With a flick of his wrist McCarter ushered Manning

and James to his side, then he trotted across the open end of the car park and made himself small against the end of the brick wall. A quick look revealed another small parking area and a brick wall with decorative arches. A shady, enclosed garden area lay beyond. He reached the parking area in two strides and peered through one of the arches in time to see a couple emerge from the house. The woman was still talking in English. "Here is the garden. We just love it."

She was young, maybe mid twenties, and attired in conservative Western attire, baggy trousers and a blouse of several layers of lightweight material. The man who followed her onto the glazed brick patio, under a roof of vine-covered lattice, was wearing an easy smile. He was in neutral, tropical-weight business casual, with a sport jacket over an opened-collared shirt. Dark-skinned, maybe really an Egyptian, but McCarter couldn't tell for sure.

The young woman led her companion across the garden to a pair of wooden chairs hidden in the shade of a tight grouping of low trees. They began to whisper, heads bowed together.

The door to the house opened, and an older woman emerged with a small tray. She wore a silk blouse, carrying herself with the proud confidence of a lifetime spent in the upper class. The woman exchanged a few quiet words with the two on the bench as she set down a platter.

By the time the snack was set out, McCarter had made the dangerous bolt across the parking area to the rear corner, where he crouched at the wall. If those in the garden had been looking, they would have spotted him through the arch's brick openings.

The couple began to speak urgently when the older

woman went inside. McCarter cursed beneath his breath. He could barely hear the conversation, and what he could hear he didn't understand.

What was he missing here? What was bothering him? As he glanced across the empty drive, he frowned, thinking hard. Twenty feet away, Manning was impatient and shrugged. James was keeping one hard eye on the interior of the car park.

Another word or two came through. Something was gnawing at him—what was it?

Then he knew. He grimaced. Suspicions confirmed, he thought, as he touched the tiny headset switch that turned on the omnidirectional auxiliary microphone on his headset. He heard the distant garble of the conversation come through his headset.

"Stony Base, take a listen," he said.

The others were getting it, too. James had his hand to his headset, adjusting it minutely and staring into space. Then he nodded.

When the pair was clearly involved in conversation, McCarter took the opportunity to race back to the car park and join the others.

"Don't tell me you got something out of that?" Manning said.

"Enough."

"That was Hebrew," Price stated.

Manning said, "Oh. Oh, yeah."

"I dialed in Katz," Price added. "He made out only a few words. Nothing useful."

"So how close are we to being sure this is the Coldman moles?" James asked, directing the question at McCarter. The ex-SEAL wore no expression, and if he was as eager to move as Manning was he didn't show it. James knew this decision was weighing heavily on the Phoenix Force leader. It was unthinkable to allow poor choices to result in civilian death at the hands of this team.

"We're at ninety-nine percent," McCarter said firmly. "Stony Base, we're moving inside, and we'll keep it soft for as long as possible. My original directive still stands—no deadly force until I'm convinced these are the people we want."

James nodded shortly, without hesitation. Manning thought the evidence was more than sufficient to justify a full-fledged assault on the place, but he knew well enough when not to insert his opinion.

The voices were moving in the garden, speaking Arabic now. The couple entered the building, and McCarter waited ninety seconds before going in after them.

CHAPTER FOURTEEN

Nibal Eissa was pacing the parlor when Azza and the newcomer entered. He had asked Azza to take the young man away while he conferred with the others, but the conference had solved nothing.

Eissa wasn't in a lounging mood, and he hated the fresh-faced punk who was trying to pull off the cool and unruffled facade.

"Justify your presence here." It was an order, and it was so to-the-point that it nearly cut through the young man's emotionless exterior.

"Mr. Eissa, I won't justify myself to you—"

"You will."

"I didn't make the decision to join the Cairo cell. You want a full explanation, then go to the people who did make the decision."

Well, the kid was good so far. His Australian accent was perfectly understated. Even when he spoke his broken Arabic it was with a Cairoese accent and Australian overtones, in keeping with his cover story. A cousin, raised since boyhood in Sydney, returning for an extended holiday with his uncle's family in Egypt.

"You know I can't do that," Eissa retorted, careful to keep his voice low as he walked and held his arms folded on his chest. "You're my only link to them.

Therefore I hold you accountable for their rash actions.''

"You can't hold me accountable," the young man said, contempt edging into his voice. "And I won't allow you to treat me like an underling, Eissa."

He went under the name Gamal Shadi. It didn't matter what his true Israeli name once was. If he was like the rest of the cell the old identity was dead and buried. But maybe Shadi wasn't like the others. He didn't have the subtly natural behavior of the long-term mole.

"Listen close, Shadi," Eissa said, his pacing stopping abruptly. "This cell has been out of touch for months. That's fine, because contingencies were planned for years ago. We don't need support. We don't need more intelligence. All we needed was the device. We didn't bargain for you."

"I'm here to *assist*," Shadi insisted, seeing himself surrounded by stony faces.

"You are a fool. This cell has been in place two years. We're flawless as natives. At best, you'll be in the way. At worst you'll expose us. You're not up to par."

"I've trained with the best and I'm good at this. And my cover story is designed for my skill level. Any significant error I make can be explained by my background—and I won't make significant errors. Most importantly, I've got skills the rest of you lack."

Eissa smirked. "Yes, you've said that ten times and have so far failed to explain yourself."

"I have told you as much as I am permitted to tell you of my background," Shadi said with finality. "I will say no more."

"You will say more or you will be alone," Eissa promised. "These people will follow me."

Shadi was stunned when he realized the weight of the words. "You're committing treason if you do."

"Wrong."

"You've sworn to do this task. You've pledged an oath on your own blood to do this. And yet you would walk away from Coldman as easily as that?"

"I won't walk away from Coldman, I will walk away from you, and I will do so because of the pledge you just mentioned. When I took that pledge, I devoted myself to see it to its end and I will. If I see you as a hindrance to this cell and its goal, then I will remove you from it. Orders from above are now secondary to the pledge I made."

Shadi looked from face to face. He was in a room full of women. The only two other men were Eissa and the agent going by the name Halim, posing as Eissa's son-in-law. But all the women were ex-Mossad or from some other special operations training background. All were experienced moles, and in Egypt it was much easier for a woman to pull off the subterfuge than a man, since a woman could limit her social life to her extended family and it would seem quite normal. All these women were coldly determined. Even the young woman Azza, who had been so kind to him, was nodding, her expression set. His mind looked for options swiftly, and none came to him.

"Then I must tell you what you want to know." He paused. Eissa looked impatient for him to get on with it.

Shadi thought this was a scary bunch of lunatics. He knew if they did consider him a hindrance they wouldn't just kick him out of the club. They'd try to kill him, their own countryman, without hesitation. There were four very skilled agents in this devoted little fake family. They just might be capable of over-powering him.

"I'm the Last Resort," he commenced.

"The Cairo cell is the Last Resort," Eissa countered. "The doctrine spells this out."

"The doctrine isn't the final word within the Cold-man organization," Shadi explained patiently. "The founders developed a top-level addendum to the master strategy years after the organization came into being. It was the Last Resort to the last resort, in a way."

The older women posing as Nibal Eissa's wife said, "You are a liar. There is no such thing."

"There is," he replied, and he would have gone on.

"You have a letter for me," Eissa said shortly, holding out his hand, and Mona regarded Eissa with suspicion.

"Did you expect this?" she demanded.

Eissa didn't answer, but opened the sheet of folded ivory stationery that Shadi handed him. Staring at the page he muttered, "Last Resort."

COLDMAN CAME into being in the 1970s, growing out of the friendship of a pair of Israelis, one a Mossad officer, the other a general in the Israel Defense Forces. After years of watching the inability of their nation to halt the Arab attacks against the Israeli people, they came to the opinion that the entire Arab world would inevitably unite against Israel. It would be a force too big, with battle fronts too numerous and widespread, to fight successfully. Israel's allies would be reluctant to come to her defense—it would be impolitic to create animosity with so many nations, especially when those nations controlled most of the world's oil. The rules of the Arab alliance would certainly spell out sanctions against all members of any alliance set against them. NATO would be impotent.

The two men developed a simple objective for their fledgling organization: if Israel went down, the entire Arab world would be brought down, too. Maybe not wiped off the face of the earth, but at least reduced to bankruptcy and chaos.

Both men were privy to knowledge of the old Coldman test project. Funds were funneled into a secret facility for optimizing the weapon. It had to be capable of wiping out massive populations, but it also had to be man-portable, because Coldman's best chance for success depended on manual delivery.

The Coldman Objective, which had never been written down, called for all members to vigorously promote a First Protocol, which meant Israel's official counteractions to the Arab threat. It was unlikely the First Protocol would succeed, and even when they were drawing up this law the Coldman pair knew it was lip service. Weapons of mass destruction would be required.

The Second Protocol was to be secret, small-scale incursions with devices that were configured for delivery from the air. This plan was deemed untrustworthy in the 1970s, when airspace was becoming easier to monitor. In the twenty-first century, it became clear this was virtually impossible. It seemed half the world's military aircraft were over this part of the world, and all tracking information was being shared globally.

The Third Protocol was what Coldman had always called its "Last Resort"—highly trained, well-equipped, extremely well-funded moles, planted in every significant Arab nation, waiting for the order to act, an order that had come just weeks ago and had precipitated the hastily planned faux vacation to Australia. This enabled delivery of the Coldman device. There had been surprise and consternation when the Cairo cell learned they were being burdened with a new member on board.

"Is he legitimate?" Mona demanded.

Eissa nodded. "I've heard rumors. This—" he waved the sheet of stationery "—confirms it."

"We're the best," Mona protested. "What can he do that we can't do?"

Eissa looked pointedly at the newcomer. "That's for our friend to answer."

"I've been trying to answer for the last five minutes," Shadi protested. "If you will allow me to speak?"

Eissa made a small gesture with his fingertips for him to proceed.

"My job is to detonate the Coldman device at all costs," Shadi said. "Regardless of its staging. I'm trained to carry the device in readiness so that it can be used if there is no other option except capture."

"We have the same orders," Eissa said, intrigued despite his anger.

"You are ordered to, yes," Shadi said. "Trained to, equipped to, no. Let me show you."

With that, Shadi opened the carry-on he had with him at all times, just as Eissa had never allowed the two Coldman suitcases out of his grip, and the third, in the hands of a man posing as his son-in-law, never out of his sight. Shadi's gym bag was small and lumpy, and what he removed looked like the army bedrolls Eissa made for himself with his extra field gear back in his soldier days. What the man unrolled appeared to be nothing more than the work clothes of a telephone lineman and a few personal electronics devices.

Without apology or explanation, Shadi stripped to his boxer shorts and pulled on the pants, zipping them up the inside of both legs to the crotch, and then he began threading a belt through the hoops at the waist. "The material is made of body armor components, designed for a combination of ballistic protection and long-term wearability. You can wear it under environmental extremes. It won't absorb a lot of water if it gets wet. It's light enough to run in. The shin guards are pretty standard military ballistic protection and will absorb multiple 9 mm rounds. The rest of the suit is mostly Ultrax armor, from Verseidag-Indutex, but the panels are configured around airtight cells. I inflate them with this." He had buckled the belt, then pulled snaps from behind the belt, snapping them into the leather. "The buckle is a battery and will activate the compressed gas cylinders. When the suit inflates, it's hard to walk around in but its level of ballistic protection is temporarily tripled or quadrupled."

"So what?" Mona demanded.

"The shirt is the same technology. I put it on, I snap it to the belt, now it is active. In case I am attacked, I'm protected neck to ankles."

Mona rolled her eyes and tried to elicit silent support for her disdain from the others, but they were staring at Shadi with surprise. When she looked at the man again she saw him inserting a needle into his forearm and clipping the IV tubing to a band on his arm. The tube went into a small, flat metal device the size of a matchbook sewn into the armband. When the connection was made the device activated, showing a tiny green light.

"Adrenaline pump," Shadi explained. "There is a lot more to it than that, but essentially it injects a mixture of adrenaline and amphetamines. I also have pain-killers. I've been tested on the mixtures and I know what to use when.''

"This guy is some sort of a Batman wannabe," Halim muttered. "I have news for you—we don't need a utility belt when we go out patrolling Gotham City. We also don't rely on drugs.''

"I don't rely on them, either.''

"Then what is all this, you freak?'' Halim demanded.

"It's designed to keep me alive and functional under the worst possible circumstances. Allow me to continue.''

Eissa cut further complaint from Halim with a nod, and Shadi continued. "This is the key to the uniform,'' he said as he donned what looked like a high school student's backpack with empty clips and harnesses. "The buckles are hollow plastic shells containing sealed, two-part, self-curing liquid plastic compounds in sealed glass tubes. When I put on the pack, I bend the plastic to break the tubes and the compound components mix. They flow and harden in ten minutes. The straps are stainless-steel filament-reinforced. Once the backpack goes on, it will not come off, ever, without a hacksaw.''

"The harness is designed to hold the Coldman device,'' Eissa said matter-of-factly.

"Of course.''

Halim, Mona and the others were looking at one another, seeking an explanation, and it was Mona who finally demanded one.

"Allow me,'' Eissa said. Shadi nodded. "This man was sent here to take over the transport of the Coldman device in the event our security is compromised. It's better that the device be activated anywhere in Egypt than not at all, am I right?''

Shadi nodded.

"Once it is attached to his body, he can activate it as needed. Once it's attached it can't be removed. In case of battle this man's orders are to save the device and himself for as long as possible. Deliver to the staging place if he can, if not, activate it. He is uniquely protected against being shot. He is trained and equipped to narcotize himself for continued performance even if severely wounded. Even if he is dying, he can dose himself with adrenaline, keep himself alive long enough to activate the Coldman device."

Shadi nodded again, frowning, dead serious.

"A real one-man death dealer," Halim muttered, but he was slightly awed by the suicidal intensity of the young man. "Why weren't we told this kind of excessive measure was being put in place?"

"I'm a new development. The current field director came up with the idea for the type of operative I am," Shadi said.

"That figures," Halim said disdainfully.

"We don't trust the field director," Mona said. "He's got questionable judgment. You're evidence of that."

"The plan is a good one," Shadi told her.

"No," Eissa said. "It's not good at all. It's impulsive. It's rash. And Coldman has always been a very patient organization. We give full measure to our undertakings. It's the sign of a poor leader when he makes a radical change to the plan without informing the operatives who will be burdened."

"I will not be a burden," Shadi protested.

"Does the board of directors even know about you?" Eissa demanded.

Shadi shook his head. "I have no idea."

Halim made a derisive snort. Mona shook her head with pursed lips.

"So what do we do about him?" Azza asked.

Eissa thought about that, then nodded, frowning deeply.

He was about to announce his decision when the walls began to scream.

CHAPTER FIFTEEN

The alarm screamed and David McCarter spotted the runner, tracked him and triggered the submachine gun, stitching him across the midsection with a quartet of 9 mm rounds and dropping him out of sight. The Briton stepped into a short hallway off the carport. The next gunner was approaching fast, his back flat to the wall. He didn't anticipate the attackers' coming inside, and when he met McCarter's gaze it was already too late.

The Briton triggered the Heckler & Koch MP-5 SD-3 submachine gun, the factory-installed sound suppressor making a sound like heavy fabric being ripped apart as the bullets exploded from the muzzle. The close grouping collapsed the guard's chest, and he toppled, his mouth open in shock.

James was a step behind McCarter and triggered his weapon across the shady entrance to an arched doorway. The rounds chipped off the brick, but one penetrated the decorative wood latticework window. There was a cry and thump, and McCarter shouldered the door. The man on the floor was trying to make a shattered elbow target a stubby box of a weapon, but McCarter triggered first, a head shot that flopped the man onto his back.

McCarter pulled into the entrance hall just as a spray

of automatic rifle fire filled the arch. He watched as the rounds thudded into the corpse and tore chunks off the bricks.

Behind him Manning gestured at a second doorway, and McCarter nodded. The big Canadian and James went through, low and high. Fifteen seconds ticked by peacefully.

"Phoenix Three here," Manning said in a low rumble. "We're at a door. We should be looking right up the barrel of your playmate when we open it."

"Then open it carefully."

McCarter heard the squeak of the door, somewhere to the right of the bloodied corpse, and then the twin coughing of suppressed submachine-gun fire. A moment later Manning appeared in the entrance and ushered the Briton in.

The Phoenix Force leader found himself in a sitting room designed like a courtyard, with low benches and a refreshment table, a small ceramic tile fountain and stairs to the upper level. Over the blare of the alarm he could hear the tinkle of water. McCarter held back the others with a raised fist, waiting....

The small metallic cylinder landed on the tiles between the legs of the dead man, and McCarter tossed himself into the others, jamming his fingers in his ears and squeezing his eyes shut. Even after he had put the brick wall between himself and the blast, the sound of the flash-bang grenade drilled into his skull, creating instant, throbbing pain.

But he propelled himself to his feet the instant it was over. He could hear Barbara Price on the headphones. He tucked the earpiece in place. "...if you can, Phoenix, report."

"Loud and clear," Manning whispered, and James

nodded, grinning. They still had their hearing and sight. Maybe the people upstairs could be persuaded they didn't.

McCarter groaned loudly in the direction of the stairwell. "Osman, help me!" It was poor Arabic, but he gave it the tongue-in-cheek treatment to distort it. The enforcement arm upstairs had no reason to suspect they hadn't incapacitated their intruders.

With a rush of feet three Egyptian gunners burst in and didn't have time to be surprised that their invaders weren't deaf and blind. The Phoenix Force trio unleashed brief, vicious fire that cut them down.

James grabbed one of the AK-47s and drilled bursts into the walls and floor. The trained Mossad agents upstairs could very well recognize the distinctive AK-47 fire and assume their men were alive and kicking.

"Up we go, mates," McCarter ordered.

RAFAEL ENCIZO HEARD the gunfire and sought it out in the wildly swinging images in his field glasses. On a roof across the street from the Eissa house, they wouldn't hear the suppressed Phoenix SMGs. There was nothing for him to see. What few windows weren't shuttered were three stories up.

"Rafe!" Hawkins said. He was just a few feet away but was monitoring street activity, leaning on the low brick wall above the crowded Old Cairo street.

Encizo looked down. Something was happening on the street. People were making way for small knots of men moving from building to building, zeroing in on the alley to the Eissa entrance. They were armed: AK-47s and shotguns.

"Hell of a neighborhood watch group," Hawkins

muttered. "They must have hired and equipped every badass in the hood."

"Too bad these people don't know they're protecting the enemy. You can bet the local crime boss would refuse if he knew the truth," Encizo said, then tapped on the radio. "Phoenix Two here. We have thirteen or more armed reinforcements coming to assist our friends with the suitcase. I'm going to try to keep them from going through the front door."

"Phoenix One here," McCarter replied briefly. "Keep me apprised."

Encizo and Hawkins had gone on recon heavily armed. It had been a pain trying to appear casual as they barged up the stairs of the dilapidated building with canvas-wrapped armloads of heavy metal, but Encizo was glad now. The sniper rifle would have been the first item left behind, and he was going to make it work for him.

The Remington Model 700 had a balanced design, accurate and durable enough for most field operations, which was why the U.S. Marines had adopted it as its official sniper weapon, designating it the M-40 A-1. If he'd been shooting long-distance, Encizo would have been wishing he had a more precise piece of technology. But firing across the street with the 700, equipped with the 10x Leupold scope, would be like shooting fish.

He waited until the knot of gunners entered the alley and headed for the gate. With a single stroke of his finger he unleashed a 7.62 mm round into the flank of the lead man. There was never a doubt in his mind that the shot was nearly perfect, and it achieved almost a magical effect. The man toppled, screaming and leaking blood. Encizo adjusted his view until the Leupold scope was filled with a stunned-looking face, and this time he went straight for the kill. He stroked the trigger less than two seconds after the first shot and sent a single 7.62 mm shocker through the bridge of the gunner's nose, barreling into his brains. When the back of his head exploded and he crashed into the dirt with an ugly grunt escaping his lungs, the screaming man was forgotten. The third round plowed into the group as they fled back to the street, but missed the target when the men bolted.

There were shouts of confusion, and the gunners retreated into buildings as Encizo took another man down with a round through the rib cage.

Out of targets for the moment, Encizo sat with his back to the wall on the red-hot surface of the roof and began calmly reloading the Remington's 5-round magazine, leaving Hawkins to keep an eye on the chaos.

"Found us yet?"

"Not yet," Hawkins said. "They're looking to the Eissa house as the source of the sniper fire. Bet they think it's been taken over. Maybe we should just drop leaflets explaining who the Eissas really are and what their intentions are toward Egypt."

"Sure, then they'd be on our side," Encizo said reasonably.

"More of them making a try at the gate."

Encizo was already raising into firing position and found a larger gang of gunners flattened against the wall around the Eissas' lower level. They thought they had four inches of solid brick between them and the gunner, so the sniper couldn't see them or shoot them.

It was a bad assumption. Not that they'd live to realize the error. Encizo used vicious trickery on the group, sending the first 7.62 mm round into a gunner in the middle of the line, who decorated the wall with the contents of his skull before dropping. That sent the entire group into a stampede, the ones in the front of the group bolting for the cover of the gate, only to find themselves grouped into an easy target for the unseen killer. One after another they were cut down by shots to the head and back, and then the survivors got smart and retreated into the street, leaving the dead and dying carpeting the alley and washing it with blood.

The last thing Encizo spotted as he pulled back was another tight knot of gunners in the street almost directly below, looking right up at him.

"We're spotted," Hawkins confirmed. He'd been waiting for the moment somebody found the source of the sniper fire. The gunners moved into the middle of the street, bringing up their assault rifles. Hawkins was better and faster than all of them, and reaped the gunners with stuttering bursts from the M-16 A-2. A few rounds were fired from the group while the survivors dispersed, but none came near Hawkins.

He pulled back and sat down hard next to Encizo. "They're on to us," he said, then came the rattle of autofire and the sound of rounds breaking brick chips and grit just a few inches from their backs. "Call me Master of the Obvious."

"Cover me, M.O.," Encizo said as he slapped the loaded magazine into the Remington, then he and Hawkins rose over the wall and the little Cuban targeted the fresh wave of gunners heading for the gate at a brisk trot.

Hawkins found two men with AK-47s tucked behind an abandoned vegetable stand. The Egyptian gunners triggered brief bursts before being driven behind their cover. Hawkins scanned the streets as he thumbed a

40 mm round into the breech of the M-203 mounted under the barrel of the M-16. There were no civilians in evidence. They had more sense than the local toughs. Hawkins targeted the vegetable stand and triggered the grenade launcher.

As the high-explosive round propelled itself along the barrel of the M-203 the barrel rifling started it spinning, which helped it stay on target. When the HE hit, it performed its function as advertised, the blast hurling the gunners away and dumping their remains in the street.

Encizo triggered one round after another in a steady rhythm with deadly consequences for the Egyptians. Their charge of the gate was broken, and another flight was in progress. Two more dropped before the magazine emptied. Hawkins caught sight of stealthy activity directly below, then it was gone.

When they were again sitting low and reloading, backs to the wall, Encizo said, "Did you happen to notice the welcome committee at the front door?"

"I saw them," Hawkins replied. "I'll guard your back."

"Good," Encizo said, but it wasn't good. He couldn't fire into the alley without exposing himself to half the street. There would be more guns aimed at his firing position.

As Hawkins headed for the black slab of plywood that served as a trapdoor entrance to the interior of the building, Encizo rose slowly from a crouch, then he jerked to his feet, fired a single round at the gate and dropped again. A pair of rifle bursts sailed overhead. He'd missed with the round, and worse, he had witnessed a pair of gunners, maybe more, finally getting through the gates.

He touched the radio.

"Phoenix Two here," he reported. "Sorry to say my net didn't hold. Company's already arrived. You ready for them?"

There was no answer.

CHAPTER SIXTEEN

Calvin James found some satisfaction in using the enemies' weapon of choice against them. His grenade packed a little more punch than the flash-bangs that had been whipped down at them. The safety pin was already pulled, the spoon clamped down by his thumb. In a corner of his mind a strange thought came and went: how many times in his life had he been standing there holding a live grenade? More than he could remember.

Then he heard the small army descending in a rush. It wasn't the stampede of amateurs, but the quick approach of trained operatives acting on a decision. This time the decision was bad. James emerged from the bottom of the steps with the deadly egg in one hand. He triggered the submachine gun into the steps at their feet, bringing the men in front to a panicked halt while the men in the rear struggled to get their weapons on him over their comrades' shoulders and heads. The Phoenix Force commando used the delay to calmly, precisely send the bomb flying up and arcing right. The Coldman enforcers were reacting as fast as humanly possible, but none of them succeeded in getting a weapon trained on James before he had ducked out of sight again.

James could picture the moment of chaos on the steps. The indecision. No way of escape and no time for it, anyway. From what he heard in the half second that followed—cries of animal rage, crashing of bodies and feet—some tried to scramble up past the grenade while others tried to stumble down the last flight of brick stairs. In the end it didn't matter for any of them.

When the fragmentation round went off, its jacket transformed into a swarm of flying metal pieces that ripped through human flesh mercilessly. The cries were gone in the instant of the burst, and the clomp of feet became the limp thumps of bodies. James reemerged, and across the landing Manning and McCarter came out of hiding. The big Canadian didn't flinch from the job at hand. Without hesitation he triggered his submachine gun at the thrashing figure that was coming to rest with his top half still on the bottom step. The man was the enemy, and the bullet was a mercy round.

James's mode was battlefield neutral. There wasn't leeway for human response to the sight of the bloody human remains, but he didn't fail to notice that the dead were all men. He reached the top of the stairs in time to see a woman running out the rear door of a large, low-ceilinged sitting parlor. She glared at him over her shoulder just before she was gone.

Angry. Not afraid. What had she been looking at? James saw heavy drapes that covered an exit on the next wall, the drapes moving as if from a recent gust of wind. There was no wind.

"Down," he said, and he and Manning dropped as the angry woman came into the door firing an automatic weapon—a short, controlled burst that split the wood where James had been standing the moment before.

McCarter came up behind them on all fours and rose just far enough to sight the woman over the roomful of expensive furniture. He came down at once, avoiding another burst.

"She's covering somebody who just left through the door with the curtains," James said.

"That would be Nibal Eissa making off with the Coldman device," Manning said grimly.

McCarter gave a meaningful glance in the direction of the woman. He had given the order to neutralize the threat without uttering a word.

Manning was on his feet, triggering the Heckler & Koch MP-5 SD-3 at the distant door before the female agent could respond, and she went down silently. She was as much a potential mass murderer as the men they had killed. She deserved no better, and Manning was too professional to feel sorry for her simply because she was female. There was a rustle of movement, and someone dived inside, low and quick, retrieving the weapon from the hands of the dead woman and withdrawing like a frightened eel into its sea burrow. She was back in a flash, and the AK-47 spit at Manning.

The rounds were wild and didn't come close, and Manning held his ground, sending back a brief warning burst through the open door. He heard rapid talking in a language he couldn't identify.

"Cover me," James said.

Before he could move, three women came through the entrance in leaps. Manning anticipated the third one in line and targeted her while she was airborne. The rounds chewed into her skull and shoulders, and she was dead before she hit the ground.

A cry of rage rose from behind a heavy carved cabinet the size of a refrigerator, and the first two female agents emerged from either side with their rifles blazing. Manning dropped to a crouch.

"We've got to go after Nibal Eissa," James said.

"I don't trust the decor to absorb a frag," Manning stated as he pulled an impact CS grenade from his combat webbing. He lobbed it overhead without sighting his targets, an impossibility with the constant weapons fire going on. The device hit the floor with a metallic clunk and burst open, filling the far end of the room with smoke clouds. The women started to hack and cough.

"Go," McCarter ordered.

James and Manning went for the draped exit with the Briton covering their rear, and when the first woman stumbled from the smoke he put a round in her neck, sending her crashing into a table that collapsed in a shower of gray glass and splintered reeds. Then her companion appeared in the smoke, firing by sound at McCarter. It took guts to target his gunfire without even trying to open her eyes. McCarter got her before she homed in on him, punching her in the chest with a triburst of 9 mm rounds. She doubled over and fell on her face as her spasming lungs were squeezed flat with a grunt.

McCarter recognized that profile. It was the young woman from the garden. What a waste of a life.

As he followed Manning out the draped door, holding his breath to avoid the tear gas fumes drifting his way, McCarter heard the sobbing of the wounded woman and an overlapping gasp, and his suspicion was confirmed. She was alive. She'd been wearing armor. He'd seen only a small gout of blood in the wound in the second before she went down.

"Phoenix One here. Talk to me," McCarter said.

There had been a call from T. J. Hawkins a moment before. He had chosen to ignore it until he had time to talk. Hawkins reported their situation briefly.

"Reinforcements coming through the front door," McCarter relayed to Manning and James, although they'd probably heard it in their headsets.

"Yeah, great," Manning grumbled.

The walkway took them to a rooftop garden over one end of the house. It was screened from Old Cairo by third-story walls on one side and by potted palm trees and vine-draped lattices on the others. The garden hugged a small inner square of the roof, a cool oasis just inches from the blazing heat of direct sun. Trickling fountains tucked among the plants and furnishings couldn't drown out the stomp of feet and agitated shouts below. There was no sign of Nibal Eissa. James spotted a reed trapdoor in the floor, beyond the cool shade of the garden.

"Sounds like a bleeding soccer mob down there," McCarter said. "We'll need to do some dirty work if we're going to get that device. Incapacitate the doers and scare off the hired help."

McCarter tossed a pair of grenades over the roof ledge at the same moment Manning opened the trapdoor with a yank and James sent his phosphorous device into the opening. As the grenade went in, a volley of heavy-caliber machine-gun fire came out. Whoever had been waiting for them just below quickly changed tactics when the grenade sailed by.

The Phoenix Force warriors heard pounding footsteps and knew the machine gunner was coming up the ladder. Manning fired a burst from the MP-5 SD-3 that he expected would send the guy plummeting into the opening again. But the man, wearing a motorcycle helmet or some such, flopped forward and rolled as the blast of the grenades came up from below, deceptively feeble.

He managed to roll just fast enough to stay ahead of the stream of rounds Manning sent chasing after him, then twisted and leaped to his feet. It was an acrobatic move, so quick and light it looked bizarre when performed by the man in heavy loose clothing and full-face shield. By the time he was on his feet again, Manning had his measure. This time he triggered the submachine gun directly into the face shield and watched the burst snap his head back like he was knocked with a crowbar. Helmet staggered a step before he gained control of the fall and twisted into it, hitting the rooftop and bounding back to his feet as if he had springs on his hands.

Helmet had his weapon in play, but no target. His assailants seemed to have disappeared, and he spun his body trying to find them. Then there was another impact, out of nowhere, sending him down yet again.

James's on-the-fly assessment of Helmet told him he was dealing with an extremely dangerous man, especially in hand-to-hand combat, and even more so because of his head-to-toe body armor. James followed his strike at the man's padded neck with a quick shot at the shins, preventing him from landing on his full body and rolling away. There was a blink of time when the man was incapacitated, and James made his best use of it, bringing his foot down hard on his adversary's hand and feeling the bones crack.

The IMI Micro-Galil jumped out of the broken hand, and James's opponent twisted off his back to reach the assault rifle with his free hand. By then James had his fingers under the guy's helmet at the back of his neck, and he yanked hard, pulling a couple of feet of flat electronics cables out from under the man's clothing and armor.

James's opponent looked surprised, as if he found this turn of events interesting, but he bounded to his feet without hesitation and dragged against the cables. James was ready for it, twisting and drawing down, and his opponent's inertia carried his lower half forward as the rest of his body tried to keep moving. James felt the roof shake when the guy crashed on his face. With a heave the Phoenix Force commando pulled his captive to the nearest trellis support, and before he had a chance to struggle free the electronics cable was wrapped around the support and the prisoner's neck. Tightly.

James had almost forgotten his companions, who'd been covering him but unable to fire their weapons during the hand-to-hand battle without risking their teammate. McCarter covered the guy while Manning knelt over the dangling helmet. "What is *this?* He's wired like the Six Million Dollar Man."

"No time for that," McCarter said, his eyes alert on the walkway from which they had just come. "Let's get that device."

James glanced at the walkway, wondering what the Phoenix Force leader was wary of, then McCarter reacted, firing at the corner and chipping away brick.

"Azza Eissa," McCarter said. "Or whatever her real name is."

"The hot one?" Manning asked.

"Yeah. I was pretty sure I only winged her, and then I heard her put a bullet in the head of her wounded sister just a second ago. After you."

James went down the ladder first, followed by Manning, and McCarter last after emptying a magazine at the fleeting shadow that he glimpsed now and again at the corner.

It wasn't far down, and they stepped into the hell they had created.

CHAPTER SEVENTEEN

Most of the men at ground level died without knowing what it was that killed them.

A few moments earlier they were rallying in support of their employer. They had been promised a good fee for serving as bodyguards-on-call. Once, two months back, the alarm had been given, and the hirelings from this corner of Old Cairo had rushed in, armed with the weapons their employer had provided them and only half-believing they would actually get the princely sum the employer promised. When they arrived and found that the alarm wasn't real, that it had been a drill, there was universal outrage—until the cash came out.

Nibal Eissa paid them, in full, for responding to the alarm.

"Now you know my word is good—and my money," he told the men, wearing a big smile. "And now I know I can count on you when I need protection."

Protection from who? The rumor that came from one of the house staff was that Eissa had somehow earned the wrath of an Israeli businessman and crime lord. The Israeli had tried to do business with Eissa through an Australian company he owned. Eissa found out about it, found he was being cheated by the Israeli and exposed the man's corruption. It was an affront to all Jews, of course, to call any Jew a cheat, and this one had crime connections around the world, and the Israelis just might try to get an assassin, or an army of assassins, into the Egyptian home of Nibal Eissa.

The men chose to believe the story was true. After all, Eissa had local government friends. It stood to reason that whatever he needed protection for, it wasn't possible that he was the corrupt one.

The payment from the drill was gone fast, and the hired guns began hoping for another attack on Nibal Eissa. Or at least another drill.

When the alarm sounded, Eissa's gunners came running again. When the bloodshed started on the street, the prospect of easy money vanished, and some of them stayed to fight back. After all, there were just two men in the sniper's nest, and the gunshots from inside didn't sound like an army.

Those who made it inside Eissa's grounds had just begun to organize themselves when they heard the shout of "Grenade!" Then there was hell on earth.

The grenades burst like fireworks, each fiery point containing a white-burning metallic speck that touched and burned. The three phosphorous devices blanketed the men, and they dropped to the bricks clawing and tearing at their own flesh. Whatever the phosphorus touched it ate through. Flesh was nothing to it. Bone didn't stop it, nor did water or steel. Nothing would stop it from burning until the phosphorus itself was consumed.

Those with multiple hits were the lucky ones, dying quickly. Those with fewer hits suffered for what seemed like a long time.

Calvin James knew a moment of regret. He knew it

was some sort of a despicable irony that these Egyptians died protecting an enemy who wanted to destroy them as a nation and a people and had died at the hands of those who would stop the genocide if they could. There was no way to reason through it.

There was one unarmed man still standing at the gate, in shock, unable to make his legs work to flee the horror. James watched him carefully as Manning and McCarter stepped off the ladder.

Then there was a rumble of a car engine, and James started to run. Eissa's car was behind a brick wall and far enough away that the blast could have missed it, and missed Eissa, too. James slapped a full magazine into the submachine gun and found himself staring at the driver of the big Mercedes—Nibal Eissa.

Eissa hit the gas as James triggered a burst, going for the front tires and watching them deflate slightly. They were run-flats. He went for the windshield and watched the rounds bounce off. James heard the crunch of bodies under the wheels of the Mercedes as he emptied the magazine into the front end of the car, hoping without hope that somehow a round would sneak through the shielding and damage anything vital.

James's magazine emptied while Manning and McCarter were lobbing more grenades at the back end of the car. Maybe Eissa saw the commandos in his mirrors and knew what it meant, because he stomped on the accelerator and shot through the gate, crunching a side into the brick and slamming into the shocked survivor. The body somersaulted over the luggage still strapped on top and flopped off the trunk, and then the grenades came, so close the dead man could have reached out and caught them like fly balls.

The body was obliterated, and the rear of the Mercedes shredded and bounced, then it was gone. They heard the squeal of tires when it reached the street. Nibal Eissa had escaped.

James was cold, empty, vaguely horrified. He felt like that shocked survivor had to have felt in the minute before he was run down. The Coldman device had slipped through their fingers. Eissa would be especially cautious from this point on.

Could they possibly track him down a second time?

James didn't think so.

And if they didn't, the device would be used. And Egypt would be—what?

What exactly would the device do? Then he focused on the scattered corpses, frozen in their agony, their bodies still smoking from black craters. This was what Coldman would do.

"Look around you," James murmured.

McCarter and Manning, each wearing his own brand of hollow disbelief, didn't even bother to ask him what the hell he was talking about.

HAWKINS PLACED the flash-bang grenade on top of the woven reed trapdoor, releasing it carefully so its own weight would keep its handle depressed, then he retreated quickly.

"That'll buy us an extra minute or two," he said with a grin.

"Won't help us with the guys in the street," Encizo said. A handful of gunners was milling below, shouting threats and obscenities.

"Our timing's got to be good," Encizo said.

"No time to practice," Hawkins remarked. There were voices below the trapdoor. "Let's just do it."

They did it, running side by side at the edge of the

building and launching themselves from the short wall. They were in the air and coming down again in a heartbeat, feet skidding on the loose dirt and brick fragments on the roof of the next building, and they heard the shouts below.

They never slowed, but ran for the ledge to the next rooftop. Hawkins realized the gap between the buildings was half again as far as the first easy hop, and the last time he felt his robe slowing him down. He put on an extra burst of speed, found Encizo matching him stride for stride and they launched themselves together into space.

Hawkins felt like he was airborne for an hour, and the building came up to meet him like a behemoth rising out of the ground in a monster movie. He revolved to dissipate the impact and suddenly stopped, safe, in a crouch, his shoulder throbbing a little where he had rolled on his weapon.

"This robe nearly killed me."

"It'll make you invisible when we get back to the ground," Encizo replied.

The metallic clank of the rolling flash-bang grenade came from two buildings away where the trapdoor opened. The grenade was one of Cowboy Kissinger's custom jobs, with adjustable fusing.

Encizo saw Hawkins looking between the rooftop and his watch as they made their way to the access opening in the roof.

"How long?"

"Fifteen seconds," Hawkins said.

"That's a pretty long time."

"Yeah."

Hawkins and Encizo entered the stairs and watched

unseen as others clambered out, arguing with one another.

"Now," Hawkins said.

They both ducked inside. The detonation was less than a firecracker and a camera flash from where they were, but when they looked out again they saw the four men sprawled on the rooftop, grabbing their blasted ears and squeezing their eyes shut.

A minute later Hawkins and Encizo were on the streets of Old Cairo, strolling along as if they belonged there.

CHAPTER EIGHTEEN

Bandar-e Anzali, Iran

The bakery closed early, and the delivery truck rolled out of Bandar-e Anzali with Amir Kadivar at the wheel and a box of festive halvah loaves close at hand. The cover story, in case he was stopped, was that he had a crate full of them for a big wedding celebration that was to take place in Masuleh.

Masuleh was as close to a tourist destination as could be found in the northwestern corner of Iran. The picturesque, traditional village in the Gilan province clung to a mountainside so steep that the walkway for one level was often the roof of the homes on the level below. Tourists in Iran came to Masuleh for the novelty and for the breathtaking vistas, but mostly in summer for the cool weather. Iran wasn't as universally arid and hot as the Western world assumed, but there was plenty of desertlike heat during summer. At thirty-four-hundred feet above sea level, Masuleh summers were mild.

At noon the truck was firmly wedged in the lunch-time pedestrian traffic of Rasht, and by midafternoon the temperature inside the windowless back end of the vehicle had dropped from scorching to merely sweltering. That was when Kadivar's assistant passed out for the second time.

Weakened by the blow to the skull, infuriated at being bound and almost unbearably uncomfortable during the worst afternoon heat, he'd begun to shout. When he was gagged he began to thrash. He had been retied, so tightly he could have been rolled like a rug, and all he could do was bend a few inches in either direction. He went through some sort of paroxysm that ended when his eyes rolled back into his head and he passed out, then came to and consumed a quart of water that Kadivar gave him a sip at a time through the straw so that his gag wouldn't have to be removed. It revived him enough to send him into another squirming, red-faced fit.

Rosner, cuffed alongside him, peered into his face.

"He's unconscious again."

"Wash, rinse, repeat," Blancanales said. It got a grin from Hermann Schwarz.

"You people are heartless," the sub crewman said bitterly.

"*We're* heartless, Mr. Mass Murdering Maniac?" Schwarz asked.

"I think this is making him crazy," Rosner said. "He's hungry and sick, and you've got to give him some freedom."

"No."

Rosner's head twisted hard. Carl Lyons was standing at the curtain divider to the truck cab, and the submariner went from angry to meek in an eyeblink. Lyons scared him like no man he'd ever met. Rosner was regretting not staying in the sub and letting himself get depth-charged by the Iranian shore patrol. It would have been preferable to being under *his* control.

"He's too dangerous," Lyons added. "We know this for a fact."

"Our friends at home come through with some IDs?" Blancanales asked.

"We know what he's been doing under his last few names, anyway," Lyons said. "What his training and experience were before 1997 is still unknown, but he was trained well enough to commit three or four assassinations for Mossad."

"Where?" Schwarz asked.

"International, all of them."

"What does it matter where the hits were?" Rosner asked, his ire rising again.

Schwarz shrugged. "Any Israeli with a sniper rifle and a support team can off a Palestinian in the occupied territories and call it a kill. It doesn't mean he's a skilled assassin. International executions are a different matter. Gives us a whole different perspective on the guy."

Rosner didn't seem to move but he somehow scooted himself a little away from the trussed-up killer, hugging his splinted arms tightly to his chest as if chilled. Every word he heard seemed to send him further into his shell. An inexplicable burst of courage made him blurt suddenly, "What will you do with us when this is done?"

"That remains to be seen," Lyons said.

Which didn't comfort Rosner at all.

LYONS DIDN'T HAVE a clue what he was going to do with their prisoners when the time came. He couldn't consider freeing them until Coldman was neutralized, and he couldn't kill them until he was sure they had given up all their secrets. The sub crewman, Rosner, was a basket case and had no more intelligence to bargain with. The older guy, Amir Kadivar, was trying to convince Lyons he knew nothing about Coldman's potential for mass murder. He thought it was some sort of a biological weapon designed to spread a nonfatal disease throughout Iran, weakening her if and when Israel was on the brink of being lost to a coalition of Arab armies. Rasool Far was a question mark. Kadivar claimed Far knew nothing more. Lyons didn't trust any of them, but he was most leery of Far.

"You going to give us a heads-up on the Coldman team?" he asked Kadivar as the mountain light softened into dusk and the hot, straining truck engine heaved a sigh of relief to reach level ground again. They were on one of the lower-level streets of Masuleh, which sloped above them for hundreds of feet, some houses almost built on the roof of the house below. In reality the structures were imbedded in the mountainside, and some people used the roof of the next lower home as their front yard and sidewalk. Parts of the town were accessible only on foot. Many of the homes were brick multitenant buildings.

"You would have to torture anything more out of me," Kadivar said.

"No time for that," Lyons said. What little conversation there had been between the two of them during the long hours on the road had become almost mutually respectful. Lyons found himself wanting to believe the man when he claimed he would never be party to genocide, even if it meant killing the hated Arab to save the beloved homeland of Israel.

"Okay, Barb, let's have whatever you've got."

Kadivar strained to hear the voice from Lyons's earpiece but didn't catch a word. Lyons jotted down a few non-English words and memorized the rest.

Minutes later Kadivar found himself trussed up in the rear of the truck with his fellow Israelis.

"'THERE'S NO Hilton?'' Blancanales asked.

"Tourists stay mostly in guest houses," Lyons said. "What we're looking for is part of a row of six small villas operated as guest rooms.''

"Sounds like those Route 66 motels from the fifties where each room is its own cabin," Blancanales observed.

"Yeah, but these are maintained to look like one-room versions of other houses in the town. Supposed to provide an authentic Masuleh experience.''

They were hiking along a path that skirted a far end of the town, trying to stay inconspicuous. The sun was still up, but the town was in the mountain shadow preceding true dusk. Lyons wanted to fix the Coldman team before dark. The guest house they were heading for was a likely target since it could be easily defended, which trained Mossad agents would appreciate, but it was just a guess. There were other places to stay that would fit their tourist cover.

Would the moles be comfortable enough in their roles to chance the close contact of a guest house, putting them in a multifamily building? Well, maybe.

"There.''

The sign was small and hand-painted, but the houses had a fresh look that came from regular maintenance. The grounds were landscaped, and the porch under the overhanging roof had the gloss of new paint. There were people milling about outside, lounging in wooden chairs and watching the spectacular mountain view grow soft. They had the look of tourists, new clothes and a subtle interest in their surroundings that a local wouldn't have. The cabin at the end, the most remote, was dark and quiet.

"Looks right," Schwarz observed. "No more town in that direction. Approachable from this end only. It's damn remote, though. A long way from transportation when you need a quick escape."

"We go in quiet," Lyons said. "No weapons until we know this is the Coldman team. We might find nothing. This might be the first of several dead ends. We could end up searching every guest house in town."

Schwarz turned his gaze down the mountainside and found that, from up here, the village looked a lot bigger than it did from the bottom.

BLANCANALES ALWAYS found it an interesting challenge to blend with the locals, but tourist towns were a piece of cake. Iran or Idaho, the locals were used to mildly strange folk strolling their streets, and a lot of behavioral mistakes had to be made before they got suspicions. The people of Masuleh had visitors from every diverse corner of Iran, and the city folk from Tehran were odd enough, so Blancanales had no problem looking like just another vacation visitor. Of course he didn't let them see that he was loaded down with enough weaponry to annihilate half the town's population.

When darkness came he was in position.

HERMANN SCHWARZ avoided the locals at every step. There was no way he was going to pass himself off as Iranian. He didn't speak Farsi or any other language that might be common in the area. His hair was brown and getting lighter every day he spent in the harsh sun, and that pretty much ruined any hopes he ever had of passing himself off as a native.

There wasn't much trouble avoiding contact with the residents of Masuleh because they largely took to their houses as darkness closed in. Schwarz decided it was pretty smart to confine your rooftop walking to daylight hours.

He found the big, narrow, apartment-like building he was looking for and waited for a burst of conversation from inside before venturing onto the plank roofing that served as part of the walkway. It was normal enough to have traffic overhead, he knew, but he didn't want anyone to notice that he stopped halfway and stayed there.

A storage crate stood in front of him, as big as a chest freezer and about as solid, with enough room between it and the roof edge for Schwarz to post his watch. There were lights along the walkway on the guest house level but not here. He wouldn't be spotted unless a passerby carried a flashlight.

The strain of a small engine signaled the arrival of dinner for the cabin guests. The old motorcycle had a small engine that putted slow and hard as it was steered sluggishly through the hairpin curve to the top tier, towing a rusty barrel bolted to eight-inch rubber tires. Schwarz was amused to see it was engineered with a pretty elaborate system of springs on a jointed framework for four-way suspension. The result was that the barrel could be towed over the rocky humps and boulders that made the paths irregular and still not spill its contents.

Lamb for dinner, Schwarz noted from the aroma as

he watched the first cabins receive their covered bowls and platters. Schwarz's stomach growled. He'd eaten dry rations and halvah for breakfast and lunch and could use a real meal. But he was accustomed to being food-deprived in the field.

The dark cabin lit up, and Schwarz saw people arriving just in time for their dinner. He counted four men entering the cabin with their trays. The light was in the middle of the room, and eventually they all walked far enough back to take their faces out of shadow. The sub crewman, Rosner, had said four were in the Coldman group. It was hard to believe the guy was lying, he was so freaked out.

Lyons and Blancanales got on the radio long enough to check in. Everybody was in position. Schwarz reported his head count.

Schwarz waited, his knees beginning to throb from the plank roof, his back strained from holding the crouch. The family beneath his feet went silent, and a hush fell on the town. A few televisions were muted by the night. The four guys in the guest cabin were among the last to go to bed. Finally the lights were turned off.

Schwarz flipped the field glasses to infrared and found himself seeing a big white sphere. What the hell was that? He switched to low-light and realized he was looking at some sort of a chimney for a gas heater on the front end of the house. Maybe the ground was too rocky to vent it out the back. Enough starlight was coming through to make low-light glasses workable, he decided, and used them to monitor the cabin for half an hour. Nobody came or went. Lyons radioed.

"Pol and I are going in."

"I'll keep an eye on things." Schwarz had been relegated to cleanup duty. With little room to maneuver, Lyons had decided it would be best for just two to enter the cabin while Schwarz watched for reinforcements and nabbed any runaways. He had the H&K submachine gun. It was suppressed, making it the best choice for use in the middle of the close quarters of the sleeping town, but it still raised a hell of a racket. The Beretta 93-R was also suppressed, wearing Cowboy Kissinger's custom silencer. The pistol was quieter than the MP-5 SD-3 and just as deadly.

He watched with his glasses on low-light as the distinct shapes of Lyons and Blancanales made their approach on the guest cabin from either direction.

"Check," Lyons said quietly. What he was checking was the radio's operation. He knew Schwarz would alert him the second he noticed anything.

"Clear," Schwarz responded.

His neck was stiff from holding himself rigid on the field glasses, but he couldn't rest. Blancanales had come over the rocky mound that marked the dead end of the avenue. Lyons was just paces away. The windows of the cabin were motionless. He flipped over to infrared to see if it would show him anything different.

It did.

"Don't take another step!" he radioed hastily.

But the steps were already taken.

Schwarz shouldn't have been amazed at what he was seeing. The infrared beams rose from two tiers below in an ever widening spread to catch the reflectors mounted above the windows on the front of the guest cabin. Infrared Perimeter Intrusion Detection couldn't be seen by the naked eye, so the beams could be larger than laser detectors, but the principle was the same. The beam went out and was reflected back to a sensor.

When it was interrupted, the alarm went off. IPID-type systems were easier to deploy quickly, especially with mirror components that received self-alignment instructions via RF from the sensor computer.

There was a blare of noise, and the lights popped on. Lyons bolted to the cabin door and kicked it with the bottom of his foot so powerfully the dead bolt was left stuck in the door frame. Lyons went in, followed by Blancanales.

Schwarz heard shouting, then bursts of gunfire.

ONE OF THEM kept a handgun under his pillow, but he was too sleep-slowed to react well. He aimed for the door when it opened with a crash and anticipated the intruder, but the shot was wide.

Lyons targeted the shooter, who was sitting up on a narrow cot under a dingy blanket. The MP-5 SD-3 fired a suppressed burst that punched into the shooter's chest, pushing him back on the cot as if he were going back to sleep.

The man closest to the door had rolled off his cot and crouched behind a cast-iron gas-heat stove that half-covered him. He had his hunting rifle up and tracking, turning the weapon on Blancanales, as the two Able Team commandos fired simultaneous bursts.

That left two men cowering in their cots, pleading for their lives in rapid-fire language that was incomprehensible to Lyons and Blancanales. The commandos exchanged a glance. Something wasn't right here.

"Speak English?" Blancanales asked.

The words silenced the survivors. "No little English," one of the men stuttered out with great effort. *"Talysh."*

"What did he say?" Lyons demanded.

"They're ethnic Talyshi," Blancanales said. "Why are you here?"

The two of them rattled back and forth between themselves, trying to make sense of the question while avoiding the gruesome remains of their former friends. "Bodyguards," one man said.

Lyons was looking for the suitcases that contained the Coldman devices, but he knew he wouldn't find them. The only luggage was a small nylon Nike gym bag from the distant past. He yanked it open and dumped out a pillow of powder in heavy plastic. "Who are you supposed to be guarding?"

"Guard those!"

Lyons hadn't expected an answer, and he followed the man's finger, darting onto the porch. Lyons disabled the blaring alarm box with a sweep of his hand, taking the plastic device off the wall.

"Able Three, what happened, briefest!"

"Able Three here—it was infrared perimeter. The stove kept me from watching the cabin on IR."

Lyons saw the reflectors on the wall the moment he knew what to look for, then dragged on his goggles while striding away from the lights of the cabin. The beams were still there, solid bars of light coming right at him and blinding him to whatever was going on in the room. It was a large house in front of him, two tiers down. Second floor, fourth window from left. When the goggles came off the IR beams vanished like something turned invisible.

"Gadgets—"

"Already on my way."

"They wholesale heroin to other ethnic Talyshi in Azerbaijan," Blancanales explained when Lyons reappeared. "The Israelis hired them as decoys."

"It worked," Lyons retorted. "Forget them. Let's go." He was trying to guess elapsed time—three minutes since the alarm sounded?

More than enough time for an escape.

CHAPTER NINETEEN

Schwarz stepped off the edge of the building, plummeted nine feet before his feet landed on the wooden balcony and rolled out the impact. The balcony lurched and came loose, pulling on whatever bolts or stays were supposed to be holding it to the wall, but Schwarz didn't wait for it to collapse before descending the stairs in three flying steps. At the next descent he found a stone staircase to the lower tier. He leaped down the stairs, feeling the night moisture on the rocks through the soles of his shoes.

Then he was on level ground and across a narrow ledge of earth that was level with one corner of the stone building on the lower tier that was the source of the infrared beams. The ground canted away, allowing half the back end to be exposed on the mountain side.

Schwarz jogged onto the roof to a place above the window he wanted, the collapsible grappling hook already in his hands, pulled from a pack on his belt. At the touch of a release button the flukes snapped into position and locked in place, and Schwarz jammed them into the soft wood beams framing a brick ventilation funnel.

He paid out the line as he stepped over the edge and descended to the window in a single leap. Landing against the stone, he heard a snap from inside the room. A drawn breath. Somebody was there, moving fast. Schwarz hated to believe in dumb luck but...was it possible the Coldman agents were still here?

Only one way to find out. He kicked away from the wall and swung through the open window, dropping the line and pulling at the Beretta 93-R as he crashed to the floor.

The man was crouched on the floor trying to close a suitcase, and Schwarz knew he'd hit pay dirt. He reacted to the Able Team commando with the cool, efficient motions of the professional, but Schwarz had more notches in his belt and better reaction time. He triggered a 3-round burst. The 9 mm Parabellum slugs took the Israeli in the groin, stomach and sternum, dropping him. Instantly there was another burst of fire from outside the cramped bedroom. Schwarz launched himself to his feet as the business end of an AK-47 poked around the corner, moving too cautiously. He stepped into the line of fire just enough to target the hands. He was firing on the fly and couldn't control the powerful rise of the 93-R when the next triburst erupted from the gun, but the first 9 mm round was on target and took a third of the hand bones apart so violently they could never have healed. The gunner recoiled, backed against the wall and spent the final moment of his life staring at the ruin at the end of his forearm. Schwarz nailed him to the mortared stone.

There was movement down the hall, and Schwarz saw the brief image of man with a rifle-mounted grenade launcher. He dived into the room he'd come from and landed on the Coldman suitcase. He squeezed his eyes shut and was collapsing into a ball when the round slammed against the stone in the hall and blew apart.

A hail of steel knives chipped the stone. Schwarz found a narrow section of wall chewed up like tattered paper. The fragmentation grenade had exploded too soon for the deadly shrapnel to reach him. He hefted the Coldman suitcase to the window and grabbed a grenade of his own. He couldn't risk anything deadly in a house full of civilians and opted for a timed CS round that hit the floor with a hollow metallic thud.

The short countdown gave Schwarz no room for error. He groped outside the window for the grappling line and looped the heavy-duty spring lock at the end through the plastic handle of the suitcase, which was too big for the spring lock. He let the Coldman fall out the window, then came the pop of the smoke grenade from the hall. Clouds of tear gas filled the room around Schwarz, who squeezed his eyes shut as he yanked himself out the window. He used his feet to close the wooden shutters, locking in the tear gas.

Schwarz pulled himself up hand over hand, then felt the rope get jerked through his hands. Somebody was hauling it in, and his hands were dragged over the rock ledge, scraping off skin and crushing his flesh. He endured it, propped his torso on the roof edge and grabbed for the 93-R handgun with his free hand. The dim starlight showed him a gleam that had to be the barrel of a weapon, and he fired at it. He didn't have time to adjust the weapon to single-round fire, and the recoil almost carried the weapon away from him. In the darkness he could make out a body collapsing, then a beam of light cut across the rooftop and nailed Schwarz like a cornered convict.

Before he could target the light an AK-47 chattered from behind the flashlight. The Able Team commando retreated fast, making a wild grab for the rope and letting the gun fall. The friction burned his hands, but he squeezed, coming to a halt.

The pain was intense, but he ground his teeth and forced himself to keep moving. He saw the dark shape of a human head poke over the roof edge. They saw him. Schwarz twisted his hand in the rope so he could hold on one-handed, then snatched the Mk 23 out of its holster. When the head showed itself again he would drill it. There was a surprised shout, and it pulled back too fast. The .45 caliber rounds bounced off the wall and sent rock shards flying, but Schwarz knew he'd missed.

He felt the rope lurch in his hands. These guys just didn't give up. He had to free the Coldman from the line, buy himself a few more seconds. He aimed at the rope underneath him and fired once, but another lurch wobbled him, skewing the shot, and he found himself pulled another four feet closer to the roof. Schwarz knew what was coming and couldn't do anything to stop it.

The hard rope turned to soggy string.

They'd dropped the slack.

This was gonna hurt.

"OH, SHIT," Blancanales breathed as he rushed to a halt on the rise where he could see the rooftop and hoped to provide Schwarz some cover. It was too late. He witnessed Schwarz getting flipped off the rope like a fisherman dislodging a hooked trash fish with only a flick of the wrist. It was unreal, seeing it happen in the near darkness, no longer punctuated by the flashes of gunfire.

Then Schwarz righted himself in midair, like the cat falling in slow motion in old slow-motion science films, and tried to get his arms around the dangling suitcase. The impact when the commando and the Coldman device met was terrific. It was an impossible catch, but for a heartbeat Blancanales thought that Schwarz had locked on.

Then Schwarz tumbled off and crumpled on the hard earth like a marionette with its strings sliced.

CARL LYONS FOLLOWED Schwarz's route to the rooftop when he saw his teammate. Falling. Gadgets came down like a ton of bricks, then clawed at the dangling suitcase like he was going to take it with him or rip it shreds so nobody else could have it, either.

Then Schwarz lost his grip on the suitcase and hit the ground hard.

Lyons jogged onto the roof and headed for the close knot of silhouettes hauling at the rope. They heard him and turned on him.

Well-grouped, Lyons thought with savage satisfaction. Easy pickings, Gadgets.

The MP-5 began its throaty coughing, and the deadly 9 mm Parabellum rounds carved an eternity symbol, a sideways figure eight that took all three killers to the rooftop in a messy pile.

A head and shoulders popped out of the roof, and Lyons dived and rolled as the shotgun blast chased after him. He expected to feel his backside burn with buckshot, but the pain didn't come and he landed flat. With a twist he found his target, sending five 9 mm rounds skimming the rooftop and plunging into the shotgunner.

He heard an exclamation and recognized the language of the ethnic Talyshi, easy enough to distinguish from Farsi. The drug distributors had to have hired out half their organization as mercenaries to the Israelis.

There was a brief conversation, then three gunners popped out of the roof and fired into the darkness, triangulating for full coverage, only to find themselves eating 9 mm shockers. One dodged back into the skylight, only to have both his companions collapse lifeless beside him.

Lyons was exposed and helpless. He had to get to cover, but first he had to finish Schwarz's work—cut the line on the dangling suitcase. He snatched out his combat knife but found himself dodging a sudden burst of AK-47 fire.

The blind burst was followed by another and another, homing in on Lyons. He scrambled to the far corner of the roof and onto the upper-tier avenue, where the AK-47 gunner lost him in the blackness, then disappeared before Lyons could get off a shot. He reappeared just long enough to target the grappling hook, which slipped away.

They were retrieving the suitcase. Lyons moved along the street and peered into the darkness below him, between the building and the mountain face. The suitcase was laying there with no visible damage, but Schwarz was gone.

He had no easy way down. If he climbed alongside the stone wall he'd be a target too easy to miss, and already a recovery crew was approaching. Lyons took a solid stance and laid his right wrist on his left forearm, aiming his Mk 23 at the trio that hurried into view. His intention was to pick off the easiest targets, then he heard one of the men issue an order in Farsi. Lyons found him. As all the villagers had retreated to their homes for the night, it had to be one of the Coldman agents.

Lyons's mouth grew taut as he acquired his target and squeezed the trigger. The .45-caliber round slammed into the Israeli at the collarbone level and cut into his torso at a steep angle, prompting the Talyshi mercenaries to drop the suitcase and fire blindly at the street above. Lyons moved a few paces and took down one of the Talyshi guards, leaving a sole survivor.

But the reinforcements were arriving, and when the Able Team leader made his next attempt, he was spotted before he could fire the gun. The kill order and the onslaught of rounds came seconds later.

Lyons's quick glimpses revealed the enemy carefully sliding the suitcase in the car and hoisting the bodies in after it. The Israeli was still alive, writhing as he was carried away by wrists and ankles. Lyons tried for the Israeli in charge of the rescue unit, and his round hit the hidden body armor protecting his chest, sending the man staggering back and falling before jumping up and fleeing around the building. The Mk 23 triggered twice more before the area was empty of life.

As if someone turned the sound on, Lyons heard the wail of a siren, the cries and screams of frightened people and murmurs of the town as it woke to an unexpected disturbance.

"Able Two?"

"Able Two here."

"Gadgets?"

"I tucked him away. Not much I can tell you now. I just stumbled on some transport, and I'll see if I can bring these guys to a halt."

"Swing by and get me."

"Negative. I'm two tiers down and that'd cost me five minutes."

"Understood. They've retrieved the suitcase, Pol."

"I think Gadgets wanted it for himself."

"Yeah, I think he did."

"Think I'll try to get it back for him."

"Yeah, do that."

Lyons commenced to jog along in search of a ramp or stairs to the next level, looking for any available vehicle. He hadn't found either when he heard the squeal of tires and a long boxy car without lights pulled away from the front of the Coldman house. It was gone.

Out of the darkness rose a throaty diesel drone, then the sputtering of the diesel engines. The treaded monstrosity blinked into existence when the headlights came on, a yellow mass of earthmoving equipment.

The excavator spun in place, and Lyons saw Blancanales working the control knobs and levers.

Lyons felt a wave of disappointment. The excavator could have been used to hem in the Coldman car, but Blancanales was late. The car was gone. The vehicle's brief head start was more than enough. The diesel powerhouse and earth-gripping treads on the excavator weren't designed for speed. But Lyons was thinking inside the box.

Blancanales was way out of it. He steered the thirty-three-ton excavator at the nearest ledge and drove right off it.

CHAPTER TWENTY

Carl Lyons couldn't believe what he was seeing, or hearing, when the excavator tilted and vanished over the tier rim with a sound like a bridge collapse. He raced for a footpath and skidded down to the lower tier, then sprinted to the place where Blancanales went over.

The descent to the next tier wasn't as steep as he thought, and there was no twisted wreckage at the bottom, just the retreating rumble of the big diesel and it spluttering exhaust.

Lyons used a few precious seconds to reconstruct his mental map of this bizarre burg. It was like no other town he'd known, tiered like paddies but none of the tiers equal, each level following and augmenting the jagged contours of the geography.

The pause gave him an idea for catching up to Blancanales. He'd go down by going up. Maybe he'd have time and maybe not, but he couldn't think of anything better.

The young man who delivered the guests' suppers parked his motorcycle at the shabbiest cabin, and Lyons assumed the delivery man traded his room for his services. The bike was still there.

The people of the tier were milling about trying to

watch the activity below, but when one of the gunman inexplicably returned they fled in terror into their homes, which was just fine with Lyons. But the boy with the motorcycle wasn't cowed when it came to his property. He burst from the front of the cabin when he saw the big American grabbing his bike.

"No!"

The kid was maybe seventeen, and a scrawny, underfed seventeen, at that. Lyons wrenched at the hitch and let the barrel trailer fall to the ground.

"Sorry, kid, I've got to have it." Lyons swung a leg onto the seat.

"You not have it!" The kid straddled the front tire. He wouldn't let Lyons simply make off with his property and livelihood. The kid knew from looking at the warrior that he'd lose a fight, even without the gun dangling off the thief's shoulder. And the combat knife at the hip. And the handgun.

All in all Lyons thought it was a pretty ballsy move, but right now he didn't have time to deal with it. He wasn't going to hurt this kid, who was a civilian guarding his personal property. But the Able Team commander had to assist his teammate.

Lyons's hand plunged into his front pocket for his roll of Iranian currency, which Stony Man Farm supplied as a matter of course for expenses in-country. Meals. Bribes. Travel arrangements. Well, this was travel arrangements. He thrust the wad at the youth, who took it with a wrinkled forehead. His eyebrows climbed higher and higher as he fanned the bills.

"Is it a deal?"

"It is a deal, sir!" It was too much money to even make the kid smile—he was blank with awe. How much was that in U.S. dollars, anyway? Lyons didn't give a shit. "Give me the key and get out of the way."

The kid pulled a single key out of his shirt pocket and dropped it in Lyons's hand, strolling dazedly into the cabin without looking back. Lyons brought the bike alive and twisted on the handle, groaning in frustration at the results. The ancient, underpowered motorcycle chugged along like it had all night to get where it was going.

Well, Lyons didn't have all night and maybe he didn't even have a few minutes, but fisting the accelerator and playing with the gears coaxed no more speed out of the bike. He uttered an obscenity under his breath and squeaked to a halt as he decided on a new course. There was no room for a U-turn on this part of the tier path, so his hoisted the bike off the ground with both hands and walked it around in a 180.

Lyons kicked the motorcycle into a roll and fed it gas, then headed for the steps he'd used to come up. He'd take a page from Blancanales's book. As the front wheel nosed onto the first step, Lyons was sure that was a big mistake, but it was too late now.

The first jolt rattled the front end, and then the rear wheel fell onto the first step with a crash, and Lyons steered the motorcycle off the irregular stone steps, riding alongside them. The motorcycle slammed into imbedded boulders and caught in grooves carved by rivulets of rain runoff, and for long seconds the Able Team warrior's concentration was absorbed in the split-second reactions that came one after another until he unexpectedly found himself on the level of the next tier. He shook some tension out of his shoulders, adjusted his grip and steered for the next cliff edge, finding the path torn by Blancanales's excavator was less rutted and steep.

It was on the third descent that he found the best combination of brakes and gears, and he was able to tear his eyes away from the ground in front of his tire for a glance below. There were the headlights of the escape car, on the far right now as it rounded the last hairpin curve and steered onto the lowest tier. The way was opening ahead of them. Where was Blancanales?

Lyons turned. Stone buildings were built into the mountainside directly in front of him, and the brief gap between them would be a sheer drop. Urging the motorcycle to its fastest speed, he drove along the edge of the street, watching the landscape below. The closely set buildings meant that the earth left exposed between them was cut to a sheer drop. There was no way down except for the road at the far end and a twisting column of stairs, which Lyons would never get the bike down.

The problem was forgotten when he saw the excavator. Blancanales's shortest-distance approach had managed to get to the lowest tier ahead of the Coldman team—whether they knew it didn't matter because it was their only way out of town unless they ditched the car.

HUGGING THE FRONT of one of the mountain-inlaid apartments and hidden from Lyons, the excavator lurched into the avenue with a rumble of diesel and the whine of hydraulics, the big treads flinging mud and rocks.

Blancanales thought wryly that Gadgets Schwarz should have been here for this. The excavator was a high-end piece of work, with a turbocharged diesel and three speeds, making it faster than expected, even though it toted an extra-heavy, eleven-ton counterweight. The Komatsu people thoughtfully provided English plates and instrumentation as standard equipment.

Blancanales stretched the thirteen-foot, nine-inch shovel arm to its maximum extension while weaving the excavator across the avenue like a drunk construction worker on a joyride. The Coldman vehicle slowed, as if the driver couldn't believe what he was seeing, then raced ahead, steering for the gap the excavator couldn't fill. Blancanales raced the diesel, and the machine lurched in the direction of the gap and then stopped with a sickening grind of gears, reversing just as the Coldman driver swerved to the rear. Blancanales bluffed the bluffer. The Coldman driver had to choose the cliff edge or the excavator.

He chose the excavator, and the car crunched into its rear end, steam spraying in a cloud from under the V-shaped metal piece that had been the hood.

The excavator rotated, and Blancanales fired controlled bursts of 5.56 mm rounds that spiderwebbed the windshield and pocked the rear doors as they flew open, shattering their windows, too. Then he swatted the boxy Russian sedan with the excavator shovel, closing the open door. The front passenger window imploded violently, raising shouts from inside. They all had to be pincushioned with glass.

There was movement on the uncrushed side of the car. A man exposed himself just long enough for an overhand pitch—a fastball right to Blancanales.

The Able Team warrior triggered the M-203 mounted under the barrel of his M-16 A-2, which was loaded with a 40 mm antipersonnel buckshot round. The results were all he hoped for. The round transformed the grenade launcher into a powerful shotgun, and the blast of buckshot ripped through exposed flesh before the man put muscle behind his toss. The flayed hand went limp, and the grenade bounced heavily on the roof of the car. For a moment the Able Team warrior thought he'd made a terrible mistake—the Coldman device was inside the car. Would a grenade blast set it off? But the round rolled down the street and burst harmlessly.

Blancanales extricated himself hurriedly from the trap of the operator's cage as another grenade was lobbed at him from behind the protection of the car door. Blancanales saw it coming. He took a risky step on the dirty, greasy front arm of the excavator and jumped, landing in a crouch behind the shovel. When the blast came there was a crack of ripping steel, and metal pieces rocketed in every direction, inches from Blancanales's scalp. The deadly shrapnel that would have torn away his flesh and bone bounced noisily off the shovel. The excavator lurched from the blast, and he got a good shove from the shovel.

Blancanales sprinted into the open just long enough to take cover behind the nearest parked car.

Footsteps. Someone bolted from the Coldman wreck. Something about the figure told Blancanales it wasn't one of the Talyshi mercenaries. A burst of machine-gun rounds peppered the vehicle and sent him behind cover, but not before he'd seen enough.

Headlights were coming, somebody arriving home late to Masuleh, unaware their peaceful hometown was now a war zone. The Able Team commando crabbed to the front of the car for a shot on the runner, but it was too late. The Coldman agent stopped the car with waving arms, then exposed his weapon and went on the offensive. With a yank he opened the door and dragged out the driver, an old, scrawny man with floundering legs, and from inside came a half-stifled cry of terror. A woman or a child.

Blancanales was helpless.

The Israeli gave the man his instructions with a machine pistol imbedded against his neck, and then the driver was put back behind the wheel. The Coldman agent walked inside the crook of the open door, the weapon trained on the occupants. The message was crystal clear.

Blancanales felt the cold anger of failure, his mind spinning through every wild plan he could conceive. No strategy gave him a chance of freeing the hostages and taking down the Coldman team.

He could have put a buckshot round into the civilian car, which would leave the Coldman team trapped. Two dead civilians would be a tiny price to pay to prevent the use of the Coldman device, which might end the lives of tens or hundreds of thousands of civilians.

It was a price too high for Blancanales to pay.

Maybe he would regret the decision. Maybe this would be Able Team's last chance to bring the Coldman team to ground in Iran. Maybe a day or a week from now, Tehran would be a city of corpses.

He squatted there, watching, and let the escape happen.

LYONS WATCHED, TOO, and he hated it. The hostages left no room for action. There was nothing worse than being rendered inert.

The car turned, then backed close to the broken hulk of the excavator, and the woman hostage was brought into the open, standing with the gun against the back of her head. Then the Coldman team emerged from the wreckage of its sedan, keeping weapons leveled at the car shielding Blancanales as they transferred to the hostage vehicle.

One man was calm, as if unaffected by the wild flight, and he assisted another whose hand was wrapped in a blood-soaked rag. The last man was agitated, his head jerking from side to side as he sought danger in the darkness, and his features showed he was one of the Talyshi mercenaries.

They toted the familiar titanium suitcases.

Lyons turned away. He had turned the bike off so as to remain silent. He walked it away, down the road, gaining speed as the incline increased. He put his leg over the seat and steered it through the darkness, barely making the hairpin turn that took him down to the bottom tier.

The hostage car brake lights flashed on, then were gone, and the car pulled away, heading into the streets of the newer section of the city, built on flat acres blasted out of the mountainside in recent years. Lyons started the bike and put on speed, thinking wryly that the little bike had decent acceleration with the assist of a slope. When he raced past Blancanales, he was looking for more bodies.

"Able One here. I'm after them, Pol. The hostages still in the car?"

"That's right, Ironman. Nice bike."

"I could pedal faster. I'm going to hang back and hope the hostages get dumped on the roadside."

"Yeah, and then what?"

"Then I improvise."

He groped behind the seat and yanked the wires on the brake lights. The headlights were off, and he drove in darkness through the short streets of the new part of town, keeping a quarter mile back. There was just one downhill road out of town, and there was no chance of losing them yet.

The car slowed, and Lyons drifted in neutral. The interior lights blinked on as the brakes flashed, then he saw the hostages exit the car in ungraceful heaps. The car sped away. The woman was sobbing, and the man was holding a gash on his scalp.

"Any other hostages left in the car?" he asked, coming to a halt. The were startled by his appearance and just stared at him. Maybe they didn't understand him. Lyons didn't know Farsi.

"More hostages?" he demanded.

"No," the man said with effort. "Just her and me."

Lyons was already gone, accelerating with gravity's help. The getaway car was a featureless box of a vehicle with a rectangular rear window, oversize like all its windows. The headlights provided enough light for Lyons to make out the silhouettes of the occupants as he closed the distance. One of the men in the rear was moving his head rapidly, agitated. That would be the Talyshi merc. Lyons wanted the Coldman agents first, and targeted the other rear occupant with the MP-5 SD-3 propped on the handlebars.

The nervous mercenary turned and looked out the rear, and his paranoia was what killed him. He spotted the motorcycle closing in on the car and shouted a warning. The driver swerved as Lyons fired, and the Heckler & Koch submachine gun fired a long burst of 9 mm rounds through the rear window, emptying more than half the magazine at the rate of 800 rounds per minute.

The Talyshi merc took two rounds to the skull, but

before Lyons could adjust his aim, the Israelis were below the seats. He had to be satisfied with filling the interior of the car with as much damage as possible as it careened wildly from shoulder to shoulder. The road curved and narrowed to skirt another mountain ledge, and Lyons was sure the car would plunge off, but the driver twisted the wheel and took the turn almost sideways, then gunned around the mountain.

Lyons rounded the corner seconds later and saw the distant headlights of the highway a few miles downhill. Once the Coldman car was on the highway they could go anywhere. The highway could take them west to Mahabad, east into Tehran, both reachable by dawn. They could arrange boat passage on the Qezel Owzan river or hop a train on the rail line that ran alongside the river for a hundred miles then branched out into the heart of Iran. Lyons had studied the topography. He knew the expert Israeli agents would use their skills to stay evasive and render themselves invisible among the civilian population of the country.

It was now or never. Silently begging the motorcycle for more speed, he used a straight stretch of pavement to change out the magazine in the MP-5 SD-3 and adjust it from automatic to 3-round burst. The bike responded with higher RPM as the slope grew steeper, and Lyons came up fast on the car. The driver had just subdued its wild swerving when Lyons triggered a controlled triburst at the spot where the driver crouched low in his seat. The swerving started all over again, and Lyons heard commands being shouted, but without panic. He got to work on the tires, accelerating at the rear right and sending a burst at the rubber, but was driven off when handgun fire came at him over the back seat. He braked quickly and sent the next burst inside the car, and was disappointed to see the tires still holding air.

Then he saw the body.

The Talyshi mercenary was being manhandled out the rear window, and Lyons fired into the corpse, hoping to penetrate. The corpse kept coming, grotesque and bloodied and looking worse as the jagged glass still in the window frame tore at it. Then the driver stomped the pedal, and the car jolted ahead, just enough to get the Talyshi to slide off the back end of the car and hit the road rolling like a log. Lyons veered to avoid it.

But the corpse was only one of three items bouncing on the road, courtesy of the Israelis, and Lyons had a choice to make—drive into the dead Talyshi or over the two bombs. Either way he was probably a dead man. He took the route into the body, front wheel slamming into the cadaver at sixty-eight miles per hour with the shock of a train collision, and when the impact came Lyons was thinking his crappy little motorcycle could go pretty fast, after all.

CHAPTER TWENTY-ONE

Rosario Blancanales didn't want to think about it. The nightmare scenario was this: he was the only one left.

He'd been inside the parked car and had it wired a minute after Lyons went downhill. But Blancanales hadn't been able to catch up to the chase. He heard the twin grenade blasts and slowed when he came to some very bad roadkill and the wreckage of the motorcycle.

The twin craters showed him where the bombs blew. The remains of the motorcycle were a hundred feet farther down the road.

He squinted into the yellow glow from his headlights, convinced he was about to spot the remains of Carl Lyons. Not many minutes ago he'd been hiding the limp, barely breathing form of Hermann Schwarz. It had taken all his willpower to abandon Schwarz and go after the Coldman team. Schwarz would have told him to do so, but still…

There was no corpse.

The motorcycle was a mess, its left side sheared by the pavement like it had been pushed against a belt sander. The trail of parts went back about twenty feet from its resting place. But the evidence showed the bike had gone into the corpse to avoid the grenades.

No way Lyons could've kept the thing upright after that. Was there?

"Ironman?"

He'd been radioing frequently and getting no answer. He received none now.

When he left the car, the smell of friction-burned metal and incinerated rubber was like the smell of corruption. He strode to the edge of the pavement and darted his flashlight beam into the scrub and bushes that filled the ditch.

A hand rose out of the branches and gripped the flashlight head. Blancanales found himself hauling in two hundred pounds of dark, dazed muscle. What he landed had to be Lyons, but it looked a lot more like the cadaver in the road. Lyons was etched with scrapes and abrasions on every inch of exposed flesh, and bled slowly from his temple and shoulder. He looked angry and defeated. He looked grim.

He walked stiffly a few paces and extracted the MP-5 SD-3 out of the roadside scrub, examined the bend in the barrel, then sent it flying into the night.

"Let's go get Gadgets," Lyons said.

SCHWARZ WAS STILL in the rocky stash where Blancanales put him.

There was a pulse. The Able Team commando exhaled long and low, feeling some measure of tension escape him. He was generally an optimist, but for a minute there the scenario on the road had seemed so real—Gadgets and Ironman both dead, and he the only one left. It was almost too good to be true that they were both alive.

He used the emergency first-aid kit from his pack to clean his teammate's wounds. He felt the bones and the base of the spine. Nothing broken as far as he could tell, nor swelling under the skull. But Schwarz had hit hard, twice—against the dangling suitcase and against the unforgiving ground. If there was serious cranial swelling it would kill him fast, and Blancanales was ready to cut into Schwarz's skull then and there if he thought it would save him.

Finally he used the smelling salts, and Schwarz gagged and blinked awake.

"Get that shit—"

"Shut up." Blancanales put a hand over Schwarz's mouth.

Schwarz focused on Blancanales, on the night sky, on the piles of rocks in which he lay.

"What's your name?" Blancanales demanded.

"Rosario Bl—" Again the hand was on his mouth.

"No time for that crap. Answer the question," Blancanales demanded.

Schwarz nodded and answered the questions. He knew his name. He could count the number of fingers. He could name an impressive number of animals. When Blancanales tried to put him in a fireman's carry, Schwarz told him to go to hell and descended through town on his own two legs, becoming steadier every minute.

Lights were on everywhere. Schwarz heard a woman crying. Terror had visited Masuleh.

They rendezvoused with Lyons on the bottom tier, and Schwarz's unasked question was answered. He'd been wondering why Lyons hadn't helped fetch him. The man was a mess, bloody and bruised.

The town didn't have much of a police force, and the patrol cars were avoided easily enough. Able Team's van was parked in a lot for visitors, well lit and mostly empty. A rust-coated squad car with a single blue revolving light reached the lot a minute ahead of Able Team, and a pair of uniformed officers used their flashlights to look into the parked cars. The bakery van stood out like a sore thumb. The cops couldn't see inside. A second police car brought reinforcements before the van doors were forced open.

The three Israelis were right where Able Team had left them, tied motionless on the floor.

"There goes the gear," Schwarz muttered.

Lyons looked at his watch. "We'll retrieve the gear in a few hours."

Schwarz was too tired to argue.

IT WAS the biggest crime wave in Masuleh in years, but a lull in the excitement finally came deep in the night. The prisoners had been questioned, the confiscated hardware inventoried. Official word came from Tehran—no one was to touch anything. Revolutionary Guard forces and intelligence personnel would arrive by midmorning.

The commander of the Law Enforcement Forces post in Masuleh knew an opportunity to avoid a screwup when he saw one. He put two men on guard duty in the one-room police station while he went home to get sleep and a shower. He wanted to be sharp when the higher-ups arrived.

The two young men left in charge at the station were immersed in quiet conversation, so Rasool Far was able to work unnoticed.

First to get the key. It was a useful device, although not exactly ingenious—a sharp piece of flat, jagged metal, three inches long and a quarter-inch wide, narrowing at the tip. A cheap lock pick at first glance, but there was nothing cheap about it. It was titanium alloy and hadn't been embedded in his rubber shoe sole, but molded there. All his shoes had them.

Rubbing the sole on a rough patch of the concrete floor, he guessed he could have the device extracted in twenty minutes, depending on how rapt the young officers were in their conversation.

But then the Americans came back.

Their timing couldn't have been better.

Far watched the dark-skinned man come through the front door without a sound. There would undoubtedly be backup for him if he needed it, but he didn't. He'd chosen a moment when the officers were facing away from the door. He stood at their backs without making a sound. The first one slumped in his chair when the American cracked him in the neck. The second one tried to get to his feet but was hauled back into his chair by the wire that fell in place around his neck.

The gag came next, and then the plastic cuffs, and in seconds the young officer was as helpless as the prisoners in the cells.

Rasool Far almost laughed out loud when the other two entered the police headquarters. They looked like they'd been rolled down the mountain and dragged back up on a rope. For all his efforts he couldn't keep the grin off his face.

"Laugh it up," said the sandy-haired one. "You're the one in an Iranian jail cell."

Far's smile stayed where it was as the Americans retrieved their equipment from an aluminum cabinet.

Rosner, the minisub crewman, watched silently. He didn't know what the Americans would do, and he wasn't sure if he was more fearful remaining in Iranian hands or being under the control of the dark-souled killer with the grim, horrifying face. He decided he'd rather take his chances with the Iranians.

Amir Kadivar, the Israeli spy who had been posing as a baker, said to the American leader, "I've been thinking this over. I believe you're on a fool's errand."

The one called Ironman just shrugged.

"Are you going to kill us before you go?" Kadivar asked.

"No. I wanted to take you along for the ride, but my companions talked me out of it. They said you wouldn't talk. Your compatriots are too low on the totem pole to know anything useful." The American commandos headed for the door.

Kadivar nodded thoughtfully. "I will tell you something you should know."

The one called Ironman stopped and looked at the single jail cell, a six-by-six cage in a back corner. The three Israelis, even the wounded sub crewman, sat on benches with their hands cuffed in front of them and leashed to the floor on eighteen-inch chains. "So tell me."

"Israel wouldn't stoop to genocide."

"Some Israelis would."

"Not members of Mossad."

"You're naive to believe that."

"Maybe you're right," Kadivar said contemplatively. "We have our maniacs like everybody else, and more motivation than most peoples."

The American waited, and Kadivar knew the man understood he was rationalizing the betrayal he was about to perpetrate. But the rationale eased his conscience, and anyway he was done. "The target is in Tehran," he told the American.

Kadivar's assistant, the mole who went by the Iranian name Rasool Far, jumped to his feet with a rattling of chains. "Don't do it!" he grated in Farsi.

"Tehran's a big city."

"I will tell you where the device will be. Come closer."

"Amir, no!" Far pleaded.

The other two commandos were on their guard, and the commander asked carefully, "Tell me out loud."

"They can't hear what I say," Kadivar said of his fellow prisoners. "We'll all be questioned mercilessly in the coming days and maybe tortured, especially Rosner. They'll know he's an Israeli. Soon they'll know everything he knows."

The American came closer with his handgun at the ready, and his companions trained their weapons on the occupants of the jail cell. He came close to the bars. Far glowered and didn't interrupt while Kadivar whispered into the American's ear.

Lyons nodded, then stood.

"That's all I know." Kadivar shrugged.

"That's enough," the American said.

He left without a backward glance.

WHEN THE Americans were gone, Far got back to work. Now more than ever he needed to get out fast.

His work had a new intensity, and it wasn't long before he scraped enough rubber off his shoe to feel the scratching of the tiny hook at the end of the device. The hook would grip the floor and extract the device from its rubber molding.

The older agent was sitting with his head hanging, as if weary with the world. The sub crewman was watching him curiously but had given up asking him what he was doing.

The police officer in the chair was the first to figure it out, and he started shouting against the gag, thoughtfully provided by the Americans, whom Far also had to thank for immobilizing the officers. Far could work fast, no need for concealment. He had the device in his fingers and the lock on the cuffs picked in half the time.

The crewman whispered, "Wow!"

Kadivar looked up, face a mixture of chagrin and surprise. "Good work, Rasool!"

Far backhanded Kadivar with the device still clenched in his fingers. The cut opened the older spy's cheek from mouth to ear. "You are a traitor."

"I did not want to be party to mass murder," Kadivar slurred. "I think what the Americans said might be true."

"Of course it is true," Far retorted.

Kadivar glared at him, blood pouring down his face. "You're a part of it?"

"You are, too, old man. You were too good at your job to not be a part. We needed people who could be Iranian effortlessly. But we also knew you'd never see the wisdom of our way."

"There is no wisdom in mass murder."

"These kinds of arguments were finished a long time ago," Far said with a grimace. "Now we're in the implementation phase of the operation. Thank you for your help."

"I did not help you."

"You did," Far said. "You just sent the Americans to Tehran."

Kadivar considered that. "Tehran is not the target?"

"Not anymore. Once I'm in touch with Tel Aviv we'll switch to the alternate target. The Americans will have a nice, uneventful stay in the glorious capital of Iran."

"I see," Kadivar nodded. "And now I will die."

"Yes."

"Spare these men. They're guilty of nothing."

"They're guilty of witnessing this."

Kadivar cast his eyes at the floor. "Then get on with it, Rasool."

Far leaned over the old man and hissed, "My name is *David*."

Then he used the razor edge of the device on Amir Kadivar's neck.

Rosner opened his mouth to shout, but the device opened his windpipe and silenced him, although he thrashed for a full fifteen seconds. The unconscious officer was next—he had to die, just in case he wasn't *really* unconscious. Finally the wide-eyed young policeman, who had been shouting into his gag for the last five minutes.

Far grimaced as the shouting diminished. He owed the American commandos a great big thank-you.

SCHWARZ DIDN'T KNOW a lot about the selection of cars in the quiet end of the new section of town. They needed something nondescript, but he hoped it would have more horsepower than the golf cart engines he was finding under the hoods. Finally he settled on a Soviet-designed military jeep. It was old but looked well-maintained. The engine wasn't filthy, and the ground under it wasn't oil-soaked. The tattered canvas roof made it look more decrepit than it was.

"I'm not promising it'll get us all the way to Tehran," he said.

Tehran? Hell, Schwarz didn't even know if the thing would start.

Blancanales and Lyons jogged to the rear and pushed

the vehicle forward as Schwarz steered it out of its parking place and into the shadows. The streets were finally quiet, but the city would still be restless after the previous evening's mayhem.

No alarm sounded before they were at the end of the street and starting on the long downhill road to the highway. Lyons and Blancanales jumped in, and they rolled a half mile before Schwarz popped the clutch, bringing the jeep to life. He was satisfied at the sound of the engine purr.

"I'll drive," Lyons said.

"I'm fine," Schwarz argued.

"You're probably concussive. I'll drive."

It was still predawn when they emerged from the mountains at the highway, which was devoid of lights for miles in either direction. The sign showed arrows and directions in Farsi, which were unreadable. Schwarz knew one said something along the lines of *East,* or *Tehran.*

When Lyons pulled the jeep onto the highway, he followed the other arrow. Blancanales had been dozing off, only half attentive, but his eyes opened and his brows knitted. "Ironman, we going southwest?"

"Yeah."

"Tehran is east."

"Yeah."

"You know something we don't?"

"Yeah."

Blancanales nodded and went back to sleep.

CHAPTER TWENTY-TWO

Tel Aviv, Israel

Joseph Devorha was excited, even nervous. He'd been keyed up since the security fiasco with Ori Flatt. That had shaken the confidence of the Coldman board of directors. They wouldn't replace him, not now, not when the purpose of the organization was on the verge of being fulfilled. Still, he knew that he had failed them. He'd never made such a bad mistake.

Now things were getting worse, bad news following bad news out of Iran. The minisub that had inserted the Iran team went incommunicado, then, according to its passive homing device, it returned to the docks at Bandar-e Anzali in Iran and disappeared. The mystery had been solved with the phone call from Devorha's most trusted mole, David Segev. Segev was a friend from college and now was an Iranian mole going by the name Rasool Far.

Devorha contacted the Iranian team at once with orders to change to the backup itinerary. The U.S. special operations team, whoever they were, were on their way to Tehran and would take the quickest routes. Devorha mapped a route for his team to avoid those routes, to avoid the unlikely event of the two cars passing each other on the road and the U.S. operatives recognizing the Coldman agents.

That took care of that, he thought, but he didn't feel confident for some reason.

When Segev-Far called again to deliver a more complete accounting of events, the Coldman director sent him to monitor his team.

"They won't even know you're there, David," he told his old friend. "But you'll be with them in case there's more trouble."

"Where would the trouble come from?" Segev demanded.

"Who knows? The U.S. team was a surprise. Maybe there will be more surprises coming."

"I'll need a better car. Something not stolen and fast."

"I'll have someone in-country rendezvous with you soonest with a set of legal wheels."

"This means I'll be in place if and when the device is activated," Segev said emotionlessly.

Devorha had always had faith in Segev as a man of diamond-hard emotional constitution. Would he shirk from sacrifice? "How do you want me to respond to that, David?"

"I want you to say goodbye, my friend."

"Goodbye, David. You'll be remembered as a hero."

His friend chuckled in response, but somehow it sounded more like Rasool Far than David Segev. "So put me on a stamp," he said. "Lead the people well, Joseph."

Devorha thought about the sacrifice his friend was making. Segev was one of the rare breed of intelligence agents that came only out of Israel.

Israel survived because of her superb intelligence organizations. Maybe there was no other nation in the world that could say such a thing so definitively, but of Israel it was true. She was a state on the brink of collapse since the day she came officially into being, in 1948. That collapse would undeniably have come if not for the effectiveness of Mossad.

The Central Institute for Intelligence and Security, known as Mossad, operated mostly outside Israel. The number of Mossad personnel undercover in Arab nations would have surprised the world. If the director of Mossad learned the total even he would be surprised.

That amused Joseph Devorha, who was a few rungs below the director on the ladder of Mossad seniority but who was the one man, in fact, who did know precisely how many Mossad agents operated in the field. He deployed many of them.

He also was responsible for a few Shin Bet undercover agents. Shin Bet was named after the Hebrew initials for General Security Services, and its responsibility was internal counterintelligence. There had been a startling number of terrorist attacks against Israelis thwarted by Shin Bet, and even more startling was the number of attacks that it had allowed to proceed in the interest of better intelligence. The head of Shin Bet knew nothing about the undercover operatives on his staff who Joseph Devorha secretly coordinated.

There was the Intelligence Corps of the Defense Forces, Mossad's sometimes rival, and the tiny Research Department of the Foreign Ministry and the Israel Police Force Special Investigations Department. All dealt with internal or external intelligence, which were one and the same in the unsettled nation of Israel, where the future makeup of the population and the borders was anybody's guess and the obsession of many.

Devorha controlled agents in every branch, as had his father before him.

Nachman Devorha was one of Mossad's classic intelligence geniuses, a master of playing the intelligence game to manipulate the politics of the world to favor Israel. That was to say, the Jewish population of Israel. Devorha the elder was a member of a small clique that met socially and discussed the good of Israel and the good of the world. They were like professors, Devorha the elder would explain, gathering on Friday night after a week of answering inane questions from ignorant Ph.D. candidates. Only when they were in the company of one another could they stretch their intellectual legs. The only difference was that Devorha the elder and his cronies talked politics and Arabs and the good of the State of Israel.

Masterstrokes of political orchestration were conceived at these meetings. Some had furthered Israel's interests, and some had saved her from being decimated. There was only one major backfire, called the Lavon Affair after it became public knowledge. A good idea—blow up U.S. and British information offices in Egypt to swing more sentiment away from the Arabs and to Israel —ruined by poor security. Prime Minister Ben-Gurion had resigned as a result of it. It brought shame on Israel, the world had said. If the world only knew what had been accomplished since then.

The clique had gone more or less undercover after Lavon, becoming a secret organization inside Mossad. There were no clear goals, but opportunities were seized when they presented themselves. It took the tri-

umph of the war in the mid-1960s for the informal
group to get serious again.

They were getting older, and only four remained.
They saw what the optimistic fools around them failed
to see. The future held more wars in store for Israel.
Despite her god-given ascendancy to this holy land, she
was like a pure pool of fragrant water floating on a
bath of rancid oil, and it would take great and constant
effort to keep the oil from consuming her. There might
come a day when the sheer numbers and simplistic per-
sistence of the Arab would be too much for Israeli intelligence to outwit.

Coldman was formed, although the organization
wasn't named then, its first step being to make itself
self-sustaining with the adoption of attractive goals and
philosophies to foster active recruitment. Those philosophies proved to be inconstant.

The most mainstream Coldman philosophy was
based on the right of the nation of Israel to survive,
with the Coldman strikes regarded only as a last-ditch
effort to even the odds. If Israel was faced with impending destruction at the hands of the Arabs, then it
wasn't immoral or unethical to take drastic steps to
reduce the might of the Arab world enough to make
the resurrection of Israel a possibility.

The right to self-defense was difficult to debate, and
it was this point of view that motivated most members
of the Coldman group. It could be discussed dispas-
sionately, without resorting to the theological justifi-
cation that made it questionable among the international political community, which was where it might
some day be put on trial.

Another perspective flourished, and maybe it was the
true conviction held in the heart of many Coldman

members who didn't admit it. It was based on Bible interpretations providing the nation of Israel divine rights, making the presence of other religious groups an insult to God and the evidence of their existence stains on sacred land. They strove to purify Israel.

As director of the Coldman organization as it now existed, Joseph Devorha could speak to any and every argument. He could reason with the young, dispassionate men and women who made up Coleman's core of field operatives, or stage a passionate tirade for the benefit of the elderly, bitter Israel Defense Forces general who saw Coldman as his only real legacy. But Devorha believed none of it, for at heart he wasn't a religious man but a soldier, a field captain who devoted his life to furthering the advantage of his side.

As a young man learning from his father how to direct the organization, he had been idealistic, but now his overriding goal was simply to bring Israel, his side, to a position of military dominance. Coldman was a means to this end, and he had no intention of waiting for Imminent Defeat, the Coldman trigger point detailed in the Coldman Doctrine.

There was a board of directors for Coldman. He didn't even know who all of them were, but they issued his orders. They had never told him to use Coldman to bring the Arab to his knees, but Devorha knew—he *knew*—that they would applaud him when he did it.

There would be a backlash against Israel if it perpetrated this atrocity, and when the backlash came Devorha would emerge from hiding in the depths of Mossad and make himself known to the world as the man who pulled the trigger. He would take the blame. He would describe how he acted alone, without official sanction from the Israeli government. The nation of Israel would be off the hook.

Israeli humanitarian overtures toward the Arab nations would insure they remained in the good graces of America and most of Europe. Anti-Israeli sentiment would linger for years, maybe decades, but anti-Israeli fomenters would be hamstrung by the perception of Israel's innocence in the Coldman affair.

Devorha himself would be an instant hero among extremist Israelis, the ones who had been preaching Arab annihilation all along. As the chips fell, as Israel realized how ideally Devorha had orchestrated events, he would become a favored son.

Israel would be slow to make its affections public, and there would be people around the world who would see him as a monster, but as years turned to decades, Israel would embrace him openly.

Today he was turning thirty-six years old. On the day he turned fifty-six, Devorha predicted to himself, he would be the leader of the nation of Israel or dead from the bullet of an assassin. Each was just as likely.

CHAPTER TWENTY-THREE

Stony Man Farm, Virginia

"Stony Base? Talk to me."

"Proceed to the given target, Phoenix One."

"I said it sounds like busywork."

"We're working on something better."

Price muted the mike on her headset and looked discouraged.

"We are?" Kurtzman asked.

"Let's make the effort."

"It's not a lack of effort that's the problem. It's the lack of options."

"How do you track one car in a city of fifteen million people?" Price demanded in frustration.

"Let's get the cops involved," Akira Tokaido suggested from a workstation nearby. He was scanning the data coming in from Cairo dispatch and finding it to be a meager supply of information.

"I've thought of that," Price said. "Too risky. These people are determined and suicidal, and they might detonate the device if they thought they were about to be arrested."

Tokaido turned to face Kurtzman and Price, pulling out the tiny earbuds and looking past them thoughtfully at the wall-mounted display showing an intricate map of Cairo and its sprawl, one of the world's biggest cities.

The young hacker shook his head. "Yeah, they might be maniacs, but they're also cool customers. Mossad-trained, in the field for a long time, you know. Overreacting, that's amateur stuff. So what if the cops are looking out for them but not to arrest them? What if it's to protect them?"

"Where are you going with this?" Kurtzman asked.

"I have no idea." Tokaido grinned.

Price's hand hit the table with a loud slap. "Let's make it work. I want an idea. I don't care how farfetched. I want some excuse for asking the Cairo police force to be on the lookout for the Eissa Mercedes or any other vehicle registered to the Eissa family."

Kurtzman nodded, then abruptly shook his head. "So we're going to ask the Cairo police to do—what? Stop the Eissa car and deliver a message?"

"Offer protection," Price suggested.

"From?" Kurtzman looked brighter.

"The same maniacs who attacked the villa in Old Cairo just and hour ago," Price replied as she stabbed a code on the nearest workstation. "Business competitors. Rival families. Doesn't matter if we make it sound legitimate."

"And how do we do *that?*" Kurtzman asked.

"Hal," Price said into the phone, "we need your help."

Garden City, Cairo

"HELLO, HAL, it's been a long time," said the Ambassador. "How's the wife?"

"Hi, Dan. She's still pining for what might have been."

The U.S. Ambassador to Egypt met Helen Brognola at one of the rare social events the Brognolas attended. It was a D.C. affair a while back. The ambassador took her for a spin on the dance floor, sending her back to her husband with a warm glow on her cheeks. The private joke was that the ambassador had come within inches of whisking Mrs. Brognola off to Cairo.

"Tell her I think of her every day," the ambassador said.

"I guess if I took her out dancing occasionally she wouldn't be so easily impressed by any slick operator in an expensive suit," Brognola growled.

The ambassador laughed, well aware of Brognola's dislike for the Washington social scene. He also knew why Hal started showing up at them in the year after the last presidential election.

It had been an unpleasant time at the Department of Justice. The new President appointed his top-level cabinet in record time, but it took him a full year to appoint his mid-level cabinet, leaving the leftovers from the previous administration in place while the new blood was painstakingly installed. No department suffered worse than Justice, where the extended political game-playing was insufferable. What made it worse for Brognola was the need to play along. That meant attending more than his usual one or two dinner parties a year.

"I'll bet you're glad that's over."

"Dan, you and I both know it's *never* over," Brognola said. "The pre-2004 backstabbing is already in full swing."

"Glad I'm in Egypt," the ambassador said, giving Brognola the opening he was waiting for.

"So am I, Dan. I've got a problem. Nothing major."

"A problem I can help with?"

"A problem that the Cairo police can help with."

The ambassador considered that, turning to part the blinds keeping out the afternoon sun. "I know some of the brass, but I wouldn't say I'm well-connected."

"It's not a huge favor."

"So ask."

Brognola asked.

Stony Man Farm, Virginia

"I TOLD HIM I was doing a political favor for somebody else and that I was still paying penance for not kissing all the right rear ends after the last cabinet shuffle."

"Will he do it?" Price asked.

"Oh, he'll do it," Brognola said confidently. "He said he'll wave around an invitation to the next embassy soiree. Your problem lies in relying on an overworked, underpaid police force, with too few personnel watching over too many people."

"Understood," Price said, and ended the call.

She stood behind Tokaido's workstation. He was watching the transcription of the electronic messaging system used for the most important emergencies and bulletins across metropolitan and suburban Cairo. The outbreak of violence in Old Cairo had rated only a mention.

Then their message appeared. It was a simple request from a high-level police official, whose name meant nothing to Price. She hoped it would inspire the patrol officers and tourist police. It asked any officer coming across the Eissa Mercedes or other Eissa car to provide a security escort and to radio for further instructions.

"Think this'll work?" Tokaido asked.

"It doesn't feel strong," Price admitted with a sigh, "but it's the only plan we've got."

Gezirah Island, Cairo

THE ISLAND on the Nile River was a place of seclusion amid the metropolitan sprawl. Fifteen stories above it was one of the most expensive views in Cairo. T. J. Hawkins didn't have time for the glitter of the Nile, the distant vision of the Great Pyramids or the splendor of the suite itself. He headed directly for the desk and the laptop, which came alive with the touch of a key.

Behind him Encizo checked the bedroom and the bathroom, finally stepping onto the balcony. There was no sign of recent occupation. One of the Eissa women called the suite home. It was unclear if she was one of the group that had gone on the so-called vacation to Australia. They did know this was the last Eissa residence in Cairo to check out, and unless they came up with a lead they'd be spending the rest of the day sitting around looking at each other.

The hotel was wired for ethernet, and Hawkins found himself instantly on-line. He opened a Web browser and typed in an IP that dumped thousands of jumbled characters across his screen in seconds, then blanked out and dumped them again. The automatic refresh on the page kept the window open while Kurtzman followed the trail backward from the Farm.

"We're in," Kurtzman said.

"How's it look?" Hawkins asked.

There was a grumble from behind Kurtzman that

sounded like Akira Tokaido. "Pretty tight," Kurtzman said. "Lots of safeguards."

Hawkins made a quick inventory of the hard drive applications, looking for software to surrender control of the PC and make things easier for the Farm. He didn't see what he wanted, but a word processing file popped up, named Friends. He opened it, found a list of names and addresses in English and described it to Kurtzman.

"I've opened it up at this end," Kurtzman said. "Could be interesting. I'm sending it to Carmen for cross-referencing with known moles, but it seems too easy—"

"We've got them!" Tokaido shouted off mike.

"What's Akira got, Bear?"

"Cairo cops found our friends," Kurtzman replied.

"You had the *cops* looking for the *Israelis?*"

"Yeah. A courtesy escort in light of the troubles at the villa this morning."

"You've got to be kidding. The police will want to take them in for questioning."

"They don't. My guess is Eissa is one of those people who spreads around a lot of cash for help keeping a low profile. That works in some parts of the world."

"Don't kid yourself, Bear," Hawkins said. "It works everywhere. Give me the location."

"It looks like they're on the highway. They're halfway to Hulwan. I guess they're leaving town."

"I guess we'll be, too," Hawkins said.

Persian Gulf, USS Carl Vinson

STUCK INSIDE the high-security lab deep inside the Nimitz-class aircraft carrier, Jack Grimaldi felt like he might as well be buried underground. He was essentially in prison, without so much as a porthole for a view. He wasn't even sure he was going to be needed. They were just keeping him where he was in case another quick delivery errand was needed. Until then he was confined in his closet-size berth or wandering the labs trying not to get in the way.

"Worst cruise I've ever been on," he complained when Dr. Shorn emerged from one of the off-limits testing chambers. Sandra Shorn and Grimaldi had developed an easy friendship, with a hint of further interest, but this time she didn't smile. Dr. Claire came out behind her, and then Grimaldi turned to see Admiral James Weyer pass through the security at the lab entrance. He and Grimaldi had shared the promised belt of Jack Daniel's, but he was looking very sober now.

"Okay, I'm here, Doctor," the admiral said.

"You have a right to know what you're transporting, Admiral, otherwise we'd have to keep you out of this," Dr. Claire stated.

"Understood. Let's hear it."

"One moment."

Claire led the group into the working interior of the lab, where the phone's indicator showed a steady red conference light. "Okay, we're all here, Barb."

"Okay. We have Aaron as well as our contact in the Justice Department."

"Hello," Hal Brognola said, but before any of Grimaldi's group responded, the big Fed continued, "he's ready, Barb."

"Patch him in."

There was a short click. "Sir?" Brognola asked.

"I'm here," said a new voice.

The admiral cocked his head shortly.

"I've got the preliminary report from Hal," the speaker continued. "I wanted to hear this one from the horse's mouth, so to speak."

Admiral Weyer thought he'd recognized the voice. Now he was sure of it, and it showed on his face. Suddenly he was in less of a hurry to get his answers, but the Man was impatient. "So, give it to me straight."

"Mr. President, we've analyzed the contents of the Coldman device," Dr. Shorn said. "It's highly sophisticated. Design, manufacture, materials all point to a highly engineered weapon."

"What nuke isn't highly engineered?" the Man asked.

"By global standards of nuclear weapons, this is far beyond what we would expect to see from any terrorists out of a Third World nation," Shorn clarified. "The manufacturing techniques alone must have cost millions to develop. The design itself is unique."

The Man said, "That's fine, but I want to know what it *does*."

"We found cobalt impregnated in the foam casing," Shorn said grimly. "This is a salted bomb."

"Meaning what?" Grimaldi asked, although he had a feeling he knew.

"Good question, whoever the hell *that* is," said the President of the United States.

"Meaning the fissionable material that would have been used to encase the second-stage fusion fuel on a more standard weapon has been replaced with a salting substance, in this case cobalt," Kurtzman explained. "During the detonation of the device, neutrons breed with the cobalt, and a radioactive isotope is created.

That provides a wider spread of radiation. More people die.''

"You're understating the case, Aaron," Shorn said. "Whoever made this device used cobalt 60. It's lethal and it lasts. The fallout will blow around for weeks before it settles, depending on where it goes off. The number of dead? I can't begin to estimate.''

"This is a unique weapon," Claire added. "The cobalt bomb was proposed more than fifty years ago as a possible doomsday device, but it's never been done as far as we know. Now somebody actually made one.''

"Jesus H. You telling me these are doomsday devices?'' the President demanded.

"No, sir. The cobalt salting was added to make the most lethal possible weapon in a man-portable form,'' Shorn said, her voice calm and reassuring compared to the scarcely perceptible waver in the Man's voice. "The amount of cobalt contained in the foam is small. But if the device functions according to its design— well, we're talking thousands of square miles of fallout-affected geography. Land that would be unlivable for years.''

"Thousands of square miles?'' Kurtzman asked carefully, as if he were verbally stepping around a sleeping cobra.

"That's the point,'' Shorn said. "This device is a far cry from what Leo Szilard suggested in 1950. What we thought was some sort of blown foam explosive material is actually a manufactured structure of hexagonal cells. They must have employed proton beam chiseling, or some other micromachining technique we don't even know about. We think it will give them enhanced detonation. The cobalt particles will be ultra lightweight, and they'll hang in the air for, well, we can't predict how long. Even on a dry day in the desert without wind these particles will stay airborne for hours or days. It will be catastrophic to human life throughout the area of coverage.''

"How catastrophic? How many human beings we talking about here?" The President's Texas accent was becoming more pronounced as the conversation proceeded, Grimaldi noticed. Any other time and he might have found something funny in that.

"Depends, sir." Claire spoke up. "The weather at the time of the detonation has everything to do with the spread of the contamination. On a calm day over level ground, it could contaminate forty thousand square miles, which equates to a circle two hundred miles wide. Everyone inside would likely be fatally exposed to radiation—those that survived the initial blast.''

"What's Baghdad? Ten million people, in and around? You saying all ten million would be dead?"

"Yes," Claire said. "Dr. Shorn was very serious when she said cobalt was long-lived and lethal. Most isotopes produced by fission have short half-lives. Tantalum-181 will only last 115 days. Zinc-64 will last less than 250 days. Gold-197 not even three days—"

"Get to the point," the Man demanded.

"The point is cobalt 60 has a half-life of more than five years. If the device we now possess had done what it was designed to do, Baghdad would be more than dead, it would be uninhabitable again in our lifetime.''

There was silence. Between the Office of the President of the United States, the lab on the USS *Carl Vinson,* and the hidden base of the world's most secret special forces organization, no one spoke for a long moment.

It was the Man himself who broke the silence. "You know, I don't think I really believed they could do it. Shut down the Arab nations, I mean." He sounded as if he were talking to friends, comrades in the face of adversity. All the political posturing, all the guarded behavior that Grimaldi found suspicious in politicians was absent. This was a human being sharing his awe and concern with those around him. "I guess they really can, unless somebody can tell me I'm wrong."

"You're not wrong, Mr. President," Hal Brognola stated. "If that weapon detonated in Baghdad, Iraq would have been half-depopulated, minimum. The nation would cease to exist, and it would splinter into small states. If the device in Egypt is detonated anywhere near Aswan, even if it doesn't take out the dam and disrupt the Nile flow, the water supply will be poisoned for a century. Seventy million people will be an impossible number for all the humanitarian efforts in the world to save. We don't know the target in Iran. We can assume Tehran, which means Iran loses a quarter or a third of her sixty-six million population and falls into anarchy. No more Iran, just some disjointed Persian states."

"Tell me how Israel comes out of this if both the Egypt and Iran devices go off."

"She's comes out ahead militarily," Kurtzman said. "Who'll stand up to her? The Saudis, maybe? Other Middle Eastern militaries will go down if they try to engage Israel in full-scale war."

"Israel will get nuked," Grimaldi said, voicing his thoughts.

"You again, whoever you are," the President said.

"Of course it will. Some Muslim nation with nuclear capability will guess or assume Israel's behind it. They'll be so mad they'll nuke Tel Aviv, and you can't blame them for doing it."

"The Coldman strategy may have anticipated that," said a new voice. It was Yakov Katzenelenbogen. Grimaldi hadn't even realized he was in on the call. "At least some of the Coldman people seem intent on using the devices only as a last resort—as in *after* Israel is defeated by the Arab nations. The thinking is that Israel will rise again, in years or decades, but the Arab nations will stay fractured, divided by radioactive walls that will keep them from consolidating for centuries. There's another Coldman niche that believes the use of the devices will be the catalyst for bringing on the biblical end times, in which Israel becomes Earth's dominant nation. Genocide in God's name."

Grimaldi, normally an easygoing guy, felt weighted with these grim words, thinking about when genocide had been perpetrated in the name of God in recent history. He knew he wasn't alone in considering the grim irony of history's most famous victims of genocide spawning a plot to perpetrate atrocities on a scale even more grand.

It couldn't be permitted.

"So how do we stop it?" Grimaldi demanded.

"You again," the President said. "Always with the right question at the right time. I need aides like you. Interested?"

"No, thank you, sir," Grimaldi replied, not even sure if it was a serious request or an attempt to dispel some of the gloom.

"Another intelligent response. Hal? What more can we do?"

"Alert the Egyptian and Iranian governments." Sandra Shorn spoke matter-of-factly, as if putting her thumb on an obvious but overlooked answer.

"We'd be at war with the Iranians within the hour," the President retorted. "If we point the finger at Israel, the Arab nations will rip her apart and the Coldman devices may or may not go off before that happens. If we take responsibility for the devices, we might save Israel but we become the Great Satan that Iranian extremists always claimed we were."

"Why should we even consider shouldering the blame when Israeli's the guilty party?" Claire asked.

"To save millions of lives," Katz retorted vehemently. "This is an act of terrorism by extremists. The state of Israel doesn't sanction this. This isn't the will of the Israeli people as a whole."

"The actions of a nation are never the actions of all the people, or even most of the people," Claire mused calmly. "It's not the place of the U.S. to take the fall when an ally commits a crime against humanity."

"I'd rather not go there, at least not yet," the Man said. "Hal, I've got to explore other possibilities, but your people remain our most viable option as of right now."

"Understood. We'll do our best."

"I know you will," the Man said, but unspoken was the rhetorical question, *Will your best be good enough?*

None of them knew if it would be.

CHAPTER TWENTY-FOUR

Northwest Iran

There were roadblocks, staffed by Iranian law enforcement at first, then regular military ground forces. They were easy to circumvent. By driving without lights on the mostly empty, unlit highways Lyons spotted the roadblock lights from a mile or two away and pulled their transport far enough off the road to be hidden. Then it was a matter of simply making an overland hike.

The roadblocks were set up outside towns and villages and were only staffed enough to check incoming traffic. Once into town they would find a new vehicle and drive it out without getting stopped.

"Sooner or later our luck is going to run out," Schwarz observed as distant jagged mountains turned gray in the predawn light.

"Then we'll deal with it," Lyons said.

Yeah, maybe they'd deal with it and maybe they'd end up in an jail cell. "I wonder if Iranian prisons are as bad as Turkish prisons."

Lyons shot him a look. "Don't worry about it. The next village should be our destination."

"You sound pretty sure."

"As sure as I can be."

"I don't know if I'd put any trust in that Mossad agent."

"He's dead."

Schwarz looked at Lyons, who continued squinting into the darkness for the pavement. Blancanales sat up in the back seat, where he'd been sleeping. "Did you say he's dead, Ironman?"

"Amir Kadivar figured out that his assistant was a part of the Coldman core," Lyons said. "Before we reached the police station, Rasool Far had been working at getting to a lock pick. Kadivar knew Far would get free and murder them all. Cops, Kadivar and the sub crewman."

"He told you all this?" Blancanales asked.

"He told me enough," Lyons explained. "I figured out the rest. He made a show of letting me in on the target for the Coldman team, but when he was whispering he gave me the rest of the story. The secondary target. He perpetrated a charade for Rasool Far. Didn't let on that he'd figured him out."

"For the purpose of what?" Schwarz asked.

"That way Far wouldn't suspect that he'd given me the secondary target, as well. Once Far got free and killed them all, he'd alert the Coldman HQ to switch to the secondary target."

"He could have alerted the Masuleh cops before we got there," Schwarz observed. "They'd have been able to stop Far before he got to his lock pick."

"To what end?"

"To save his skin!"

"He was more interested in stopping mass murder," Lyons said. "I think he was still pondering the problem when we showed up and his course of action became clear."

"So he knew he was about to be killed and he allowed it to happen to bluff Rasool Far," Schwarz said, a touch of admiration in his voice. "Pretty noble, if it's true."

"Yeah," Lyons said.

"You believe it is."

"Yeah. Call it a hunch."

Schwarz said nothing more, but he glanced at Blancanales, who shrugged in the darkness and slumped back in his seat.

Schwarz didn't like hunches, but he trusted Lyons's. The man had the instincts of an experienced intelligence strategist. If he thought the story was true, then it probably was.

"The primary target was Tehran, as was to be expected," Lyons offered. "Golestan Palace. It's a complex of buildings and gardens in Tehran. Now it's a museum, as well, so it would make sense for tourists to go there. These guys play their cover roles to the hilt. Especially now that there's a general security alert in this quadrant of the country, they'll play Arab tourists to their own advantage. An advantage we lack."

"But it's a disadvantage, too, if they stick to tourist destinations," Blancanales said.

"That becomes a disadvantage only if someone is looking for them. As far as they know, we're on our way to Tehran."

"Where are we actually headed?" Schwarz asked.

"Ali Sadr is our next stop," Lyons said, nodding toward a sign on the side of the road. The English-language legend in small print was almost visible enough to read, now that the sky was lightening.

"Did that say caves?" Schwarz asked.

"Yeah," Lyons said. "Caves."

THEY WERE OFF THE ROAD five minutes later when they spotted the glow of taillights ahead. Lyons had been about to ditch the vehicle in favor of overland travel anyway, knowing they were close to their destination and more exposed with every passing moment. Schwarz flattened a tire and the spare in the trunk, just to keep up appearances should it be discovered anytime soon.

Then they were marching through the woods and scrub, keeping as far from the highway as possible without losing their direction into the village.

The village of Ali Sadr made good economic use of its caves, which were only discovered in the midtwentieth century. They were scenic but sterile. The deep underground lakes contained no fish. There were vast natural cathedrals but no bats, with no signs of habitation by anything bigger than albino cave bugs. Still, when sight-seers had their fill of museums and an endless procession of mosques, they came to Ali Sadr for a change of pace.

The roadblock here looked more serious than those they had come across during the night.

"Revolutionary Guards," Schwarz said as he picked out the uniforms in his field glasses. Perched uphill behind a boulder, the Guards were close enough that the still morning air carried loud voices to them. "They're being pretty thorough."

"Not good enough to unmask the Coldman moles," Lyons stated.

"I think you're right," Blancanales agreed. "If for no other reason than they'd probably have shut down the roadblock if they caught some guys sneaking in with nukes. Does it look like they know what they're looking for, Gadgets?''

"No. They're thinking small. They're opening luggage and shaking out socks and stuff. They know something is up, but they don't know what.''

"Let's get into town.''

"Let's give it a few, Ironman,'' Schwarz said without tearing his eyes away from the glasses. "I think I just recognized the driver of the car that's next in line.''

"Gadgets, you did get brain damage. That's not them.''

Schwarz didn't argue, but he didn't look away, either.

"They have to be hours ahead of us,'' Lyons said.

"They stopped and changed cars like we did,'' Blancanales suggested.

"You couldn't recognize somebody in a car that far off,'' Lyons added. "When did you even see him?''

"He shot at me in Masuleh,'' Schwarz said.

"And now you think you see him again?'' Lyons wasn't convinced.

"Yeah. Check it out.''

Blancanales and Lyons looked through their glasses, and Schwarz was proved right when they saw the suitcases coming out. Three of them, appearing to be old, battered aluminum. In actuality they were titanium shells filled with foam explosive materials. Schwarz felt his chest grow tight with tension as the scene at the roadblock played out. The distant little figures seemed to be moving in slow motion.

The Revolutionary Guards were interested in the suitcases. The Coldman moles weren't interested in their interest. They surrendered their luggage for inspection, then began going over a colorful brochure. Their dress and features were unexceptional. Schwarz wouldn't have been able to pick them out of a crowd in this country. They were just three Iranian guys out on a road trip.

One of the Revolutionary Guards extracted something from the shell of one of the suitcases. A wire dangled from it. He barked at the Coldman moles, who stopped chatting and looked curious at the soldier's intensity. The Guard barked again. The words were loud enough that the Able Team commandos could hear their insistence. He wasn't asking politely.

"Uh-oh," Schwarz said, as one of the Coldman agents grinned and reached for the device in the soldier's hand.

Schwarz wondered if he was about to die, alongside Ironman and Pol and every tourist and resident this side of Tehran. If the moles knew they were made, they wouldn't hesitate to activate the device. Even unassembled the thing would blast them all to eternity and spread enough radioactive dust to kill thousands.

The Coldman agent never stopped grinning. His hand pulled away from the device in the soldier's hand, and they heard its rasping screech.

"Britney Spears," Lyons said. He made out the distorted downbeat coming from tortured boom box speakers.

"I'd have preferred a lethal dose of radiation," Blancanales muttered as they watched the guards move on to the next car in line. "Kind of clever combining an audio system with a weapon of mass destruction."

"So they go into town, they go through all the tourist motions, see the cave and all that," Schwarz said as he watched the Coldman team repack the cases.

"Where do we make our strike? Fudge shop? Souvenir stand?"

"I think we leave them alone for now," Lyons said. "Too risky here. If the Iranians have Revolutionary Guards at the roadblocks, they'll have the town crawling with soldiers, too."

"On the other hand, if they go belowground with the device, it will be the safest opportunity to take them out," Blancanales said. "Even if it goes bad and they manage to detonate, where better than in a cave? The blast will be partially contained."

"Pol, you're talking about killing thousands of civilians instead of hundreds of thousands," Schwarz said. "I'd rather kill zero. Especially since we'd be among the casualties either way."

"Good point," Blancanales admitted, but a heavy wad of doubt sat in his stomach. It was a risk. Able Team was good at taking such risks, but Able Team wasn't infallible.

But, as Gadgets had said, if they failed he wouldn't be around to live with it. An optimistic viewpoint, he thought wryly.

Stony Man Farm, Virginia

"I'M NOT GOING to tell Able no." Barbara Price spit the words. "Let's look for alternatives."

"We're doing it," Kurtzman replied, then added with a touch of defensiveness, "I didn't say we were giving it up."

"Okay. Sorry. What are the alternatives?"

"So far they're few and far between. Trouble is the U.S. keeps a pretty small inventory of UAVs in the field. There aren't many, and they're limited in their capabilities. Flying speed and distance are factors. The Pioneer can't get to Al Sadr soon. When it did, it wouldn't have much range left.''

"Why not airdrop it?" Price demanded.

"We can't stealth drop a Pioneer, and we can't fly over Iran with a Tomcat or a helicopter without starting an international incident.''

"What can we drop without being detected?''

"We're exploring the options.''

Price showed her concern. "That's a very politic response.''

"Sorry. I don't want to sound conclusive. Barb, we're looking.''

Price walked away slowly, her fingers drumming her thigh. In her fancifully embroidered white Western-style blouse and her worn, faded jeans she looked like a cowgirl with a lot on her mind. The setting, one of the most advanced electronic information gathering centers on earth, couldn't quite dispel the impression.

The Computer Room was stuffed with equipment and had the too-cold atmosphere and constant rush of air from the cooling system needed to keep the hardware comfortable. The vaguely ominous mainframes and drives were only a part of the total computing package, since parts of it were now stored throughout the facility. In total it was an information technology facility of a immense scope.

All this was lost on Price. She wanted an answer a machine couldn't give her. But the people in this room weren't helping, either, which wasn't a failing on their part. They were the best. The smartest. The most skilled.

So maybe an answer was there. Maybe she just needed to squeeze it out, like the last brushful of toothpaste in a flattened tube. Price strode deliberately to Carmen Delahunt, who looked up from her monitor curiously and raised her brows when she read the determination on her colleague's face.

"Tell me how to get the Iran Coldman traced. I want a feasible answer right now."

Delahunt was taken aback. "That's what we've been—"

"No excuses, I want the answer now."

Delahunt looked angry for a moment, then retorted. "I-Gnat!"

"Can't do it. None in the vicinity." Kurtzman broke in with a shrug.

"Bullshit!" Delahunt retorted. But she looked surprised with herself.

Price looked at Kurtzman, and now the faintest smile played on her lips. "Carmen says 'bullshit.'"

"I've checked it out," Kurtzman said, but his words slowed to a halt. "But come to think of it, I haven't completely checked it out."

"All right!" Akira Tokaido said to himself, but everyone heard him. "I *love* hacking into the CIA!"

Washington, D.C.

THIS TIME Hal Brognola wasn't asking for favors, he was making demands, in the form of orders from the President of the United States. Even the Central Intelligence Agency was beholden to the commander in chief, but you wouldn't think so from the director's response.

"This isn't a request," Brognola said shortly, interrupting the CIA head. "This is a courtesy call. We're doing you the favor of letting you know that we're temporarily making use of I-Gnat AC6B.''

There was an intake of breath. "Hal, how the hell do you even know about that device, let alone its classified serial number?''

"How I know is classified.'' Brognola regretted that, because he would have enjoyed explaining that his staff of hackers had penetrated Langley's electronic security and taken inventory of the agency's global UAV deployment.

"I'm the head of the CIA! What better security clearance do you want?''

"That's also classified.'' It was the kind of thing the CIA always said to everybody else, and Brognola couldn't help but feel some satisfaction at feeding Langley a spoonful of its own medicine. "Sorry about this,'' he added, but knew he didn't sound sincere.

"I bet you are. What's the target?''

"Classified.''

"How am I supposed to issue orders to my operational crew without knowing the mission?''

"We'll use a non-CIA crew.''

There was a pause, then a short snort. "No. Uh-uh. No way, Hal. That bird's too valuable, and you *can't* have a qualified crew.''

"We'll handle it.''

"You won't handle it! You don't know how! Even the GAAS guys don't know what all we've done to some of these birds! You put that thing up without one of my trained people, and it will come down in pieces. Then is DOJ going to buy me a new one?''

"Yes, we will. Listen, I know this is a slap in the face but it's a done deal. The orders have been delivered.'' There was a sort of splutter but Brognola barreled on. "To make it up to you I've been authorized to throw you a bone on this one, if you let me."

The spluttering stopped. The outrage transformed to guile, and Brognola could almost see the man's poker face through the phone lines when he said, "What kind of a bone?"

"If our plan is successful, you'll get a comprehensive report on what is going down in the Middle East."

"How comprehensive?"

"I'll give you the other side's details, not ours," Brognola said. "You'll know players, you'll get a timeline and documentation, you'll get physical evidence. You'll get nothing on our field personnel or their tactics."

"What's that going to do for me after the fact?"

Brognola said, "I make you an oath—it'll provide three or more major avenues of investigation."

"None of which will be new to us," the Langley head complained.

"Believe me, it will be stuff you've never heard of."

"You said 'if the plan is successful,'" the CIA man said. "What do I get if your plan fails?"

"You get months of watching network news footage of the murder of a million human beings."

The director thought about that. "Yeah. Okay, Hal," he said finally.

Brognola hung up and reviewed the conversation in his mind, wondering if he'd played his cards as skillfully as he thought.

The CIA director couldn't have halted an Executive Order, but he could have stalled its execution in various ways. It was good to have his grudging cooperation. The report Brognola would send Langley would be carefully constructed to reveal nothing about Stony

Man Farm or its operations. And the CIA surely knew there were U.S. intelligence and special operations agencies about which it knew nothing. Brognola had been careful not to make himself look like one of the organization insiders, but the director would logically assume he was.

What would that mean? Would the CIA take it upon itself to uncover a secret agency that interfaced with the Justice Department's Hal Brognola?

They probably would. It would be very illegal, but it would surely happen.

If there was one thing the CIA hated, it was being out of the loop.

Persian Gulf

ADMIRAL JAMES WEYER pushed into Jack Grimaldi's berth without knocking as the Stony Man Farm pilot was buttoning a blue flight suit, devoid of insignia. The suits were his attire of choice. If you asked him about it, he would launch into a story about Albert Einstein wearing an identical outfit day after day so he wouldn't have to waste any of his immense brainpower to co-ordinate his outfits each morning. He would say it with the trace of a grin that proved he was being self-deprecating.

He made the same grin now. "Hey, it's my favorite drinking buddy."

"Your friends are real string pullers, aren't they?"

Grimaldi's grin was gone. The admiral was looking at him a little too harshly, his stance too stiff. "When they need to be."

"Not sure I understand why they need to be."

"Are you asking me for a debriefing?"

The admiral enunciated slowly, "I'm not cleared to get a debriefing."

"Sorry about that."

"But it is my duty to know everything that goes on on this vessel that is pertinent to the activities of the crew. You'll leave out nothing in that regard. Understood?"

"Understood."

"Cough it up. Anything I don't already know."

Grimaldi leaned on the bulkhead and tried to come up with something to make the man more at ease. "You were at the conference call. You've got most of the story."

"Somebody mentioned Iraq during the call. All I know about is Iran and Egypt. Anything you can tell me there?"

Grimaldi thought about it. Giving away Stony Man Farm secrets was something he wasn't about to do, but this man did deserve to know the rest of it. "The Coldman organization originally had three targets. The Iraqi team was tracked down first and was taken out of action en route to Baghdad. As you heard, that was their target."

The admiral nodded, shoulders loosening by a millimeter, and he ushered Grimaldi out the door. They spoke in low voices during the fifteen-minute walk through the massive sea carrier.

"Your people took them down inside Iraq?"

"It was a U.S. team that nabbed them on Iraqi soil," Grimaldi admitted. "They managed to take them down before they could activate the devices, which was something, since we think their orders are to activate rather than surrender."

"Orders from whom?"

"We don't know. We're sure there are upper-level Mossad people running Coldman. We think there are higher-ups from the other Israeli intelligence agencies and the executive branch."

"How far up?"

"We don't know."

The admiral stopped in the hall and looked at Grimaldi, piercingly. The pilot endured it. The admiral finally admitted, "I guess you don't."

"I've been straight, Admiral," Grimaldi said. "I've held back only what I had to."

The admiral nodded. Although he wasn't used to playing escort to civilians on his own ship and didn't like cloak-and-dagger types, he liked this civilian straight shooter. He just hoped the team behind the man could do the job.

"I've been thinking about the phone conference with the President, and it's keeping me from sleeping," he said in a confiding voice that surprised himself, because the only people he spoke to like that were his father and brothers. "I've been thinking about the possible outcomes if these devices are detonated. If hostilities break out in the Middle East, it won't be a Desert Storm. It will be bigger. It could go nuclear all around."

Grimaldi nodded. "This carrier will be at the front."

"We'll be the one launching most of the nukes. And a few minutes later somebody will figure that out and we'll be on the bottom of the Persian Gulf. And if the explosion and the heat don't do the trick, then it just might be the fall that kills us, because if we get nuked the Gulf will get burned dry for miles in every direction."

Grimaldi pictured it. Millions of tons of Gulf water

transforming into superheated steam during the nuclear blast and billowing away, leaving a blackened crust where the sea floor had been. How long then until crushing waves rushed back in from the Gulf of Oman to fill the void?

"Don't worry about the fall, Admiral," he said. "I guarantee you, the explosion *would* do the trick."

They were strolling through a flight control suite and came to a set of doors labeled Authorized Personnel Only. Weyer nodded to the MPs, one on either side of the door and one at the desk outside it. The man at the desk took an electronic thumbprint to verify Grimaldi.

"One more thing I want you to know."

"Yes, Admiral?"

"I do like my boat."

"I understand," the Stony Man pilot said, and he felt the weight of responsibility that rested on this man's shoulders. If the situation reached the point of a nuclear exchange, what this man did and didn't do might decide the outcome.

He hoped it wouldn't come to that.

CHAPTER TWENTY-FIVE

Persian Gulf

Four men and two women, dressed as civilians, made up the carrier's I-Gnat crew. It had to have been maddening to get kicked out of their own playground, but it couldn't be helped. The signature on the orders might have helped. Still, Grimaldi felt vaguely uncomfortable with all six of them sitting on the other side of the soundproof glass watching him work. They were waiting for him to screw up. He felt like a DJ at a radio station with very poor ratings.

He waved once. Nobody waved back.

"We've got you, Jack," Aaron Kurtzman said in the headphones. "I'm seeing all your displays."

"Almost seems too easy," Grimaldi said. "I was sure somebody would try to screw things up, just to put us in our place."

"You're not the most popular guy on the ship?"

"I'm the least popular guy in the whole Middle East at the moment. It's that Sodomy guy in Iraq, then me."

"Uh-uh. I spoke too soon," Kurtzman said. "There's a controlled shutdown of some kind occurring. All our links to the system are freezing up."

A small red warning light flashed atop one of the

monitors. It was the only display of any kind visible to the operators in the waiting room, and Grimaldi watched their faces light up. He was concentrating on the controls and feeling helpless as the communications links turned themselves off one after another. Tiny windows on his display showed *Scheduled Communications Security Maintenance Initiated. Delay?* The only problem was that a built-in script of some kind made Grimaldi's cursor inoperable when he scrolled over the Delay option.

"These jerks gonna shut us down before we get started?" he growled.

"We're on it," Kurtzman said. "Yeah. We got it."

Like magic, Grimaldi saw an Override window appear and vanish and take a Maintenance window away with it. This repeated until all Maintenance windows were gone and the red light atop the monitors turned dark. Grimaldi gave another wave and a smile to the crowd in the waiting room. Now they were pissed off. A beautiful young blond woman sneered and gave him the finger.

"That's very ladylike, honey."

"I beg your pardon?" the deep, studious voice of Huntington Wethers asked.

"Talking to my fans, Hunt."

"I hope so, Jack," Wethers said. "We're up and running and we're ready for go."

"I see nothing."

But suddenly Grimaldi did see. A test pattern display to his right flickered alive and showed him a figure in ear protectors who jogged out of his view. That left him looking at the deck of the carrier. He found all the readouts from the robot aircraft were where they should be, so with a final check with the Farm he instructed the I-Gnat to take off.

She did it all herself. Grimaldi just watched the screens. When he saw the unmanned air vehicle hit a sudden head wind, he made a grab for the mouse to make a manual adjustment, only to find the craft had performed the function automatically.

In the good old days, like the 1990s when unmanned aircraft were first used successfully on a wide scale, the robots were piloted from the ground. They were even called Remotely Piloted Vehicles or RPVs back then. Now they were Unmanned Aerial Vehicles—UAVs— and they flew themselves, tracking themselves with GPS, communicating their data and receiving new orders via satellite links.

Grimaldi was engaged with familiar display windows—altitude, wind speed, GPS position, fuel gauge, attitude adjustment, automatic pilot—but there wasn't much he needed to do about it.

The unmanned I-Gnat aircraft had been one of the CIA's best tools for gathering intelligence around the world for years. The UAV was made by California's General Atomics Aeronautical Systems and equipped with synthetic aperture radar developed by Sandia National Laboratories. This imaging technology had been miniaturized into a system called Lynx that weighed just 115 pounds, making it ideal for I-Gnat. The unmanned CIA aircraft was eighteen feet, nine inches long with a forty-three-foot wingspan, and a power plant sufficient to lift it to a 25,000-foot cruising altitude.

The synthetic aperture radar allowed the aircraft to send back images with four-inch resolution or about 10 cm—as good as NRO's most capable spy satellites.

Better still, the imaging system saw through cloud cover and could even penetrate heavy rainfall. Another advantage was its flexibility compared to an orbital satellite. You could fly it where you wanted it, and its stealthy profile kept it hidden.

Its history of successes was impressive. It was used to keep an eye on troop buildup in Serbia, and it watched terrorists controlling a Japanese embassy in Peru in the late 1990s. The UAVs had been used by Stony Man Farm previously, and it didn't take Grimaldi long to spot recent CIA upgrades.

"We have electronic tagging capability," he said to whoever was listening.

"That's why we're using her," Wethers said. "We hope it's as good as the CIA claims in its internal reports."

Grimaldi watched as the aircraft moved over Iran. The view wasn't much from four miles up.

He walked to the door and leaned out.

"Got a problem?" asked the beautiful blonde.

"Yeah. A problem," Grimaldi agreed.

There were smiles.

"No coffee—can you tell me where to find some?" he asked, and the smiles were gone.

Stony Man Farm, Virginia

"STONY, THE CAR IS PASSING the checkpoint," Carl Lyons radioed.

"We've got the target," Kurtzman replied. "Hold on for a confirmation."

The I-Gnat's synthetic aperture radar shot out pulses quickly and continuously, comparing consecutive pulses to one another. The result was high-resolution-image output that equaled that of a virtual antenna the size of the distance the aircraft traveled between pulses. Atmospheric interference could easily be compensated for. What was most useful was the programmed Coherent Change Detection function that identified moving objects and even allowed them to be tracked.

Kurtzman watched the car settle into a cruising speed of about sixty-eight mph. With his workstation tied into the control systems on the carrier in the Gulf, Kurtzman applied an electronic lock on the car. The lock was software-based and relied on keeping the vehicle in sight at all times, but that wasn't a problem for the I-Gnat unless the Iranians chased her away.

Under normal circumstances that wouldn't worry Kurtzman, but the high level of air alert throughout the Middle East meant there might by eyes watching the Iranian skies capable of spotting the low profile I-Gnat.

For now they were in good shape. Sparse cloud cover meant the synthetic aperture radar could operate at an optimal Ku-band frequency without interference. The lock would stay reliable until the car reached heavy street traffic, after which Kurtzman's confidence level in continued tracking was low.

"I've got a Possible Pursuit message," Grimaldi relayed. With the UAV locked on target and on automatic pilot, he was on hand only to take manual control if a quick getaway was needed.

Kurtzman saw it, too. Sure enough, there was a vehicle about a quarter mile back that appeared to be pacing the Coldman team.

"Here, I'm going to pan on it and play back," Grimaldi said

"Good idea."

A moment later one of the auxiliary screens showed

a different angle on the view below. The second car could be seen going by the military checkpoint, then accelerating up to ninety-four miles per hour.

"He's in a hurry," Grimaldi muttered.

But not for long. When he closed in on the back of the Coldman team, he slowed quickly to a pacing speed. That had been two minutes ago. Back on the primary screen the live feed showed him still in place.

"You going to mark him, too, Bear?"

"You read my mind, Jack," Kurtzman answered as he clicked on the second vehicle and added an electronic marker to it. The display showed that it was a Priority Level Two mark. If the cars diverged the UAV would stay with the Coldman car, at Priority Level One.

"Able One, you seeing a tail on the Coldman team?"

"We saw a car not far behind it. Not long enough to say that it was a tail. You sure it is? There's just one way out of this town if you're not going to Tehran."

"Understood. We'll watch and save our judgments for later."

"Aaron," Wethers said from his workstation. "We've got interferometric mode capability. May not be any good, but why not take a look at what that vehicle looks like in 3D?"

"Can't hurt," Kurtzman agreed, although the imaging system's 3D mode was still in beta testing. A moment later a rendering appeared on screen.

"Isn't that a Chevette?" Wethers asked. He fed the rendering into software that would convert it to a widely used commercial format, then he launched a comparison search. "Well, no, it's a Soviet-era design made in Khazakstan and Russia until 1989. It's got a one-point-one-liter engine.''

"Somebody forgot to tell the driver," Kurtzman said. "He just pushed that thing past ninety."

"A ONE-LITER ENGINE?" Schwarz asked.

"I think this one may have been tweaked," Kurtzman added.

"More than tweaked. I bet there's nothing under the hood that's still factory," Schwarz said. "It's having no problem keeping up with the Coldman guys in the Audi."

"Who'd bother to drop that much effort into a car like that?" Blancanales asked.

"Somebody who didn't want to look like he was even capable of trailing a team of terrorists," Lyons replied. "This confirms our suspicions, Bear."

"We're already working on it. It might help to have the plate numbers."

Fifteen minutes later the opportunity presented itself, and Lyons steered their latest transport off the road. Theirs was also Russian-made but fifteen years newer—a Lada Niva SUV appropriated in the night from a small farm outside Ali Sadr. It didn't complain much about the rough earth and weed-hidden rocks. When Lyons brought the SUV skidding to a halt, Schwarz ejected himself from the back seat and jogged up a boulder-strewed hill. By the time he reached the top his head was pounding. He spotted the Coldman team following the long curve the road took to avoid this rocky patch of real estate.

They were already putting distance between him and the hill, and Schwarz flipped open the multipurpose tripod and made quick work of focusing the video pickup he'd mounted on it. Plugged into his wearable computer, it was already recording digital images as the Coldman pursuer drove into view below him and began receding. Schwarz swore under his breath when the video image snapped into view on the tiny right-eye LCD monitor, blurred beyond use even with the focus and zoom on the video pickup supposedly being controlled by the CPU in his pack.

Then Schwarz noticed that the rest of the world was also blurred.

"That can't be good," he said through an exhale, squeezing his eyes shut and then forcing them to focus. The world became clear again.

"I'm sending it now, Bear," Schwarz said as he isolated the best fragment of video and shuttled it to Stony Man over their encrypted communications link. He took an easier pace returning to the SUV.

Finally, when he was crawling into the back seat, Kurtzman said, "Yeah. Crystal clear. You do good work, Gadgets."

"I know that."

It took only a few minutes of fast driving to erase the lead their prey gained during the stop, and by then Price was on the line. "No leads here, Able. The plates are supposed to be on a courtesy van on a hotel in Esfahan."

"Stony Man, we've got another forty miles of empty highway," Lyons said. "Let's make our move. We do the tires on the tail and that will take them out of the picture. Then we go for the Coldman team."

"What's your plan there?" she asked.

"We'll pull alongside and put a flash-bang round through the window," Blancanales said. "It'll incapacitate them without destroying the device."

· "What if they crash and the car burns?" Price posed.

Lyons and Blancanales looked at each other for the answer. "You tell us," Lyons replied.

"The titanium cases will transfer the heat readily. They'll melt the foam and create toxic radioactive fumes that will escape under high pressure. You won't survive."

"So we have to wait until they decide to pull over?" Blancanales demanded.

"You have any ideas, Pol?" Lyons asked.

Blancanales lowered his brow, then shook his head. "I don't."

"Gadgets?"

Schwarz didn't answer.

Blancanales glanced into the rear.

"He sleeping?" Lyons asked, unable to find Schwarz in the mirror.

Schwarz was drenched in sweat and lay facedown on the rear bench seat with one arm dangling on the floor. He looked limp, like a man who'd been shot in the back.

"Oh, shit," Blancanales said.

CHAPTER TWENTY-SIX

Salwa Bahri, Egypt

Rafael Encizo didn't know much about where he was, but he knew it smelled bad. He'd been in some pretty horrific situations, but this was turning out to be one of the worst-smelling days of his life, starting with waking up in the rear of the rental SUV, after a night of fitful sleep, to find T. J. Hawkins snoring on his shoulder and fogging him with morning breath. Not long afterward he was slogging through the streets of a poverty-stricken village on the banks of the Nile in Upper Egypt, searching for the latest in a long list of Mossad safehouses and trying to avoid the raw sewage in the streets.

That safehouse had been abandoned, like most of the others they'd investigated in a long night spent driving south out of Cairo. They had to have made eight probes between midnight and five a.m.

Stony Man's plot to get the Cairo police involved hadn't succeeded one hundred percent, but it got them on the right track.

Phoenix Force caught up to their informant, a Security and Tourist Police officer outside Hulwan, parked in the shade of a palm in the parking lot of a gaudy roadside refreshment stand with signs in English and German. It was strictly a tourist place. A can of Coke was three dollars, but the officer had treated himself. Nibal Fissa was gone.

"Wrong man," the policeman said, smiling widely. "I waited to tell you. He was not the man you were looking for."

"Oh. You hung around to tell me that, did you?" McCarter asked.

"Yes. I thought I would do you the favor, since your request came through official channels." The officer toyed with the worn looking grip of his machine pistol, and he adjusted the green armband that identified him as Tourist Police.

"How exactly did you know this wasn't the person we were looking for?"

"He told me so."

McCarter glared at the cop. "I hope you earned a nice fee from our friend in the Mercedes."

The Egyptian assumed a mask of amusement, but he didn't meet McCarter's eyes. "Sir, you must be joking!"

"I sure wish you had done what we asked, friend," McCarter said. "Now we'll have to make you some trouble."

"What do you mean?"

Hawkins was already out of the SUV and taking rapid-fire snapshots of the officer and his car. They'd been half expecting this.

"I mean you took a bribe," McCarter said. "You sold us out."

"You have no right to call me a thief!" the officer returned, his gaze flitting from McCarter to Hawkins's picture-taking.

"I'm not going to be the one calling you a thief," McCarter told him. "We're sending our report and our photos to the American Embassy. The ambassador, who made this request personally, will send it to his friend who serves as your police chief or whatever you call the guy in Cairo. The head guy. He'll send it to a district supervisor, and he'll send it to your supervisor, and everyone is going to be very angry at you. Then what do you think is going to happen when you explain that you were just being helpful?"

The officer was almost trembling. Bribe-taking was no big deal, but bringing embarrassment on one's supervisors was a career-ending mistake.

"If you do that, I'll be without a job."

"Then I think you had better tell us the truth. All of it."

THE TRUTH WAS the officer had been paid about $300 to point the "people from the embassy" in the wrong direction. The officer was supposed to say Eissa and his family took the nearby turnoff to Egyptian Highway 23. They mentioned taking the 401 back north to the big Highway 03, then east to the port city of As Suways.

In reality, Eissa's car drove south, continuing along the Nile, and Phoenix Force had gone off after it, beginning a long night of searching safehouses. Kurtzman had unerased a list of them from the laptop in the Gezirah Island apartment—actually it had been parts of several automatic backup copies of the list, too fragmented to have been noticed by the software employed to permanently erase deleted files.

Almost immediately they knew they were on the right track. The first safehouse showed evidence that the Eloons had been there less than an hour before. The evidence was a litter of soiled bandages, used gauze and a woman's silk blouse that was torn open on one side and crusted with hours-old blood.

At dawn they decided to separate, each Phoenix Force commando getting his own rental vehicle and spreading out across the eastern bank of the Nile.

These safehouses were unmanned but provisioned with food, first-aid kits and sometimes weapons. Most had never been and never would be used. Phoenix Force needed more. They needed to know a destination.

Which was why Rafael Encizo was trying to step only in the dry places in the alley behind a mud-brick house in Salwa Bahri, and trying not to breath the fumes coming off the wet spots.

It was just past nine a.m., and the temperature was already closing in on one hundred. He leaned against the wall beside the shuttered window that faced the alley and dragged an arm over his forehead to wipe the sweat, and he listened.

There had been no sign of life, nothing to make this safehouse different from the others, but there was something itching his instincts. He was in traditional Arab robes for whatever benefit they could offer as a disguise, and the submachine gun was in his hand, tucked under a fold of cloth.

Encizo felt something like a bump coming through the heavy cushion of the dried mud-brick wall. It was subtle. He edged closer to the window until he was just out of sight of whatever was behind the loose weave of the reed shutters.

After a minute there was another bump, and Encizo

pictured a glass bottle being set down on a wooden tabletop.

He moved deeper into the alley. The shadow-shrouded door at the far end, where it backed against a building on the next street, started to open.

A puff of cigarette smoke issued from the door and drifted skyward, followed by another.

The man emerged, tucking the mini-Uzi into the back of his loose pants, and Encizo grabbed him around the throat. The Phoenix Force warrior pinched the throat closed, lifting and propelling the man across the alley into the adjoining mud-brick wall. The impact jolted the building and rendered the smoker unconscious. Encizo settled him in the alley muck and appropriated the mini-Uzi, then stepped inside.

It was surprisingly cool and dark, and Encizo squinted into the shadows as he moved to a shady corner. It took long seconds for his eyes to adjust, and by then somebody inside was worried about the noises. A quick word was spoken, a question, then a tall robed figure appeared from the front of the building. A mini-Uzi targeted the brightness of the door. Encizo stepped into him and lashed out with his stolen weapon. Hand bones crunched, and the Uzi clattered to the floor. Before the man could cry out Encizo stepped into him, shoulder to chest, and shoved his elbow through the man's gut.

The robed figure went to all fours, and Encizo dropped his body weight onto one knee in the middle of his back, which flattened the man. The man in the robe wasn't about to get up and shake off the trauma.

The Cuban moved quickly through the door, finding a dark room with closed shutters. A glass of some amber beverage sat on a short table, next to newspapers and a tiny television. In the next room were cots and an imitation of a European antique wardrobe. Encizo saw the wardrobe quiver slightly. Somebody was hiding inside.

He stepped into the next room and found himself at the front of the home. A small sitting area, more cots. The door was rarely used, bolted and secured with a wooden doorstop. Nobody else here.

Encizo waited. Whoever was hiding in the wardrobe didn't know he knew the person was there. That someone was hiding bothered him. Some local? A hired maid or cook scared by the sounds of violence? He shot the bolts, removed the doorstop and unlatched the door.

Whoever crept out of the wardrobe and into the front room was blinded when Encizo yanked the door open. Since he was behind the door he got none of the direct light, just a perfect view of the sneak.

The small man had a scarred face and a scraggly, pointed beard. His crusted eyes squeezed shut against the onslaught of the sunlight. He backstepped into one of the cots, one arm windmilling for balance while he pushed out the other to fire a palm-size revolver. Encizo delivered the hand a crushing blow that sent the revolver to the floor.

Encizo grabbed the little man, now squeaking in pain, and manhandled him onto his back on the convenient cot, then gave him a few feet of distance.

It was a little runt of a man, filthy enough to bring his own unique stench to the smell leaking in from the streets. He groaned, holding up the hurt hand and spitting out a stream of invectives.

"Speak English."

"Fuck you, American!"

"Where's Eissa?"

If he spoke any more English, Runt wasn't about to let Encizo know about it. He glared, then sprang up at the machine gun pointed at his chest. Encizo had seen it coming and lifted the barrel of the Heckler & Koch out of his reach, then brought the stock into the man's face when he collapsed on the cot, which upset him onto the floor.

"Did Eissa come here?"

"Who is Eissa?"

"Have it your way." Encizo rotated the man onto his stomach with one foot, then had him in cuffs in seconds.

"You're hurting me!" Runt squealed.

"That's nothing." Encizo brought him onto his back again, hard, which smashed his hurt hand underneath him. The man's jaw spasmed.

"Did Eissa come here?"

Runt sneered.

"Don't protect him. The man is a Mossad agent."

Runt grinned, his eyes darting. "I know that, but they don't." His eyes darted to the front of the house.

Encizo heard the newcomers outside and fell deeper into the darkness as they kicked the door. Two of them jumped inside, covering the room with their AKs. Runt shouted in Arabic, and they turned on the dark end of the room. They fired into the darkness but didn't survive long enough to find their target. Encizo returned a pair of bursts that took them down. Another figure came and went in the door just long enough for a burst that came closer to hitting Runt than Encizo. The ugly little man shouted angrily as he tried to struggle to his feet.

Encizo heard heavy steps from the rear of the house

and knew he was about to be squeezed. He snatched the little man off the floor, shook him violently to shut him up and sent him through the door.

Runt staggered dazedly and fell flat, then Encizo followed him out. The pair of gunners had their attention on Runt. Encizo took out the man on his left, then whirled and caught the other as he was squeezing the trigger. The Cuban saw his mistake. This guy had a shotgun. He should have been the first to go. He directed his next burst at the hand on the stock of the weapon and hoped for the best, watching the shotgun flash as the triburst slammed into the trigger hand and forced the barrel's aim downward. The rounds continued into the gunner and sent him to the ground.

Encizo felt his legs throbbing and forced them to work through whatever damage there was. He whirled again, covering the street, which was abandoned. The locals knew when to disappear.

As the gaunt little man got to all fours, Encizo pushed him down, which unleashed an epic decree of Arabic invective. The Cuban cut it short, using the collar of the man's robe as a handle and pushing him against the wall of the Mossad safehouse, facing him toward the front door. Voices from deep inside were getting angrier as they inventoried their dead comrades.

Two rushed into the street, discovered their mistake when they spotted Encizo and his prisoner, and turned their weapons on them both. The fact that Runt was in between didn't provoke any hesitation, and the little man shrieked. Encizo triggered the MP-5 SD-3 with the barrel resting on Runt's shoulder, the suppressed sound of the bursts shutting him up. The AKs clattered to the ground along with the gunners. The earthen street was baked so dry and hard by years of desert sun that the puddles of blood didn't soak into it.

The shouting told Encizo at least two more were inside, and he wasn't worried about them. They had no way out except the front door and through the alley, both in his line of fire. He pulled back the submachine gun without releasing his hold on Runt's collar, giving the little man a jab in the spine with the hot suppresser. "Your friends don't seem to like you any better than I do," Encizo observed. "They were gonna shoot you to get me."

"They are pigs!"

"Yeah, well, they aren't anything anymore. Time to talk."

"Talk about what?"

"Your right ear." Encizo shoved the suppressor against it. "Where is Eissa and his team?"

"How should I know?"

"They were here."

"They left an hour ago."

"How do you know they're Israelis?"

"I guessed."

"But you didn't let on or you'd be dead."

"I am no fool. I will give it time. When things settle down, I will let Eissa know that I know who he is, then he will see I can keep his secrets and he will pay well for my service."

"Yeah, I guess that would prove you're a real loyal type of guy," Encizo replied. "Never mind the whole part about betraying your country to the enemy."

"What secrets could the Israelis possibly steal from Egypt that would make a difference?" Runt asked contemptuously.

"He's not a spy," Encizo said, and had the urge to

give this guy the whole story—the potential for mass death and starvation, the destruction of Egypt—but then he knew it would be a waste of breath.

"Where did they go next?"

"Another house, a place to hide the one who is shot."

"Where?"

"I don't know."

"Where?"

"Why would they tell me that? I say I do not know!"

"You shouldn't know anything," Encizo said. "But you seem to have overheard a lot."

There was a scuff of shoes from above, and Encizo realized the men inside had some way onto the roof. He twisted and walked Runt farther into the street, aimed overhead and waited a heartbeat. The gunners jumped to their feet and pointed their weapons into the street. Encizo fired before they realized he was on to them. One knelt and slumped out of sight while another threw his hands into the air, sending an old desert rifle sailing away before he pitched over the edge and tumbled to the ground. Except for the robe, he looked like a stunt man in a Western movie overacting a dramatic death.

Runt heard the submachine gun cycle dry and made his move, twisting out of Encizo's grip and delivering a vicious kick at Encizo's stinging shins, but the Cuban avoided it with a step to the side, allowing the MP-5 to fall, then dragged Runt into his knees.

"Okay, Runt, I've had enough of your town's hospitality. Where did Eissa go next?"

"Do...not..." Runt gasped, then he looked into the

face of the Phoenix Force commando and changed his mind. "It is in Daraw. I do not know the address."

"The one who is shot—why didn't they just leave him here with a guard?"

"Did not trust us. It is a girl. The other house has no one working it. They said she was safe there because no one knows the place."

McCarter was in Daraw. Encizo needed to get in touch with the Phoenix Force commander and give him a heads up, if it wasn't already too late.

Encizo had one last question. "Why did Eissa have you people here? What's your purpose?"

"To get rid of you. But Eissa said it would be many men."

Sirens made Runt start to struggle again. It was about time the cops showed up, Encizo thought, and rapped Runt on the head with the stock of the MP-5, then tossed him unconscious on the remains of the man from the roof.

The Salwa Bahri law was going to poke through this mess and pin some of it on Runt, at least, and maybe make him the fall guy for all of it. The man was destined for some extended time in the infamous Egyptian prison system. Encizo slipped away wondering if it would have been more merciful just to kill him.

CHAPTER TWENTY-SEVEN

Daraw, Egypt

David McCarter was inside the safehouse in the town of Daraw, twenty miles to the south of Encizo, and he knew he wasn't alone.

Bloody bandages littered the floor in the kitchen. The remains of prepackaged meals eaten in haste littered a counter. It was a European-style flat, one of two in a duplex in the front corner of a small complex. Near the town's growing business district, it was still remote enough to offer a hidden drive for unseen comings and goings. Both flats in the duplex had been rented with Mossad funds, according to Stony Man's intelligence. The adjacent flat had proved to be empty.

But not this place.

At the bedroom door he took in the sight of a woman on a bed, under a white sheet, which had been tucked under her bare arms. Bottles of drugs and first-aid paraphernalia were scattered on the bedside table, along with bottles of water and boxes of food.

Her eyes popped open, and her hands moved under the sheets. McCarter dived to the floor and avoided the rounds that punctured the wall beside his head. He was on his feet as the woman tried to target him again, hampered by the sheet, and she cried out when he slammed the Mk 23 on her gun hand. He grabbed her handgun through the sheet and yanked both weapon and sheet off, flinging them into the corner.

McCarter stepped back, keeping the Mk 23 between him and her.

The woman was nude except for the mass of gauze and white tape adhered to her lower rib cage, and she made no effort to cover up.

"You're the one who shot me," she said.

McCarter didn't answer.

"Come back to finish the job?"

"If necessary."

"I'm going to take my pills. If you don't like it, shoot me."

She poured a palmful from a topless bottle and swallowed what had to have been ten tablets, washing them down with a half bottle of water. Then she fell back on the mattress, exhausted.

"What's the plan?"

"Like I'd tell you anything." She shot the words back.

"You've got nothing to lose."

"Or gain."

"I'll get you to a hospital."

"I'm bleeding internally. I'm not pulling through this one, mate," she said scornfully.

"You've lived for more than fifteen hours since getting shot. The bleeding can't be all that bad. Since you're not comatose, I'll bet you'll last long enough for them to pump you up with a couple pints of blood. Once that stabilizes you, they can go in and fix the leak."

"You make it sound so easy."

"It could be. Just come up with some answers. Think of it as purchasing sixty more years of life."

"Not interested. I'd rather just lay here and fade out, you know?"

"No," McCarter said. "I don't know at all."

"You know, no man's ever bested me. Not at anything," she said with a long sigh.

McCarter went to the table and took the pill bottle. Sedatives, prescription strength. The label said fifty, and the bottle was empty.

"You've already killed yourself, I see."

"Didn't want you to get anything out of me," she said, grinning sleepily. "But I wouldn't mind if you took advantage of me in other ways, Mr. British." She put her hands behind her head to lift her bare breasts.

"Screw a dying girl?" McCarter said. "Don't know if I've had a more repulsive come-on in my life."

The woman wasn't insulted. "Oh, come on, Mr. British. Why not indulge us both? You want this body to go to waste?"

"It's already a waste," McCarter said. He'd been tempted to take her to the hospital, whether she fought him or not. She was young. She had to be redeemable, no matter what came before now. But he knew it was too late for her.

"Listen, you can't allow yourself to go with this on your conscience. You can stop it now. Just tell me what you know. What's the plan?"

But it was too late. She was unconscious. It wasn't the ten pills he'd watched her take, but the forty pills she'd downed before he got there.

McCarter pulled out the headset and got on the radio, hoping the town was big enough to support one of the cell phone formats the system would access automatically. Hawkins had their main vehicle and its communications computer, a sort of multiformat mini-switching station, and he was on the line a moment later.

"Phoenix One, hold on," Hawkins said. "Rafe, David's on the system."

"Phoenix One, you in Daraw?" Encizo said. "I've got an alert that there'll be one of the Coldman agents at the safehouse there."

McCarter was listening to Encizo, but he was watching the pathetic figure on the bed. Too young. Too beautiful. Her stomach rose shallowly, then fell deeply, and didn't rise again.

"Am I too late, Phoenix One?" Encizo asked.

McCarter said, but to himself, "Yeah. Too late."

CHAPTER TWENTY-EIGHT

Luxor, Egypt

Gary Manning decided that it was a better thing to be poverty-stricken in Luxor than in Cairo, but not a hell of a lot better.

Somebody knocked on the heavily shaded window of the rental Suburban. Manning could see the hand but not the person it belonged to until he rolled down the window. The kid was under three feet. The squeegee was almost as tall as he was.

"You've got to be kidding me," he said before the kid could say a word.

The kid hadn't expected an English-speaking white man, but the sight of Manning got him excited. Nobody had more money than American tourists. "Wash car five dollars!" he blurted.

"Don't have dollars."

"No problem. Thirty-five pounds."

"Thirty-five Egyptian pounds is more like ten dollars U.S., but the point is, you could never reach my windows."

The kid had used up his working knowledge of English and didn't know what Manning was talking about. "Wash car! Wash car!"

"No, thanks," Manning said, and rolled up the window. There was a small sound as the kid slapped the Suburban angrily and walked away with his squeegee and a bucket of gray water.

He felt sorry for the boy, but if he paid the kid the Suburban would be surrounded by every peddler in the neighborhood trying to get his share of tourist money.

The safehouse was silent, a small mud-brick hovel among the endless haphazardly scattered hovels that made up a sort of suburb of Luxor.

The safehouse was somewhat unusual in that it had a garage, with steel doors that unfolded like hinged window shutters. The doors were padlocked. There had been no sign of movement.

Manning glanced in the side mirror and spotted the car window washer gathered with a knot of other boys, none of them older than eight. One of them was squinting at the Suburban. Was he jotting down the license plate?

Why would he do that?

Manning rolled that over in his mind. Well, if these kids spent their days on the streets, they'd be good at monitoring the comings and goings of strangers. Their services would be a cheap buy. Information they gathered would be useful to lots of people. Maybe the cops or local crime organizations or both. It might even be Eissa who employed them, although there was no evidence any Coldman team spent much time here. There was nothing to show they had used the safehouse today.

Manning stepped out of the car.

The kid with the pencil and the three-inch ringed notebook hurried to the group, but the boy with the squeegee, the youngest of them all, stepped forward with a broad smile.

"Car wash?"

"No, thanks. Any of you speak English?"

The kid with the notebook gave him a wary nod.

"You take the numbers of all the cars that come through?"

"Why do you want to know?"

"I want to buy some information."

That got their interest. Even the car washer knew the word "buy."

"Okay. I will sell you information."

"Tell me what kinds of things you write down in there," Manning said, nodding at the notebook.

"Anything strange," the kid said. "Cars and people. Police times."

"You mean police patrols? When they come through here?"

"Yes. And when strange police come and when they come through here when they are not supposed to."

Manning got the picture. "I'll bet there's a man in your neighborhood who pays you to write these things down."

"Yes," the kid said very cautiously.

"I don't want you to tell me who he is," Manning said. He had better things to do than harass the local crime boss. "But I do want you to tell me if you wrote down anything about a car that came to that house today."

The kid followed Manning's finger to the Israeli safehouse.

"No person lives there," the kid said uncertainly. "But someone did go there today."

"And?"

"They went away again."

"And?" The kid clearly had more to say on the subject.

"They came in one car and left it in there. They left in a different car."

Manning grinned. "Write it down in your note-book?"

The kid grinned, too, and hard-bargained Manning out of fifty Egyptian pounds. When the deal was done, Manning had the notebook page in his front pocket, but he didn't put the wad of cash away. The boys eyed it. Manning was thinking that Stony Man Farm could afford to buy this bunch a higher standard of living for a day or two.

"I've got another offer, and it's for all of you." He told the English speaker to translate his request. They took the money and departed, promising not to return for one hour.

Manning wasn't taking the kid's word for it that the Eissas had come and gone. He approached the white-washed mud-brick house from up the street at an angle that exposed him to none of its shuttered windows.

What Manning didn't see was the young man in a window of a nearby house, watching him through the telescopic sites of a tripod-mounted weapon.

Halim Eissa. The undercover Mossad agent swore beneath his breath.

Only one of the commando team had showed up. That was no good. Halim Eissa had hoped to get the drop on the whole gang, bombard them with enough 40 mm HE grenades to wipe them off the face of the earth. As far as he was concerned, they were all that stood in the way of the success of the Coldman cell in Egypt.

Well, at the very least he was going to get some answers out of the lone man. Then send him to hell.

When Manning was at the garage, he checked for a gap to see through, but found none. He listened at the windows, making a full circle around the house without seeing signs of occupation.

A hard kick with the bottom of his foot sent the front door flying open. Manning followed the door in, covering the empty living room, then made a quick circuit of the tiny house. There was no sign of recent occupation. The Coldman team had come and gone fast, stopping just long enough to switch vehicles. Nevertheless he devoted five minutes to a thorough search, looking for anything that would help them out. The search might have saved his life.

By the time he left the single bedroom his eyes were accustomed to the shady gloom of the interior, which enabled him to spot the unlooked-for dot of red against the back wall of the living room.

He froze. The dot didn't move, and it was coming in through the front door, still standing wide open. A security laser didn't make sense. What else could it be but a laser aiming device?

Manning retreated into the bedroom and used his field glasses to probe the windows of the houses on the street. He found the gunner tucked into the darkness of a nearby window. The big Canadian made out just a slice of the man but could tell he was watching the Coldman safehouse with his own binoculars. He didn't know Manning was watching him.

The Phoenix Force commando knew it wouldn't take long before the guy got suspicious. He had to work quickly to turn the tables. He regretted leaving the M-16 A-2/M-203 in the Suburban, but it wasn't as ideal as the MP-5 for a room-to-room probe. Manning would make do with the highly accurate Mk 23.

The hardest part would be getting a clean shot. He opened the window glass, then used the razor edge near the tip of the combat knife to score two of the reed shutter slats—not easy to do without making the shutters move. Then he waited for the gunner to look away slightly so he could pull out the shutter pieces. The opening was about three inches square.

He took a stance with his gun arm braced by his forearm, the only supported stance that allowed him to see and fire through the small opening. At the moment he found his mark, his mark found him. Manning saw the man adjust his binoculars quickly, looking at the bedroom window, and he knew his shutter handiwork had just been noticed. He fired before the man could pull himself from the line of fire.

Then Manning bolted from the safehouse.

HALIM EISSA FELT the floor rush up to his body even though he didn't feel the gunshot. He was weak, weaker than he had ever felt before. He was helpless.

With one hand he pulled the paper tab out of his pocket and gripped it between his teeth, careful to avoid the swollen pocket in the middle. With the other hand he attempted to push himself to his knees.

There was blood on his hand, and his arm wouldn't work. The shot was in his right shoulder, and it wasn't a mortal wound. Halim Eissa felt a wave of relief, then panic. He might live, and he wanted to live!

But he couldn't allow himself to be questioned by the commando. He used his left hand to push himself off the ground, then walked on his knees to the tripod, using one of its legs to drag himself to his feet.

The commando was sprinting out of the safehouse. Their eyes met, and Eissa grabbed for the trigger on the grenade launcher as his adversary fired an on-the-run burst from the submachine gun, forcing Eissa to drop. The Israeli heard the detonation of the HE. The paper tab in his teeth was getting soft from his saliva, and he used his tongue to position the little liquid-filled pouch between his teeth. Then he waited.

MANNING DIVED and rolled as he heard the grenade expel from the launcher. He was still trying to curl into a low-profile ball when the round hit the safehouse and exploded, showering him with debris. Then he was on his feet again. A quick glance told him the house was obliterated, but the mud walls had turned to powder in the explosion. His body might end up black and blue from the fallout, but he wasn't slowed.

When he crashed into the gunner's house, he found the man lying on the floor trying to reach the handgun holstered under his one functional arm. When Manning arrived he gave it up.

The Coldman mole chewed on something, swallowed it, then spit out a soggy wad of paper.

"I sure am sorry to see you," Halim Eissa said.

He was dead in seconds.

Manning stood over the corpse, feeling as if he had failed. He had nothing except a semicredible license-plate report on the Coldman vehicle. It wasn't much to go on.

He sure hoped somebody had better luck this morning than he did.

CHAPTER TWENTY-NINE

Luxor, Egypt

"We have nothing," Manning complained.

"We do have that license plate," Barbara Price replied coolly.

"Well, we have a license plate, no problem then," Manning said. "Just call in the Egyptian cops for an assist. They were so helpful last time."

"It got screwed up, but it did get us going in the right direction," Hawkins suggested.

They had reassembled in Hawkins's rental Toyota Landcruiser GX9 to present one dismal field report after another. The mood was gloomy. Hawkins's comment made nobody feel better. Parked Nile-side in the lot for a minor tourist attraction, some monument erected by a New Kingdom pharaoh three thousand years ago, they found no comfort in the day that was unfolding around them. It was so stifling hot that the interior was in the nineties even with the Landcruiser's air-conditioning compressor straining at the rivets.

Stony Man Farm, Virginia

BARBARA PRICE FELT the mood of gloom halfway across the planet.

"All right," she said. "Let's go over our list of leads."

Manning barked, "License plate. There. The list is done."

"I think we've given full value to the self-pity angle, so let's move on to something new, okay?" she said. She was in the War Room with Kurtzman and Katzenelenbogen, pouring over printouts of any and all evidence they had come up with. It was Kurtzman who jumped in.

"We still have our most important lead," he said. "We know the target."

"The dam?" Price asked.

"I don't know how much faith we can put in that now," David McCarter told them. "They know they've got somebody hot on their tail. Why risk a direct strike on the dam?"

T. J. Hawkins spoke. "Yeah. They can blow the thing anywhere in Lake Nasser. The result is the same. It leaves Egypt without usable water. The fallout from the weapon will contaminate the lake and all the water passing through the basin for years."

"Years? I don't think so." It was Encizo. "We're talking about particles, right? Wouldn't the particles get washed downstream? Wouldn't lake contamination clean itself up?"

"Yeah, I guess it would." Hawkins sounded unsure. "Depends on the water flow. Nasser is a lake. I don't know if there's a real positive current from the feed on the south end to the dam at the north. Hell, I don't know what I'm talking about. Aaron?"

"Not my area of expertise, either, but Rafe, you might have brought up an important point," Kurtzman said. "What would the bomb do to the lake? The answer might show us what the Coldman target is."

"You're right, Bear," Katzenelenbogen said. "Ori Flatt told me the target was Aswan, but that might have been just some general statement he overheard. Maybe the target wasn't the dam at all. Maybe all they needed to do was get a bomb into Nasser. If the water flow is too slow to clean the lake, it would do the job the Coldman organization wants."

"You're right, and we need some outside expertise to clear this up," Price said. "We have to answer this question soonest."

"I don't buy it," Calvin James said. "Sorry, but Nasser is too easy a target."

"Too easy?" Price asked.

"Lake Nasser is two hundred miles long, and the last fifty miles of it is in the Sudan," James said. "If the Israelis wanted to poison the lake, they could have figured out a way to get the devices into the southern end of the lake in Sudan. They wouldn't go to all the trouble of planting moles in Egypt. It doesn't add up."

Kurtzman nodded. "You're right, Cal. Not only would Sudan access have been easier, it would have been more effective. The contamination would have covered the lake from one end to the other. It would have been a lot more sustaining."

"On the other hand," James continued, "I think we might be on to something."

"Such as?" Price asked.

"I'm not sure," James said slowly. "Something's missing. There's a puzzle piece I think we overlooked."

"I get the same feeling, Cal," Katz agreed. "Maybe we've been jumping to too many conclusions."

"We need some consultation on this. We need to computer model it," Price said. "Might tell us something, might be a waste of time."

"Right now," Manning said, "what else have we got?"

They all knew the answer, but Manning offered it anyway. "We got nothin'."

Denver, Colorado

KENNETH MORGENSTERN picked up the phone and heard a voice out of the past.

"Dr. Kenny, how are you these days?"

"Whoever you are, you sound just like this guy I knew named Hunt Wethers. But of course he vanished off the face of the earth and was never heard from again, so who are you?"

It was the kind of thing Dr. Kenny said to old friends who hadn't called in a while. Not that he'd been dialing up Hunt Wethers too often. But he'd been very busy.

"I need a favor from you, Dr. Kenny."

"You need to borrow money?" Another one of the kind of things Dr. Kenny liked to say.

"A professional favor."

"Wow. That's unusual. You sure you remember what my profession is, Hunt?"

"I remember. You specialize in archaeogeology."

There was a knock on the door, and two men in dark suits and shaded glasses entered the cramped, chaotic office.

"Dr. Morgenstern?" one of them asked. No, demanded.

"Yes, I'll be with you in a minute. Have a seat."

They pulled out badges.

"Hunt, hold on, I think I'm about to be arrested."

"We're Department of Justice, Doctor."

Morgenstern took a few seconds to process that. "And?"

"I sent them, Kenny," Wethers said.

"*You* sent them?"

"They have a confidentiality agreement I would like you to sign."

The agent put away their badges, and one of them pulled out a thin tube of paper that unrolled into a document. Some sort of a contract. The stationery was from the United States of America Department of Justice.

"You want to explain this to me, Hunt?"

"Glad to, Kenny. But I can't go into details. We're in a hurry."

"In a hurry to do *what?*"

Huntington Wethers started explaining.

Stony Man Farm, Virginia

"I'M E-MAILING YOU the IP you'll need to patch into Bertha Blue. That's what we call the IBM mainframe here," said University of Denver geophysicist Kenneth Morgenstern. "I included my personal password and user name so you'll have full access."

"We're already in, Kenny," Wethers said. "User name *HuntW*."

"Oh. So you are. I see your login. Well, I'm pulling up what you need. Shouldn't take long."

"How long is long?"

"Kenny, that's my co-worker," Wethers explained. "Call him Aaron."

"Hello, Aaron. Just a few minutes. Most of the software we'll need is already built, of course."

Kurtzman was about to say more when the light for the third line blinked and added the newcomer to the conference call.

"Dr. Jules, thanks for joining us. Dr. Morgenstern is already on the line with us."

"I hope I can be of help. I'm a bit surprised by all this," Adam Jules said.

"You and me both, Jules," Morgenstern said. "What's your field?"

Wethers broke in. "Dr. Jules is a weapons researcher at Aberdeen. Dr. Morgenstern is a geophysicist at the University of Colorado. I hope you both understand why this is serious and why time is crucial?"

"Yes, sure, Hunt, don't get your panties in a bunch," Morgenstern said. "Here you go."

The wall display showed a tight translucent gray grid and the image of Lake Nasser. In the lower right-hand corner was a white window full of alphanumerical strings. "Impressive, Doctor," Kurtzman said.

"It's nothing," Morgenstern said. "You seeing this, Jules?"

"They've got my PC patched in. I'm seeing it," Dr. Jules said. "But what does it do?"

"It models the behavior of the river," Morgenstern explained. "We've got every major lake, ocean and river in the world on this system. And most important creeks, washes, arroyos, what have you. We have records of flow, historical behavior data, everything you could want. Billions of datum, all to model water behavior and potential for misbehavior. Floods are always our biggest concern, but we're also watching for possible course changes. Rivers change course a lot more frequently than we think they do. It's how they are. But it's disastrous for somebody who is living where the river wants to go. We've got T3s dedicated to bringing in meteorological data, but that all gets sent preprocessed by NMS.''

''That's fine, but what do you need to do to model the dispersion of suspended particles?'' Kurtzman asked.

''I don't need to do anything. The programming is in place.''

''It is?''

''What do you think dirt is, Aaron? It's particles. How a river carries and deposits its dirt has a lot to do with how it behaves over the course of time. So, yeah, we know how to model the distribution of particles. Just tell me how big they are, what they weigh, how they're shaped. All that.''

''That's why I'm here,'' Jules said. ''It gets theoretical, since it's never been done, but here are my best estimates.''

For the next five minutes the conversation was beyond the understanding of the two Stony Man cybernetics experts. Morgenstern and Jules talked atomic weights and adhesion characteristics of near-microscopic particles.

Barbara Price came in with Hal Brognola and Yakov Katzenelenbogen, and they silently took seats to view the demonstration. Finally some sort of consensus was reached by the scientists, and Morgenstern plugged in his numbers.

''It's quick and dirty, but under the circumstances I don't know how we could get much more accurate, no matter how much time we had,'' Jules said. ''Not without actually studying a cobalt detonation.''

"Let's hope we never have that opportunity," Wethers intoned.

"So here's your first model," Morgenstern says. "This shows us what would happen if the bomb went off in the center of the lake anytime over the next ten days. We're reasonably certain what weather conditions will be like because they don't change much in that part of the world. We know water volumes going into and out of Nasser."

A small sphere of blue dots materialized at a point over the center of the long, jagged lake. It drifted, then was gone as the time lapse showed an hour passing every five seconds.

"The cobalt's spreading south as well as north," Dr. Jules noted.

"Sure it will," Morgenstern said. "Lake Nasser doesn't flow fast enough to prevent it. A lake that big, you get all kinds of different water currents."

The blue dots were moving into the Nile River, the particles thinning out. The simulation speeded up, and it showed a nearly consistent saturation of cobalt particles from the dam to the Nile Delta in under a week.

"Can you speed it up even more, Kenny?"

"Sure."

The days and weeks began to fly by, and the blue in the lake dissipated. The Nile became less blue as the particles were carried into the Mediterranean, which diluted them. An environmental disaster for the Med, Kurtzman thought, but by the end of the simulation it was clear that Egypt was relatively clear of contamination in less than a year.

"Dr. Jules, tell me what residual radiation would look like on this," Kurtzman said.

"Can't do it. There's no data on which to base an

estimate. With the particles washed away, the land might actually be livable again. Might.''

"Hold on, please, Doctors." Kurtzman turned off their microphones so the Stony Man team could converse freely. "Model A is a bust. Coldman wants Egypt out of the picture for a lot longer than a year."

"I agree," Price said. "Let's see Model B."

Kurtzman turned their mikes on again and asked Morgenstern to proceed. The screen blanked out, then the computer-generated Lake Nasser was back. This time it showed the device detonating in close proximity to the Aswan Dam and destroying it utterly. The dam blast was demonstrated by the appearance of a blue cloud. It drifted and settled, and the water became contaminated. The blue discoloration of the Nile stretched all the way to the delta. Onscreen it took no time at all, although the real-time count was several days.

If this model was programmed to count mortality rates, Kurtzman wondered, how many would it show? Twenty million dead? Thirty million? Then over the following weeks and months, how many more? Another twenty million?

Then something surprised him.

"It's cleaning itself out faster," he observed.

"Of course it is," Morgenstern said. "They blew the dam. The water's pouring through fast. The Nile stays agitated, and the cobalt doesn't settle. The Nile's back to normal in just a few months. By normal I mean the river reverts to its natural, predam cyclic pattern of floods."

"Hold on, please." Kurtzman killed the microphones again.

"Now I don't know what to think," Kurtzman said in frustration, turning to the others.

"I thought we had it figured out," Price said. "Model A is clearly more deadly to Egypt. But not deadly enough."

"In terms of the radiation danger, A's the winner. Model B has the most long-term impact, though," Brognola said. "The radiation is gone, but so is the dam. The water supply is insufficient for the population."

"I considered that," Huntington Wethers said. "What I know about the population along the Nile and the possibility of alternate water sources, well, I make a rough estimate of thirty million dead in the first year. Maybe forty million. That's half of Egypt. The compromised Nile will support the population that is left in Model B. There will be hot spots where water gets trapped after the initial flood tide, but most of the land is livable. Yes, it is horrific, but it's over and done with, and Egypt survives."

"If we know that, then Coldman knows that," Brognola growled. "Lake Nasser or the Aswan Dam make no sense as a target, not when they could better cripple Egypt by simply detonating the device in the middle of Cairo."

Yakov Katzenelenbogen had been silent, but he sat up suddenly. "We went with computer modeling to find out what pieces of the puzzle we were missing," he said, impatience evident in his voice. "Let's let the people who know tell us what those pieces are, for God's sake. Aaron, turn us on."

Kurtzman turned on the microphone.

"Doctors, you don't know me. Call me Yakov. Kenny, I have a feeling you've got a Model C for us."

"I've been waiting for somebody to ask, Yakov. I started thinking like a terrorist and came up with my own target. I haven't viewed the model, but I know what we're going to see.''

"So what's the target?'' Dr. Jules asked.

''The Aswan Iron Plant,'' Morgenstern said. ''You nuke it, and you disrupt substrata for miles. The dam gets destroyed just as completely as in Model B, but that's just one of many openings that get punctured by the blast and the unsettled geography. Instead of a single wall of water tearing down the Nile channel, you've got several flood tides going who knows where.''

''Let's see it,'' Katzenelenbogen said.

Without another word, Model C began to unfold. The now-familiar blue sphere materialized, not on the dam but close by. The brownish-blue water began to ooze out of fourteen distinct new openings on the northern end of the massive man-made lake.

The water turned blue as the particles settled, and the Nile flooded north with the unstoppable momentum of millions of tons of pent-up energy. Some water streams came to flat desert, where they spread and slowed, depositing cobalt 60 in vast lakes. The water dried and was gone in days as the simulation progressed. The cobalt remained.

Other streams found low places in the land where they formed new lakes, trapping the cobalt temporarily, only to overflow, and the stream continued north. Within a few hundred miles of the lake all the independent water flows had come to a halt or rejoined the Nile River. With the force of four rivers in place of one, the Nile burst over her banks again and again, contaminating millions of acres of land. From Aswan to Cairo, every city was flooded.

The flooding abruptly halted, leaving a blanket of contamination.

"We're at twenty-three days," Morgenstern said. "Most of the water is in the Nile Valley, but the volume is so great the river cut itself a straighter path. You see where some of the old meanders have straightened. Now it's really moving fast. Wow. Look at that."

The blue that had been shading the waters of the computer-modeled Nile began lightening, and then it was gone in just a matter of days. But the unprecedented flooding had turned the digital Egypt blue in an irregular path miles wide and hundreds of miles long.

"Here's the scenario," Morgenstern says. "My model shows fourteen containment breaks, some in the substrata, that allow Nasser waters to spread north. Could be less. Could be more. Most of them will reseal as the rock settles, but a few will be eroded by the flow until they're permanent. In other words, these holes can't be plugged."

"I'm seeing eighty-five to ninety percent of the inhabited Nile Valley made unlivable—contaminated or surrounded by contamination," Dr. Jules said. "No Egyptian population center will survive except the oasis towns and the Gulf coast cities."

"Alexandria may or may not be livable, depending on the new water channels that develop in the delta," Morgenstern added. "I can figure out the possibilities if needed."

"Thank you, but I think we know what we needed to know," Price said. "Thank you for your time, Doctors."

"I hope we've helped," Dr. Jules said. "Good luck."

"Yes. Good luck. I'll be watching the news," Morgenstern added. He sounded like he wanted to say more.

What more was there to say?

CHAPTER THIRTY

Stony Man Farm, Virginia

Kurtzman was staring at the screen and holding on to the arms of the wheelchair as if he were about to hoist himself up and start pacing.

Yakov Katzenelenbogen entered the Computer Room. "Okay, let's see it, Bear."

Kurtzman nodded at the screen.

Katz leaned across the computer expert to squint at the screen. It didn't take long to read, but he read it many times. It was Arabic.

"I didn't want to trust my translation software," Kurtzman said.

"It says, *This day it becomes cold at midnight.*"

"Then I guess my translation software got it right."

"I got your message. What's happened, Aaron?" It was Barbara Price, coming through the door in a hurry.

"E-mail message came in to the laptop at the Eissa hotel suite in Cairo. We've been monitoring it and grabbed the message."

She glanced at the screen. "It doesn't say much."

Katzenelenbogen straightened. "It's a timetable."

Western Iran

IT WAS CARL LYONS WHO made the decision to operate, but he let Rosario Blancanales do the actual cutting. The operation happened in a rocky niche, where they parked hidden from the road in a place where the iffy satellite connection was stable. A Navy surgeon on temporary rotation at Stony Man Farm talked Blancanales through the procedure. The night was cool, but Blancanales couldn't stop sweating.

"It's not as hard as it sounds," the doctor said reassuringly. They had located the swelling, shaved off a patch of hair and drenched everything in rubbing alcohol to sterilize it. "It's just a simple cut to relieve the pressure."

"A simple cut into Gadgets's skull," Blancanales said under his breath. Then he made the cut.

They shot Schwarz with antibiotics and watched him in shifts throughout the night. No more fever bothered him, but he didn't regain consciousness. The Navy doctor told them everything sounded fine from the vitals they were constantly relaying to him.

It was almost noon when they got the news that the Coldman team, still under I-Gnat watch, was pulling out of their campsite a few miles down the road. Able Team was on the road in minutes, with Schwarz laid out in the back seat.

"I'll take it very personally if he doesn't pull through," Blancanales said.

"We might not pull through ourselves. Then you won't have anything to worry about."

They closed to within a mile of the Coldman car to find its mysterious tail still in place, and the trio of vehicles, each unaware of its companions at the rear, continued west across Iran in no particular hurry.

The unmanned aircraft started to struggle to stay locked on the vehicles as traffic grew dense around the city of Tabriz. Finally it grew befuddled, and the I-Gnat turned and headed home.

The city streets were crowded with people and cars. Lyons muscled the Niva SUV through the city traffic, struggling to keep the Coldman car in sight without announcing his presence. The Israelis started to play games, stopping in one place, waiting a while, driving somewhere else.

"Maybe they're stalling for time," Barbara Price suggested after she explained the e-mail intercepted from the Coldman PC in Egypt. "They don't want to get to their staging place too soon and risk attracting attention."

It was hours before the car stopped for good, in front of some low-rise apartments. The tail car pulled past the Coldman team and was gone.

The Israelis climbed from the vehicle and took the suitcases from the trunk as if they were simply unpacking after a holiday. Lugging the suitcases into the apartment, they didn't see Able Team's SUV, which was parked around the block.

"Nobody's home," Lyons observed. "That building looks condemned."

Blancanales felt Schwarz's neck. "He's still alive."

"I'll take that as a good omen," Lyons said. "Let's go get a nuke."

It was a residential district, and in the encroaching dusk they didn't look out of place walking along the roadside. The locals didn't notice them. The man in the tail car, parked around a hidden corner, watched them warily as they walked right toward the place he was staking out.

When the pair strode to *his* building and drew their weapons, Rasool Far's worst fears were realized.

The device was at risk.

His reason for being there was to reduce that risk.

He went stalking the hunters.

Aswan, Egypt

THE ASWAN Iron Plant was built on a deposit of iron ore estimated at 380 million tons. The density of the deposit made the huge project appear to be financially viable when it broke ground in the late 1990s at an estimated construction cost of $700 million. The expense was shouldered by three international steel conglomerates sharing ownership with a host of small players with minor stakes in the plant.

By mid-2001 the Aswan Iron Project was at a virtual standstill, its chairman and deputy chairman jailed on accusations of profiteering and funds misappropriation. The shell facility progressed slowly as debates over the viability of the project surfaced. New evidence came to light showing the level of impurities in the ore was much higher than originally reported. The project was too expensive to complete and too expensive to abandon.

Years after the megaproject broke ground it remained in limbo. What work did progress at the site was strictly maintenance, enough to keep the equipment from deteriorating while the stakeholders wrangled over the problem.

Calvin James was watching one of the maintenance workers from almost a mile away. The man strolled lazily through the silent, grimy hulks of conveyors and earthmovers. He was the only thing moving for miles, and James thought he looked like the last man on Earth in a science-fiction movie about the aftermath of nuclear war.

Then the last man on Earth fell dead.

James squinted into the field glasses, silently telling the maintenance man to stand up, brush his trousers, laugh at himself for tripping over his own two feet. Then the blood began to puddle around the fallen man.

"Phoenix Four here," he whispered into his mouthpiece. "They've arrived."

"Locations?" McCarter asked.

"Unknown. I just watched them take out a maintenance worker. I never saw the sniper. Wait a second." James peered into the glasses again. The blood pooled under the man's chest. The bullet had to have entered from the back. "The sniper was south of the entrance, and that's about as much as I can tell you."

"Stay sharp."

James crept down the rocky grade to the drop-off that marked the edge of the massive quarried site. The irregular square was a mile on each side and three hundred feet deep. It seemed an unlikely target for the Coldman device unless you were aware how the special characteristics of this geology would magnify the effect of the nuke.

If Stony Man hadn't figured it out, he and the rest of Phoenix Force would be hanging around the Aswan Dam with their thumbs up their noses until it was way too late.

It might still be too late. There was no room for mistakes. He allowed his thoughts to center on the mission, the goal. It was the mission that mattered. Not regrets, not near misses. The lanky black commando's

SEAL experience asserted itself as he stepped into open space and allowed himself to plummet.

His feet hit the steep hillside of rocky rubble, and he skied it with his arms waving until he managed to skid to a halt and regain his balance, forty feet down. Then he descended with long, controlled steps that still took him down the pebbly wall faster than he could ever match on level ground, bringing him to the bottom in a miniavalanche of fist-size rocks. He bolted for the nearest office trailer and waited, listened and scarcely breathed.

The entrance into the pit had been the first big risk, but there was no way for them to get into the project site without exposing themselves. McCarter had guessed the Coldman team would be watching for trouble from the rock cut entrances, not over the walls. Still, the complete exposure made the chance of discovery dangerously high.

McCarter and Manning were coming in from the south, rappelling down a sheer cliff face. Encizo and Hawkins were entering via a channel cut in the rock for water pipes, on the west end of the site. James had volunteered for the north face insertion, where the piles of scrap rock meant he didn't need his mountain climbing gear at all.

James checked his watch. Ten minutes until the next scheduled radio check. He didn't relish doing nothing for that long.

He heard footsteps. James homed in on a man strolling by on the other side of the mobile home. He wasn't a Coldman mole or a mercenary. His oil-drenched outfit and the toolbox in his hand told James he was another of the maintenance crew. James knew the man was in mortal danger. The Coldman team was probably murdering every worker on-site to reduce the chance of problems.

He slung his weapon on his shoulder, ready to snatch the man silently. The worker could wait out the events in an office trailer.

The footsteps paused. The Phoenix Force commando dropped to the ground and looked under the trailer as the maintenance man toppled, wide eyes glimmering with confusion before the light in them died. James never even heard the shot.

He swore silently, and then it occurred to him that the corpse was sprawled in the open. Would the Coldman agents leave their murder victims exposed? Probably not. Somebody would come soon to hide the body.

It was time to start culling the ranks.

NIBAL EISSA FELT ALIVE and dead at the same time. The excitement of reaching the end of this long undertaking melded with his numb ambivalence to his own impending death, but these emotions paled beside the thrilling satisfaction of holding the power of death in his hands.

Eissa had known he might need to stay with the device until the moment of detonation. Now, on top of all his rampant thoughts, he felt himself weakening, longing to put the device and his death behind him, take a new route that offered him anything more than the termination of his existence.

But he wouldn't do it. He'd committed himself long ago, and sacrificed all those years of his life to put him, and the device, in this place at this time. He wouldn't allow that to go to waste by not being here if and when Coldman activated.

If and when were the words the people of Coldman

used repeatedly, to prove time and again to themselves that they wouldn't commit this horrible act unless the survival of Israel depended on it. They weren't like the Nazis. They wouldn't commit mass murder in the name of some philosophical or political idea, only in self-defense. Nibal Eissa realized that he had long ago ceased to believe the *if and when*. There wouldn't be an *if*.

The possibility of the Coldman leadership deciding not to use the devices was unthinkable, just as deserting his suicide post was unthinkable. It would mean all this effort was wasted.

Eissa wouldn't let it be wasted. If the leadership didn't push the button from their safe havens in Tel Aviv and Jerusalem, then Eissa would do it himself.

The last hot rays of the setting sun were gone. Gamal Shadi was coming down a ladder into the excavated hole where Eissa watched over his device like an apprehensive father.

"Dreaming of what might have been?" Shadi asked.

"Of what will be."

"We won't have Halim here with us when it happens," Shadi said. "No contact. Azza, too. Nothing."

"What of it? They're probably dead. We will be, too, in a few hours. It's sundown already."

They were at the deepest point in the quarry, where a twenty-foot deep, twenty-foot wide circle was carved from the stone around the entrance to a narrow cavern. It had been excavated for the purpose of accessing the cavern, where a cache of explosives would eventually have been detonated to make the quarrying easier. It served the same purpose for Coldman. It would channel the unmitigated force of the detonation directly into geographic layers that would react most violently to the blast.

The interior of the quarry was entirely shadowed except at dead center. The rays of the sun were being cut off by the distant quarry wall, and the heat of the Egyptian day was dissipating. Eissa realized he was comfortable, here, now, in his role as murderer of millions.

"I've read the latest reports from home," Shadi was saying. "There might be a cease-fire. A cooling-off period. We might not be using the device tonight, after all. Then we go into hiding. But I don't know how we can do that, with the mess you've left scattered from one end of the Nile to the other."

"You think I've burned my bridges," Nibal Eissa commented.

"Yes," Shadi said.

Eissa had been hoping the Coldman enforcer would show himself to be of a like mind, a believer in the Coldman device, not the Coldman philosophy. Now he could see it wasn't true. Oh, well, so Shadi would simply have to die sooner rather than later.

"How's the cleanup coming along?" Eissa asked.

"Almost done," Shadi said, his frown showing that he was still thinking about the previous topic of conversation. "What'll you do with the mercs if we're ordered out of here without detonating?"

"Pay them off and send them home. They're Bedouins. They don't care what happens in the valley."

"They're a risk."

"There's no risk. Ah, speak of the devil."

Standing at the excavation's edge was the small, hooded Bedouin who commanded the mercenary team. His AK-47 dangled from a shoulder strap.

Shadi didn't understand the language when the merc

spoke, explaining something. Eissa gave him some detailed instructions. The Bedouin asked for clarification twice. Finally Eissa was exasperated and reverted to Arabic. "Yes, yes, that's exactly right. Do it. Right away."

The Bedouin walked away.

"They *are* a risk," Shadi said when he was sure the mercenary was out of earshot.

"Let me explain why I'm not worried about them," Eissa said, strolling across to the device, where it waited, display flashing in readiness.

"Well?" Shadi said finally.

Eissa glanced up.

Shadi whirled. The Bedouin was back, and the AK-47 was aimed at him. He had his explanation. The Bedouin triggered a long burst that traveled up the front of Shadi, pushing him into the excavation wall. Finally a round chopped into his head, and Shadi collapsed.

"I told you he wore body armor," Eissa complained.

"He's dead, what do you care?" the Bedouin asked coolly.

Eissa shrugged. He couldn't argue with logic like that.

But Shadi wasn't dead at all. The man sat up, head bloodied but intact, and he reached for Eissa with a little .32 that jumped out of his sleeve. It fired like a popgun. Eissa felt his skin burn, then he fell to the ground.

Shadi pushed himself up, running in a crouch until he could free the mini-Uzi strapped on his hip, then he dropped, rolled and fired a burst that took the Bedouin in the knees, then the chest. The merc commander flopped onto his face on the edge of the excavation, gun arm dangling over the edge, the strap still tangled on his wrist. Then the AK slid off, clattering on the rock below.

Shadi hastily dropped the mini-Uzi beside Nibal Eissa and retreated to the far corner of the excavation, arming himself with the IMI Micro-Galil.

The Bedouin mercenaries started to gather seconds later, trailing the Coldman mole who called herself Mona Eissa. When she saw the corpse of the man who had been playing the role of her husband, she cried out and hurriedly descended. She threw herself on Nibal Eissa, sobbing. Shadi wondered idly if he actually was her husband.

As the woman was extremely upset, Shadi realized that she hadn't been expecting death for either of them.

"You're a part of the conspiracy," Shadi said accusingly in Hebrew. He didn't care what the Bedouins heard or thought.

"What?" She looked up with red eyes.

"The entire cell has been planning all along to get out of Aswan before the device detonated," Shadi said calmly. "No wonder you resisted my addition to the team."

"You don't know what you're talking about."

"It was convenient that your two young people came up with reasons to get left behind," Shadi observed. "First Azza gets wounded, and Nibal insists she's too sick to continue traveling with the team, then Halim has to stay behind and deal with the pursuers. Here we are at the end, and half the cell survivors are absent."

"Halim and Azza are dead, or they would be here," Mona insisted. "And you have the nerve to accuse us? When did the trouble start? This cell was operating flawlessly until you came onboard. It is clear who brought us to the edge of failure!''

Shadi was taken aback by the accusation. He hadn't thought of it that way, but in fact the special forces team had begun harassing them the day he joined the Cairo cell. Was he really to blame?

''It doesn't matter now,'' he declared.

''Doesn't matter?'' she demanded.

''They're dead.'' Shadi lowered his voice. ''They'd be dead tonight, anyway. We will all be dead.''

''There's no guarantee the word will be given,'' Mona Eissa argued plaintively. ''Then these people will have died for nothing, and the fault will be yours.''

''The fault may be mine, but the word,'' Shadi said, tonelessly, ''is given already.''

''What?''

Shadi said nothing. The sun was gone from the sky, and though a halo of brightness rimmed the nearest peaks, the quarry was filled with despairing dusk.

''I have always defended the Coldman ideal,'' Mona said. ''I've always maintained that Coldman was a last resort only. But I was wrong, wasn't I? It was always meant to be used to destroy our enemies.''

''Of course.''

Her head drooped, her strength and confidence leaking out of her as she stood disconsolately over the corpse of Nibal Eissa.

''So do it,'' she said. ''It's ready. Push the button.''

''Base is on-line and will detonate both devices at midnight,'' he said. ''Dual detonations will create more confusion and a less cohesive response.''

''Response?'' she hissed.

''Humanitarian aid. We want it delayed as long as

possible so the impact will be greater. In the first few hours a coordinated medical response might save thousands.''

''Well, we can't allow that.''

''They argued over money, I think.'' Shadi's voice suddenly became loud and clear, and he still looked like he was talking to Mona Eissa, but he was actually telling this to the Bedouin mercenaries.''

''What do you mean?'' one of them demanded. ''Do we still get paid?''

There was sudden discontent in the merc ranks, and it made Shadi grin. He had their measure. Their leader was sprawled dead at their feet, and they were worried about their paycheck. He rummaged in Eissa's pockets and found a roll of cash wrapped in rubber bands.

''Here's your money, including the shares of those still on patrol and your commander's share. Divide his pay among yourselves if you like.'' Shadi counted out the bills, bound the roll in one of the rubber bands and sent it arcing up to the Bedouins with an underhand toss. For minutes the mercenaries squabbled and grabbed until the shares were distributed.

Shadi spoke again when the quarreling stopped. ''You can take your money and go if that's what you want, but as the new commander of this operation I have a new offer—I will pay you again, just as much as before, if you'll work for me the rest of the night as planned.''

Shadi neglected to explain that they would all burn in nuclear fire before they could possibly spend the cash. The mercenaries didn't need to discuss it among themselves before accepting his generous offer.

Tabriz, Iran

HERMANN SCHWARZ SAT UP suddenly, which was a huge mistake. It was a full minute before he could focus his eyes past the blinding pain.

There was a familiar taste in his mouth. He was doped up—that explained why he felt dopey. He wished Pol was around so he could tell him that great pun.

Where was Pol?

Where, for that matter, was the United States of America? 'Cause this wasn't it. His first clue: a street sign in Farsi.

He was in Iran, he remembered. They'd been driving cross-country. He'd knocked his head at some point. Schwarz felt the spot and found stitching, and the flesh was hot. The agony from the touch of his fingers almost blacked him out again.

Did he catch a bullet in his head? Or did the stitches have something to do with the earlier knock? Then he recalled passing out in the car.

It all came back to him, every step of the mission, and he knew what had happened to his head. Pressure build-up, slow but deadly. When he went down for his unexpected nap, Blancanales or Lyons was forced into the role of surgeon. That would explain why he was doped up.

So where were Blancanales and Lyons now?

Then Schwarz saw somebody he knew. One of the Coldman moles. In an eyeblink Schwarz remembered everything he had learned about Rasool Far.

Far was heading into what looked like an abandoned apartment building on some street in some Iranian city. Lyons and Blancanales had to be inside. Was this the staging place for the Coldman device?

Everything fell in place, including Schwarz's obligation. As soon as Far was out of sight, the Able Team commando armed himself from the clutter of equipment on the floor of the back seat.

Every move hurt. Like hell.

CHAPTER THIRTY-ONE

The interior had been gutted, and the place was used as some sort of an enclosed market, with stands and kiosks and a few storefronts. It had to have closed down in an abrupt bankruptcy more than a month earlier, judging by the ripeness of the abandoned produce and meat. Carl Lyons and Rosario Blancanales breathed mostly through their mouths to avoid the stench.

From the floor above them they could hear the quiet conversation of the Coldman team, the sound carrying so clearly they could make out a few words. It was mostly Hebrew. The Coldman agents were past caring about blending in.

"Able Three here. Talk to me. Please. Somebody."

Lyons and Blancanales pulled into a side room where being overheard would be less likely.

"Gadgets, what's going on?" Lyons demanded in a whisper.

"I've been trying to raise you guys forever. Think I had my buttons mixed up. I'm inside the building."

"Gadgets, you're drugged up. Get to cover and sit this one out."

"You need me, Ironman."

"You're a danger to yourself right now."

"Not as dangerous as Rasool Far."

Lyons considered that. "Okay. What about him?"

"He's tailing you. Just went up the back stairs."

"Shit!" Lyons hissed. "Gadgets, do nothing. Stay there. We'll handle this."

Blancanales scanned the mess of junk that filled most of the second floor. He pointed. Lyons squinted into the darkness, seeing nothing in the dim light coming through the dirty windows. He flipped down his glasses and switched to thermal, and then he found Far. The Israeli agent was crouched in shadow, frowning and scanning the blackness. His lack of night-vision gear was a disadvantage.

But the fact that Able Team had to operate in perfect silence was the thorn in its side. There were more moles upstairs, suicidal and determined to carry out their orders. Any clue that the enemy was in the building with them might be enough to force them to activate the Coldman device immediately.

"No firearms," Lyons said in a voice that was below a whisper.

Blancanales nodded, then turned on his heel and found something he remembered seeing on the floor. It was a piece of heavy reed, like bamboo, maybe once part of a retail stand. Four feet long, slightly flexible. Blancanales bent it experimentally. No cracking. It was tough. He knew how to use a weapon like this.

The Able Team warrior silently dropped his pack and his MP-5 to the floor, donned his glasses and stepped into the blackness.

The goggle lenses could be controlled individually, and Blancanales set one for thermal to track Rasool Far while keeping an eye on the depth of the shadows with the other. Far carried a handgun, a 9 mm semiautomatic, with another tucked in his pants at the small of his back. One shot would get the attention of Far's comrades upstairs, no question.

It had to be a silent kill.

Far was probing the dark recesses, taking his time to search thoroughly while Blancanales gained on him with maddening slowness. He didn't get close enough until the Israeli was standing outside the small side chamber that hid Carl Lyons.

As Far prepared to make a quick entrance and take out anyone he found hiding inside, Blancanales moved to his quarry's back. They were both surprised to hear movement behind them.

It was just a scrape. The sound of shoes. Far glowered at the blackness, then he saw Blancanales with his peripheral vision. He whirled, and the Able Team commando heard the intake of breath that might signal a shout. He rammed the end of the cane into the soft spot just above Far's collarbone. The Israeli gagged and stumbled, still choking as he pushed the handgun at his adversary. There was a flash of steel, and the big Randall combat knife slashed out of the darkness and chopped through the flesh of Far's wrist, deep into the bone.

Blancanales dived for the gun, getting a free hand between the floor and the falling weapon, catching it with a small thunk.

Rasool Far clutched his half-severed hand to his chest and gagged on his ruined trachea, and somehow had the presence of mind to make a run for it. When his staggering feet brought him to the stairs, he came to an unsteady halt. Gadgets Schwarz held him at bay with an eight-inch blade. Far's good hand went for the gun at his back, and Schwarz rushed in, forcing the blade between Far's ribs while reaching behind him to clamp down on his gun hand. Schwarz held him in a silent assassin's embrace until the life was gone from the body.

"WE'LL TAKE THEM" Lyons mouthed to Schwarz, who shrugged.

Lyons and Blancanales crept up the steps, and the Coldman team was sitting there, as if waiting for them.

Their only antagonists were hundreds of miles away, looking for them in Tehran. What did they have to worry about?

The surprise appeared on their faces as the submachine guns started to fire, but it was over in seconds. Blancanales and Lyons examined the bodies carefully, looking for any signs of life. There couldn't be any error. There couldn't be any chance one of them could get to the device.

After Schwarz joined them, they slid the bodies down the stairs for good measure.

"It's set," Schwarz said, peering at the fully assembled Coldman device sitting on a bare spot on the floor. The oversize connection conduits made it look like some sort of air cleaner.

"For when?" Lyons asked.

"It's not set for time. Look, it has a mobile phone switchbox." He indicated a plastic electronic component plugged into the top of the weapon. Sure enough, there was a cell phone fitted into a cavity, and a backup phone in an identical cavity beneath it.

"Are you shitting me?" Lyons demanded. "Somebody is going make a *phone call* to detonate this thing?"

"Yeah," Schwarz said. "Please push two if you would like to kill one million innocent civilians."

Lyons stared at him. Blancanales shook his head as if stunned.

"Well, why not?" Schwarz said. "It's a reliable communications system, it can't be easily traced, the infrastructure is in place. And all this thing needs is a single command—blow up."

Blancanales said, "Gadgets, you mean somebody can call at any minute and do the deed?"

Schwarz nodded.

"You know how to disable it?"

"Sure."

"Well, do it," Lyons ordered.

"No, I've got a better idea," Schwarz said.

Aswan, Egypt

CALVIN JAMES WAITED for the body to be fetched. When the pair of mercenaries had their hands full of the corpse's ankles and wrists, he came out of hiding just long enough to press the muzzle of the Mk 24 into the nearest mercenary's back and pull the trigger. The .44-caliber round erupted from his chest at almost the same speed at which it left the handgun and plowed into Merc Number Two.

Then James was alone with three corpses.

He wasted no more than sixty seconds pulling the dead men into his hiding place behind the trailer, just so they weren't all out in the open. Moving cautiously, homing in on the center of the quarry, he reported his activities to McCarter.

He was signing off when he heard the gunshots. First

a quick barrage of automatic fire, probably an AK, followed by a quick shot from a smaller caliber weapon.

"Any of you responsible for the gunfire?" James radioed.

The team reported in quickly. James was the only one who had heard the shots.

"They're having a falling out," McCarter observed. "That's not good."

James knew it wasn't good at all. If they were falling out, it was probably because somebody had decided not to do the deed. When the battle finished, somebody else might feel compelled to detonate the device here and now, before more rebellion arose among the ranks.

James was running from cover to cover. A brief gap in the machinery and temporary buildings showed him his destination: the excavated cavern entrance. Stony Man's intelligence said this was the likely detonation point.

A small army of mercenaries gathered around it, then began breaking up, heading in different directions. Almost to a man they were counting currency as they walked past his hiding place and fanned out among the quarry junk.

James played the image in his mind. The mercenaries had been paid off. Maybe they'd been told to go home or stand guard. They wouldn't know what the real purpose of the device was, or they wouldn't be here.

James briefed McCarter.

"We see them, Cal. We're trapped," McCarter said. "We can't back you up for ten more minutes without engaging these blokes first."

"You start a firefight, and whoever is still guarding the nuke is going to blow it for sure."

"We'll wait them out, then. Sneak past and join you as soon as we can."

"Egypt might be dead before then," James said. "I'm going in."

James crept toward the excavation until his cover ran out, then he ran. He was within thirty yards before someone emerged from the excavation.

It was a woman, older, black-haired. James recognized her as the mole who posed as Nibal Eissa's wife, going by the name Mona Eissa. Stony Man never uncovered her real Israeli identity. As she pulled herself to the surface she swatted at her wet cheeks, then said something over her shoulder in Hebrew. She sounded bitter.

She froze when she saw James. He continued striding toward her at a fast, long-legged pace.

Mona Eissa cocked her head slightly, her tear-brightened eyes flashing. James had the odd feeling she was making some sort of choice. Was it possible she was doubting her loyalties to the Coldman Project, weighing the monstrous sin of genocide against a lifetime of loyalty to a nation and cause?

It took her seconds, and when the decision was made he witnessed the change in her. It was like watching a matted, scrawny alley cat become a snarling, vicious predator in the blink of an eye.

"Intruder!" she shouted as her hands flew to the automatic rifle dangling from her arm. She had the kind of speed that came from endless years of combat training. James was faster. The MP-5 SD-3 coughed briefly, taking her in the chest with a quartet of rounds and killing her instantly.

James bolted to the lip of the excavation, spotted the occupant and launched himself into open space. The man in the pit dodged away as James came down, but a midair tae kwon do kick landed on the side of his head, sending him into a running stumble that ended when he collapsed heavily to the ground.

James hadn't had time to prepare for the landing and hit too hard, feeling one ankle twist, but he rode out the momentum as best he could and pushed himself to his feet.

The Coldman device was there. The Coldman agent shot his hand out, and the Phoenix Force warrior glimpsed a silvery missile. He twisted his body on his injured leg and felt the bright sensation of steel slicing shallowly into the skin of his chest before sailing past. James triggered the MP-5, sending a burst of 9 mm Parabellum rounds into the runner's chest and upper arm, driving him forcefully into the rock wall. He didn't fall, but painfully tried to target his adversary with the Galil. James triggered a burst at the man's skull and watched him collapse.

He raced for the Coldman device, sitting next to the ugly gash of the natural cavern, and tried to find the connection he knew would disable it. He didn't see it and he didn't dare make a mistake.

The Phoenix Force warrior didn't have time to find the part he needed before the ''dead man'' was moving again.

James covered him with the MP-5, trying to figure out why he wasn't truly dead, then made out the skull-tight armor protecting the head. It had deflected much of the force of the rounds. The guy still had a half-crushed cranium and had to be mortally wounded.

Even so, he was moving, pulling on his sleeve. He was wearing what looked like an IV, and when he squeezed the exposed bladder taped to his forearm, the liquid flowed into his veins.

The man trembled violently and sat up, then glared at James and pushed himself into a furious crawl, covering the distance to the fallen Galil before James could quite believe what he was seeing.

Shadi lunged for the weapon, but James unleashed a barrage of rounds that drained the magazine. The merciless beating pounded against Shadi's armor, smashing his rib cage, churning his organs, setting off an avalanche of internal bleeding.

Shadi was wired on a cocktail of adrenaline, painkillers and amphetamines, and that itself would have killed him in ten minutes. Now it somehow kept him alive and conscious and trembling. When James stomped on his gun hand and appropriated the weapon, Shadi tried to speak. Blood bubbled out by the pint.

There was a rustle, and James whirled, facing a pair of mercenaries on the lip of the excavation. One of them reacted by bringing his weapon into play, and James took him down with a quick burst from the Galil. The other Bedouin had more sense. His bosses were dead, so the job was finished. That was more or less the message he shouted to every merc within earshot.

James returned to the Coldman device and removed a panel cover that showed him the connector he was looking for. He pulled it, turning off the triggering mechanism. The red display dimmed. He'd let Hawkins and Manning take care of dismantling it.

It took the commando team a full three minutes to assemble along the lip of the excavation, where they took in the sight of the bodies and the dead device. Hawkins muttered something about James going solo, since the rest of Phoenix Force was obviously just so much baggage.

James didn't hear the remark. He was standing over Gamal Shadi, who continued to tremble like the ground was quaking beneath him.

James honestly didn't know if the man was alive or dead.

Tel Aviv

JOSEPH DEVORHA JUMPED out of his seat when the red exclamation point blinked over the error message on his display. The error had to be wrong.

The diagnostic routine started automatically and offered a short explanation. The problem wasn't within the computer but with the Aswan device. When the error occurred, the device initiated an error report phone call to the host computer.

Should the host computer initiate active communication with the device?

Devorha frantically clicked "Yes."

The call went through. It was picked up. The diagnostic inquiry started to go through its tests, then got cut off by a human voice.

"Go to hell, you son of a bitch."

The connection went dead.

As impossible as it was to believe, the Aswan device had been disabled.

Devorha had argued for activating the devices the moment they were on-line. The board of directors had vetoed his suggestion. Simultaneous activation. On schedule. By the book. It had been planned this way from the start.

But Devorha did have the authority to override the

edict in an emergency, such as now. The Coldman plan was already severely compromised. Just one-third of its intended weapons could be utilized. Maybe that would be enough. Maybe the terror and chaos out of Iran would humble the Arab world.

The window for the Iranian device still showed all systems normal. Without further hesitation Devorha clicked the button labeled Activate.

Tabriz, Iran

"ABLE, WE'RE getting the call!" Kurtzman shouted into their headsets.

"We're not hearing it, Bear," Schwarz replied, leaning over the phone box.

"Trust me, it's coming through! Okay, we picked it up!"

The three Able Team commandos looked at one another in the darkness, their eyes drawn inexorably to the device on the other side of the room, now surgically detached from its electronic control system.

"They must have turned off the audio on this end," Blancanales said. "Can you imagine sitting here and suddenly hearing the call come in? They wouldn't want one of their guards doing something impulsive."

They waited in the darkness. With the bomb. And the phones. And the dead men on the floor below.

"He did it," Kurtzman said. "The son of a bitch. He just pressed the button."

The three Able Team commandos watched the device, as if expecting it to react somehow.

Schwarz wondered if it was possible for a hunk of

machinery to have emotions. Because, swear to God, he could feel anger coming from the Coldman weapon.

It had been denied its purpose.

Tel Aviv

JOSEPH DEVORHA WATCHED the monitor showing a video feed from an Israeli meteorological satellite. The video feed it sent was used on network and global weather reports every night. This night it would show something more than swirling clouds.

His feed was digital overlaid with white graphics indicating national borders and important cities. He was about to see Tabriz, Iran, flash brightly, then become shrouded in black smoke.

But it didn't happen.

He angrily pointed a remote at his office television, preset to receive the satellite feed out of a Tabriz news station.

The station was still on the air.

He looked at the computer screen. The Tabriz device had been activated, as far as his PC was concerned. He initiated a diagnostic call to the device.

Like the repeat of a horrible nightmare, a human being answered the call. It wasn't a member of the Coldman Iran cell, but a voice as grim and deadly as the grave.

"Mossad Field Director Joseph Devorha," the voice said, "you can expect a visit from Israeli internal affairs officials very soon."

They knew who he was. They knew where he was. They had reported his actions and his location.

Devorha snatched at his desk phone and stabbed the buttons for his most ardent supporter, the retired Israel Defense Forces general who had viewed Coldman as his personal legacy. The general would protect him—

somehow. The phone was picked up, and a brusque recorded voice told him the line was disconnected.

He started to dial office numbers one after another. The Coldman directors had to be in their offices to witness the climactic moments, but none of them picked up. Did they know? Had the news started to spread already?

He dialed the phone number he had been instructed to never call. The man who picked up was one of the most powerful men in Israel, a man with global name recognition.

"This is Devorha."

"Who?"

"Joseph Devorha!"

"How did you get this number?"

"*You* gave it to me."

The man on the other end of the line, the chairman of the board of Coldman, chuckled unpleasantly. "I don't think so."

And he hung up.

Devorha was being abandoned. The directors would deny being directors. The chairman would laugh at any suggestion that he was the chairman. Joseph Devorha would take the fall for them all.

He heard footsteps in the hall outside his office.

Devorha reached for the .38 revolver in his desk as fists pounded on his door. The steel barrel tasted cold and bitter.

The door burst open, and for a half second he looked into the faces of his fellow Mossad agents, who would arrest him and force him to reveal his shame to his peers. Devorha couldn't face it.

He knew he was a coward. He couldn't face that, either.

So he pulled the trigger.

James Axler
Outlanders®

SEA OF PLAGUE

The loyalties that united the Cerberus warriors have become undone, as a bizarre messenger from the future provides a look into encroaching horror and death. Kane and his band have one option: fix two fatal fault lines in the time continuum—and rewrite history before it happens. But first they must restore power to the barons who dare to defy the greater evil: the mysterious new Imperator. Then they must wage war in the jungles of India, where the deadly, beautiful Scorpia Prime and her horrifying bio-weapon are about to drown the world in a sea of plague....

In the Outlands, the shocking truth is humanity's last hope.